HEART
ON
THE *Line*

Books by Karen Witemeyer

A Tailor-Made Bride

Head in the Clouds

To Win Her Heart

Short-Straw Bride

Stealing the Preacher

Full Steam Ahead

A Worthy Pursuit

No Other Will Do

Heart on the Line

A Cowboy Unmatched from *A Match Made in Texas:*
A Novella Collection
The Husband Maneuver from *With This Ring:*
A Novella Collection
Love on the Mend from *With All My Heart Romance Collection*

HEART ON THE *Line*

KAREN WITEMEYER

BETHANYHOUSE

a division of Baker Publishing Group
Minneapolis, Minnesota

© 2017 by Karen Witemeyer

Published by Bethany House Publishers
11400 Hampshire Avenue South
Bloomington, Minnesota 55438
www.bethanyhouse.com

Bethany House Publishers is a division of
Baker Publishing Group, Grand Rapids, Michigan

Printed in the United States of America

Library of Congress Cataloging-in-Publication Data
Names: Witemeyer, Karen, author.
Title: Heart on the line / Karen Witemeyer.
Description: Minneapolis, Minnesota : Bethany House, a division of Baker
    Publishing Group, [2017]
Identifiers: LCCN 2016050054| ISBN 9780764230394 (cloth) | ISBN
    9780764212826 (trade paper)
Subjects: | GSAFD: Christian fiction. | Love stories.
Classification: LCC PS3623.I864 H44 2017 | DDC 813/.6—dc23
LC record available at https://lccn.loc.gov/2016050054

Scripture quotations are from the King James Version of the Bible.

This is a work of fiction. Names, characters, incidents, and dialogues are products of the author's imagination and are not to be construed as real. Any resemblance to actual events or persons, living or dead, is entirely coincidental.

Cover design by Dan Thornberg, Design Source Creative Services

Author is represented by Books & Such Agency

17 18 19 20 21 22 23   7 6 5 4 3 2 1

To Wyatt and Wes.

Wyatt—
Your sweet disposition, punny sense of humor,
love of God, and kind spirit inspired this latest
hero. Someday a godly woman is going to
recognize what a treasure you are and snatch
you up! Keep flashing those dimples, and
remember you'll always be your mama's hero.

Wes—
My favorite glasses-wearing, bicycle-riding,
technology nerd.
25 years, and we're still going strong.
You are my rock, my best friend,
and the romantic inspiration
behind all my fictional heroes.
Real life with you is better
than any story.
1 · 4 · 3

The Lord seeth not as man seeth; for man looketh on the outward appearance, but the Lord looketh on the heart.

—1 Samuel 16:7

PROLOGUE

The cheerful tinkle of a bell alerted Grace Mallory to the arrival of a guest. Immediately setting aside the ladies' magazine she'd been perusing, she rose gracefully to her feet, smoothed the front of her bodice, then put on a welcoming smile. It wouldn't do for a patron of the Oxford Hotel to be kept waiting.

It had been hard enough to get this job in the first place. Her father had to call in a favor with one of the investors to get her on staff, and she wasn't about to give her supervisor any excuse to let her go. Thankfully, the predominately male clientele of Denver's most progressive hotel seemed to enjoy conducting business with a young female telegraph operator once they deemed her skill satisfactory.

But this man didn't have the look of her usual client. He was still wrapped in a snow-dusted overcoat, scarf, and hat, as if he'd come in off the street rather than from one of the guest rooms.

"Good afternoon, sir," she said to his back. He'd yet to turn around. "How can the Western Union office serve you today?"

He closed the door and turned the lock.

Grace's throat pinched and her heart thundered in her chest. "What are you do—?"

The words, along with her fear, died away when the customer turned. A pair of familiar brown eyes gazed at her from above the striped blue scarf that covered half his face.

"Daddy?"

He grabbed at the scarf with frantic hands as if it were choking him. "Have to send a wire. Now. The rumors are true. All true."

"Calm down." Grace rushed around the counter to help her father unwind the scarf and brush the snow off the shoulders of his coat. "What rumors?"

"The Haversham estate. There's another heir," he said as he pushed away her helping hands and marched up to the counter. "A child by the first wife. A girl." He pulled his fogged-over spectacles from his eyes and rubbed the lenses clean with the edge of his scarf. "She's the rightful owner of Haversham House. Not the son."

Grace gasped. There'd been talk of another heir ever since Tremont Haversham died three months ago. Whispers, innuendo, but no name, no proof. Grace had assumed the rumors were built on wishful thinking by the miners' families.

When his father's health declined a year ago, Chaucer Haversham had taken over the running of the Silver Serpent Mine in Willow Creek only to have it plunge into ruin after President Cleveland repealed the Sherman Silver Purchase Act and the bottom fell out of the silver market. Whether it was stubborn pride, blind ambition, or even a noble desire to keep his father's company in operation, Chaucer refused to close the mine. Instead, he demanded longer work hours from his miners with no additional compensation as he switched from mining silver to the more commonplace minerals of lead and zinc. Conditions were said to be deplorable, but with so many out-of-work miners, no one dared complain for fear they'd be replaced by one of their neighbors.

"Quit your woolgathering, Gracie."

Grace dashed back around the counter and grabbed a telegraph blank. Herschel Mallory was a scholar by nature. Quiet. Kind. A bit absentminded. She couldn't recall the last time she'd seen him so worked up.

"Who do you want to wire?" she asked, pencil poised.

"The Pinkertons."

Grace hesitated. "But doesn't Chaucer Haversham have a pair of Pinkertons on his payroll to keep the miners in line and prevent strikes? Wouldn't they support his claim, no matter what proof you've uncovered?"

"I want you to wire the Philadelphia office. A Detective Whitmore in particular."

She jotted the name down on her form, needing no further explanation. Tremont Haversham had grown up in Philadelphia and married his first wife there—a woman of whom his wealthy family did not approve. At least that was the version of the tale Grace had heard. The woman died in childbirth. The baby, too, or so it had been believed. Brokenhearted, Haversham returned to his family and within a year took a second wife, a woman of means and social standing this time. One who knew how to push her husband into a position of power, leadership, and great financial triumph. One who had given him a son.

"Found your report to Tremont Haversham dated October 12, 1892." Her father slung his satchel up onto the counter as he dictated his message. The bag thumped against the wooden shelf with the sound of heavy books. "If female still alive, she is rightful heir to Haversham fortune. I have documents to prove her claim. Need to dispatch to you immediately. Please advise. Herschel Mallory."

Grace finished scribbling the message then looked into her father's frantic eyes. "What did you find, Daddy?"

As a scholar and professor of literature at the University of

Denver, Herschel Mallory had been hired by Chaucer Haversham to catalog his father's extensive library in the family's Denver mansion. A mansion Chaucer had inherited but never visited. From what Grace had heard, he avoided Denver altogether, preferring the estate in Boston where his mother maintained a residence.

Tremont and Caroline Haversham had lived apart for the last decade, Caroline seeing to the raising and education of their son while Tremont oversaw the mining operations. Apparently the situation suited both parties, a state Grace had always considered rather sad. She'd never met Chaucer Haversham, but she couldn't help feeling a little sorry for the young man who'd been separated from his father during the very years he was coming of age. She would have been lost without her own father. He meant the world to her—his love and acceptance never in question.

Grace's mother had been her mentor, teaching her to pick out the dots and dashes of Morse code as a child in her telegraph office, then guiding her in the ways of womanhood and domestic responsibilities. But when she died two years ago, the shared grief of that loss had bonded Grace and her father as tightly as if the broken halves of their hearts had been melted down, reshaped, and forged into an unbreakable, interlocking design.

It was that closeness that had her senses on full alert when her father fiddled with his satchel strap instead of answering her question.

She reached out and covered his fidgeting gloved hand with her bare one. "Tell me, Daddy. What did you find?"

"Proof, Gracie." His gaze met hers, and the mix of dread and determination in his eyes set her stomach to cramping. "Proof that Haversham's first child didn't die with her mother. Proof that Haversham tried to find her. Proof that the odd wording of his will makes his daughter an heiress and his son simply a business owner."

"You found this proof in the library at Haversham House?"

Her father nodded.

"But if the documents are Mr. Haversham's property, what can you possibly do about it?"

He dropped his gaze.

"Daddy?"

He jerked his hand away from her touch and paced away from the counter. "The documents were *Tremont* Haversham's property, and he's dead. If Chaucer's not the true heir of the Denver mansion and its contents, then the documents don't really belong to him, do they?"

The knots in Grace's stomach twisted. "What did you do?"

"Nothing you need to concern yourself about. I just borrowed a couple books from the collection. Chaucer plans to sell them off anyway. It's what he did with the art—had an appraiser come in a week after his father's funeral, then sold the finer pieces at auction by month's end. He has no respect for his father beyond the price to be fetched from his belongings." Herschel paced back toward the counter. "The books I took were ordinary editions. Nothing of monetary value. He won't miss them."

Suddenly, the full satchel on her counter held a whole new significance. "You can't just take them!"

Her father's face hardened. "I can't stand by while an injustice is perpetrated, either. Tremont Haversham was my friend, Gracie. More than a friend. If it hadn't been for his influence, the university would have let me go during that dark time after your mother passed."

Grace dropped her head. She remembered that time. Both of them steeped in grief. She'd been young with no real responsibilities, and her father hadn't noticed or cared if the house went uncleaned or if dinner had burnt. But the melancholia had brought Herschel Mallory to the brink of unemployment. Papers and exams had gone ungraded for weeks. His clouded mind turned his organized lectures into meandering, meaningless forays. Students had stopped

11

attending. Parents had complained. Board members had threatened. Only Tremont Haversham had spoken on her father's behalf. Had taken him aside and reminded him of his responsibilities, made him see that destroying himself would only dishonor his wife's memory. He had to pull himself together for his daughter's sake.

She glanced around her tidy little office with its elegant oak furnishings and carpeted floor. Her stomach swirled. She owed Tremont Haversham a debt, as well. He was the investor responsible for hiring her. The hotel manager had insisted on a male operator even though she'd proven more skillful than the other applicants—until Mr. Haversham had convinced him to reconsider.

Grace's father reached across the counter and captured her hand. "Tremont Haversham had a daughter. One stolen from him. One he desperately tried to find before his death. One, I believe, he loved very much." His eyes softened as he looked at Grace. "I know what it is to have a daughter. And if anything ever separated her from me, I'd move heaven and earth to get her back."

Moisture gathered behind Grace's eyes.

"She needs to know her father loved her, Gracie. To have something to remember him by. I owe him that much at least." He paused, then released her hand to pat the top of the leather satchel. "There are letters, too. Love letters between Tremont and his first wife. Chaucer would burn them if he knew of their existence. I can't let that happen. The daughter deserves a chance to know her parents."

Grace stared down at the telegraph blank, legal technicalities warring with moral responsibility.

"Send the wire, Gracie," her father urged, his voice gentle.

She met his gaze a final time. The love in his eyes melted away the last slivers of icy indecision. She nodded, sat down at the key, and started tapping.

Two days later they waited in a rented, second-floor room in a nondescript boardinghouse. Across the street stood the café where her father was scheduled to meet the agent Detective Whitmore had sent to collect the documents. Whitmore had warned them not to trust anyone else with the evidence. Not even the postal system. Several parcels delivered to him over the last few months had shown evidence of tampering, and he had yet to discover the culprit. Best not to risk such valuable information falling into the wrong hands.

"Are you sure we can't just turn the documents over to the marshal?" Grace clutched her father's suit coat to her chest, the coat she was supposed to be helping him into.

Her father shook his head and glanced over his shoulder at her. "As far as the local law is concerned, the books are Chaucer's property. They have no obligation to investigate whatever may have been found inside. They'd simply return the items, and Chaucer would destroy them.

"Detective Whitmore is right. We can't trust anyone else. I'll not hand the books over to anyone other than Whitmore or the man who carries his recommendation." He attempted to smile, but the sad twisting of his lips did nothing to reassure her. "Come, Gracie. Help me on with my coat."

Grace obeyed, sliding the wool sleeves of the slightly rumpled sack suit jacket over his arms and up onto his shoulders. She stepped around him and tugged on his lapels until the coat hung evenly on his slender frame, then smoothed them flat against his chest.

"Everything will work out for the best," he said. "You'll see. The only people who know about this meeting are Detective Whitmore and the Pinkerton agent he sent."

And the telegraph operator who received our message as well as any others listening in on the line. Grace kept that disquieting thought to herself. Telegraph operators signed contracts of confidentiality, after all, vowing only to reveal message contents to intended parties. But operators were human. Susceptible to bribes or threats.

As were Pinkertons. She still didn't like the fact that they had confided in the same agency that had men working for the Silver Serpent mine. Chaucer Haversham's pockets were deep. All it would take was the quiet promise of a payday spread by the agents already in his employ to convince someone in the Philadelphia office to pass on any suspicious information.

But none of that could be helped. Her father was too noble to abandon a quest once begun. He was going to see this through, come what may. So she would see *him* through.

"You're a good man, Daddy." Grace glanced up from buttoning the top button on his vest. He always had something on his person coming undone—buttons climbing out of their holes, watch chains tangling, scraps of paper falling out of his pockets. She forced a smile to her lips. "Be careful."

He smiled back, then leaned in and placed a kiss on her forehead. "I will, pet." He winked at her then stepped over to the chest of drawers near the door to fetch his satchel. He lifted the leather strap over his head and fit the bag against his right hip, tucking it close to his belly. Then he settled his dark gray fedora on his head and straightened his posture. "Be watching for my signal."

Grace nodded. "Forehead, you'll bring him here. Glasses, I'm to take the box and head for the carriage."

He grinned. "That's my girl." He reached for the door handle and let himself into the hall.

Grace moved to close the door behind him, but he stuck his head back through the opening. "Whatever happens, Gracie," he said, "God will see us through."

Her throat grew tight.

"I love you, girl." His gaze held hers for a heartbeat, then he spun away and marched down the hall.

"I love you, too, Daddy," she whispered as she closed the door

14

with a quiet click. It would take him a few minutes to descend the boardinghouse stairs and exit to the street, but Grace rushed to the window anyway, her gaze darting between the street below and the café window across the way. Pedestrians meandered along the boardwalks, a few dashing between wagons and men on horseback to cross to the other side. The bustling scene matched that of any other Thursday morning, but Grace's pulse throbbed a ragged rhythm anyway.

Please watch over him, Lord.

As determined as Herschel Mallory was to turn the documents over to the Pinkertons, he was still approaching this meeting with caution by not taking the actual books with him. His satchel carried old literature tomes from his personal library. The Haversham books rested in a pink-and-white hatbox pilfered from Grace's closet, a disguise they'd decided most men would overlook.

Her father had reserved a table next to the large plate-glass window at the front of the café. If the agent showed adequate proof that he'd been sent by Whitmore, her father would remove his hat and use his handkerchief to wipe his forehead, signaling Grace that all was well. If, on the other hand, the agent roused suspicion, her father would instead use his handkerchief to clean the lenses of his glasses. That was the signal for Grace to collect the bags they'd packed that morning along with the all-important hatbox and exit through the alley, where they'd paid a driver to hold a carriage for them. She was to purchase a train ticket to Colorado Springs and wait for her father there.

Movement beneath her window caught her eye. A man approached the street, his fedora as familiar as the gray sack suit covering his shoulders. Grace touched her fingers to the chilled glass, wishing she was there beside him, holding his hand.

He paused, waiting for a freight wagon to pass by, carefully avoiding the brown, snowy slush that splattered the edge of the boardwalk, then started across the street. At the midway point, a grubby young boy dashed directly in front of her father, causing him to pull up short to avoid a collision. Her father's hand instinctively dropped down to protect his satchel from the likely pickpocket, but it wasn't the satchel he should have guarded. In that same moment, a shot rang out. From where, Grace didn't know, but the muffled *pop* sliced through her heart like the sharpest blade.

"Daddy!" She jumped to her feet, her palms pressing desperately against the window. She pounded the glass. "Daddy!"

He pivoted toward her as he fell, his gaze meeting hers for one brief moment.

"No!" Her horrified scream echoed through the room as the man she loved more than any other crumpled to the ground, a dark stain spreading across his vest.

Amid the chaos of people screaming and running for cover, the grubby urchin returned to her father's side, not to help but to snatch the satchel from around his neck. The little devil!

Grace pushed away from the window. She had to get to her father. But a movement caught her eye before she turned away. Daddy was reaching for something.

She plastered herself back against the window, needing to understand whatever he was trying to tell her. His awkward movements brought tears to her eyes, but he finally managed to bring his arm up high enough to pull his spectacles from his face.

Grace's tears fell in earnest now. She shook her head in silent denial, even as comprehension settled over her. He didn't have a handkerchief, but with his last breath, Herschel Mallory rubbed one lens of his spectacles, leaving a red smear across the glass.

The signal was clear.

Run!

I

A mos Bledsoe! Get out of the street before you run someone over with that infernal contraption!"

It took a great deal of mental fortitude, but Amos managed not to roll his eyes at the pretty debutante holding court on the boardwalk outside the dressmaker's shop. His mama had drilled manners into him at an early age, so he chose instead to release the steering handle with one hand and doff his hat to her as he politely slowed his pace.

"Miss Dexter." He even offered a smile, though the effort did nothing to soften the indignation on the face of the lady in question. He nodded to her ever-present companions as well. "Miss Berryhill. Miss Watts."

"I declare." Harriet scrunched her nose as she waved a gloved hand in his direction. "If God had meant for mankind to ride upon two-wheeled devices, he wouldn't have created horses. Just look at you wobbling about. Anyone with half a brain knows that for a vehicle to be sturdy it needs *four* wheels."

"What about a pony cart, Harriet?" Miss Berryhill ventured,

17

her forehead crinkling. "My Aunt Bea rides in one all the time and never has any trouble."

"That's because it's attached to a *pony*. A creature with *four* legs," Harriet huffed. "The animal keeps the cart steady."

Amos had to admit she'd been quick with that rejoinder. As much as he disliked her for so actively disliking *him*, he couldn't discount her intelligence. He just wished she'd use it for something other than belittling him in public. It seemed her favorite pastime.

"Bicycles are quite safe, I assure you," Amos countered, determined to continue on the path of higher ground. "Even young women ride them. They're quite the rage back east. Haven't you seen the pictures in *Harper's Bazar*?" All right, so perhaps he'd hit a divot in his higher-ground travels. He couldn't resist prodding her a little. "My sister said a bicycle costume from Paris was featured on *Harper's* cover back in April." He nodded toward the dressmaker's shop. "I'm sure if you haven't seen it, Mrs. Ludlow could let you peruse her copy."

He'd never thought it would come in handy to have a sister dedicated to keeping up with the latest fashion trends, but seeing Harriet Dexter flounder for a reply suddenly made all the dull evenings spent in Mother's parlor, listening to female dither about fabric and patterns, well worth the torture.

"Really, Amos!" Harriet sputtered. "How vulgar you are to speak of . . . of split skirts and . . . bloomers in mixed company. Why, I'm appalled. Simply appalled." She sniffed and immediately set off down the boardwalk in the opposite direction. "Come, girls. I see a gentleman more worthy of our time. Oh, Roy!"

She waved, and a cowboy standing outside Yeidel's Beer Hall touched the brim of his hat. Right before spitting a juicy wad of tobacco over the railing to mix with the mud of the street.

Definitely a fine specimen of gentleman-hood. How could Amos possibly hope to compete?

Taking refuge in mental sarcasm usually removed the worst of rejection's sting, but a prick or two remained. It always did. Even after years of practice.

Amos shrugged and remounted his bicycle. He pedaled with more vigor than usual, eager to increase the distance between himself and his latest female failure. Today's episode shouldn't bother him. After all, it wasn't as if he *wanted* Harriet Dexter's attention. The woman was a shrew of the first order. It was a matter of pride, he supposed. No one liked to be perceived as lacking. Or constantly passed over in favor of a version of manhood he'd never achieve.

A block past Main and Austin, traffic lessened considerably. Shops gave way to schools, churches, and finally dwellings. Lucy's home was another three blocks down on Morton Street, which gave him far too much time to ponder the vagaries of the feminine mind before dinner.

If these were still prehistoric times, when the breadth of a man's shoulders directly corresponded to one's likelihood of survival, he could understand a woman preferring a cowpuncher like Roy Edmundson over him, despite the man's tobacco habit and bent toward liquor. But this was the modern age, a time of scientific discovery and industrial advancement. Yet women still flocked toward the largest muscles and deepest bank accounts available, completely overlooking the benefits of intellect and integrity.

All right, not *all* women. There were a few out there with sense enough to see past a fellow's appearance and status. Lucy. His mother. Amos shifted his grip on the handlebars as he maneuvered around a particularly bumpy section of road. Surely there were others. He pictured the ladies at church who were always ready with a smile for him and a kind word. Gems, every one. Of course, they were all over fifty.

Amos quirked his mouth into a wry grin. Apparently it took a certain level of maturity and wisdom to appreciate his masculine attributes.

His smile faded. Surely Miss G didn't fall into that category. Not that she wasn't mature or wise. She seemed to be everything a man of intellect would want in a woman. Unless she were old enough to be his mother.

That utterly depressing thought brought Amos up short, and he nearly rode into the shade tree outside his sister's house. He corrected at the last second to avoid the collision and vigorously applied the brakes.

How many months had he pinned his hopes for future happiness on the mysterious Miss G? The lady of sparkle and wit who entertained him with stories of outlaw attacks, quilting fiascos, and a budding romance between a reluctant shop owner and the freighter who carted her goods. He'd been following that tale with particular interest, his own hopes lifting at the prospect of a man's persistence paying dividends in winning a maiden's heart. But what if the delightful Miss G was a matronly, grandmotherly figure and not the young woman he'd always pictured? Such a turn of events would be devastating, for he was already more than a little in love with the operator from Harper's Station.

That was the peril of being a telegraph operator: one could strike up a conversation or a friendship—or something more— with someone dozens of miles away, a person one had never seen. How easy it would be for this person to misrepresent themselves, to claim to be a young, unmarried beauty when in fact she was a middle-aged mother of five with poor hygiene and a twisted sense of humor. He'd even heard tales of male operators impersonating females to play pranks on their comrades. Amos had worried about falling victim to just such a joke when he'd first stumbled upon Miss G on the lines after hours a few months ago. She'd been so sweetly reluctant to start up a conversation with him, however, that he couldn't cast her in the role of malevolent trickster.

He *had* done some investigating, however. Her station abbreviation, Hs, stood for Harper's Station, a town he'd never heard of. This initially raised his suspicions, until he put his best sleuth on the case—his mother. She had relatives and gossip contacts all over the state. Within a week, he'd learned that Harper's Station was some sort of women's colony started up by a lady banker and her maiden aunts. Which assured him of Miss G's gender, at least.

Her age remained a mystery since he'd never be so gauche as to ask. He'd gathered hints, however. For example, she hadn't mentioned a husband during the course of their conversations, nor children. The only reference to family he could recall was that her mother had taught her telegraphy when she was a child, which left the impression that she was still a young woman. And though she'd never specified, he inferred from her omissions as well as her choice to dwell in a women's colony that her parents were no longer part of her life. Dead, perhaps, or estranged? He could only speculate.

The one thing he knew for sure was that she was possessed of a superbly pleasant nature and made him feel as if she looked forward to conversing with him as much as he did with her. Which was a considerable amount. So considerable, in fact, that he spent nearly every evening listening to her tapping on the sounder and responding in kind. Never had he enjoyed another's company so much.

But what if Miss G was nothing like the image he had built up in his mind? He didn't expect a great beauty, didn't really even want one. Just a woman of somewhat youthful age and passable features, but who could brighten a man's world with her smile. Whose quiet demeanor would soothe a man's spirit at the end of a long day. Whose witty observations of life would entertain and banish boredom. She'd already proven to be proficient at the latter two qualities. It was fear of her failing on the former two that kept him from pursuing a personal meeting.

Reality rarely bore up well when compared to a beloved fantasy. On the other hand, one couldn't make a life with an idealized figment.

"You planning on loitering out here until the sun goes down," a familiar female voice prodded, "or are you going to come join us for dinner?"

"Bossy as ever, I see," Amos teased. His sister might be three years younger, but she'd never shied from ordering him around. He grinned, stepped over his bicycle's crossbar, and pushed the vehicle up to Lucy's front porch. "I don't know how Robert puts up with you."

"Same way you do," she sassed, tossing the dish towel she held at his head.

He dodged with a chuckle and snagged the cloth out of the air. She was right. Both he and Robert loved her to distraction. Amos never would have given Robert permission to marry her if he didn't.

"Mama's already inside," Lucy announced as Amos ascended the front steps, snapping the dish towel at her skirt. She gave a little squeal and grabbed for the towel. "You beast. Stop that."

He let her take it from him then swooped in to kiss her cheek. "What's for dinner?"

"Fish entrails and monkey brains."

Amos faced the open door and breathed deeply. "Mmm. Amazing how such exotic fare smells just like sausage and onions."

Lucy pushed at his shoulder. The effort was easy enough to withstand, thanks to the balance and fitness he'd gained from cycling, but he made a show of staggering sideways to please her.

"It's not as if you would notice what we're eating anyway, as far as your mind was from here a few minutes ago. You should just go see her, you know, instead of tormenting yourself with questions you can't answer."

Amos glared at her. "Mother should never have told you about my inquiry into Harper's Station." His sister was far too clever and too much of a matchmaker to let a juicy tidbit like his friendship with a mysterious female telegraph operator go unexplored.

Lucy shrugged. "I had most of it figured out already. You spending less and less time here after dinner, always needing to swing by the office on your way home. I never expected it to last this long, though." She elbowed him in the ribs as they walked into the front hall. "Something tells me you're smitten, big brother."

A denial rose to Amos's lips as warmth crawled up his neck. Thankfully, his nephew saved him from telling a bald-faced lie.

"Unca 'Mus! Unca 'Mus!" The two-year-old boy ran like a runaway train straight for him, arms outstretched, grin wide.

Amos's heart surged with love as he bent down to scoop up the rascal. "Harry! My goodness, but you're getting heavy." Pretending to struggle in lifting the tiny sprout off the ground, Amos grunted and groaned. They ran through this routine every night, and it never got old. How could one resist such an enthusiastic welcome?

Harry, of course, went straight for the glasses as soon as Amos settled him in his arms. Amos had given up trying to avoid the inevitable about six weeks ago and now just let it happen. It was easier that way. Lucy would scold and pry the spectacles out of Harry's slobbery fingers. Amos would blow a buzz of air against Harry's neck until the boy giggled uncontrollably and squirmed to get down. Once the little monster ran off, Lucy would hand Amos the glasses. He'd unbend the wire frames, rub the lenses clean, then join the rest of the family in the dining room.

Tonight, however, his sister held his spectacles for ransom after her son ran off to pester his grandmother. When Amos raised a brow at her, she simply looked at him, all teasing gone from her face.

"You'd make a great father, you know."

"Lucy . . ." Amos shook his head. He didn't need this tonight. Not after facing down Harriet Dexter and her maids-in-waiting.

His sister meant well, but nagging him to marry only made things worse. It wasn't like he was *trying* to stay single.

She touched his arm. "She's out there, Amos. The right lady for you. And she'll be a better match than you can even imagine. God will see to that. All you have to do is find her."

Amos blew out a breath, a sarcastic laugh escaping with the air. "She's hiding awfully well, sis."

She patted his back then held out his glasses. "Maybe you've been looking in the wrong places." She strolled ahead a few steps before swiveling for one last parting shot. "You might try Harper's Station. I hear there's a surplus of females there." Her mouth curved into a smirk. "Might increase your chances with less competition around. I'm sure your *friend* at the telegraph office could make some recommendations."

"Why, you . . ." Amos lurched forward, a growl rumbling in his throat.

Lucy shrieked and ran off, no doubt straight into her husband's arms. The perfect refuge for such a disgustingly happy married woman.

Yet her words lingered, urging Amos to take a risk—to attempt to turn a fantasy into something real and lasting. What was the worst that could happen?

2

It's hard to believe, isn't it?"

Grace Mallory smiled at the soft comment from Emma Shaw as the two of them slowed their pace on the boardwalk outside the café, not wanting to encroach on the scene playing out in front of the general store.

"Another prayer answered," Grace murmured, her joy true and deep at the sight of her friend finally opening herself to the possibility of love. "She deserves to be happy."

"Amen to that." Emma drew to a halt, a smile blossoming across her face.

Grace stopped as well, her own lips curving at the sight of Victoria Adams—shopkeeper, single mother, and former proponent of the never-trust-a-man-for-any-reason philosophy—standing in the circle of a man's arms. A very tall, muscular man, whose slouch against the freight wagon at his back did nothing to disguise his massive physique. The complete adoration on his face as he looked down at the woman in his arms, however, made his size completely irrelevant.

That was what every woman wanted. Evidence of a man's love, his devotion, his unwavering dedication. Malachi Shaw looked at Emma that way. Grace's father had looked at her mother that way. And now Mr. Porter looked at Tori in the same manner. Grace's heart warmed with delight for her friend, yet also panged with a strident chord of envy. Would *she* ever be the recipient of such a look?

The vivid image of the last look her father had given her as he lay dying in a cold Colorado street answered her question. Women in hiding didn't have beaus. *Couldn't* have beaus. Not if they wanted to ensure their suitors stayed alive.

Emma touched her arm. "Grace? Are you all right?"

Grace immediately smiled to erase any evidence of her melancholy thoughts. "Of course. It's just that seeing Tori and Ben together reminds me of my parents. My father used to look at my mother that same way."

Emma nodded and turned her attention back to the courting couple. "I envy you your memories. The aunts have told me stories about my mother and father's courtship, and I have the pocket watch my mother gave him with her love note inscribed inside, but I can barely recall their faces, let alone the way they used to look at each other."

Grace squeezed Emma's hand, thankful for the reminder that she wasn't the only one who had experienced loss and hardship. "I imagine they looked at each other in much the same way you and Malachi do now."

Emma's cheeks grew rosy, but her smile shone even more brightly. She squeezed Grace's hand in return. "I hope you're right. Because when Mal looks at me with love in his eyes, I feel like I can accomplish any task, endure any hardship, and overcome any obstacle, as long as he's by my side."

"I think you've proven that in the last few months," Grace said with a soft chuckle.

Emma joined in the laughter. "Yes. Too much proof, as far as I'm concerned. Hopefully we won't put the theory to such an extensive test again anytime soon."

Remembering the life-threatening attacks against Harper's Station a few months ago, Grace heartily agreed.

"Thanks again for joining me for dinner tonight." Emma slipped her hand free and rubbed her arms against the brisk wind that swept over them. "Betty always insists on feeding Malachi on the days he works for her. Thankfully the new coop is nearly complete. Once the laying hens move in, I'll be able to claim my husband for evening meals again."

Grace smiled. "It was my pleasure."

Ever since her marriage, Emma had gone out of her way to assure the ladies of Harper's Station that her new status as a wife in no way affected her dedication to their community. If it hadn't been dinner at the café tonight, Grace was certain Emma would have arranged another time for the two of them to chat. And not just about telegraph business. Emma might be a banker and the town manager, but first and foremost, she was a friend. The kind who welcomed a runaway, grief-stricken girl with open arms and gave her not only a job but also a home.

The wind picked up, causing the temperature to dip as the sun plunged toward the horizon. A shiver coursed over Grace, urging her to make a quick dash back to her rooms at the telegraph office and the stove that waited for her there.

It wasn't just the stove she was eager to return to. She cast another glance at Tori and Ben, warmth infusing her cheeks as he leaned close and brushed a kiss across the shopkeeper's cheek. Grace might not have a man to hold her, to stand by her side, or to kiss her good night, but she did have a particular friend. One who corresponded with her nearly every evening and who might, even now, be calling her on the wire.

She glanced toward the small clapboard building on the

outskirts of town. Anticipation surged inside her, despite her attempts to stifle it.

This was too ridiculous. For all she knew, Mr. A was a middle-aged dandy who wore a girdle to contain his generous belly and doused himself in suffocating amounts of strong cologne. She could probably overlook the girth, but the cologne? She never could abide the artificial smell of toilet water. Especially since men who opted to wear such scents tended to do so in place of bathing. Having a hundred miles between them was probably a good thing.

So why was she stepping down from the boardwalk and lifting a hand to wave farewell to Emma?

"I'm going to get out of this wind," she heard herself say. "Give Malachi my regards."

Emma nodded. "I will." Only a slight wrinkle in her brow hinted at her curiosity over Grace's eagerness to depart. "Have a good night."

"You, too." Reinforcing her excuse, Grace tugged her shawl more tightly around her shoulders and jogged toward her rooms.

When she pushed open the door, the heat from her stove washed over her in gentle welcome. She slipped off her shawl, folded it over her arm, then turned to click the lock into place. Even in a town full of women she trusted with her life, Grace never retired without locking the front door and checking all the windows. She made her rounds hurriedly tonight but still inspected every latch to make sure it was secure.

The sounder in the office was quiet. No tapping coming through the wire yet. Mentally insisting she was *not* disappointed, Grace hung up her shawl, exchanged her less comfortable heeled button boots for a pair of soft kid leather slippers, and put on a kettle for tea.

By the time she had a steaming cup in hand, the first tappings echoed though the office doorway. Her silly heart leapt at the sound, but she forced her feet to move at a sedate pace from her private chamber, which served as bedroom, kitchen, and sitting room, into the office.

She always kept the doorway open at night, in case an emergency message came through, but Western Union operators were not required to work after hours. They were, however, given the privilege of conversing with one another when not on the clock. Many stayed late or arrived early to do so. Very few conversed as late in the evening as this, though. Most were home with their families by now, so there was a greater chance of privacy. That was one of the reasons she allowed herself to indulge in these nightly chats with Mr. A. The late hour didn't bother her, since she lived in the same building where the telegraph was housed, but what about her companion?

He spoke often of his mother and sister, his nephew. He had family, people who cared about him. So why did he spend his evenings conversing with her over the telegraph wires? Could he be as lonely as she was?

Dot. Dot. Dot. Dot. Three unit pause. Dot. Dot. Dot. Seven unit pause. Dash. Dash. Dot. Seven unit pause. ·-   ·-·   ·
-·--   ---   ··-   -   ····   ·   ·-·   ·

Hs. G. Are you there?

It was Mr. A. She'd recognize his quick touch at the key anywhere. So crisp and precise. A metronome couldn't create spaces any more rhythmic. She'd long admired his deft hand at the key. Setting her tea on the table, Grace slid into her office chair, a giddy tickle in her stomach despite her best efforts to maintain a sense of detachment.

Yes, Station Dn. I'm here.

Excellent! I worried I had waited too long to call. Dinner at my sister's took longer than expected.

I hope you didn't rush away on my account, Grace tapped. She touched the key, intending to reassure him that she could answer his call anytime, since her personal chambers were only a couple steps away from the office, but such a detail seemed too intimate to share, even with someone she'd corresponded with for several months. She settled for a more generalized reply. *Family ranks higher than friendship.*

Not when they insist on driving one to distraction. I was eager to escape. Believe me.

What dastardly plague did they set upon you? Grace grinned as she tapped out the words. Mr. A always seemed to have a humorous story to tell about his family, his life so wonderfully normal that whenever she listened to him, she managed to forget all about danger and unseen foes. For a few blessed minutes, she was simply a girl talking to a young man, no worries in sight.

I dare not tell you, for fear of spreading the contagion. It seems to strike the women around me with alarming regularity.

Intrigued, Grace leaned forward. *Surely the distance between us will serve as adequate protection.*

My mother and sister have both been afflicted for some time, I'm sorry to say, but tonight their symptoms worsened.

That sounds dire, indeed. Did you call a physician?

No point. There is only one cure to their ailment. And apparently I must administer the healing dose.

Then you should do so at once, Grace replied, grinning as she reached for her tea. Mr. A never failed to entertain.

I would, of course, he said, *but I find the key ingredient in the required elixir to be frustratingly elusive.*

Can you not simply visit a druggist?

I'm afraid not. You see, the item I must find in order to cure this plague of interference is . . . a wife.

The tea Grace had just sipped spewed from her mouth to splatter over the table in front of her. Coughs spasmed in her throat.

A wife?

A strange fluttery sensation danced through her belly. He wasn't married. Why did that knowledge please her so well? Her hand trembled as she reached for the key. She had to make some kind of response. But what should she say?

I'm sure they only have your best interests at heart.

They do. But a twenty-eight-year-old man doesn't want his personal life dictated by his female relations.

Twenty-eight. A man in his prime. A man who was suddenly sharing more personal details with her than he ever had before.

Grace dabbed at the spilled tea with a handkerchief, her mind spinning. Was he fishing for details in return? She wanted to reciprocate. It was what a friend would do. Yet she couldn't afford to say too much.

I can't claim as many years of experience dealing with meddling relations as you can, but a couple friends of mine recently decided that marriage is not without its advantages. Thankfully, they have so far avoided seeing me as a matchmaking prospect.

Grace yanked her hand from the telegraph key and made a fist, her heart pumping in a wild rhythm. Details cloaked in vagueness. Would he understand what she'd just revealed? The wire remained silent for an eternally long moment.

Count your blessings, he finally sent, his usually metronome-like precision stuttering slightly. *Perhaps we could meet sometime to commiserate. I would—*

Clear the line, a brash staccato tapping interrupted. *I need to break in. This is an emergency.*

Grace nearly jumped from her chair at the pounding intrusion. It exploded across the wire like cannon fire in a still forest.

Proceed, came the answer from Mr. A. Immediate. Meticulous. All hint of personal vulnerability gone.

Grace replied in kind, though she feared her touch on the key had yet to reassert its professional tone.

Hs. Cs station has a message to relay. Are you on the wire?

A message from the Colorado Springs station? Grace shivered

as she lurched forward to answer. *Yes. This is Hs station. G on the wire. Go ahead.*

Message relayed from R as follows: He knows where you are. Coming for you. Sorry.

Everything in Grace stilled. Numbness spread from her mind to her limbs and finally to her heart. Her day of reckoning had arrived.

Chaucer Haversham had found her.

3

Amos stared at the telegraph that had fallen eerily silent. What was happening on the other end? Was Miss G in trouble? And how should he respond? It was his sworn duty not to speak of anything he learned via the wire. All communication was confidential. But he couldn't just ignore what he'd heard. It was too ominous.

If Miss G fled, how would he ever find her again? And if she didn't and the mysterious *he* caught up with her? Amos's hands clenched into tight fists. He had to do something. Had to help her somehow.

He glared at the wires leading from the telegraph, up the wall, and outside. If only he could travel via those same wires to Miss G's side. To hold her, comfort her, protect her from whatever villain threatened.

Why now, God? Why are you snatching her away from me at the very moment we started to connect on a more personal level? Is this your way of telling me I'm destined to be alone?

The wire crackled, and tapping ensued.

Hs? Is there a reply?

Amos bent forward in his seat, circling both arms around the telegraph as if he could comfort his lady through his posture. All of his energy centered on listening for Miss G's reply.

Hs? the sender repeated after several seconds ticked by with no response.

Message received. No reply. Hs off.

"No," Amos groaned. "Don't sign off. Not yet."

He waited for the other operator to sign off. Then waited another painstaking, time-crawling minute to ensure privacy on the line.

G? Are you there? he tapped.

"Please be there," he begged under his breath. "I need to know you're all right. Don't shut me out."

He fingered the key again. *Please. I want to help.*

He sat there for twenty minutes, waiting for a reply that never came.

She was gone. Just like that. The very moment he'd found the courage to open himself up to the possibility of a meeting, another man swooped in and plucked her from his loose-fingered grasp.

Amos flopped backward in his chair, suddenly more drained than if he'd ridden his bicycle along the MKT rail line all the way to Wichita Falls.

The perfect woman. One who actually enjoyed conversing with him, who made him laugh, who brightened his evenings. One who was younger than he . . . and *single*. A woman—not a relative or aged church member—who made him feel like he wasn't a mistake, like he had value, purpose.

Amos straightened. Planted both feet on the floor.

Purpose.

What if God had not been taunting him with what he could never have? What if God had directed his evening at Lucy's to run later than usual for a specific reason? To ensure that he was on the wire when that emergency message came through. What if God had allowed him to feel closer to Miss G than ever before right as that message hit the wire so that he'd be invested?

Invested enough to take action.

Amos surged to his feet. He set his chin, then grabbed his coat and locked up his office. He had a bag to pack, a replacement operator to find, and a family to say farewell to, all before the first train left in the morning.

Grace ignored the siren call of the telegraph. *Please. I want to help.*

If only it were that easy. But Mr. A didn't know what helping her would mean. A vision of her father falling in the mud-riddled street, a red stain spreading over his chest, filled her mind. She couldn't drag her new friend into this danger. Nor could she risk the safety of her current friends. She had to warn Emma.

Stomach swirling, Grace retrieved her shawl, slid her palm down the side of her skirt to ensure the derringer she always carried in the garter holster on her right thigh was still in place, then stepped out into the night.

The cold wind stung her face and flapped her skirt, but she bent into the force of it and lengthened her stride. Time was of the essence.

She trudged toward the old stagecoach station that Emma had converted into a home for herself and her two maiden aunts, Henrietta and Alberta Chandler. After Emma and Malachi married, they chose to stay in the station house with the aunts until they could build a home of their own. Mal had an area cleared in the empty field across from the church and had started framing out the walls, but with all his other duties, it would likely be a few months before he finished it.

Having the Shaws still close at hand would be a blessing tonight. Grace tightened her grip on her shawl and marched on.

Once she reached the station house, she climbed the front porch steps, paused to take a deep breath, then knocked. A kind-faced woman with a loose bun of graying hair at her nape opened the door.

"Miss Mallory. What brings you out at such a late hour, dear?" Alberta Chandler ushered Grace inside. "Is there trouble at the telegraph office?"

"I'm afraid a matter of some urgency has come up. Is Malachi . . . ?" The question dissolved, having become irrelevant. A tall man with fierce eyes stepped into the parlor, his boot heels clunking against the floorboards as he approached from the hall.

"Grace?" His gaze darted to the front window behind her as he reached for the gun belt hanging on a nearby wall hook. "You need help?"

Her stomach danced with nerves. She hated being the center of attention—especially when that attention came from a man with his hand wrapped around a weapon—but there was nothing for it. Trouble was on its way, and the marshal of Harper's Station needed to be prepared.

She gave a jerky nod, shame making her chest ache. Her secret had put these people in danger. Friends who had blindly taken her in, never guessing what price their kindness might demand. Yet these same friends had successfully ousted a murderous outlaw and overcome a businessman's scheme to ruin the town's commerce. If anyone could stand strong in the face of difficulty, the ladies—and the rare occasional gentleman—of Harper's Station could.

Grace straightened her shoulders and lifted her chin. "I need to have a word with you and Emma. If she's available."

"I'm right here, Grace." Emma strode into the parlor from the kitchen. Her sleeves were rolled up, and her ink-stained fingers suggested she'd been tallying household accounts. A long tress of dark hair had fallen loose from its pins and hung across her forehead. Emma tucked it behind her ear as she stepped into the room. Her hand grazed Malachi's arm as she moved past him, the movement natural and affectionate, yet her compassionate eyes never left Grace's face. "Whatever you need, we're here for you."

Henrietta Chandler followed on Emma's heels, her sleeves also rolled up. She held a dinner plate in one hand and a dish towel in the other. Her face glowed with righteous purpose. "Should I get my bloomers?"

Grace couldn't help but smile just a bit. Lord love Aunt Henry. She was always ready to battle the forces of intellectual darkness for the cause of women's rights, her famous bloomers being her armor of choice. "I don't think the bloomers will be necessary tonight, Henry. I just need to talk."

One brow rose on the eldest Chandler sister's forehead. "If it's serious enough to summon Malachi, it's serious enough for bloomers. I'll fetch 'em as soon as I finish the dishes." Which she set to immediately, spinning about in a swish of skirts to march back into the kitchen.

Bertie Chandler's amused gaze met Grace's. "Henry's been complaining that things have been dull around here lately. You know how she loves a good crusade. She's been itching for an excuse to don those awful pantaloons for weeks." Bertie shuddered, eliciting a chuckle from Grace, no doubt Bertie's intent from the beginning. She had a gift for putting people at ease.

And it worked. Emma joined in the quiet laughter, and even a bit of the vehemence dimmed from Malachi's expression when he smiled along with them.

Grace's nerves hadn't completely abated, but the release gained by laughing, even for the briefest of moments, slowed the frantic pace of her swirling stomach.

"Come," Emma said as she took Grace's arm and led her toward the parlor's sofa. "Sit down and tell us what happened. It must be a new development, since you didn't say anything at dinner."

"Yes." Grace swallowed the last of her reticence as she took a seat. Emma sat beside her, close enough to offer support without smothering. Malachi sat in the chair catty-corner to the sofa and leaned forward, his forearms on his thighs.

"Did you receive a telegram?" Malachi inquired as Bertie discreetly disappeared into the kitchen.

Grace nodded. "I have reason to believe that the man I've been hiding from for most of the last year has discovered my location. He's coming for me. And his coming might put Harper's Station in danger."

She turned to look at Emma, not wanting to witness the disapproval in Malachi's eyes. He was a good man, but protecting the women of Harper's Station was his priority. Emma and the aunts, in particular. The secret Grace had kept from all of them had put the people he loved in jeopardy.

"If you could just retrieve the items you placed in the bank vault for me," Grace blurted, "I can leave by morning. If anyone arrives looking for me, you can assure them that I've gone."

Emma stiffened, her expression changing from that of patient listener to offended tigress in a flash. "Didn't you once say that you were done running? That Harper's Station was your home?"

"Well . . . yes." Grace darted a glance at Malachi. His expression was as fierce as his wife's, yet not with the disapproval she'd feared. It looked more . . . protective. Of *her*.

"Then there'll be no more talk of you leaving." Emma folded her arms across her chest and glared. "If you think I'm going to let you face this threat alone, you are sadly mistaken."

"Emma's right." Malachi's deep masculine tones vibrated with authority. "You've got a better chance here with us. We stand together, Grace. No matter what comes. That's what Harper's Station is all about." He leaned back and crossed one booted foot over his knee. "Besides, if a man is after you, he'll stand out like a sore thumb the minute he steps foot in town, which gives us the advantage. You're safer here than anywhere else."

Grace shook her head—not in argument, but in amazement over the staunch support being offered. Emma didn't catch the difference, however. Her expression grew more mulish.

"You're not leaving, Grace, so don't even try to argue. Let's move on to the explanation of who this man is and what he wants with you."

Grace wanted to jump up and hug her friends, but she'd never been the type to throw herself at others, preferring quiet observation over demonstrative displays. So she squashed her rioting emotions and gave a simple nod of acquiescence instead.

It seemed to suffice. Emma loosened her arms, and Malachi uncrossed his legs. He slapped his palms against his thighs as he leaned forward, his alert gaze pinned to her face.

Grace swallowed. "His name is Chaucer Haversham, and either he or someone acting on his orders shot and killed my father."

"Oh, Grace." Emma reached across the sofa and clasped Grace's hand. "I'm so sorry."

"What does he want with you?" Malachi asked, his tone kind even as he probed for specifics.

Grace focused on the level-headed marshal instead of his sympathetic wife. She needed to concentrate on the problem, not her loss, if she hoped to get through this explanation without breaking down.

"He wants the same thing he tried to get from my father— documents that prove he is not the only heir to the Haversham fortune. My father discovered them while doing an inventory of the library in Haversham House. If those documents come to light, Chaucer Haversham stands to lose over half of his newly acquired inheritance."

Malachi let out a low whistle and rubbed a hand over his jaw. "And you have these documents, I assume?"

Grace nodded. "They're locked up in Emma's safe at the bank."

Malachi's gaze flew to his wife, his thoughts clear on his face. He was assessing the likelihood of Emma being in the line of fire when Haversham arrived.

Emma didn't seem to notice her husband's intense regard. She was too busy puzzling through what Grace had said. Her forehead crinkled. "I don't understand. You didn't give me documents to hold. You gave me books. Worn copies of *Guy Mannering* by Sir Walter Scott and *Oliver Twist* by Charles Dickens. I thought they were rare items you were holding onto for investment purposes."

Grace shook her head. "My father said the books themselves are of no particular value. That's why he didn't think they'd be missed until after he had a chance to meet with the Pinkerton agent hired by Tremont Haversham to find the daughter he had believed dead for twenty-five years. The documents are secreted inside."

"Then let's retrieve them," Malachi announced, bracing his hands against his knees as if preparing to rise. "I can deliver them to the Pinkertons. Haversham can hash out his inheritance mess in the courts. Getting rid of the documents gets rid of the threat. Problem solved."

"I'm afraid it's not quite that easy." Grace looked from Emma to Malachi, then dropped her gaze to her lap. "I've been through those books a hundred times, and I can't find evidence of any documents. Just a handful of scribbled notes in a few margins. I trust my father's word. I know he found something—something he died to protect. I just don't know what or where it is."

4

I should have brought my bicycle," Amos muttered under his breath as his mule veered off the road for the seventeenth time to munch on some scruffy-looking vegetation that must be the mule equivalent of catnip.

The livery nearest the depot in Seymour had been woefully picked over. He'd had a choice between a green-broke mustang with demon eyes and a mule the proprietor had dubbed *Will*. The name had sounded friendly enough until Amos mounted and discovered it was actually short for *Willful*. The beast refused to take direction or instruction, and while Amos was not the best of horsemen, even he knew that when he tugged the reins to the right and nudged with his heels, the animal beneath him was supposed to move right. But not Willful. The contrary beast simply ignored his commands and moved from one scraggly snack to the next with no respect for the urgency of his rider's mission.

Amos had kicked the animal's well-rounded girth, tugged the reins, and tried every encouraging sound from tongue clicks, to friendly *get ups*, to authoritative commands. He'd even gone so far as to whistle and make embarrassing kissing noises while rocking uncomfortably forward in the saddle. Nothing worked.

The mule would only move when he was good and ready, and he was never ready until he'd eaten all the roughage within three feet of the road.

"For pity's sake," Amos muttered. "I can walk faster than this." He leaned his weight into the left stirrup and rose up to dismount.

At the same moment that Amos pulled his foot from the right stirrup, Will raised his head from his snacking and set off at a bone-jarring trot. Amos nearly tumbled to the ground. Thankfully, his years of cycling had honed his balance. It wasn't pretty—a death grip on the saddle horn, an awkward forward lurch resulting in a mouthful of hairy mane, and a series of lopsided shifting as he felt around for the stirrup—but he succeeded in staying aboard.

"Nice try, Willful. But you can't defeat me that easily."

As if rising to the challenge, the maniacal beast increased his pace just as they crested a hill. A large hill with a rather steep descent.

"Whoa, now." Amos tugged on the reins, knowing it was pointless but having to try anyway. "Slow down, boy. No need to rush . . ." His words hit a crescendo and transitioned into a cry of alarm as the mule plunged down the hill, ears back, neck stretched.

Amos pressed into the stirrups and leaned backward in the saddle, holding onto his hat with one hand as he tried to keep from toppling straight over Will's head.

Just when he thought he might survive with his bones intact if not his dignity, the mule zagged to the left, turning the gently curving corner at the bottom of the hill into an angle so sharp, Euclid could have used it to demonstrate the principle of perpendicularity. Unfortunately, Amos's trajectory followed a different path, one more likely to demonstrate Newton's laws than Euclid's.

Newton's second law of motion had him continuing along the linear path dictated by the hill instead of the corner. Then the law of universal gravitation kicked in and slammed his airborne personage to the ground with a force that returned Amos to the law of motion. Or non-motion. His resting body definitely wanted to stay at rest. It hurt too much to move.

But his aches and pains didn't matter. A young woman was in need of his aid somewhere around that bend. He'd not let a few bruises and a bit of dirt keep him from his course.

Amos planted his palms against the hard-packed earth and lifted himself from the ground, wincing at the ache in the shoulder that had taken the brunt of the impact. Once he staggered to his feet, he made a hasty inspection—a difficult task when one's spectacles dangled from one's right ear. Thankfully, the lenses had been spared. After a quick reshaping of the wire frames and a rub from his handkerchief, the eyeglasses were back in place and the world around him returned to focus.

He brushed off the worst of the dirt and took a moment to straighten his collar and retrieve his hat. Then he marched around the bend and promptly stepped in a still-warm pile of mule manure.

He couldn't look. All he could do was smell. Amos tipped his face toward the heavens and flung his arms up in protest.

"Are you trying to tell me something, Lord?" He pulled his hat from his head and glared at the cheerfully blue sky. "If so, could you just make the mule speak like you did with Balaam and save us both the aggravation?" A snuffling sound brought Amos's gaze down to Will. The horrid beast was munching on more of those leafy weeds. "I always considered Balaam a brute for beating his donkey," Amos said as he pointed a finger at Will, "but I'm beginning to understand how one might be driven to such action."

Although . . . Balaam's donkey had tried to warn his master away from the path he had chosen. Was Willful doing the same? Warning Amos away from Harper's Station?

Lord, are you telling me to turn back, or did I just get stuck with the most cantankerous mule known to mankind by happenstance?

43

"And how am I to know the difference?" he muttered as he trod to the edge of the road and scraped the worst of the manure from his boot sole onto a rock. Needing something softer to clean the leather sides with, Amos spied Willful nosing around a new clump of his favorite snack. He smiled.

Walking straight for the bush, Amos nudged Willful out of the way and wiped the rest of the droppings off onto the cluster of tasty vegetation. He looked up at his nemesis and raised an eyebrow. "It's not so funny when the things *you* care about get contaminated, is it?"

Will stopped chewing and stared at Amos. Then he turned and headed down the road as if he hadn't a care in the world.

Well, he hadn't. He was a mule.

A mule carrying all of Amos's belongings.

"Whoa, now," Amos called, slapping his hat back on his head and hurrying after the departing beast. "You're missing a passenger."

The Lord must not have been trying to warn Amos away from Harper's Station, for a true miracle occurred at that moment. Willful came to a halt in the middle of the road and stood as still as an oak tree on a windless morning while Amos mounted. And as a further answer to prayer, when Amos tapped his heels to the animal's flanks and clicked his tongue, Willful actually moved. In the right direction.

Amos whispered a prayer of heartfelt thanks and vowed not to complain about the slow pace. As long as he kept moving forward, he might just make it to Miss G's telegraph office before sundown.

Ten minutes later, the first buildings of the town came into view. Amos straightened in the saddle, his heart suddenly thumping against his ribs.

He'd made it.

She was there. Somewhere. His Miss G. Waiting for him.

Well, perhaps not waiting for him, as she didn't know he was coming, but still. She was there. In one of those buildings. Alone. Frightened. In need of a brave young knight to rescue her. And while his steed might be a sorry excuse for a mule, and his armor might be a bit dusty and aromatic, his quest couldn't be more pure, his intentions more noble. As soon as he found the fair maiden, he'd offer his protection and perhaps his name if she turned out to be even half of what he'd imagined.

As he passed a large house and corral, he spied telegraph wires strung on poles. He traced the wires with his gaze and quickly spotted the small wooden building that served as the termination point. The telegraph office.

With a gentle tug on the reins, Amos steered Willful to the right. He was still fifty yards away, his imagination churning with possibilities—was her hair brown or blonde; did she have blue eyes or green; was her figure tall and slender or short and curvy—when the mule balked. Amos frowned.

"Not now, Willful," he grumbled, so full of anticipation over the meeting about to take place that he nearly missed the meeting being thrust upon him.

By a gray-haired woman with steely eyes and a Colt revolver aimed at the side of his head.

Amos turned his face toward her, raising his hands at the same time. "I mean no harm," he said as he got his first full glimpse of the woman. Correction—*women*. There were two of them, though the second looked about as frightening as a grandmother with a plate of cookies. Probably because she *did* have a plate of cookies. Much less threatening than the Colt.

"Get off of that there mule, stranger, and state your business," the taller one ordered. "I don't like the looks of you." She wrinkled her nose. "The smell of you, neither."

Amos's neck heated. "Sorry. I had a bit of a mishap on the journey—"

"I don't care about your journey," the virago interrupted. "I care about your destination. And why you thought coming here was a good idea. Now get off that mule. And keep your hands where I can see them." She pulled back the hammer on the revolver and eyed him like a seasoned soldier taking aim at an enemy.

"Yes, ma'am." Moving slowly so as not to spook her, Amos dismounted as best he could with his arms still raised. His left foot got hung up in the stirrup for a nerve-wracking moment, but with a couple hops and a lean into Willful's side for balance, Amos managed to tug his boot free and plant both feet safely on the ground. He turned slowly to face his welcoming committee.

"What's your name, dear?" the grandmotherly one asked, scooting closer to examine him, curiosity lighting her eyes. Curiosity and a healthy dose of wariness. None of the outright hostility of her companion, though, thank heavens.

"Amos Bledsoe." He tentatively tipped his hat, casting a hasty glance at Revolver Granny as he did so to make sure he didn't need to duck a bullet. His eyes widened slightly. Were those *bloomers* she was wearing?

"And your business?" Revolver Granny demanded. Bloomers or not, she had a steady hand with that gun. Not a single tremor. He wished he could say the same about his knees.

Cookie Granny frowned. "Really, Henry, must you be so brusque? He's not even carrying a weapon."

"Not that we can *see*." Revolver Granny—Henry?—eyed him up and down, no doubt searching for any suspicious bulges. "He could be hiding one under that coat."

"I'm not, I swear to you," he assured them, taking hold of the edges of his jacket and lifting outward to prove it.

"Hands away from the coat, mister!" Revolver Granny thrust her weapon an inch farther into the rapidly shrinking space between him and the barrel of her pistol.

Amos immediately released his jacket.

"Now, state your business."

"I'm looking for a friend of mine." He swallowed. A friend whose name he didn't even know. Not exactly a mark in his favor. "The local telegraph operator."

Cookie Granny shook her head. "Oh, dear. That's unfortunate."

Unfortunate? Why? Had something happened to Miss G already?

"I told you he was a ruffian, Bert."

Cookie Granny's name was Bert? Had he hit his head when he fell off the mule? That would explain a lot. Willful's sudden good temper. The strange old ladies with men's names and bloomers and . . . cookies.

"I'll go fetch Malachi before dropping off the cookies at the café," the one called Bert announced as she turned to leave.

"I'll keep him covered until Mal gets here." Henry grinned as she adjusted her grip on her weapon. "Won't be long, if I know that boy. We protect our own around here, mister. When my nephew gets through with you, you're gonna rue the day you ever set out to find Grace Mallory. You hear me? . . . Why're you smiling?"

Amos couldn't help it. His lips refused to turn down. He might be about to meet his Maker, but that particular problem paled in comparison to the other, more pertinent piece of information he'd just learned.

Her name was Grace.

5

A groaning hinge followed by a rush of cool air told Grace that someone had opened the door to the telegraph office, but she didn't look up. She was too busy scribbling down the message coming across the wire.

The telegrams that came in from Emma's New York broker always demanded her full attention. One missed number or decimal point could drastically change the entire meaning of the financial picture being painted. Thankfully, he always followed up with written correspondence, but sometimes the reports didn't arrive until after action needed to be taken at the stock market.

The sounder quieted, and Grace finished scrawling the last of the information. She read over what she had written. Everything made sense, but like any good operator, she always sought confirmation.

Lifting her hand to the key, she tapped. *Please repeat.*

The telegraph clicked away, and Grace followed each word with her pencil on the message blank. She found a word she'd omitted and a misspelling of an investor's name, but all the numeric information was accurate. She wrote in the corrections, then signed off.

Message received. G at Hs.

Task complete, Grace set aside the message—she'd have to copy it in more legible script before handing it over to Emma—and stood to greet her caller.

The marshal stood in her doorway, his attention on the town outside her office. Grace couldn't tell if he was looking at something in particular or just scanning for trouble in general. He was certainly exuding vigilance. Gone was the cheerful handyman who made his rounds with a ready grin and an eagerness to assist with whatever the ladies might need. In his place stood a lawman on high alert, expecting trouble. *Her* trouble. Grace pressed her hand against her abdomen to steady her breathing and her nerves.

"Mr. Shaw." She forced a smile to her face, hoping it would add a pleasant tone to her voice and disguise her unease.

He turned to regard her, then shut the door and took two long strides toward the small window near the counter. He hunched slightly in order to maintain an unobstructed view of the street, his height being greater than that of the paned glass.

"What does that Haversham fella look like? Can you describe him?" His gaze slashed back to her for a long moment, his intensity cutting through her like a blade.

"I—I don't know. I never met him. He avoided Denver. Any time he spent in Colorado took place at the mine in Willow Creek, a couple hundred miles southwest of us."

"Ever meet the father?" Mal asked before swinging his attention back to the window.

Grace attempted to recall Tremont Haversham's features. She didn't exactly move in the same circles as the silver tycoon, but she'd seen him from a distance in the hotel a few times. "He was tall, I believe. Broad shoulders. Square jaw. His hair was streaked with gray but dark underneath. He always dressed in the highest fashion and carried a cane with a silver knob on top. But why do you need . . . ?"

"Sons often take after their fathers in looks," Malachi clipped out.

Her heart pounded in her chest as the ramification of those words soaked into her half-numb mind. "Have . . ." A sudden thickness clogged her throat. She swallowed and tried again. "Have you seen someone suspicious?"

Lord have mercy. So soon? She thought she'd have at least a day or two to prepare.

"Yep." Malachi turned back to face her, his piercing gaze doing nothing to soothe her rioting nerves. "Henry spotted him coming into town and pulled her pistol on him. The scoundrel admitted right to her face that he was lookin' for you. I locked him up in the new jailhouse."

Good heavens. Thank the Lord for Aunt Henry and her revolver. Grace's legs quivered and threatened to give way. She clasped the table edge in front of her and slowly lowered herself into the chair.

"He don't look much like what you described, though. He's kind of scrawny with sand-colored hair and spectacles. Not one for fancy clothes, neither. He's wearin' a suit, but it's not tailored. And he rode into town on a mule of all things. Not exactly a wealthy man's choice of mount." Malachi rubbed his chin, a frown etching lines into his brow. "'Course, Haversham could have hired someone to take care of business for him. But even then, I would have expected a gunslinger-type, not a fellow who looks like a store clerk. He wasn't even carrying a weapon."

"That *is* odd." Whoever had shot her father had definitely known his way around guns—rifles, especially—to take down a man in a crowded street from a great enough distance to avoid detection.

The marshal finally abandoned his post at the window and stood across from her desk. He fiddled with the pint-sized canning jar that held the three sharpened pencils she kept on hand for customers. The wooden shafts clinked against the glass as he twisted the jar back and forth.

"He claims to be a friend of yours," Malachi said as he set about organizing the pencils according to height. "Amos Bledsoe." He finally met her eyes. "Ever heard of him?"

Grace shook her head. "No. I don't think so." All her friends were women. And most lived here in Harper's Station.

"He said you might say that."

Grace frowned. "What does that mean? Either I know him or I don't. How could I be friends with a man whose name I don't recognize?"

Malachi set the pencil jar aside and leaned an elbow on the counter. "That's what I figured. Told him the story was cagey, but he insisted I ask you. Said he met you on the wire, whatever that means. Goes by A. And claims to be from Denison, not Colorado."

"Denison?" Her voice trembled.

The marshal shrugged. "That's what he said."

It couldn't be. Could it?

Mr. A? Here, in Harper's Station.

Grace slowly pushed to her feet, so many emotions swirling through her that she felt a mite dizzy, but the thought of her mysterious Mr. A being in Harper's Station, a few short yards away . . . well, she just couldn't sit.

Last night he'd hinted at the possibility of a meeting, but then the message from the Colorado Springs office had arrived and cut their conversation short. Cut their relationship short too, or so she'd thought.

Could this Amos Bledsoe actually be her Mr. A? The man who made her laugh and eased her loneliness on long evenings. Who had a wonderfully interfering mother, a teasing sister, a down-to-earth brother-in-law, and an adorable, glasses-grabbing nephew, all of whom she'd secretly adopted, at least in her imagination, to fill the aching void of family in her life.

How had he gotten here so quickly? He would've had to take the train first thing this morning, and they'd just spoken last night.

Could he be an imposter? Had Haversham learned of her friendship with Mr. A and sought to use that to his advantage? To trick her into giving up her information?

The idea was farfetched. Only local area operators would be able to listen in on her nightly conversations, not operators from as far away as Colorado. But if Haversham had gotten to Rosie, her mother's old telegraph colleague in Colorado Springs—the only person in Colorado Grace had stayed in contact with—he could get to others. Coerce them into helping him.

Rosie wouldn't have given up Grace's location unless Haversham had left her no choice. He must have threatened her family. Grace had made Rosie promise to give Haversham whatever he asked if that happened. She wasn't about to let him destroy another woman's family as he had hers. The fact that Rosie still found a way to get a message of warning to Grace last night proved her loyalty.

"You all right, Miss Mallory?" Malachi straightened and started moving toward the half door at the end of the counter that separated her inner office from the waiting area. "You look a little shaky there."

"I'm fine. Really." In truth her insides were spinning like a weathervane in a tornado, but the marshal didn't need to know that. "I'm just a little surprised. I *have* corresponded with a telegraph operator in Denison, and his call sign is an *A*, which could stand for Amos." She moved toward the connecting door herself, grabbing her shawl from the back of her chair as she went. "Perhaps I should take a look at this Mr. Bledsoe. See if I can verify his claim."

Malachi met her at the end of the counter, his face still schooled in serious lines, but his eyes danced with a touch of humor that didn't quite fit the lawman persona he'd been projecting moments earlier. "I'd be happy to escort you, ma'am." He offered his arm.

Normally, Grace would have pretended not to notice the gesture. Such attention embarrassed her, made her feel far too visible when out in public. Yet at this particular moment, she doubted she could make it to the jailhouse under her own power. As wobbly as her legs were, she'd likely hit a divot in the ground and end up sprawled in the middle of the road. Better to be seen on a married man's arm than on her face in the dirt.

Besides, if it truly was her Mr. A waiting in the marshal's jail cell, she'd certainly not want to meet him with a torn hem and dust smudging her cheeks. A first impression could only be made once.

At the sound of the outer door opening, Amos jumped off the cot and hurried toward the bars at the front of the cell. He hooked a finger around the edge of his collar and tugged at the suddenly too-tight band. He stretched his neck above the starched tourniquet and inhaled a lungful of stale air.

Steady, man. Steady.

The marshal pulled the door wide, then stepped aside to allow a woman to enter ahead of him. Amos caught his breath and tugged his derby from his head.

She was dainty, barely over five feet, he would guess, with a tiny nip of a waist. She dressed as if wanting to avoid notice, her black skirt free of any trim or adornment except for a thin silver buckle that held a black belt in place at her waist. She wore a pleated blouse with thin, dark green stripes and a simple black bow tied at her neck. A pale gray shawl slipped down her shoulders to rest in the crook of her elbows as she moved into the room, closer to the bars separating him from her.

Thick brown hair framed her pale face, curled back in some kind of twist that, while simple, also flattered her delicate features.

A spattering of freckles danced across the bridge of a nose that sloped gently and turned up just a tad at the end.

But her most arresting features were her eyes. Large in her face, like those of a doe in the forest, their deep brown color drew him in. Soft. Gentle. A little afraid. Yet a fire burned there, too. He'd seen the same depth in his sister's eyes, hidden behind the teasing light she usually showed the world. If someone were to hurt a member of her family or someone she cared about, all evidence of the affable Lucy would vanish in a flash, leaving the tigress to take over. His gut told him Miss Mallory would act much the same.

The tiny woman said nothing, just stared at him through the bars, taking his measure. Suddenly Amos recalled his sorry state of repair. The stench of mule manure from his boot, though faded now, seemed to strengthen and rise around him in a cloud. He'd dusted most of the dirt from his clothes, but he knew he still looked rumpled and unkempt. At least his hair was in decent shape. He'd just had it trimmed last week. It wasn't much to recommend him in the appearance department, but then, he'd never expected to win a lady's heart with his looks.

"So." The marshal cleared his throat, reminding Amos of his presence. "This the fella you've been corresponding with, Miss Mallory?"

She took a step closer, her face moving between two bars, leaving his view of her completely unobstructed. She blinked, a slow fluttering of lashes that made his gut tighten. When his gaze met hers, a rosy glow spread across her cheeks. She ducked away from his regard as if embarrassed, then slowly raised her head again, resuming her scrutiny.

Yep. Inner strength. She'd not be one to shy away from what needed to be done.

"Miss Mallory?" the marshal repeated.

She tilted her head. "I won't know until I talk to him."

Amos tugged on his jacket and raised his chin, offering her the most winsome smile in his limited arsenal. "Miss Mallory. I'm Amos Bledsoe, Western Union operator from Denison, Texas. We spoke just yesterday—"

She shook her head, cutting off his introduction. "Not that kind of talking," she said as she reached into her hair and extracted a black pin.

Amos frowned, then immediately brightened as he saw her stretch the *u*-shaped wire over the first finger of her right hand.

Not only was his lady lovelier than he'd let himself imagine, she was clever as well.

6

Grace willed her hand not to tremble as she fit the hairpin over her finger. A difficult task when her insides were jumping about as if she'd swallowed a family of crickets.

The man in the cell reminded her a bit of her father. His sack suit was walnut brown with a thin pinstripe, and while the buttons were all neatly done up, wrinkles creased the fabric. Her father had never given his clothing much thought. He'd just thrown on whatever had been at hand, preferring to expend mental energy on his academic pursuits. The man in front of her, however, seemed more conscious of his appearance. His shirt cuffs had been tugged down to show just a hair below the edge of his coat sleeves, as fashion dictated. His collar points were starched, and the knot of his tie hung perfectly straight. What an odd mixture of fastidious care and rumpled mayhem.

And what was that smell? Grace struggled not to wrinkle her nose. She'd never noticed the marshal's office smelling like a livery before. The odor seemed to grow stronger the closer she came to the man in the cell.

But no matter. She wasn't here for a social call. She was here to determine this stranger's identity. She peered up into the man's face, past his spectacles, and into his eyes.

They were blue, his eyes. And earnest. And just a tad unsettling.

Breaking the contact, Grace straightened her shoulders and took a step forward, intent on tapping out a message on the cell's crossbar. But a hand grabbed her arm and tugged her backward.

"Don't get too close, Miss Mallory," the marshal instructed as he gently steered her away. "You can do your talkin' from back here."

Actually, she couldn't, but Malachi didn't know that. And why would he? He wasn't an operator. She glanced around the office, her gaze zeroing in on the desk. A tin cup rested on its surface. That would work nicely.

Smiling at the marshal, she stepped away from his hold and moved toward the desk. "May I?" she asked, indicating the chair.

Malachi looked at her oddly but nodded. "Be my guest."

"Thank you." She swept her skirt aside and settled herself on the seat before reaching for the coffee cup. She peered inside and frowned. Still half full. She glanced around for a place to dispose of the beverage, but there were no potted plants or conveniently located knotholes in any of the nearby floorboards.

Without giving herself time to think better of it, she lifted the cup to her lips and chugged down the cold, bitter brew in one long gulp. She grimaced and nearly choked on the awful stuff, but she got it down.

"You . . . ah . . . want a fresh cup?" Malachi asked, the shock on his face rather comical. "I got a pot on the stove in the corner."

"No, thank you." Her reply emerged more as a rasp than actual words. How did he drink that swill? It tasted like boiled shoe leather. "I just need the cup."

She promptly turned the tin cup on its side and hovered her hairpin-covered finger above it. She glanced past the befuddled marshal to the man waiting expectantly in the jail cell. He was gripping the edge of his jacket, holding it away from his body.

He'd fitted the bottom button between the first two fingers of his right hand and held it an inch above the iron crossbar.

Grace turned away and bit the inside of her cheek to contain the smile trying to edge its way onto her face.

He knew exactly what she was about and was ready to respond.

Focusing on the silver cup in front of her, Grace began the test. *Call me like you would on the wire.*

A series of dull raps came from across the room, the cloth-covered button muffling the sharpness of the reply. *Dn calling Hs.* The sound might be off, but the rhythm wasn't. It only took the first few clicks for Grace to recognize the sender's unique style. To an untrained ear, one tapping pattern might sound like any other, but to an operator, the rhythm, tempo, and phrasing combined to form an auditory signature.

Mr. A's signature.

But even if Amos Bledsoe was indeed her Mr. A, he still had some explaining to do, and Grace wasn't about to let the opportunity to quiz him pass her by.

Who's filling in for you at Dn?

Dorinda Mansfield, came the immediate reply. No hesitation. No unsteadiness to interrupt the rhythm. *She worked the telegraph at the railroad depot until she married two years ago. Her husband agreed to let her cover my shifts.*

The quickness of his response and the assured way he tapped it out gave the impression of honesty. And she had to admit, she liked the fact that he trusted a female operator to cover his post. Even though the field of telegraphy employed more women than nearly any other, male operators tended to believe themselves superior. Probably because they received larger wages for the same work, an inequity that Henrietta Chandler railed against on a regular basis. Thankfully, Amos Bledsoe didn't seem to share that supercilious view.

The practice of paying women less for the same work *was* unfair, but if the telegraph companies couldn't hire women at a smaller wage and thereby increase their profits, they probably wouldn't hire females at all. The cheaper rate opened doors that Grace needed if she was to support herself.

Describe your family to me, she tapped out on the tin cup, continuing the interrogation.

He named them all and gave a brief description of each in that tongue-in-cheek style of his that was so endearing. He gave details she recognized from previous conversations, and when he was finished, he'd successfully removed all doubt that he was anyone other than her Mr. A from across the wire.

The tapping faded and a throat cleared. Grace started at the non-rhythmic sound and jerked her head up. The marshal stood in front of the desk, his shoulder propped against the wall to his left, his forehead etched with lines of confusion.

Poor man. It was rude to carry on a conversation in a language others in the room couldn't follow, but it was the only way for her to confirm Mr. Bledsoe's identity.

"You two done . . . *talking?*" He tipped his head toward the man in the cell, but his eyes remained fixed on Grace.

She really should continue the rest of this interview in spoken English. But she had one more question she wanted answered. A personal question that she'd rather Malachi not be privy to, yet one that would play a significant role in deciding what action she took once Mr. Bledsoe was released.

"Almost," she hedged as she stole a glance at the man in the cell.

He met her gaze straight on. His lips twitched a bit, hinting at some inner nervousness, but he didn't shy away from her, and that forthrightness stirred her admiration. He didn't rail at the injustice of being thrown in jail when he'd committed no crime. He didn't demand release or threaten retaliation. Not even in his coded communication, which the marshal clearly didn't understand. He simply stood on the other side of the bars with calm dignity, ready to give her whatever answers she required. This was a man of integrity and courage.

A man whose motives she needed to excavate just a little further.

Amos held Miss Mallory's gaze despite the clenching of uncertainty in his abdomen. Did she believe him? Would she welcome his help? Or had he made a complete fool of himself by jumping on that train this morning?

He'd arrogantly assumed Miss G to be alone and in need of his protection. He'd thought to woo her gentle heart with a valiant rescue. But the Harper's Station women's colony apparently had a lawman—who was actually a *man* and seemed to know his way around firearms, judging by the holster slung low on his hip and the gun case in the corner with an assortment of rifles and shotguns at the ready—and at least one gun-toting she-wolf on the prowl to keep its residents safe.

Miss Mallory didn't need his protection.

Yet as he looked at her, he couldn't manufacture the desire to leave. He wanted to be her champion, yes, but more than that, he simply wanted to be with her, to explore who she was beneath that lovely exterior. To discover who they might be together.

She looked away, dipping her chin back toward the desk. Then she started tapping, and as he decoded the soft percussion into words, his heart thumped a more forceful cadence in his chest.

Why did you come? she asked. *What do you hope to gain?*

Amos swallowed and took a moment to wipe the clamminess from his hand before answering. How much should he divulge? They barely knew each other. Until today, their acquaintance had only existed over the wire, where anonymity created an illusion of safety, of comradery.

He sensed his response would dictate the future of their relationship. There would be no going back. It would either move forward, or it would die. And the woman seated across the room from him would dictate the direction it took. The same woman who had revealed *nothing* of her own feelings or thoughts beyond what little he could read on her face.

The woman who was in danger and didn't know who she could trust.

Amos squared his shoulders and reclaimed his grip on his suit coat button. He was going to have to crack his chest open and expose his secrets to her. Nothing else would suffice for gaining her trust. She might still send him away, but at least he'd know that he'd done all he could.

Holding the button over the bar, he carefully tapped out his reply.

I came because I care about you. After that cryptic message last night, I was worried you were in danger. That you might need my help. He gazed at the desk, willing Grace to look at him.

As if she felt his silent plea, she raised her head and turned until her eyes finally met his.

I see now that you have friends and protectors here, but I'm not ready to leave yet. You mean something to me, G.

Her eyes widened slightly, and he feared he'd said too much. Then again, maybe he'd not said enough.

I've felt friendship grow between us, he continued, *a friendship that left me wondering if there could possibly be more. I've wanted to meet you for several weeks, but until last night I was too afraid to suggest a meeting. Too afraid I'd disappoint you, and you'd end our evening discussions. Or that you'd turn out to be a fifty-year-old grandmother who only chatted with me because she had trouble sleeping.*

A burst of laughter escaped Miss Mallory before she could raise a hand to cover her mouth and contain it. The soft, throaty sound warmed his insides and gave him hope that perhaps not all was lost.

The marshal frowned and looked from her to Amos and back again, but thankfully he didn't interrupt or demand explanations.

I want a chance to get to know you, Miss Mallory. To see if perhaps we can get along as well in person as we do over the wire. And to offer whatever assistance I can to aid you in your current predicament.

She twisted away from him again, hiding her face as she quietly straightened the marshal's desk. She placed the coffee cup right side up, removed the hairpin from her finger, and rubbed the spot that had surely been pinched the last quarter hour. Then she slid the pin back into her hair, smoothed her hands over the blotter on the marshal's desktop, and slowly—gracefully—pushed to her feet.

"What do you want me to do with him?" the lawman asked as he shoved away from the wall and moved to meet her in the center of the small room.

Amos released his jacket button and stepped back from the bars, trying to maintain as much dignity as possible.

"I'm convinced he is who he claims to be," she said.

Amos desperately wanted to scratch the suddenly violent itch that flared around his collar. Why wouldn't she look at him?

"But I think we should leave him here until I have a chance to address the ladies at the town meeting tonight. You know how some of them get when unknown men roam the streets. I think it would be better if I warn them about him before turning him loose."

She was going to leave him locked up? Amos tried not to be offended, but he was a law-abiding citizen whose only crime was wanting to help a lady in distress. A lady who had plumbed his depths without offering him an ounce of insight into her own state of mind.

Miss Mallory glided to the door, then paused and glanced over her shoulder. Not at Amos, but at the marshal. "I'll stop by the café and ask them to send dinner over for him."

Then she left. Without a single glance in Amos's direction. With no word to him. Not even a hint as to her reaction to all he had shared.

The marshal strode up to the bars. Amos expected a scowl or a series of threats about leaving Miss Mallory alone, but Mr. Shaw surprised him. The smile he offered felt almost conciliatory.

"Don't worry," he said. "The meeting's in less than an hour. You won't have to wait long." He tipped his hat back on his forehead and leaned his shoulder against the barred door. "The women around here run a strict democracy," he explained. "Everyone gets a say about what goes on in town. Grace is playing things safe by having you cool your heels here until she can explain your presence to the others—some of whom ain't too fond of our kind, I'll warn you—but she's the cautious sort. And not without cause." He aimed a pointed look in Amos's direction.

Amos nodded, understanding the unspoken message. Grace Mallory had endured hardship, the kind that changed a person. He'd have to be patient if he hoped to woo her.

Mr. Shaw knocked a knuckle against the bar. "Might as well get comfortable." He tilted his head toward the cot against the outside wall. "I'll make a fresh pot of coffee so you don't have to drink yesterday's leftover sludge with your dinner." He chuckled and shook his head as he walked toward the small wood-burning stove in the corner. "I still can't believe she drank that stuff. I know it was vile. I only drink it because I hate wasting anything edible."

As the lawman's friendly rambling dwindled, Amos tried to get comfortable on the cot. He rested his head against the wall and let out a heavy sigh.

Then he heard it. A gentle rap from the other side of the wall as if someone were knocking on the brick. Knocking in a discernible pattern.

.. -- --. .-.. .- -..

-.-- --- ..- -.-. .- -- .

I'm glad you came.

Amos smiled, the weight pressing down on his chest lessening considerably at the four small words echoing through the wall at his back. He stretched his hands casually over his shoulders as if to pillow his head, but before he laced his fingers together, his knuckle rapped out a quick reply.

-- . - --- ---

Me too.

7

Helen Potter filed into the church with the rest of the ladies who had gathered for the town meeting. She edged into the sanctuary, making a point to keep Betty Cooper, her employer, between her and the marshal, who stood guard at the door. With Betty as a buffer, she wouldn't have to look him in the eye.

Malachi Shaw had proven himself a decent sort, but Helen still didn't feel comfortable around him. Of course, she'd never felt comfortable around any man. Loathed most of them on sight, as a matter of fact.

Coming to Harper's Station a year ago had felt like walking into heaven. No men anywhere. She didn't care how hard the work was at the chicken farm. No men meant no fear. No worrying about where the next blow would come from. No constant strategizing how to avoid crossing a man's path. No fretting about the consequences of saying the wrong thing or not enough right things. She'd shovel chicken manure and have henpecked hands for the rest of her days if it meant never laying eyes on a man again.

But good things tended not to last in her life, and the paradise of Harper's Station's male-free environment was no different. The town's founder, Emma Chandler, had gone and married the fella she'd brought in to help rout the outlaw threatening them several months ago. That meant their colony had a male resident. A permanent resident. A voting resident. And Emma wasn't the only defector.

Victoria Adams, one of the staunchest supporters of the male-free life—a successful shopkeeper, mother, and co-founder of the colony—was actually allowing a man to court her. Helen had been devastated when she'd heard the news. She'd long admired Tori's independence and had held her up as an example of what a woman could achieve without a man at her side. Tori had been Helen's inspiration. Until she'd turned traitor.

It felt as if the women she shared a bond of sisterhood with were, one by one, changing before her eyes. Opening themselves to the influence of men. Yes, the men they'd chosen to align themselves with seemed honorable and kind—*so far*—but it still felt like a betrayal.

Helen followed Betty into one of the pews several rows from the front. As she took her seat, Katie Clark slid in beside her and leaned close to whisper in her ear.

"Have you heard about the new man in town?" The gossip bubbled out of Katie like the sticky froth from boiling rice, scalding Helen with the unwelcome news. "I heard Mr. Shaw has him locked up in the jail. I don't know what he did, but I think it has something to do with Grace. Ann Marie said Grace came into the café and ordered dinner for him. He's some kind of friend of hers, I think." A frown marred the young blonde's smooth forehead. "Not sure why he's in jail if he's a friend, but I bet this meeting has something to do with him."

Betty had brought the girls into town early so they could deliver eggs before the meeting started, saving them a trip in the morning. Helen had taken a basket to the boardinghouse while Katie had delivered to the café. Then they'd met back up with Betty and the other girls from the farm at Tori's store and helped unload the rest. Well, Helen had helped unload. Katie hadn't returned until the work was practically finished. Apparently she'd become entwined in the café's grapevine of idle chatter.

Helen gave Katie a disapproving look. "Emma will tell us what we need to know soon enough. We don't need to speculate."

Katie's bubbles continued frothing, completely unaffected by Helen's attempt to dampen them. "But aren't you curious about him and what his relationship is with Grace? She never talks about him. About anyone from her past, actually. He could be an old suitor or a long-lost brother who's been searching for her for years."

"Or he could be a confidence man using his relationship with Grace to talk his way into our midst so he can empty our pocketbooks and leave us destitute," Helen snapped.

Katie shook her head, a familiar sadness creeping into her expression. "Why must you always expect the worst of people?"

"Not people," Helen corrected as she twisted in her seat to face forward. "Just men."

"You know that's not normal, right?" Katie whispered.

Helen pressed her lips together in a tight line. She wouldn't have answered anyway, but the fact that Emma Shaw was moving toward the podium gave her the perfect excuse to remain silent.

Normal? Probably not. But smart was better than normal. A smart woman could protect herself, avoid confrontations before they happened, and escape the inescapable. Smart equaled safe. And safe was the pinnacle Helen aspired to achieve.

Katie was so young, so naïve, so unrealistically romantic. If the girl ever left Harper's Station, she'd end up used and abandoned by some charming rogue in less than a month. She lived on fairy-tale dreams of handsome princes and chivalrous knights in a world of rattlesnakes and coyotes. Helen might only be three years older in age—twenty-five to Katie's twenty-two—but she was ancient in terms of experience. And her experience told her that if there really was a trouser-clad outsider in Harper's Station, trouble would be right around the corner.

The room quieted as Emma Shaw ascended the dais and faced the gathering. "Thank you for coming, ladies. We have a matter of some concern to discuss this evening. Someone has threatened one of our own, and we need to apprise you of the situation so that you can be on your guard."

Helen sat up straighter, her instincts flaring. She'd made a vow when she'd first come to Harper's Station—they all had—to lend aid without question to any sister in need. This community worked because everyone relied on one another, supported one another, trusted one another. They were family. And this family stood together, no matter what.

"Grace Mallory has asked to address us tonight," Emma continued. "Please give her your attention." She stepped away from the podium and nodded to someone seated in the front row. "Grace?"

The telegraph operator stood and climbed the two steps to the stage, then slipped behind the podium, grasping the sides of the wooden stand as if it were the only thing keeping her upright. Head down, she locked her gaze on the floor a few feet in front of the first row of pews.

Helen squirmed in sympathy. She knew what it was like to prefer the shadows to the spotlight. Most of her childhood had been spent learning how to avoid notice. How to hide in dark corners and arm herself with invisibility. She'd hidden out of necessity, not temperament, but she understood the feeling of exposure when caught in the light. It took courage for someone as shy and quiet as Grace Mallory to address a group of fifty women, even if they were her friends and peers.

Grace cleared her throat and raised her focus a few inches off the ground. "A man named Chaucer Haversham has been looking for me for nearly a year. Yesterday, I received word that he has discovered my hiding place here in Harper's Station." She glanced sideways to Emma. "I offered to leave town, but Emma and Malachi agreed that I'd be safer here."

"You ain't going nowhere, Gracie," Henry Chandler shouted from the front row. Heads throughout the church bobbed in agreement, including Helen's.

"Thank you," Grace murmured as her cheeks grew pink. "You are all such dear friends. You have no idea how much your comradery means to me." She stood a little straighter and finally raised her gaze to eye level with the audience. "But you need to know the danger my staying entails. I have no proof, but I am fully convinced that this man, or someone working under his orders, shot and killed my father."

Helen gasped. A killer?

Katie reached into Helen's lap, grabbed her hand, and squeezed. Helen turned and met her friend's stare, a silent promise flowing between them as Helen squeezed Katie's hand in return. They'd look out for each other.

"I have something he wants," Grace explained. "Something that threatens his inheritance, which truly belongs to an older half-sister everyone believed had perished at birth. My father was about to turn the documents over to a Pinkerton agent but was murdered as he crossed the street to keep his appointment." Grace shifted from side to side, her focus dropping once again to the floor.

Had she seen her father die? Helen bit her lower lip. She couldn't imagine such a thing. As often as she'd wished her own father dead, she'd never wanted to witness the deed being carried out. Especially not in so sudden and violent a fashion. And if Grace had actually liked her father? It must have been awful.

Grace seemed to gather herself, straightening her spine and lifting her chin. "Haversham owns a mine in Colorado and has Pinkerton agents on his payroll, so I don't know if the agent my father was scheduled to meet betrayed us or if he would have proven trustworthy. Mr. Shaw is going to help me connect with the head agent in Philadelphia to investigate. In the meantime, I ask that you keep watch and report any sightings of male visitors to Harper's Station."

Katie suddenly lurched to her feet, jerking Helen's arm in its socket before releasing her hand. "What about the man at the jailhouse?"

Grace's cheeks deepened from pink to a burning red, but she didn't flinch as she met Katie's gaze. "His name is Amos Bledsoe. He's a friend who heard of my trouble and came to help. He might be in town a few days, but he poses no threat."

Helen stiffened, her shoulder blades bumping uncomfortably against the wooden back of the church pew.

Another man in Harper's Station. Wonderful. They were multiplying like rabbits.

It was a good thing the farm sat five miles outside of town. She'd make a point not to volunteer for any deliveries during the next week or so. The rabbits hadn't spread beyond the borders of town yet, and Lord willing, they never would. The two roosters they had strutting around the coops were more than sufficient.

"Mr. Bledsoe is visiting from Denison and has no connection to the Haversham family or the Pinkerton agency," Grace explained. "He is simply a friend, and I hope that you will welcome him as such." She glanced around the room, bravely meeting the eyes of the ladies in the audience. "Does anyone have an objection to Mr. Bledsoe being allowed to stay?"

Helen squirmed but said nothing. She didn't want another man hanging around, but she had no true grounds to object. The fact that the visitor wore trousers didn't seem like a good enough reason to ban him from town. Well, it was reason enough for her, but most of the ladies in the room weren't quite so extreme in their views.

Or were they? Helen's chest thumped as Henrietta Chandler pushed to her feet in the front row.

"Seems a mite suspicious that this fella showed up so quick after your friend sent you that telegram last night. What if he's working for Haver-what's-his-name? Maybe he's the one who told the rich gent where you were hiding."

Thoughtful murmurs echoed around the room, and Helen held her breath. *Please send him away.* But Grace shook her head, and Helen's hope withered.

"I know who revealed my location to Mr. Haversham—a woman who used to work with my mother. She has kept me apprised of the investigation into my father's shooting as well as any noteworthy items regarding Mr. Haversham's business over the past nine months. It wouldn't have taken Haversham long to discover that I worked as a Western Union operator. After that, it would just be a matter of finding local telegraph operators susceptible to bribes and having them listen in on the wires for any clues that might lead to my location."

The color flaring in Grace's cheeks faded to a more normal hue as she grew more involved in her explanation. "I took precautions," she said. "Not communicating with any of my friends from Denver, only with my mother's contact in Colorado Springs. I changed my call sign. Only sent personal information over the lines after hours in the evenings. But no plan is foolproof, and I knew there was a chance that Haversham would eventually discover Rosie's involvement. I made her promise to give up any information she had on me if he threatened her or her family." Grace looked down at the podium in front of her and blinked several times as if fighting off tears. "I didn't want him to lay waste to her life the way he devastated mine." She sniffed once then deliberately raised her chin, determination etched into her features. "When I received Rosie's warning, I knew exactly what had happened, and I cast no blame.

"Mr. Bledsoe overheard that warning, and that's what precipitated his hasty trip out here. Not many men would leave their employment and family responsibilities on such short notice to help out an acquaintance in a faraway town, but Mr. Bledsoe did just that. I believe it speaks highly of his character."

Or his manipulation skills. Helen bit the inside of her cheek to keep her pessimism from escaping.

"Besides," Grace continued, "Mr. Shaw and I both questioned him, and I am convinced he is exactly who he claims to be. He is a concerned friend, just like each of you. And right now, I need all the friends I can get."

Now Helen felt guilty for wishing the trouser-wearer away. Her shoulders drooped as Henry Chandler took her seat. No one else seemed willing to voice an objection after that heartfelt plea.

Grace stepped off the dais, and Emma took over the meeting, giving directions on who to contact if a strange man was spotted and what action to take. Helen didn't really listen. She didn't need to. Emma always gave the same lecture. Don't do anything to put yourself in danger. Don't confront the intruder. Run to Malachi for help. Etc., etc.

Instead of listening, Helen plotted ways to separate herself as much as possible from the approaching trouble. Not because she didn't want to help Grace. She did. But men in charge didn't like interference. No one expected her in town, anyway. She worked at the farm, after all.

Helen straightened as an idea took root. The pecan trees near the old line cabin by the creek on the south side of Betty's property had been showing signs of dropping when she walked out that way a couple weeks ago. Collecting the pecans would take two or three days, with all the nuts she'd seen in the branches of the bigger trees.

For the first time since they'd come to town, Helen felt a genuine reason to smile. Not only could she put distance between herself and the invading male establishment by staying at the farm, but she could nearly double the size of her buffer during peak hours of the day by sneaking away to harvest pecans.

A mess of nuts to escape the miscreants. Perfect!

8

Grace finally managed to draw a full breath after the last lady turned to leave the church. Only Emma and Victoria lingered, and Grace knew they wouldn't pester her with unanswerable questions. Would Haversham harm them to get to her? *Please, Lord, don't let that be the case.* Why couldn't she contact the missing heiress directly and turn the documents over to her? *Because I don't know the name of the woman or where she resides.* Why hadn't she asked her father where the documents were hidden before he left?

That one haunted her. She should have pressed him for details, but he'd been so focused on trying to anticipate every possible eventuality regarding the meeting with the Pinkerton agent that he'd had little patience for her questions. He'd been distracted, short-tempered, all because he loved her and was trying to protect her while still doing what he believed to be right. So she'd simply trusted him. He was her father. If he said he had proof, he had proof. He had no reason to lie. In fact, he had more reason to deny finding anything. They both would have been safer if he'd pretended not to recognize the significance of what he'd found.

But her father was not that type of man. Integrity ran thick in his veins, nourishing every thought and action. He could no more hide from what needed to be done than she could ignore a message sounding over the wire. Both situations demanded a response, and the Mallorys responded.

"Are you all right?" Victoria's soft voice gently extricated Grace from her memories. Tori placed a hand on Grace's shoulder, her blue eyes full of empathy.

Grace nodded and even managed a small smile. "No one tried to run me out of town, so I guess the worst is over."

Emma moved to Grace's other side, her brows raised. "You're an even bigger optimist than I am if you truly think the worst is over. We won't even know what the worst is until Haversham or whomever he hires arrives."

"I don't know." Grace gave a small, self-deprecating laugh. "I think I'd rather face Haversham than speak in front of such a large group again. At least then I could use my derringer." She patted the pistol in the garter holster beneath the right side of her skirt. A pistol she never went anywhere without. "I felt helpless against all those eyes staring at me."

Emma's eyes widened in disbelief. "You know all these ladies care about you."

"Yes, but not all of us have your gift of leadership." Grace met Emma's gaze. "I've always envied how at ease you are whenever you address us as a group."

Emma shrugged. "I never really thought about it. I just get up and say what needs to be said."

Grace smiled. "I know." Emma ran the town, the local bank, and pretty much any other project that required guidance. Her astounding capability would be annoying if she wasn't also the most compassionate, caring person Grace had ever met.

"Ben will be stopping by the store tomorrow to prep for a couple big deliveries," Tori said as the three of them wandered through the church door. "I'll ask him to keep an eye out for anyone suspicious in the area. If anything snags his attention, he'll get word to us."

Grace clutched the railing by the stairs, feeling adrift and in need of an anchor. For the last few months, she'd actually allowed herself to feel safe. To believe that she could have a normal life. Even a suitor—at least an anonymous one safely removed from her troubles.

Now look at her. Treading water in the middle of a maelstrom, afraid that every friend who offered her a line would be dragged down into the vortex with her. Yet without their help, she would drown.

Grace forced a smile to her face. "Thank you, Tori. Having Mr. Porter's help will be a blessing."

Emma wrapped an arm around Grace's shoulders, and Grace turned to face her. "You're not alone in this, Grace. You have allies. An entire town full of them. And we're all ready to help in whatever way we can."

Grace blinked back the embarrassing moisture suddenly blurring her vision and ducked her head as she leaned briefly into Emma's embrace. "Thank you." She straightened and looked at Tori again. "I couldn't ask for better friends."

"You've been there for us," Tori said, her voice ripe with conviction. "We're just returning the favor."

Emma nodded. "That's what sisters do." She squeezed Grace a final time then traipsed down the steps as if her simple statement hadn't just set off an earthquake beneath Grace's feet.

Sisters?

She'd never had a sister. Or a brother. And now, when her problems threatened to bring harm upon their own lives, these women surrounded her with a level of acceptance and support that truly superseded the boundaries of ordinary friendship. Only God could bring about such a blessing.

"'A friend loveth at all times, and a brother is born for adversity,'" Grace quoted softly, the familiar proverb speaking to her heart with a depth she'd not experienced before today.

Emma twisted around on the stairs and grinned. "As Aunt Henry would say, change that *brother* to a *sister* and you've got a promise to hang your hat on."

Grace shook her head in amusement as she made her way down the steps. She could hear those very words coming from Henrietta Chandler's lips. In fact, it wouldn't surprise her in the slightest to learn that Aunt Henry was secretly writing a suffragette version of the Holy Scriptures, replacing all the *mankind* and *brethren* terminology with words more suited to readers of the female persuasion.

"Although," Tori said as the others caught up to her on the path, "Grace seems to have a *brotherly* friend interested in assisting her as well."

"That's right." Emma neatly maneuvered Grace into the middle of the trio, ensuring she couldn't escape. "Why is it that I've never heard of this man before? You didn't even mention him last night when you came by to talk to Mal."

Grace stared at the ground. It looked dry enough to absorb her if she could just find a way to liquefy herself and melt into the dust. How could she explain that she'd been carrying on intimate conversations with a complete stranger? That she'd not even known his true name before today? They'd surely think her foolish, if not an outright loon. Yet these were her *sisters*. And sisters shared secrets.

"Amos and I have been corresponding for a few months. In the evenings, over the telegraph wire. We were chatting last night when the message came through from Colorado. He overheard. I didn't expect him to show up, though. We've never actually met."

Emma threaded her arm through Grace's. "And yet he rushed immediately to your aid." She glanced past Grace to meet Tori's eye. "If you ask me, there's something stronger than friendship motivating his actions."

Heat rushed to Grace's cheeks. Yet even as she squirmed under Emma's assumption, she couldn't stop a little thrill from shooting through her chest. She'd had much the same thought. After all, Amos had admitted to caring about her when she'd questioned him earlier. He said he wanted the chance to get to know her. That alluded to a possible future, didn't it?

"I agree," Tori said. "Ben found countless excuses to visit my store during the months he was trying to convince me to let him pay court. He says he was letting me get used to the idea of having him around. Something about cooking a frog in cold water that slowly warms instead of throwing the creature into boiling water and having him jump out."

Grace sputtered on a suppressed laugh that threatened to choke her. "Did he really compare you to a *frog?*"

Tori cocked a wry grin. "I've learned to look past the object of the analogy to the meaning behind it when talking with Ben. Otherwise I'd be constantly offended by how many times he compares me to a horse."

"Well," Emma said, leaning across them, "Ben does *love* his horses, so coming from him, such a comparison is probably high praise."

"True." Tori lifted her face toward the sun, a smile of pure contentment eliciting a twinge of envy in Grace's belly. Then the moment passed and the shopkeeper turned her attention fully on Grace. "No man is perfect," she said. "But if he loves you and respects you and treats you with kindness, the flaws fade away."

"Unless you're in the middle of an argument," Emma said. "Then they seem to magnify."

Grace and Tori chuckled. It was well-known that the town founder and the town marshal had occasional differences of opinion over how things should operate in the community. Differences that could become rather boisterous.

"Of course, it's a temporary condition." Emma ignored their laughter, injecting her voice with schoolmarm precision as she shared her vast wealth of married knowledge with her companions. "Those flaws shrink back down to near invisibility as soon as he says something sweet or holds you in his arms or kisses you."

Grace nibbled her lower lip. She didn't know what Mr. Bledsoe's flaws were. She didn't know *him*. Over the past months she'd built up an ideal, a fantasy in her mind of what her Mr. A would be like. An unrealistic standard impossible for any man to live up to.

She'd envisioned a tall man with midnight hair and skin tanned from working outdoors, which was ridiculous, since she knew Mr. A worked in a Western Union office. Yet that hadn't stopped her from dreaming of him having rugged masculinity, swagger, and confidence. A man with a physique that would make one's mouth go dry. A man not unlike Malachi Shaw or Benjamin Porter.

Amos Bledsoe had not been blessed with such attributes. He had his own, more subtle type of handsomeness, centered around his eyes—piercing blue, yet not in a hard way. They were honest and open and seemed to look straight into her. Even through the spectacles. His personality was just as sweet and clever as it had been over the wire. And the fact that he had rushed to her rescue *did* make her heart flutter.

But it also raised doubts. What kind of man left his job and his family to ride to the rescue of a woman he'd never met? It seemed a bit extreme. Perhaps he was *too* invested in her. Would allowing him to stay put her in a different kind of danger? Hadn't it been an obsessed admirer who killed that saloon singer down in Tarrant County? The wires had been abuzz with the gossip for weeks.

Grace gave her head a little shake. She needed to get a grip on her imagination. The man she'd met in the jailhouse earlier had been perfectly normal. Gentlemanly, sincere, and candid regarding his intentions. Intentions that still made her blood pump a little faster when she thought of them, despite the fact that he hadn't quite matched the image she'd built up of him in her mind.

A sudden thought scurried across her mind. What had he expected *her* to look like? And how far short had *she* fallen? Had he pictured her as a statuesque blonde like Tori, or perhaps a fiery, take-charge dynamo with dark curls and vibrant green eyes like Emma? He probably hadn't expected a short, shy, secretive female with a murdering mine tycoon on her trail.

A sigh slipped silently through her parted lips. She was certainly no great prize. Yet he'd said he wanted to stay. That he was glad he'd come. Even after she'd left him locked up in Malachi's jail. Surely that was worth more than a pair of broad shoulders and a wagonload of muscles.

9

"Bertie's fixin' a cot for you down in the basement of the station house," the marshal said as he unlocked the door to Amos's cell. "The boardinghouse is full up, and the ladies there wouldn't take kindly to a male guest anyhow, so we figured it'd be easier for you to bunk with us."

Amos put his hat on and stepped out into freedom. Odd how the air felt fresher on the other side of the bars. And he'd only been inside for a couple hours. What must it be like for someone who'd actually been convicted of a crime?

Feeling stiff—more from the stress of not knowing what was being said about him in the town meeting than the marshal's rudimentary accommodations—Amos rolled his shoulders and bent his neck from side to side a few times as Malachi Shaw closed the cell door behind him.

"Bertie's a good cook," the marshal continued, as if Amos might need further convincing, "and I've already instructed Henry not to draw her weapon on you again."

Wait. Those names. Was he actually going to be staying with the Revolver and Cookie Grannies?

Some of his shock must have shown on his face, for Shaw

laughed before thumping him on the back. "Don't worry. Emma and I will be there, too. We'll watch your back."

He winked, a sure sign he was teasing, but Amos's muscles knotted back up anyway. He remembered the steely look in Revolver Granny's eyes. That gaze had practically dared him to give her an excuse to fire her weapon.

Repressing a shudder, Amos stole a quick glance back through the bars. "You know, that cot wasn't so bad," he commented, only half joking. "If you left the door unlocked, I could stay here." Safely away from the crazy grannies.

"Nah. Gotta keep the room available for the real criminals." Shaw opened the top drawer of his desk and tossed the cell key inside. "Besides, you'll want the use of the parlor for your visits with Miss Mallory. Can't woo a lady in a jailhouse."

Amos speared the marshal with a look. Had he just pretended to be obtuse when Amos and Grace were tapping out their coded, private conversation?

Shaw grinned. "It's not like you can hide your intentions, Bledsoe. Not here." He shoved his desk drawer closed then leaned his hip against the corner's edge. "There's only one reason a man lingers in Harper's Station: to win a woman. A particular woman. Only two of us have managed to accomplish the feat so far, but Ben Porter and I are living proof that the impossible can be achieved if you want it badly enough."

Did he want it badly enough? Enough to sleep under the same roof as Revolver Granny and her giant pistol?

The answer came to him in an instant as the jailhouse door opened and a pair of ladies stepped inside. One walked straight up to Shaw and accepted his arm around her waist as if it were the missing accessory to her dress. But the other? She hesitated at the entrance, the early evening light casting golden highlights on her hair. Amos's heart skittered to a halt then lunged forward at a gallop.

Oh, yeah. He wanted it badly enough.

Holstered or not, Revolver Granny, I'm moving in.

Amos tugged his hat back off his head and nodded toward the delicate woman hovering just beyond his reach. "Miss Mallory. Good to see you again."

She dipped her chin in return, her lashes temporarily blocking the warmth of her lovely brown eyes. "Mr. Bledsoe." Slowly those lashes lifted, and he swore he could feel the temperature in the room escalate a degree or two. "I'm sorry about leaving you here with so little explanation. I hope you can forgive my rudeness."

"The food you sent over was tasty," he replied, not quite ready to absolve her completely, at least not aloud. "It helped pass the time."

She'd left him to stew, no doubt testing his resolve to stay the course. Understandable. She was in the path of an oncoming storm and needed to know whom she could depend on when the waters got rough. Yet he couldn't let her think he was some pansy who'd let a woman walk all over him, either. She needed a strong man to stand beside her, one she could respect and rely on. He'd been that man for his mother and sister for the past ten years, ever since his father died the summer Amos turned eighteen. He aimed to be that man for Grace Mallory too. If she'd let him.

"Did the denizens agree to let me stay, or should I prepare to battle a mob of skirted zealots bearing pitchforks and torches once the sun goes down?"

Grace's lips twitched upward in what was sure to be an adorable quirk of amusement when the marshal's voice broke in and ruined the moment.

"No pitchforks around here, Bledsoe. Our gals pack lead." He stood to his full height, bringing the lady circled in his arm with him. "Taught 'em myself."

"Hush, you," the brunette admonished, elbowing Shaw in the ribs. Not that he seemed to notice. "No intimidating the guest."

Mrs. Shaw aimed a bright smile at Amos and tried to step out of her husband's hold. He didn't let her. She shot a frown at him over her shoulder before turning back to address Amos.

A grin crossed the marshal's face the instant his wife was no longer facing him. It was all Amos could do not to grin back. He had to bite the inside of his cheek to keep his mien serious as Emma Shaw hurried to assure him of his safety.

"You are welcome to stay in Harper's Station as long as you like, Mr. Bledsoe. Grace considers you a friend. That's all the recommendation we need."

Amos shifted his gaze back to Grace. She didn't say anything, but her eyes met his, and the resulting impact to his chest reverberated down to his toes. She'd vouched for him in front of the entire town. Called him friend. Yet the way her eyes searched him now—peering past his spectacles, past the trail dust, past his disheveled suit—it seemed as if she were still evaluating him. Looking for indicators that he could indeed be trusted.

He had some proving to do. Amos stretched his neck above the starched points of his collar and jutted out his chin. He fully intended to be up to the task. Whatever that task entailed.

"So what happens next?" he asked.

Grace drew in a breath as if about to speak, but Mrs. Shaw jumped in first.

"I'm going to head back to the station house to help the aunts with dinner, and Malachi has his rounds to make, but you are certainly welcome to come get settled in the room Aunt Bertie set up for you. It's in the basement, but no one can feather a nest like Bertie. She'll have piles of warm quilts, a wash area, and probably even a plate of oatmeal cookies waiting for you."

Good old Cookie Granny. Though, the wash area sounded better than the cookies at the moment. He swore he could still smell the faint odor of mule manure wafting up from his shoe. He'd never thought himself vain since he'd never considered himself handsome, but tidy? Yes. And the lovely Miss Mallory had only been introduced to the rumpled, dusty version of Amos Bledsoe. No wonder she held herself back. She was probably worried his disreputable appearance reflected a slovenly character. He'd have to pray that second and third and tenth impressions could eventually outweigh a poor first one.

Amos tipped his head. "I'm sure the accommodations will more than suit my needs. You and your aunts are kind to take me into your home. I would be happy to pay a boarding fee, of course."

Mrs. Shaw waved her hand as if to brush away his offer. "We'll worry about that later. For now, just know that you're welcome here. Your satchel and saddlebags are already inside, and we've seen to your mule."

Willful. Amos hid a shudder. "I'll need to return that beast to Stranton's Livery in Seymour sometime soon."

"Stranton's?" the marshal broke in. "That explains it. I wondered why in the world a man with a scrap of intelligence would choose a stubborn cuss like that to transport him. I nearly threw my shoulder out yanking on that ornery critter's lead line while trying to move him away from the ladies' garden plot. Obstinate thing refused to budge."

Amos felt the pieces of his tattered manhood being stitched back together. If Malachi Shaw—a gun-toting, denim-wearing man's man—struggled to corral Willful, then Amos need feel no shame for his own failures.

"He's a handful, that's for sure." He gestured to his sorry state of dress. "I had a bit of difficulty with him myself, as you might have surmised from my less than orderly appearance." He darted a glance at Miss Mallory, pleased to see she looked sympathetic. "But I was in a hurry to get to Harper's Station, and he was the best of the horseflesh left to choose from."

"Ah." The marshal drew Amos's attention away from Grace as he tugged his wife toward the door, then gestured for Amos and Grace to go out ahead of him.

Amos plunked his hat on his head again and smiled at Grace. She offered a small, shy smile in return before pivoting to exit. He followed, his gaze taking in the slender line of her neck and the curves nipping in at her waist.

"Next time you're in Seymour, head to Bart Porter's place." The marshal's voice had Amos jerking his gaze away from the woman in front of him to focus on the far less interesting features of Malachi Shaw. "His livery is a couple blocks south of the depot, but his stock is far superior and less likely to be picked over since he's not the first livery visitors find when they get off the train. All the locals know to go to Porter's."

"Thanks," Amos said, not thankful at all to still be talking with the marshal about mules and horses when who he really wanted to talk with was the woman who'd halted a few steps away from him. "I'll remember that."

"Tori mentioned that Ben will be making a delivery run through here tomorrow," Mrs. Shaw added, prolonging the discussion. "He's Bart's brother. I'm sure he'd be happy to return your mule when he goes back to Seymour after his deliveries. He can pick you out a better mount and bring it with him next time he comes to town."

"Actually, I'd prefer a bicycle." Amos edged closer to Grace, hoping his abrupt change in subject would give him the chance to offer his escort.

"A what?"

Really? Was the marshal sabotaging him on purpose? Everyone knew what a bicycle was. The things were all the rage back east.

Amos frowned at Shaw. "A velocipede. An accelerator. A two-wheeled, man-powered vehicle. You know, a bicycle."

"You're a wheelman?" Mrs. Shaw practically bounced in excitement, which only made her husband scowl. "I've seen pictures in magazines, but I've never seen one in person. Oh, Mal, can you just imagine Aunt Henry's reaction?" She spun to beam at her husband, effectively banishing his frown. "With all she's read about how the velocipede is emancipating women, she'd be thrilled to see one in action! The bicycle costumes with their bloomers and split skirts, the freedom to go where one wills, and the independence of manufacturing one's own mobility. She'll be over the moon!" She brushed past Amos, ran up to Grace, and grabbed her hands. "I'm going to talk to Tori about placing an order. What do you think? Four? Five? I know Aunt Henry will want one, and I'd love to try one as well. Do you think any other ladies would like one? If Amos would be willing to give us some instruction, we could have a town full of bicycles! Much cheaper to maintain than a horse, and with extra health benefits."

"Don't you think you're getting a little ahead of yourself there, Emma?" The marshal's frown was back in place as he strode up to his wife. "Henry is fifty-three years old. If she gets up on one of those contraptions, she's liable to fall off and break her neck. Tell her, Bledsoe." Shaw pierced Amos with a look that demanded full agreement.

But Amos was tired of this conversation and just cranky enough to be obstinate. Maybe Willful had rubbed off on him. "My mother rides one on occasion, and she's around the same age. They're quite safe once you learn to balance."

Shaw's eyes narrowed and a muscle in his jaw twitched in a rather menacing fashion. Amos decided he'd poked the bear enough.

"Although the roads in Denison are in much better condition than what I've seen here," he added. "Ruts and erosion do make learning rather difficult."

"The area where we're building our house is flat and hard-packed," Emma insisted, unperturbed by the dark cloud settling over her husband's features. "It would be a perfect place to learn! I'm going to find Tori." She turned back to Grace. "Expect us first thing tomorrow morning with an order to wire."

Then, in a swirl of skirts, she spun around and hied off toward a large building bearing a sign that proclaimed it the general store. The marshal just shook his head and let out a sigh even as his lips curved into a smile, attesting to his fondness for the whirlwind force that was his wife.

"She's probably gonna have the entire town wheeled up by the end of the month." Shaw eyed Amos. "Why couldn't you just ride a horse like a normal person?"

Amos shrugged. "My family says I've always been a little on the odd side."

A strong hand came down on Amos's shoulder. "Then you'll feel right at home in Harper's Station." Shaw tipped his head toward Grace, the only one who hadn't jumped into this crazy conversation, yet the one who'd captured Amos's complete attention without saying a word. "You mind seeing Miss Mallory home? I gotta make sure Em doesn't bankrupt us with this new bicycle scheme."

Amos looked at the woman standing quietly in front of him, whose eyes communicated more than a person's tongue ever could. And right now those eyes seemed to have lit with the same anticipation he felt thrumming through his veins.

A chance to be alone. *Finally.* To talk through matters of true importance, like who was threatening her, and how Amos could help.

Like how well they might suit, should they decide to explore a new facet of their relationship.

Like asking permission to take her hand so he could discover if her skin was truly as soft as it appeared.

Without turning his gaze away from the woman before him, Amos answered. "Yes. I'll see Miss Mallory home."

10

Grace walked silently beside Mr. Bledsoe, thankful that he made no effort to engage her in conversation. It was coming, she knew, but for a few blessed moments, peace reigned. A peace she desperately needed in order to collect her fragmented thoughts.

Mr. Bledsoe must be told about her father, Haversham, the missing documents—everything. But as they walked together, other thoughts intruded, niggling questions that refused to be banished. Why did her belly tighten every time Mr. Bledsoe's gaze tangled with hers? And what would she do if Emma and Tori were right about him being interested in more than simple friendship? Did she *want* him to be interested in more?

She bit back a sigh. Things had been so much simpler when they merely conversed over the wire. It was safe. Anonymous. Grace stole a peek at the man at her side. Mr. A was no longer anonymous. He was real, and he was here. For her.

A little thrill coursed through her, leaving the skin on her arms tingling.

Safe might be comfortable, but it wasn't exciting. Or particularly helpful when trouble struck. Better to have a tangible Amos

Bledsoe by her side than an imaginary Mr. A who only existed in a lonely woman's dreams.

When they reached the telegraph office, Mr. Bledsoe slowed his steps and turned to her. "You live here as well?"

Grace nodded. "There are two small rooms behind the office. It's not much, but it suits me." Some might find the small wooden building's weathered plank siding and lopsided eaves ramshackle, but she preferred to view it as having character. Instead of a shade tree, she had a pole with a mess of black wires atop it in the side yard. The wires might be an eyesore, but she'd not complain. Not when they afforded her a paycheck every month. "I stayed in the boardinghouse for a short time while we had that outlaw trouble," Grace continued when Mr. Bledsoe made no comment. "Emma didn't want any of the ladies staying alone. But I found I missed my privacy." She shrugged, a little embarrassed to admit the shy side of her nature to a man who seemed so gregarious. "As soon as the trouble ended, I moved back here."

"I know what it's like to want a place where you can escape people for a while. I love my family, but after a few hours in their company, I'm more than ready to find a quiet place to hide." He laughed softly, and Grace smiled.

Silence stretched between them, and Grace edged closer to the door, not knowing what else to do. Mr. Bledsoe shifted from foot to foot. His gaze dropped to the ground.

"I don't want to keep you from your supper," he blurted, for the first time making her wonder if he could be as nervous as she was. "You must be quite hungry after facing down the masses during the town meeting."

"Actually," she said, turning her attention away from the door and back toward him, "my stomach is still knotted so tightly, I doubt I'll be able to eat anything for quite some time."

He looked up, something hopeful lighting his eyes.

Grace pressed a hand to her stomach and inhaled a long breath.

Words jabbed at her tongue, clamoring for release. It took a moment to dredge up sufficient courage, but eventually they found their way into the air. "Perhaps I could make us some tea, and we could talk for a while?"

Mr. Bledsoe visibly relaxed, and the smile that stretched across his face was bright enough to banish the evening's shadows. "I'd like that very much."

How could she not smile in response? He seemed so genuinely pleased by the idea of spending time with her. A rather amazing situation, considering her decided lack of conversational skills.

She hadn't contributed a single word to the discussion of horses, mules, and liveries back in the jailhouse. And not from lack of trying. She'd longed to say something witty or charming or even halfway intelligent, anything that might prove her to be something other than the shy, bland little mouse she knew herself to be. But each time she thought of something worthwhile to add, Emma or Malachi jumped in ahead of her. Thankfully, she was much better one-on-one. At least when conversing with other women. She'd not had much opportunity to test her skills with men, especially suitors. If that was what Mr. Bledsoe was.

Grace reached into her skirt pocket and retrieved the office key. "I'll put the kettle on," she said as she let herself in. "If you'll prop the door open, I'll bring a second chair out for you, and we can sit in my office." Between the open door and the window, there should be no perceived impropriety.

Mr. Bledsoe followed her past the customer counter and collected a piece of wood from the firebox she kept near the office stove in the corner. Returning to the entrance, he wedged the kindling scrap beneath the door and propped it open. Then he stuck his head into her personal quarters. "If you'll show me which chair you want moved, I'll carry it to the office for you."

She pointed to a blue-striped armchair she used for reading, then frowned. A small brown stain marred the slightly faded upholstery near the edge of the seat. She didn't remember that being there. Not that she could do anything about it now, since Mr. Bledsoe was already moving in that direction.

The chair was made of heavy oak, but Mr. Bledsoe lifted it several feet off the ground with no difficulty. He might look like one of her father's university cronies in his suit and spectacles, but there was nothing frumpish about his muscles.

He busied himself with examining her telegraphy equipment until she brought out the tea tray. After learning he liked sugar as much as she did, she stirred two spoonfuls into his cup, handed the white china to him on a matching plain saucer, and gestured for him to sit.

He'd been so patient and polite, giving her plenty of uninterrupted time to gather her thoughts as she brewed the tea, yet she could not put off what needed to be said any longer.

"It was very kind of you to come all this way to offer your assistance, but I'm afraid the trouble you find me in is more severe than you could have bargained for." She lowered herself into the blue upholstered chair when he insisted on claiming the less comfortable wooden chair for himself, and after an awkward hesitation to gather her courage, she met his gaze. "Please know that I will not hold you in poor esteem should you decide to return to Denison. In fact, I would recommend that you do so. Your mother and sister would not take kindly to my putting you in harm's way."

Amos's gaze hardened. "I love my mother and sister, but they do not dictate my life. So tell me what we're up against, and I'll decide what risks I'm willing to take."

Grace swallowed. What *we're* up against. He'd already included himself. And the way he spoke—so firm and determined—Grace couldn't help but consider him in a new light. The friendly, bantering Amos Bledsoe had a steel core. A strength, perchance, that a woman might lean upon and find purchase.

Would that strength continue to stand fast after he learned the truth about her situation? Only one way to find out.

Grace sipped her tea then leaned back in her chair, watching his face and gauging his reactions. "I'm afraid the story I have to tell is not a short one."

Amos sat unmoving in his chair, trying to absorb all that Miss Mallory had told him during the last thirty minutes. Her father had been murdered right before her eyes. He couldn't even fathom such a thing. To see someone you loved gunned down in the street . . . Amos couldn't stop himself from thinking of his mother, his sister. His fingers balled into a fist. He clenched his jaw and jerked his gaze toward the window, searching for control, for perspective.

What kind of courage must it have taken for her to start a new life alone? No family, no friends she could turn to without putting their lives at risk. All while the sword of Damocles—or Haversham, in this case—hung over her head.

He'd admired Miss G's warmth and quick wit over the telegraph line, but the depth of character that the flesh-and-blood woman embodied was nothing short of remarkable.

A movement across the room brought his head around as his hostess made her way back into the office. She'd gone to fetch a shawl to combat the cool air coming through the open door, but that wasn't all she'd retrieved. She clutched a stack of folded papers tied with a wide length of red ribbon. The letters her father had uncovered.

"I gave you plenty of time to make a run for it," she said, a hint of a smile playing with the corners of her mouth. "Even left the door open for you." Her eyes twinkled, and his pulse responded like the tail of a puppy who'd just caught sight of his favorite person, surging from calm to vigorous thumping in a single heartbeat.

He adored this side of her. Lighthearted and playful even in the midst of harsh trial. She hadn't acted this way with the marshal or even with Emma Shaw, at least not that he'd seen, a fact that pleased him more than it probably should. He wanted to believe he was the only one to draw out this part of her nature, that she reserved it for him alone. Because *this* was the woman who'd captured his interest on the telegraph, a woman of subtle humor and indomitable spirit. A woman he could imagine spending his evenings with for the rest of his life.

He got to his feet when she entered the room, determined to prove himself a gentleman despite his less than fastidious exterior. "I considered escaping," he teased in return as she took her seat in the blue-striped chair, "but a second trip on Stranton's mule was a higher price than I was willing to pay." He affected an exaggerated shiver. "Nope, you're stuck with me. At least until the order of bicycles arrives."

He settled back into his chair, his gaze moving from his companion's face to the stack of letters she held. As he watched, she extended the papers toward him. He caught her eye, a silent question passing between them. She nodded.

"I thought you might like to read them. There are less than a dozen, so it shouldn't take long. I wasn't able to find anything helpful to the situation at hand, but perhaps you'll catch something I missed."

He accepted the letters and laid them in his lap. Reaching for the ribbon, his mind raced with possibilities. He'd always loved a good puzzle, yet this was no intellectual exercise. People's lives were at stake. *Grace's* life was at stake.

Amos glanced up. "These are the letters Tremont Haversham's first wife wrote him during their courtship?"

Miss Mallory's brown gaze ran over him slow and deep, like chocolate icing melting over a still-warm cake. And he was definitely warm, even with the cool evening breeze blowing through the office door. He probably would be for a while, after that heated stare. Of course, she wasn't evaluating him as a suitor. Her eyes didn't flash with sudden attraction or desire. They searched and evaluated him with cautious hope, looking for signs that he would be able to help, that he could offer a new perspective or fresh insight that might lead to a solution.

Help me help her, Lord. He desperately wanted to be Grace's hero, but more than that, he wanted her to be safe. However that came about.

"Her name was Deborah Linfield," Grace explained, her soft voice floating through the room like a gentle summer breeze. "The tale I've heard is that they met by chance late one afternoon in Fairmount Park in Philadelphia. Haversham and some friends were out riding, and Deborah was walking home after a long day at the dressmaker's shop. She was an expert in beadwork, highly sought for her talent with a needle, and paid well for her skill. Perhaps too well, for that day, after receiving her wages, she was attacked, the thief waiting for her in a copse of trees before snatching her reticule.

"The story goes that she put up a fight, screaming and clawing at the man until he pulled a knife and cut the purse free of her wrist. Tremont heard the commotion, took in the scene, and rode the thief to ground. He returned the lady's purse and saw her safely home. They were instantly smitten and began a courtship that culminated in marriage less than a year later. Tremont's parents did not approve, since Deborah lacked the family pedigree necessary to fit into their exalted circles, but Tremont didn't care. He married her anyway, and the dress she wore to her wedding made the papers, the beadwork so intricate that she outshone all other society brides that season."

Amos scanned the first letter's flowing, feminine script. The prose was rife with effusive gratitude and hero worship for the man who had come to her rescue. A small twinge of envy pricked his hide. "Sounds like quite the romantic tale."

"When Haversham moved to Denver, the gossip about him ran rampant. Girls sighed over his tragic history—the man who loved so deeply that he defied his family to be with the woman he loved, only to lose her in childbirth. The fact that his second wife considered Colorado a primitive wilderness filled with primitive people did nothing to enamor her to the women of Denver. They loved Tremont but resented Chaucer as the child of the pretentious shrew who thought herself above them. Chaucer knows that if Deborah's child is indeed alive, the people of Denver will rally behind her."

Amos unfolded the second letter and ran his fingers along the page. "Perhaps Deborah mentions a friend in one of these letters, someone she might have trusted with the care of her child."

Grace gathered her shawl more closely around her. "I looked, but I didn't find any mention of people beyond her employer at the dress shop and one or two of her fellow seamstresses, none of whom sounded like intimate acquaintances. She didn't mention any towns or cities from her past, either, nor family members. From all accounts she'd been orphaned at a young age and then apprenticed to an embroiderer, where she'd learned her trade. But even if she *had* family, I don't think the child would be with them."

Amos looked up from the letter. "Oh?"

"Deborah was in the Havershams' home when the baby came. Tremont was gone on business and had not wanted her to be alone so far along in her pregnancy, though he intended to be home before the baby was born. But she went into labor two weeks early. The Havershams summoned a physician, but the man was unable to save Tremont's wife. He signed a death certificate for both Deborah and her unnamed daughter. With Tremont absent, only the doctor and Tremont's mother bore witness to the birth. If Mrs. Haversham wanted to rid her son of all traces of an unsuitable wife, she could have bribed the physician to forge the death certificate and dispose of the child. What's one more anonymous babe left on the steps of a church?"

Amos's stomach clenched in anger at the coldhearted picture Miss Mallory painted. Could someone truly be so cruel as to abandon a newborn and compound their own child's grief simply to restore their place in society? "So Tremont never saw his child?" He barely got the words past the disgust clogging his throat.

Miss Mallory met his gaze, her own eyes shimmering. "Only her grave."

Amos cleared his throat and straightened in his chair. "Didn't you say the missing Pinkerton report was dated 1892? What made Tremont question his daughter's death and seek out the Pinkertons so many years later?"

"I don't know for sure." She dropped her attention to her lap, and her fingers fiddled with the fringe on the edge of her shawl. "I remember the Denver papers speculating on the extra trips he made home around that time, the gossip mill grinding away over whether he was reconciling with his estranged wife. Then there was an obituary notice stating that his mother had passed, and the gossip ground to a halt." Slowly, Grace lifted her head, her gaze latching onto his. "Perhaps the guilt became too heavy for the aging woman, and she confessed her crime on her deathbed, seeking absolution from the son she'd wronged."

Amos whistled softly. "That would fit."

"It's pure conjecture," Grace said as she resumed twirling the shawl fringe around her finger. "I have no proof. But after nine months of agonizing over the pieces of this puzzle, this is the only configuration that makes any sense."

Her finger suddenly stopped twisting, and a new tension seeped into the air around them. She leaned forward in her chair. Amos instinctively stretched to meet her.

"If you're willing to stay, I'd like you to help me find the missing documents, Amos."

His name on her lips sped his pulse, but it was the plea in her eyes that captured his heart.

"They exist. They have to. My father wouldn't have risked his life without solid evidence. Yet in nine months of wrestling with this conundrum, I'm no closer to uncovering the Pinkerton report or the amended will. I need you to find what I missed."

Amos dropped the letter still loosely clasped in his right hand and reached across the space between them to cover her fingers. They were chilled, whether from the air or the distressing nature of the situation, he couldn't know. What he *did* know was that he wanted to warm them, to banish all cold and fear from her life.

"I'm here, Grace." He gripped her hand and rubbed his thumb in gentle strokes over her knuckles. "And I'll do everything in my power to help you."

II

Two days after the town meeting, Helen fit the handle of a large basket over her right arm and crossed through the farmhouse kitchen on her way outside. Katie and a couple of the new girls sat at the table, peeling potatoes and yakking about the latest news from town. News that centered on the most recent male interloper.

He was already causing havoc. Not that Helen had expected anything less. Men always stirred up trouble. But bicycles? According to Katie, Emma had convinced Tori to order five of the crazy things just because Mr. Bledsoe said he preferred them to horses.

Helen's stride lengthened in agitation as she left the farm behind. Wheels over horses. That right there proved the fellow was off his rocker. Who wanted to push a pair of wheels to get from place to place if a horse would do the moving for you? Besides, a horse was smart enough to stop at the edge of a cliff. A speeding velocipede would take you right over. Henrietta Chandler and her bloomers could take lessons from some crackpot wheelman if she chose, but Helen would keep her feet firmly planted on the ground, thank you very much.

The walk to the pecan grove took a good twenty minutes, and by the time Helen reached the first trees, she'd walked out much of her frustration. It was hard to stay focused on negativity when God had blessed her with such a glorious day.

She glanced at the sky, where a handful of puffy white clouds swam lazily across the bright blue expanse. So peaceful. Perhaps even happy. Helen didn't really know what happiness felt like. To her, it was simply the absence of pain. Yet when she looked at a sky like this one, something inside her whispered that there could be more. There could be joy that led to dancing, to laughter, to a place where fear could not penetrate.

Others understood it. Katie was always giggling and smiling and urging Helen to stop being so gloomy. But Katie had learned how to laugh as a child. She'd played and danced and sung songs with a mother who'd called her *princess*. Helen had learned how to hide. She'd placated and ducked and taken blows without making a sound from a father who'd called her *worthless*.

Setting her basket on the ground beneath the first tree, Helen pulled her work gloves from where she'd tucked them into the waistband of her skirt. The first time she'd gathered pecans, her fingers had been stained for weeks, and no amount of scrubbing would remove the dark brown tint from her skin. Now she made a point to wear gloves along with her oldest, darkest dress, an ugly black thing she'd worn to her father's funeral three years ago. She saved it for the dirtiest of chores. Mucking stalls, cleaning the chicken coop, gathering pecans. It seemed fitting to drag the dress she'd been assigned to wear out of respect for her dead father through manure and grime. His soul had been a cesspit.

But the day was too pretty to let ugly memories intrude. Helen directed her attention to the task of gathering pecans as she lowered herself to the ground and crawled through the leaves and debris. Shaking a handful of nuts together, she listened for the solid sound that indicated a husk full of meat. She discarded the lighter ones, flinging them away from the tree, and tossed the good ones into her basket. She did the same with her thoughts. Each time a thought of her father rose to instill anger or bitterness in her soul, she mentally flung it away and clung instead to a blessing.

Blessings like the sunshine and blue sky. The birds singing in the treetop above her head. The breeze that cooled her while she toiled. Betty and the girls at the farm. A bedroom with a lock on the door. Even that thief of a squirrel running around the base of the tree, stealing the nuts she was there to harvest.

"Get out of here, you!" She tossed a cracked pecan husk at the bushy-tailed rodent, a smile creasing her face as the rascal easily dodged her poor throw. In a flash, the squirrel jabbed a nut into his mouth, turned, and sprinted up the tree. His little claws scraped against the bark as he made his escape.

He was a marvel, moving so fast Helen could barely keep track of him. He leapt from trunk to branch to higher branch with such confidence and grace. That must be what freedom was like— jumping through life without worry or fear.

I want to trust you that completely, her heart prayed, for she knew she didn't. She was a clinger, not a leaper. Once she found a safe branch, she grabbed on and held tight with every ounce of strength she had, terrified that if she let go, she'd plummet back to where she'd come from. She wanted to leap forward in faith, but her claws were too embedded. Something would have to shake her loose. And that prospect terrified her.

Her basket half full, Helen stood, stretched out her lower back, then moved to the next tree. A large cluster of nuts lay amid the dirt and leaves to the right of the trunk, so she started there. She'd just set the basket down when an odd sound caught her attention. She straightened and tilted her head toward the noise. It was low, more of a rumble than anything.

Helen strained her ears, mentally filtering out the rustling leaves and bird chatter. Holding her breath, she poured all her effort into listening.

There! She heard it again. A growly moan.

Cautiously, she moved out from under the overhanging tree branches and scanned the area. Had an animal been hurt? Nature was so barbaric—predators targeting the weak, packs abandoning their injured. It was despicable. Yet animals in pain were unpredictable. Some were even dangerous. She should take precautions.

Wishing she'd brought her rifle along, she settled for a sturdy tree branch that fit comfortably in her hands, and walked as stealthily as she could through the fallen leaves and hollowed-out pecan husks.

"Where are you?" she muttered under her breath when the sound faded away. It had come from somewhere to the west, she was sure. But where?

She crept forward, her gaze scanning the prairie grass in a wide arc in front of her. There. A section of flattened grass to her right. Near the path that led to the old line cabin she liked to visit when she needed a place to be alone for a while. She adjusted her grip on the branch and hefted it a little higher over her shoulder. Then she set her chin and strode forward.

Reddish-brown smears stained the flattened grass. Blood. A lot of it. The animal must be incapacitated, dragging itself away from whatever had caused it harm.

Helen's heart panged in sympathy. She understood the instinct to escape, to hide and lick wounds. Judging by the width of the trail, the animal was big. Maybe a coyote or a wild pig. Both of which had large teeth and fierce temperaments. Helen slowed her approach. Perhaps she should just leave it alone.

Another moan, weaker this time, reached her ears. She steeled her spine. No creature deserved to suffer. Not even a coyote.

She pressed on a few more steps then faltered to a halt. This was no coyote. Unless they'd taken to wearing men's trousers.

Helen shook her head, every sympathetic impulse inside her hardening to stone. Was this some kind of divine joke? If so, she wasn't laughing.

"I'm not doing it," she grumbled, peering from the corners of her eyes to the blue sky that had looked so inviting mere moments ago but now felt like it was bearing down upon her with ominous intent. "You can't make me."

The pressure didn't relent. In fact, it grew heavier, pushing on her heart until her pulse throbbed in her veins.

It wasn't fair. He was asking too much.

She glanced from side to side, praying for someone else to be within shouting distance. Anyone. Even the marshal or the freighter. Shoot, she'd even take that bicycle-riding, spectacle-wearing newcomer that Grace seemed to favor.

But no one was around. Only her.

And the unconscious man slowly dying from a nasty gunshot wound to his leg.

12

Grace clutched the books to her chest, her grip tight enough to cramp the muscles in her fingers. Only about fifty steps separated the bank from the telegraph office, but she couldn't escape the feeling of being exposed. These two books represented hundreds of thousands of dollars. More than that—they represented the price of her father's life. She hadn't removed them from the bank since she'd first entrusted them to Emma and her fireproof safe a month after arriving in Harper's Station.

Perspiration dampened Grace's hairline as she walked with her head down, gaze focused on any loose stone or bump in the road that could cause her to stumble. The tickle of a sweat droplet running down her temple made her grimace, but thankfully a cool autumn breeze blew against her face, evaporating the evidence of her nervousness.

When she'd shown the books to the marshal that first night after Rosie's warning came over the wire, they'd just stood in the locked storage closet where Emma kept the safe. Malachi had thumbed through the pages, examined the spine, and even held each one upside down, giving it a good shake. No life-altering documents had fluttered to the floor, however. Not that Grace had expected them to. She'd gone through every page of those volumes on her own, multiple times, with no success. The marshal might be able to shake the books with more vigor, but no one could search between the pages any more painstakingly than she had.

Which was why she was risking removing the books from the safety of the bank. If she and Amos were to find the documents, it was going to take more than a fluttering of the pages. They would need hours. Days, perhaps. And since she was needed at her post at the telegraph machine and she didn't want to inconvenience Emma after hours, the only way she and Amos could examine them together would be in her office.

And they would examine them *together*. She trusted Mr. Bledsoe . . . mostly. She trusted the idea of him that she'd built up in her mind based on their interactions over the wire these last months. However, she needed time to get to know the real person, now that he was here, to ensure her impressions of his character were accurate. In the meantime, she wouldn't be letting these books out of her sight. They were her responsibility. Her legacy. And with danger set to arrive any moment, they were her burden to carry. No one else's.

Reaching the office, she pried one hand free from her cargo and opened the door. A quiet, precise tapping echoed from behind the counter. Amos sat at her table, bent forward over the telegraph, his face a mask of concentration as he confirmed a message that had something to do with bicycles.

He looked so natural there, working in his shirtsleeves, his dark brown suspenders contrasting sharply with the white of his shirt. His trousers were neatly pressed, lifting just a little as he leaned forward to reveal matching dark brown stockings.

Mr. Bledsoe had taken great care with his appearance the last two days. Grace grinned softly as she reached behind herself to shut the office door. The rumpled, bedraggled specimen she'd first encountered had disappeared, replaced by a fastidious man of business, one she had to admit held a certain appeal. His nose might be a tad long and his build more slender than strapping, but here, in his element, he projected a confidence and intelligence she found quite attractive.

For the first time in months, she actually believed the solution to her mystery lay within her grasp, and Amos was the reason. He was quick-witted, clever, and *invested*. In her. Grace shook her head as she came around the counter and moved into the inner office. She still had a hard time believing her good fortune. Why would a virtual stranger take such an interest in her troubles? True, they'd struck up a rather intimate acquaintance over the wire, but he owed her no favors. She'd done nothing to deserve his loyalty or admiration. Yet he'd traveled over a hundred and fifty miles to help her and seemed in no hurry to make an escape.

"Thank you for covering the wire for me while I stepped out," she said when she recognized the pattern of his sign-off code. She slipped her shawl from her shoulders and hung it up on the hook near the door to her private chambers. His coat and hat hung from a nail a few inches away, and for a moment something in her chest ached at the sight of the masculine garments hanging so close to her own. As if they belonged.

"Glad to oblige." The chair squeaked as Amos straightened to face her. His light blue gaze found hers.

Grace clutched the books a little more tightly to her breast. Eyes that shade should be shooting ice crystals through her veins, but when combined with his smile, the effect was quite the opposite. Her insides had gone warm and gooey, like a cookie fresh from the oven.

"I was trying to help Miss Adams locate some used bicycles to save on cost. She was planning to place an order with Montgomery Ward, but the Hawthorne Ladies' Safety machine they sell runs $65, more than the ladies here can afford. I told her I'd put out some feelers among some of the wheelmen I know to see if we could locate some used cycles."

"Sixty-five dollars?" Grace nearly choked on the amount. She flopped rather clumsily onto the armchair she'd opted to leave out in the office. "You could buy a *horse* for that price."

"A broken-down nag, maybe." Amos scowled a bit at her lack of velocipede enthusiasm. "It's less than half the price of a decent saddle horse. And you don't have to feed it or pay to have it boarded. All you have to do is grease the chain occasionally and rinse the dirt off the frame. Still . . . I'll concede that it's not cheap. I saved up for nearly six months before I bought my top-of-the-line Columbia. Thing runs like a dream, though." His smile returned, along with a devastating sparkle in his eyes that the lenses of his spectacles seemed to magnify.

"I can't believe Emma convinced Tori to order five of the things. She'll never be able to sell them." Grace laid the books across her lap and leaned against the upholstered chairback. "Emma can probably afford one, but nearly everyone else runs on a tight budget."

Amos winked at her. "No need to worry. When Miss Adams saw the price listing in her catalog, she called me in for a consultation before placing an order. Cooler heads prevailed, I assure you." He rested his arm on the table, looking so at home that it was a bit disconcerting. "Now, thanks to a message that just came in from George Walker of the Alamo Wheelmen in San Antonio, I have been promised three women's style Yukons and one men's Sterling, all used but in good repair, for a grand total of $100."

Grace bit back a grin. He looked downright smug. She supposed he had every right to his pride. He'd brokered an impressive deal. She might even be tempted to purchase one of the crazy things herself. Her companion obviously found a great deal of enjoyment in owning one. Perhaps she would, too.

That opinion had absolutely nothing to do with the image that had just popped into her head of his arms wrapping around her as he taught her to balance on two wheels. Nothing at all.

"It seems the Wagner & Chabot store has been looking for a way to reduce their inventory and clear out their less expensive models in order to cater to a more discriminating clientele," Amos continued, still basking in the glow of his coup. "They can have the machines on the train tomorrow if Miss Adams decides to make the purchase."

Grace finally granted freedom to the grin she'd been holding back. "How could she not, after finding such a low price? You'll be touted as quite the hero, I'm sure."

He shrugged off the praise. "I just sent out a few telegrams. Nothing heroic." Suddenly he straightened, his posture stiffening. "Telegrams I paid for, I assure you. I wrote up receipts and added the coins to your cash box."

Grace waved off his explanation. "I trust you."

He leaned forward, his face set in serious lines. "Do you, Grace?"

She couldn't bear the intensity of his stare for long, but before ducking her head, she managed to murmur a quiet, "I'm starting to." She ran her hands over the worn cloth covers of the books in her lap. "I wouldn't be showing you these otherwise."

"Those are the books your father found in Haversham's library?" Keen interest laced Amos's words, and for the first time since she'd come in, he allowed his gaze to linger on the items in her hands. He didn't reach for the volumes, though, or even ask for permission to examine them. He seemed to understand the hold they had on her, the memories they evoked, the danger they represented, and was letting her set the pace.

She appreciated his thoughtfulness, but she'd delayed long enough. Lifting her chin, she thrust the books toward him. His eyes widened slightly at her forceful gesture, yet he made no comment, just accepted the books with a level of reverence she'd not expected. The marshal had been all business, shaking things loose to try to find the missing papers, but Amos was different. He took his time. Ran his fingers over the embossed titles on the spines, turned each book over slowly, examined them from every angle.

He turned away from her and laid the books on the work table. Balancing the spine on the tabletop, he simultaneously released the front and back covers. *Oliver Twist* fell open to a page about two-thirds deep. Amos repeated the action twice more. Each time, the book fell open to nearly the same page. After the third attempt, he left the book open where it had fallen and took up the second volume.

Grace rose from her seat and came to stand behind him. She thought she'd tried every technique imaginable to uncover the books' secrets, but she'd never thought of this. She ran her fingers along the center binding seam between *Oliver Twist's* open pages. "It's like the book was trained to open here," she said, slightly awed by the discovery even though she wasn't sure how it helped their current dilemma.

"When I looked at the pages of the closed book, there were tiny gaps in certain places." Amos paused in setting up *Guy Mannering*, his palms still holding the book upright as it balanced on its spine. "The books are older and have obviously been read, so one would expect such gaps to occur. But I wanted to see if any of the gaps were more pronounced than the others."

He released the covers of the second book, and it fell open near the middle. After resetting it, he released it again. This time the book fell open to a place closer to the front. On the third attempt, the book opened to a section near the middle but slightly deeper than the first occurrence.

"That one was inconsistent." Grace frowned at the book lying open to a seemingly random page. "What does that tell us?"

Amos leaned back and crossed his arms. "I can't say with certainty." His brow furrowed slightly as his gaze moved from one book to the other. "But logic would say that if documents were stashed inside these books, the thicker of the two was stored in the Dickens. It would've caused enough of a wedge to bulge the pages away from their natural positions. The binding was strained or even slightly broken due to the internal pressure. Whatever was stored in the Scott novel was much thinner. Perhaps only a single sheet. It caused no long-term damage to the binding."

"Tremont Haversham's revised will." Excitement bubbled up inside Grace. A clue! Her first real clue! "With all his wealth and assets, it would no doubt be several pages long. That must be what my father found in *Oliver Twist*. The Pinkerton report would have been much more brief. Probably just a name and per-haps a brief explanation of why they believed her to be Tremont's missing daughter."

Amos uncrossed his arms and rolled his shoulders a bit. "I know it doesn't tell us where the documents are now, but perhaps knowing where they once were will help somehow." He grabbed the edge of his spectacles and resituated them on the bridge of his nose. "I don't know how exactly, but it's a place to start, at least."

"It's wonderful. It's more than I deduced on my own." Grace clasped his arm in an effort to reassure him, then realized the intimacy of the gesture and blushed. She started to pull away, but Amos covered her hand with his own.

"I'll not give up the search," he vowed. "We'll find those docu-ments, Grace. I swear it."

She believed him. She wasn't quite sure why, but she did. Noth-ing felt impossible anymore. Not with this intelligent man working beside her. A friend to share her load.

Perhaps more than a friend? The thought skittered through her mind at the same moment a figure moved past her window.

The marshal. And another man.

Her heart fluttered in a panicked, frenzied rhythm. The books! She had to hide the books.

Jerking away from Amos's tender hold, Grace snatched the

books from the table, turned, and fled through the doorway into her chambers. She darted around her bed, opened the top drawer of the bureau, and shoved the books beneath her cotton drawers and stockings just as the office door creaked open and masculine voices filtered in.

Slamming the drawer closed, Grace spun around and hurried back to the outer office, willing her breathing to slow despite the tightness in her chest and the pounding of her pulse. Forcing her lips into a polite smile, she slowed her step as she passed through the doorway and prepared to greet her unwanted guests.

"Marshal," she started, then faltered as her gaze fell on the tall man at Malachi's side. A man who fulfilled every heroic fantasy she'd ever concocted to pass the lonely nights.

Tall, rugged, muscular. His skin was tanned from the sun. His hair dark, his jaw square. Black leather vest, blue shirt, trousers that outlined long legs and a lean stomach. The gun belt around his waist hung low on his hip, ready for action. And every wave of dark masculinity emanating from this stranger announced that he knew how to use a weapon. This was a man of skill. Of strength. Of undeniable swagger.

His attention zeroed in on her the moment she entered the room and latched on as if nothing else around him mattered. He fingered the brim of his hat as he dipped his chin in a nod of respect, but those dark brown eyes of his refused to release her. She felt a blush rise to her cheeks, but she didn't duck shyly away from his regard as she usually did. She couldn't. He wouldn't let her. It was as if he had a physical hold on her.

"Miss Mallory?" Heavens, even his voice was dark and rich. "I'm Elliott Dunbar of the Pinkerton agency. I've been trying to find you since the day your father was gunned down in Denver. You're a hard lady to run to ground."

13

Amos instinctively stepped between Grace and the towering stranger with the far too attentive gaze. The man had every desirable physical characteristic Amos lacked. *Every* one.

And Grace had noticed.

Instead of staring at the floor as she had the first time Amos had met her and several times thereafter, she gazed directly at the stranger's chiseled features, her golden eyes wide. Rapt. Ensnared.

Amos's jaw clenched. Great. Just what he needed when he'd finally decided to court a woman: competition. In a *women's* colony. He must be cursed.

Taking a deliberate step to the left in order to block the Pinkerton's direct line of sight to Grace, Amos extended his hand over the counter. "A pleasure to meet you, Mr. Dunbar. I'm Amos Bledsoe."

Finally, the man removed his gaze from Grace and looked at Amos. He smiled, and while the expression softened the hard lines of his face, it lacked any genuine warmth. Yet he shook Amos's hand and spoke in a friendly man-to-man way that carried no hint of the derision Amos usually encountered from men of his type, especially when a beautiful lady stood nearby.

"Bledsoe. Good to know you." Dunbar pumped Amos's arm up and down, his expression nothing but amiable.

Wonderful. Not only was the leather- and denim-clad Adonis oozing masculinity like a snail did slime, but he was personable too. His kind were supposed to be egotistical oafs. It was one of the few faults lesser mortals like Amos could exploit. But while Dunbar certainly didn't seem lacking in the confidence department, he wasn't insufferable with it, either. Doggone it.

"You're a Pinkerton?" Amos asked, hoping to keep Grace disengaged as long as possible.

"Yep." Dunbar reached into his inside coat pocket and pulled out a couple sheets of folded ivory paper along with a silver badge pinned to a piece of worn brown leather.

Amos fingered the badge. Heavy. The engraving of good quality. *Pinkerton National Detective Agency.* It looked authentic. He glanced over at the marshal. Shaw gave a small, confirming nod. Amos reached for the papers next. As he opened them, Dunbar confirmed the contents.

"Detective Whitmore sent me." He stepped sideways, no doubt in search of Grace again. "I'm right sorry about what happened to yer pa, miss. There ain't a day that's gone by since then that I haven't wished I could go back and change what happened. Prevented it somehow."

"Th-thank you." Grace's voice came out whisper-thin behind Amos.

He tossed a glance over his shoulder to check on her, then immediately wished he hadn't. She had *the look.* The soft, wooly look that came over unattached females when a man of handsome face and ideal form paid attention to them. He'd seen it on his sister's face when she'd first met Robert, and on a handful of others when that cowpuncher Roy Edmundson showed up at a church social. He'd never seen it directed at him. But then, who wanted it? Wool made him itch, and a woman under the influence of *the look* could barely string two words together in a coherent sentence. Case in point, the incredibly intelligent telegrapher behind him tripping over a standard conversational nicety as if it were a complex mathematical formula.

Someone needed to snap her out of it before her sensible nature suffered permanent damage.

"Miss Mallory," he said as he moved toward her, purposely blocking her view of the Pinkerton again and seeking out a connection with her eyes, "would you like to examine Mr. Dunbar's papers?"

She hesitated, blinking.

"I already looked through his documents," the marshal announced. "Everything appears to be in order."

Amos gave the marshal a nod. "I'm sure you're right, but since this matter concerns Miss Mallory, I think she should be afforded the opportunity to inspect the paperwork herself."

"Yes." Grace cleared her throat, and when Amos pivoted to face her, he was relieved to find the wooly look quickly fading from her eyes. The sharp intelligence he so admired reasserted itself as she reached for the documents. "Thank you, Mr. Bledsoe."

"Of course." He curved his arm around her and placed his left hand against the small of her back as he handed her the papers with his right. She startled a bit at his touch, her eyebrows raising just a fraction, but she made no comment. Nor did she lurch away from him. Both encouraging signs.

He fought the primitive urge to stare Dunbar down, to announce his claim in a language all males understood. He knew better than to lay down such a gauntlet, however. Men like Dunbar tended to view such claims as an invitation to prove their prowess. Nothing tempted like the forbidden.

Besides, Amos couldn't compete with Dunbar's packaging. He had accepted that truth about himself long ago. Squaring off with such a physical specimen would only play to his weaknesses.

No, if he was to win the war, he had to alter the playing field, set aside the primitive and focus on the sensitive. Instead of pitting himself against his rival, he would discount the man entirely and focus on the person who truly mattered—Grace.

Amos planted himself by Grace's side and offered silent support as she read through the papers. He'd seen the letter of introduction Detective Whitmore had written for Dunbar, addressed to a Mr. Herschel Mallory. It couldn't be easy for her to see her father's name like that, as if he were still alive.

Her hands trembled slightly as she scanned the letter. "Were you there?" She didn't look up from the letter, but Amos knew who she addressed. "At the café?"

Dunbar dragged his hat off his head and dipped his chin. "Yes'm, I was there. Sittin' in the café, waitin' on yer pa. We never suspected . . . The street was crowded with people. It should have been safe. I . . ."

"It wasn't your fault," Grace said, still not looking up as she folded the papers back into their creased rectangles.

Amos held out his hand to take them from her, wanting to ease her burden in some way. And to keep as much distance between her and Dunbar as possible.

She handed him the papers, and her gaze finally touched his for the first time since the Pinkerton waltzed into the office. The mix of emotions swirling in the brown depths of her eyes caught Amos off guard. Grief for her father, hope that her troubles might be at an end, and confusion—over the Pinkerton's sudden appearance, perhaps? Amos had questions about that, too.

Amos's fingers stroked hers as he took the documents from her hand. Her chin lifted slightly, as if his touch had bolstered her, and her eyes sharpened into the determined focus he was accustomed to seeing.

Good.

Feeling stronger himself, he slid the papers across the counter toward the Pinkerton. Dunbar nodded his thanks and tucked them into his coat pocket, his manner polite. Except for the amusement in his gaze when Amos finally made eye contact with him.

Amos recognized that look. It wasn't one of good humor or a sunny disposition. It was the look of someone who found it funny that a man like Amos thought he had a chance with a woman like Grace. A look that said Amos was so far beneath him in masculine appeal, it was laughable.

Well, Amos knew how to deal with such looks. He ignored the offended jab in his gut and met Dunbar's amused gaze straight on. He lifted his left eyebrow just a hair and stared. Not enough to project defiance. That would only deepen the amusement. Amos had come up with a look that incorporated just enough self-assurance to cast doubt into the egotist's brain.

I'm a man of depth and integrity. Are you?

Dunbar blinked, and some of the amusement faded from his gaze. It was enough. Amos turned back to Grace.

As did Dunbar, apparently. "I understand your father had some documents to turn over to us," the Pinkerton said, striding down the length of the counter until he stood directly in front of Grace. There'd be no subtly blocking his view now. "Do you have those, miss?"

"I'm afraid they aren't . . . readily available."

Interesting. She didn't mention the books, a fact Amos found immensely encouraging. Dunbar might have stellar good looks and authentic credentials, but he didn't have Grace's trust. Not yet.

The Pinkerton frowned. "Well, I, ah . . . don't aim to frighten you, miss, but there's reason to believe your possession of those documents has placed you in danger. I'm under strict orders to collect any evidence you have and get it to Whitmore before Chaucer Haversham learns of your location."

"He already has." That grim pronouncement came from the marshal.

Dunbar glanced at the lawman beside him then aimed an unrelenting stare at Grace. "If that's the case, we ain't got time to spare. Why don't you and I step over to the café, get some coffee, and discuss how best to get those documents?"

Grace's gaze flew to Amos, then to the marshal before finally resting on Dunbar. "All . . . right. If Mr. Bledsoe doesn't mind tending the office while I'm away."

Of course I mind! Amos wanted to refuse, but he held his tongue and gave a tight nod of assent instead.

The café was a public establishment. She wouldn't be alone with the Pinkerton. But for all intents and purposes, she'd be *alone* with him. Private conversation. Cozied up at a corner table. Dunbar's long limbs crowding her space, giving him an excuse to *accidentally* bump her thigh with his knee or brush his hand along her arm. He'd no doubt fire a barrage of masculine machinations at her to find out what she knew. And as much as Amos would like to believe that Grace was too clever to fall for the detective's ploys, she'd already shown a wooly-eyed susceptibility.

She stepped over to the hook on the wall and collected her shawl. "I just need to send one quick telegram before I leave. It will only take a minute."

Dunbar nodded.

Amos frowned. What telegram? Nothing had come in except that note from the Alamo Wheelmen. He hadn't seen any completed telegram blanks lying around.

Nevertheless, she walked straight to the office table and delicately perched on the edge of the seat he had vacated when their guests arrived.

She reached for the key, but she didn't open the circuit. Did Dunbar have her so rattled that she'd forgotten the basic operations of the telegraph? Amos was about to step close and whisper the oversight into her ear when he recognized his call sign at the beginning of her message.

It took a great deal of control not to let his surprise or growing delight show. He busied himself with straightening the stack of extra telegraph blanks in the box on the near side of the table so it would appear as if he was paying Grace no particular mind.

A—When D and I are at café, take items back to E. Lock in vault. Let no one see. Will follow my father's example.

Amos instantly recalled the story she'd told about the hatbox and her father's insistence on hiding the documents until meeting with the Pinkerton to ascertain his motives.

Grace pushed back from her chair and stood. "I won't be long," she said, her eyes meeting Amos's for no more than a heartbeat, but he understood the message. He wasn't to dawdle.

"I'll take care of things, Miss Mallory."

She nodded. "Thank you, Mr. Bledsoe."

Then she left. On the arm of a man who threatened everything Amos hoped to gain. Yet it wasn't Dunbar who Grace trusted with her father's books. It was Amos. The spectacle-wearing, bicycle-riding telegraph operator who listened to her secret messages and took them to heart.

He just prayed Dunbar didn't switch her loyalties.

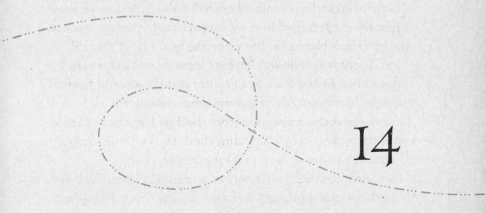

14

Helen scowled at the stranger bleeding all over the path to her cabin. "You got no business bein' here," she groused, not that he cared anything for her opinion. He was too busy dying.

Without his boots on.

Helen frowned. Gray wool stockings were the only things covering his feet. Odd. No horse, no boots. The horse could have been spooked, but the boots? Unoccupied footwear rarely bolted on its own.

Adjusting her grip on the branch she carried in case he proved dangerous when roused, Helen prodded the sole of his right foot with the toe of her shoe. His mouth tightened and he groaned, but he didn't lurch to his feet or attack her.

He posed no threat. That was good. But he wouldn't be getting up and walking out of her life any time soon, either. That was bad. Or, at the very least, inconvenient.

Blowing out a breath, Helen dropped the branch and lowered to her knees beside the fallen man. She cast one more cautionary glance at his face before turning her attention to his leg. He'd managed to tie a bandana around the wound, which had probably slowed the bleeding enough to keep him alive. But judging by his pallor and lack of awareness, he wouldn't be alive much longer without help. And thanks to an ill-timed prayer on her part, the Almighty had just volunteered her for the duty.

"What were you doing skulking around out here, anyway?" Helen muttered as she stripped off her pecan-stained gloves and pried the bandana back to examine the wound. A dark hole in his trousers that continued into the flesh below confirmed her earlier suspicion.

Gunshot.

Which begged another, more bothersome question. Who shot him? And where was that person now?

None of the ladies came out this far. Most of them rarely left town, and the ones at the farm would have said something about shooting a man. As much as that gaggle loved to gossip, they'd probably not be able to *stop* talking about it.

"So are you the good guy or the bad guy?" Helen arranged the bloody bandage back over the wound, then studied the man's face as if that would give her some insight.

She knew better than most that a man's character had no correlation with his appearance. Her father had been handsome enough to fool an entire town into believing him a saint. Ladies thought she and her mother were the luckiest females alive. And when her ma's battered body finally gave out, womenfolk lined up with food and sympathy for the widower left behind. Helen had done all she could to scare the fools away. The women might be stupid, but they didn't deserve the nightmare of living with Judson Potter behind closed doors. No female did.

Thankfully, her father enjoyed the attention from his admirers too much to settle on just one lady. And since he had Helen to work his frustrations out on at home, he kept the ruse up for nearly two years before he had the decency to drink himself blind, tumble headfirst off his horse, and break his neck.

This fella didn't have the look of a charmer, at least not from what she could tell by the side of his face not planted in the dirt. A day's growth of whiskers darkened his jaw, his clothes were practical rather than fancy, and his left stocking had a hole on the side of the heel. Helen's gaze traveled back up to his head. His hair was longish, overlapping his collar, as if he couldn't spare the time for a trim, but his mustache was impeccable. Thick, brown, and long enough to hide the top line of his upper lip, yet well-groomed and tidy.

Helen smirked. "Found yer vanity, didn't I?" Somehow that made him less formidable, knowing he had a weakness. Besides the hole in his leg, of course.

Which she really needed to do something about.

Unfortunately, grabbing his feet and dragging his carcass the last ten feet to her cabin door was probably not the best option. He looked far too heavy, and yanking on that bad leg would do him no favors. She might not want to help him, but now that she'd been assigned the task, she wasn't about to sabotage her results.

Helen glanced up the path to the line cabin and frowned at the closed door. Transporting an unconscious stranger was going to be hard enough without having to deal with a latched door. She pushed to her feet, jogged over to the cabin, and opened the door. Worried the wind would blow it closed before she returned, she grabbed the one chair the small room boasted and propped the door open.

She hurried back to the fallen man and hunkered down by his head. "All right, Mr. Mustache, you have to wake up enough to help me move you." She squeezed her arms beneath his right shoulder and lifted. "It ain't far," she grunted, barely managing to roll his torso a few inches off the ground. Heavens, he was heavy. "Just a few steps. Then you can pass out again. I promise."

His head jostled as she struggled to roll him. Another groan, louder this time, rumbled from beneath that bushy brown caterpillar on his lip, and his eyes cracked open.

121

Helen nearly dropped him, not expecting such vivid green eyes on a man with dark coloring. His gaze was glassy and unfocused, but any consciousness was better than no consciousness, so Helen doubled her efforts, determined to take advantage of whatever awareness she could wrest from him.

"Wake up, mister. I can't get you to the cabin on my own. I need your help." She spoke right next to his ear, her head bent close to his as she searched for the right leverage. "Come on. Help me!"

"Rachel?" he croaked. His body stiffened as he raised his head to look at her. His cloudy gaze meshed with hers for a breath-stealing instant, then something snapped inside him. He started thrashing, desperate to get up.

"Easy, now," Helen warned. "You're hurt." She wanted him to get up, but she didn't want him to kill himself in the process.

The stranger only clenched his jaw and continued his ungainly rise. He was half dead, yet somehow, by sheer force of will, he crawled to his feet. He could bear no weight on his left leg. Helen tried to wrap an arm around his waist and duck under his left arm as a human crutch, but he pushed her away.

No, not away. He pushed her behind him. Planted himself in front of her like some kind of crazed guardian.

"Don't worry, sis. I won't let Pa hurt you. Go hide where I showed you. Everything will be all right."

Helen froze, her heart pumping a frantic rhythm. He thought she was his sister, and he was protecting her. Despite what must be excruciating pain, he stood in her defense.

How many times had she dreamed of a strong older brother to stand between her and her father?

But he wasn't her brother. He was a stranger, out of his head from fever and loss of blood. He wouldn't be able to stay on his feet long. She had to get him to the cabin.

"I'm safe," she murmured in an attempt to calm him. "You're the one hurt. Let me help you."

He shooed away her hands. "He might come back. You need to hide where I showed you. Pa won't find you there. I'll make sure of it."

By putting himself in harm's way and taking the beating himself. She knew. Hadn't she done that herself when her mother had grown too weak to withstand her father's "discipline"?

Ma had done her best to shield Helen when she'd been a child, but over time, she grew too tired and worn out to divert her husband. Helen had been twelve when she took over the role of protector, trying to spare her mother the brunt of her father's wrath. In the end, he'd still killed her. A person could only be broken so many times before they lost the ability to mend.

"Pa's gone," she said, playing along with the man's delusion. She locked her arm around his waist and wedged herself beneath his left shoulder. "You can protect me when he gets back. If you can stand, which you won't be able to do unless we get to the house and tend that leg."

His brows peaked in confusion. "You're sure he's gone?"

Helen nodded. "I'm sure. Now let's get you to the house." She took a step toward the line shack. Then another. He hissed in pain, but limped along beside her.

"One more year, Rach," he said, his words slurring slightly and his weight growing heavier as they reached the door she'd propped open.

Helen trudged forward, afraid they wouldn't make it to the narrow bed inside if they slowed.

"Grayson said he'd hire me as soon as I turn sixteen. We'll leave that very day and never come back here again. I swear it."

Thank heavens the room was small and sparse. Just a chair, the bed, and a rickety table by the stove in the far corner. Nothing to trip over or climb around. Three strides, and she'd have him to the bed.

After one stride, his leg gave out.

He groaned and collapsed against her. Helen nearly crumpled beneath the weight. A cry tore from her lips as she staggered.

Her cry must have galvanized him, for he strained to regain his footing, releasing a primal growl that sent chills over her as he forced himself upward. Tears came to her eyes that had nothing to do with the throbbing in her shoulders as he used her body as a crutch. Her eyes misted for the man who gave everything he had to protect her. He protected her from an enemy of the past and from the burden of his weight in the present, and whispered promises of a future where they would be free.

She had no doubt this man would kill himself trying to spare her, and the certainty of it split her heart wide open. All the hatred, fear, and distrust she'd harbored for so long leaked out, leaving her raw and aching. Yet strength rushed in to fill the emptiness, like nothing she'd ever felt before.

She no longer cared who the stranger was or what he'd been doing out here. She didn't even care if he was the Haversham fellow Grace had warned them about. He was Rachel's brother. A protective, selfless man who didn't deserve to die. And Helen aimed to do some protecting of her own.

"Hold on, mister," she ground out between clenched teeth. "This ain't gonna be pretty."

Helen tightened her grip on the man's waist and lurched forward. His leg couldn't take the jostling, but she'd anticipated that. She bent over, taking his weight onto her back as much as possible as she dragged him one step closer to the bed.

Her vision tunneled until all she saw was the narrow wood bedframe and the patchwork quilt she'd made from flour sacks last winter.

One.

She gritted her teeth and scraped her right foot along the floorboards.

More.

The man went lax, his full weight coming down on her. Helen's knees threatened to buckle, but she refused to give in. She leaned forward, her focus zeroed in on the bed.

Step.

Feeling the stranger toppling and knowing she could do nothing to stop it, Helen tumbled with him, her only goal to control the location of his landing.

They fell awkwardly atop the bed, his head knocking slightly against the wall and her chin digging into his sternum. Their legs were a tangled mess, and her right arm was pinned beneath his back, but they'd made it.

Elation gushed upward through Helen's chest and erupted in quiet laughter. Praise God! They'd made it.

As she caught her breath, it occurred to her what she must look like, and a second burst of laughter bubbled out of her.

If Katie could see her now, her friend would faint dead away. Helen Potter in bed with a man. And smiling.

The world must surely be coming to an end.

15

"Come find me at the jailhouse when you're done with your visit, Dunbar," Malachi Shaw said, his voice firm, insistent. Yet his assertion of control did little to calm the panic rising inside Grace as she realized the marshal was going to leave her alone with the Pinkerton. "Male accommodations around here are scarce. We'll have to make arrangements."

Mr. Dunbar smiled and nodded. "Sure thing." Then he opened the café door and motioned for Grace to enter ahead of him. "Miss Mallory?"

She hesitated, finding it incredibly difficult to tear her gaze away from the marshal, who had remained at street level when she and Mr. Dunbar climbed onto the boardwalk. Slowly, she forced her attention away from Malachi and turned to meet the Pinkerton's dark brown eyes. His smile seemed to deepen as she looked at him, and the hint of a dimple creased his right cheek through the dark whiskers of his closely cropped beard. She immediately dropped her gaze to her feet.

Good heavens, but he was handsome. And the way he looked at her . . . Grace's stomach danced and whirled, her pulse fluttering in time to the dizzying tempo in her belly. She bit gently on her tongue, injecting just enough discomfort to clear her head. *You can do this.*

After all, her father had been poised to do this very thing—meet with the Pinkerton agent sent by Mr. Whitmore and hand over their evidence. She would finally be completing the work her father started. Yet, like her father, she intended to be cautious. She wouldn't hand anything over until she was sure the man in front of her could be trusted. And there was only one way to make that determination—spend time with him.

Lifting her chin, she aimed a smile somewhere in the vicinity of Mr. Dunbar's throat and entered the café.

Ann Marie hurried toward them across the nearly vacant dining area. The curvy brunette greeted Grace, but her eyes never strayed from the tall man near her elbow. Usually Grace didn't mind being overlooked—she enjoyed the peacefulness of anonymity. But seeing the obvious interest lighting Ann Marie's eyes made this particular oversight prick her skin like stinging nettles.

"Let me show you to a table," Ann Marie offered, moving to Mr. Dunbar's left side and smiling up at him like a besotted schoolgirl. "Would you prefer one by the window, or a more private area near the back?"

Grace blinked. Usually patrons just sat wherever they found a vacancy. The only other customer in the entire place was Daisy, the elderly lady who liked to sip tea and watch the town happenings from the front window. So why the escort? Did Ann Marie think they'd be overwhelmed by the sheer number of seating options?

The Pinkerton winked at the overeager waitress, and Ann Marie blushed. Question answered.

"A little privacy would be welcome," he said, his low voice rich and a tad . . . arrogant? He turned to Grace, and she swore she could feel his gaze touch the skin of her face as if his fingers had stroked her cheek.

A shiver ran down the back of her neck. It wasn't unpleasant, exactly. It was warm and tingly and made her insides tremble, but it also left her feeling unsettled. Such a look was too intimate between virtual strangers. They'd only met half an hour ago, too soon to have formed any meaningful attachment. Yet it might just be his way of showing attraction. She knew so little about how men courted women. And this man, in particular, seemed more potent than most.

Still . . . she'd feel better if he demonstrated at least a *little* nervousness. His abundance of self-assurance was making her lose a grip on her own.

It was so different from when she was with Amos. Mr. Bledsoe had a way about him that naturally boosted her confidence, made her feel comfortable in her own skin. No pretense, no need to impress. Just acceptance, respect, and honesty.

Grace suddenly hungered for those steady qualities. Mr. Dunbar, with his burning brown eyes and shiver-inducing smile, felt oddly . . . threatening. Like a sleek panther on the prowl. And the more sheepish she became in his presence, the more apt he'd be to pounce.

So get rid of the wool and find your gumption.

"Thank you, Ann Marie," Grace intoned softly when they reached the corner table. "I'll take tea and one of those butter cookies you make that are so tasty."

She reached for the chair, determined to seat herself like an independent woman, but Mr. Dunbar beat her to it. He slid the chair out, brushing his fingers along her arm as he did so. She jerked her gaze toward him, but he simply smiled politely at her, with nothing untoward in his manner.

She nodded her thanks as Ann Marie sidled up to the Pinkerton. "I also make an apple turnover that's light and flaky and goes real well with coffee. I got a few cooling in the back if you're interested."

"Sounds delicious. I'll take two. Along with that coffee." Dunbar winked at the waitress again, and Ann Marie nearly tripped over her own feet as she turned to make her way to the kitchen.

Grace bit back a sigh. Was that how all women reacted to this man? No wonder he exuded confidence. He was like walking whiskey, intoxicating unsuspecting females just by entering their proximity. Time to build up an immunity. Herschel Mallory's mission deserved nothing less than clearheaded focus and insightful discernment. Not fluttery distraction and a mush-filled mind.

Mr. Dunbar took the seat across from her and shined the full force of his masculine glory directly at her. Grace ordered her stomach to cease its skipping. When it didn't, she decided she needed a more assertive approach.

"How long have you worked with Detective Whitmore?"

Dunbar's eyes widened slightly, and his surprise, even as subtle as it was, buoyed her confidence.

"A few years," he answered as he leaned back in his chair. "Best mentor a man could ask for. He has a knack for finding people who don't want to be found." His eyes met hers, and he slowly leaned forward again, closing the distance between them by resting one forearm on the table near her side. The black sleeve of his coat grazed the white linen of her napkin. "That's why I was so determined to find you. Didn't want to let Whitmore down."

Grace smoothed a wrinkle from the tablecloth to give her an excuse to glance down. He was too close. Too . . . intent. But she needed to watch him as he answered her next question, so she didn't keep her gaze downcast for long. Just a heartbeat or two in order to give herself some relief from his stare. Then she banished the shy mouse inside her and raised her head. "How *did* you find me?"

Did his lips tighten just a bit at the corners? Grace peered more closely at his face, but it seemed the Pinkerton preferred to be on the giving end of scrutiny, not the other way around.

He straightened away from the table and crossed his arms over his chest. "Good detective work."

Grace waited for him to elaborate. He didn't.

This time, *she* leaned across the table. She laughed, hoping to hide her determination to excavate details. "Can you be a little more specific?"

Mr. Dunbar smiled. That swaggering, I-could-kiss-your-garters-off-if-you-let-me smile that brought a warmth to her cheeks she was powerless to stop. "Can't go giving away trade secrets, darlin'."

She might not be able to control her blush, but she had a slightly stronger grasp on her mind. That smile was a decoy. He didn't want to answer her question. Why?

Grace offered a smile of her own. One far less practiced yet, she hoped, flirtatious enough to play to his ego. "I won't tell anyone." She batted her lashes. She had no idea if such an action would help her cause or simply make her look ridiculous, but she figured it was worth a try. "You must have been quite clever to discover my hiding place after all this time. I thought for sure the trail had gone cold. What gave me away?"

He shrugged. "When I couldn't find you, I turned my attention to Haversham. He's wealthy, has lots of resources. I figured if I couldn't uncover your hiding place on my own, I'd wait to see if Haversham did. Kept my ear to the ground, used a shared comradery with the Pinkerton agents on the mine payroll to gain access to inside information. Then, as soon as I heard about the telegraph lady in Colorado Springs giving up your location, I jumped on the first train headed south, praying I'd get to you before he did."

"See," Grace said, turning up the brightness on her false smile, "I knew you were clever."

Dunbar preened at the praise, but the instant before his cocky grin returned in full force, the lines at the corners of his mouth relaxed. In relief that he hadn't been caught in his web of deception.

For he *was* lying. Of that, Grace was convinced. She just wasn't sure if he was lying now or had done so earlier.

Back in the telegraph office, Mr. Dunbar had seemed surprised when the marshal mentioned Haversham's knowledge of her location. Yet now he claimed that he'd discovered her hiding place because he gleaned the information from Haversham's men. Both scenarios could not be true. Had Chaucer Haversham gotten to Dunbar, corrupted him somehow, bribed his loyalty away from Whitmore? Or was the Pinkerton sitting across from her an honorable man who had simply been attempting to spare her worry when they first met, therefore choosing to minimize Haversham's role?

Lord, help me discern the truth, Grace prayed as she dropped her attention to her lap.

"Here we go." A cheerful voice interrupted Grace's prayer as Ann Marie arrived at the table with a tray laden with beverages and sweets.

Mr. Dunbar scooted out his chair and stood. "Let me help you with that." He reached for the tray.

"Thank you." Ann Marie allowed him to clasp the tray but seemed to forget to release her own hold. Grace cleared her throat softly. Ann Marie yanked her hands away, causing the teacups to rattle in their saucers.

Mr. Dunbar smiled, only making things worse for the poor girl. Ann Marie's cheeks looked like they were on fire, something to which Grace could easily relate.

While the Pinkerton held the tray steady, Ann Marie arranged Grace's tea in front of her with a lacy butter cookie on a small plate beside it. Then she set a second arrangement at Mr. Dunbar's place, a much stronger aroma wafting from his cup. His pair of apple turnovers dwarfed her cookie by comparison, but then, a man of his size couldn't be expected to eat like a lady. Although he could apparently be expected to *drink* like one. Grace hid a grin as Mr. Dunbar frowned at the dainty china teacup his coffee had arrived in.

As Ann Marie set out the blue sugar bowl and matching cream pitcher, the Pinkerton raised an eyebrow. "You got any real cups? That coffee'll be gone in two swigs."

Ann Marie took the tray back from him and held it close to her chest like a shield. "I'm sorry. We don't get many men in here. The marshal's really the only one, and he's taken to bringing his own mug when he comes in with his wife." Her gaze followed Mr. Dunbar as he lowered himself back into his chair. She nibbled her lip as a frown continued marring his face. "I made sure not to use the cups with flowers painted on them," she said, trying to appease. "And I promise to be attentive with your refills. Just catch my eye, and I'll bring the pot. As often as you need."

"I suppose my manhood can withstand a dent or two from drinking out of a lady's cup." He grinned up at the waitress, who nodded immediately in agreement.

"Oh. Yes, sir. You have nothing to worry about there. Nothing could dent your . . . er . . . manliness." Cheeks flaming once again, Ann Marie started backing away. "I'll just . . . ah . . . go make sure the coffee's plenty hot. For when you need a refill."

The Pinkerton dipped his chin. Ann Marie spun away and hustled off to the kitchen.

Grace lifted her teacup to her lips to hide her smile.

"Sweet girl," Mr. Dunbar said, no hint of arrogance in his tone, just gentlemanly warmth.

Grace peered at him over the rim of her cup. He shrugged in a self-deprecating manner, then grasped the teacup handle between his large thumb and first two fingers and lifted it to his mouth. A thin mustache and well-trimmed beard outlined his lips, and Grace had to admit that Ann Marie was right. Drinking from a ladies' teacup would not dent this man's masculinity anytime soon. He could probably replace his hat with a garland of woven wildflowers and still project a warrior's mystique.

But despite his charmingly roguish demeanor and the attraction that surged through her whenever his dark eyes connected with hers, she didn't trust him. She wanted to believe him worthy of her father's secrets, to let him relieve her of the burden that had been weighing her down for so long, but she couldn't. Not until she quieted the suspicious whispers buzzing in her mind. Too much was at stake to be anything less than certain.

"So, Miss Mallory," Mr. Dunbar said as he reached for a turnover, his voice casual, his movements slow and smooth. As he raised the sweet to his mouth, he paused, waited for her to look up, then pierced her with a look that, while friendly, exuded steely insistence. "Where are those documents your father uncovered?"

16

Amos paced the length of the far-too-short-to-be-satisfactory telegraph office for the tenth time, ran fingers through his barely-long-enough-to-grab hair for the third time, then flopped into the padded, Grace-should-be-back-and-sitting-here armchair.

What was taking so long? He pounded the arm of the chair with his fist as his knees bounced with an energy that urged him to do more than sit around and wait like a trained pup. But what could he do? He'd already accomplished the one task Grace had left for him—delivered the books to Mrs. Shaw and watched while she secured them in her bank vault.

Supervising the lock-up had been a straightforward, simple matter compared to finding the books in the first place. Grace's chambers were small enough that there hadn't been too many places to look, but he'd still felt guilty rifling through her personal belongings. Especially her underclothes. Even now, his neck heated at the memory of digging through her unmentionables. When he'd opened that drawer and seen what was inside, he'd quickly shut it. But after looking through the rest of the bureau, he'd realized that the top drawer had been the most disturbed, the most untidy. So he'd gone back and, as respectfully as possible, dug through items he'd only ever seen on clotheslines or in mail-order catalogs until he'd unearthed the two volumes he sought.

That had been twenty minutes ago. He pulled his watch out of his vest pocket and flicked the brass cover open with his thumbnail. Twenty-*two* minutes. Even worse. He snapped the lid closed with a disgruntled sigh and stuffed the watch back into his pocket.

As he mentally debated whether to resume pacing or start unraveling his left stocking one thread at a time, a movement outside the small window caught his attention. Grace!

Amos surged to his feet. He yanked open the half door at the end of the counter and stepped through at the same moment the main door swung inward.

And there she stood. Staring at him, eyes wide at his unexpected nearness. Her light gray shawl hung draped over one arm, the tiny pink rosebuds that patterned the dark blue of her dress brought out the youthful loveliness of her face, and her slightly wind-mussed hair made his fingers itch to stroke each wayward strand softly back into place.

He cleared his throat and tried to clear his mind as well. This was not the time for thoughts of hair-stroking or hand-holding or any of the hundred other courting ideas running through his brain at the moment. This was the time to focus on Grace and her mission.

Though if he were honest, a small portion of his attention would probably remain dedicated to determining how much competition that pretty boy Dunbar presented.

"How did it go?" Amos asked, finally breaking the charged silence stretching between them.

Grace's lashes dropped to shutter her eyes as she tugged the door closed behind her. She said nothing as she moved past him, just quietly hung up her shawl before crossing to the window to peer outside.

Gazing longingly after the Pinkerton? Or making sure no customers were approaching so they could discuss the situation without interruption? With her back to him, hiding her face as well as the view out the window, Amos couldn't tell.

"I evaded him as best I could."

The soft-spoken words sent a hard jolt of pleasure through him. He *knew* she was too smart to fall for a handsome face without searching out what lay beneath. Cloaking his jubilance in an expression of mild curiosity took considerable effort, but he managed. Barely.

"Did he press you for answers?" Amos's jubilance faded as he considered how intimidating such a large man could be. If Dunbar had threatened Grace or made her feel uncomfortable, Amos would have to take steps to ensure the two were never left alone together again.

"He asked several pointed questions that were difficult to sidestep, but he remained a gentleman." Grace turned, her gaze seeking him out. Amos immediately closed the distance between them, crossing into the main office and halting only when he stood directly in front of her. Taking no time to weigh the wisdom of the action, he reached for her hand. Her fingers were chilled from the autumn wind, and as soon as her skin touched his, all he wanted to do was warm it. He squeezed her hand gently, rubbing the back with his thumb. A slight tremor passed through her, yet she lingered, not pulling away from his touch.

"I'm here for you, Grace," he vowed. "Whatever you need."

Tiny frown lines sprouted across her brow. "What I need is an unbiased opinion of Mr. Dunbar and his motives." She tugged her hand free, then sat at the desk and fiddled with the edge of the telegraph machine.

Amos returned to the blue-striped chair and perched on the edge. "I'm not sure how unbiased my opinion is," he admitted, since he despised the far-too-handsome Pinkerton, "but I can

136

promise to evaluate everything about him with a healthy dose of skepticism." She finally turned to look at him, and Amos leaned forward, bracing his forearms on his knees as he spoke. "I would never tell you what you should do with your father's books, Grace, but Dunbar's timing in showing up here makes me wary."

She said nothing, just held his gaze. For once, he was the one who looked away first.

"I caught him in a lie." Her soft voice floated to him. Amos jerked his attention back to her face, which gave little indication of what she might be thinking.

"Did you confront him?" He hoped not. If the Pinkerton had a hidden agenda, Grace needed any advantage available to get the upper hand.

Thankfully, she shook her head. "No. And I think I hid my reaction well enough that he didn't suspect anything." Her shoulders lifted in a shrug. "It was harder to evade his direct questions about the location of the documents. I told him truthfully that I hadn't been able to find them yet in my father's belongings. He mentioned the books. Said his informant among the Pinkertons at the Silver Serpent Mine let it slip that two books had gone missing from the library at Haversham House."

Amos straightened. "He admitted to knowing Chaucer Haversham? But earlier he acted as if he'd known nothing about Haversham discovering your whereabouts."

"I know." She sighed and turned back to the telegraph, outlining the rectangular base with her finger. "That was the lie I caught him in. I just can't discern the intent behind it. Was he simply trying to spare me worry, not realizing that I already knew of Haversham's discovery? Or is his duplicity a symptom of a more serious problem?"

She blew out a breath, pushed back from the desk, and twisted in her chair to stare into the empty space above the customer counter. "I can't trust him with the books. Not yet, at least. When he asked about them, I told him I had packed them away and left them with a trusted friend. When I refused to give him the name of the friend, he encouraged me to wire that person and ask her to ship them to me." Grace turned to face him, her eyes dark and fretful. "That's when I left and came here. It was the perfect excuse—leave him to assume I'm wiring my friend."

"Without realizing that your friend is just a few steps away at the bank." Amos smiled. "Quick thinking. You probably bought yourself at least a couple days. Dunbar couldn't expect a shipment to arrive any sooner than that."

Grace's gaze dodged past him through the doorway to her private chambers then returned to his face. "The books *are* at the bank, aren't they?"

"Yes. They're safe. Locked up tight."

Her shoulders relaxed. "Thank you."

The depth of gratitude she packed into those two small words made his heart swell to what felt like twice its normal size. What he wouldn't give to slay all her dragons so easily.

Silence stretched between them. It wasn't uncomfortable, but it reverberated with the tension of a complicated situation that had no clear solution. If they could figure out Dunbar's true motives, they could decide how to proceed, but until they ferreted out the truth, they remained in limbo.

"I have two days to find Father's documents." Her tone didn't instill much confidence. "But with Mr. Dunbar hanging around town, I can't risk taking the books out of the vault." Her mouth quirked with irony. "It's rather hard to find something if you can't look in the place where it's hidden."

Amos smacked his knee with his palm and shot to his feet, determination humming in his veins. He would not allow her to be defeated by this situation. "Then we'll just have to tackle this problem another way."

The office chair creaked as Grace craned her neck to follow his movements. "What are you thinking?"

He paced over to the counter, then pivoted, leaning back against the half wall. "If we can't investigate the documents, we'll just have to investigate the man who intends to claim them."

"Mr. Dunbar? But what is there to investigate? His credentials are legitimate." Her brow furrowed, but it seemed to be more in thought than confusion. "Malachi and I telegraphed the Pinkerton office in Philadelphia the morning after I received the warning over the wire. Detective Whitmore confirmed that he's had the same man working my case since he received my father's communication all those months ago, one Elliott Dunbar. Mr. Whitmore assured us that he could be trusted. Said Dunbar was as honorable as they come."

"Yet your gut says otherwise, doesn't it?" Amos gently prodded.

Grace gave a jerky little nod. "I just wish I had evidence one way or the other. To either verify that he is the honorable man Whitmore claims or to prove he's been corrupted somehow. That Haversham got to him. Paid him off, threatened his family, *something*. But I have no proof on either side."

"Not yet," Amos conceded, "but that doesn't mean you can't start gathering the information you need to decide if he's trustworthy."

Interest lit Grace's eyes. "What kind of information?"

"Anything. Everything." Amos pushed away from the wall. He crossed the floor in five strides then sat on the corner of her desk. "We don't take anything for granted. We question everything, including Whitmore's testimony. If Dunbar has been working this case for nearly a year, Whitmore hasn't seen him in quite some time. It's possible Dunbar's no longer the man Whitmore knew."

"Not the man Whitmore knew . . ." Grace shot forward in her seat. She reached for the telegraph sounder, opened the circuit, and began tapping.

Amos translated the sounds as she set up a wired path to the telegraph office at the Pinkerton agency in Philadelphia. Once connected, she asked for Whitmore. The operator on the other end responded that the detective was not available, so Grace turned her attention directly to her cohort on the other side. A male operator, by the sound of his touch on the key, slightly heavier than Grace's, and a little faster. Almost . . . regimented, like a soldier marching to battle.

Have you ever met Detective Dunbar?

Yes.

Can you describe his physical appearance?

Tall, brown hair, mustache.

No beard?

Never seen him with one. Might not shave while in the field, though.

That earned a frown from Grace, and no wonder. Dunbar seemed the type of man who used his looks as a weapon. Such a fellow would always look his best.

What about his eye color?

Don't know. The tapping grew thicker and less precise, as if the sender were growing agitated. *Never looked close enough to notice. Why all the questions? If he's got the badge, he's Detective Dunbar. The only way a Pinkerton loses his badge is if it's stolen from his corpse. Quit clogging the line with your fretting. I have real work to do.*

Grace thanked the operator for his assistance then raised her gaze to Amos. "The description matches."

Amos frowned. "Tall. Brown hair. Mustache." He shook his head. "Grace, that description matches half the men in Texas. I wouldn't exactly call that substantive proof."

She slumped backward in her chair. "I know. I hoped to uncover something more definitive, but it seems all I've done is confuse matters even further."

"How's that?"

"I thought we only had two possible scenarios to decide between. But now it appears we have three."

Amos ached over the weariness and strain in her face that seemed to deepen as he watched. "Three?"

Grace released a heavy sigh and nodded. "Until now I thought I had two choices. Mr. Dunbar is trustworthy, or he's been corrupted, possibly coerced, by Haversham. But according to the Pinkerton operator, there's a third option."

Amos thought back over the words of the Philadelphia operator in an effort to follow Grace's logic. He had insisted Dunbar was exactly who he presented himself to be because . . . Amos's back stiffened. "The badge."

Grace's gaze melted into his. "There could be a Pinkerton agent lying dead somewhere between here and Colorado."

17

Helen sawed the stranger's pant leg with a dull serrated knife she kept in the cabin for eating purposes. After five minutes, with only a two-inch slit to show for her effort, she abandoned the knife and used her hands instead. Grabbing the ragged edges of denim, she yanked them apart as hard as she could. The fabric gave way and tore several inches straight up the front. She repositioned her hands, and repeated the motion three more times, until she finally had his left pant leg split wide and hanging open to a point several inches above his knee.

Unfortunately, her yanking on the denim tore away most of the clot that had formed over the wound on his thigh, and blood started seeping out of the bullet hole. Blood and a disturbing whitish fluid that hinted at infection.

Helen bit her lip and turned her head as an inconvenient light-headedness assailed her. She needed help. She could give him basic care, but if infection had already set in, that required nursing skills she didn't possess.

But who could she trust to keep her secret? Because her stranger *had* to remain a secret, at least until Helen figured out who he was. She might not care for Malachi Shaw's male presence in Harper's

Station, but even she had to admit that the marshal was extremely protective of the ladies who lived there. With him on high alert over the threat to Grace, he'd probably either lock the stranger up or kick him out of town without sufficient care for his wound. Helen couldn't let that happen. Not to Rachel's brother.

She pulled a clean handkerchief from her pocket and pressed it against the bullet hole. Judging by the size of the stains on his trousers as well as what he'd left on the dirt and grass outside, the stranger had lost a bucket's worth of blood. He was running a fever, mumbling out of his head, and had early signs of infection.

He represented no threat. He didn't even carry a weapon. No one traveled through wild country without a way to defend themselves from animals or the occasional outlaw, yet her stranger wore a gun belt with an empty holster. A leather sheath large enough to hold a hunting knife hung at his left hip, but it too was missing its occupant. This fella didn't even have any boots. He'd been stripped.

Whoever had shot him had made good and sure his opponent couldn't give chase. Had her stranger shot first, bringing retaliation upon himself? Or had he been ambushed?

Helen tilted her head to get a better look at the man's face as she continued pressing her makeshift dressing against the hole in his thigh. He couldn't be more than twenty-five or twenty-six. There weren't enough lines on his face or leather in his hide for him to be much older. Surely a man who would sacrifice himself for his sister when he was fifteen couldn't have hardened into a woman-hunting mercenary with no conscience in so short a time.

Helen straightened as another, more disturbing thought crossed her mind. He might not be the kind to hunt a woman for personal gain, but what if someone threatened his sister or someone he cared about? Helen frowned. Such a man would do *anything* to save the people he loved.

Maybe she ought to tie his wrists to the bedstead before she left. The iron was old, but it hadn't corroded. It would hold him, especially in his weakened state.

First things first, though. She needed to clean that wound.

Helen left the blood-soaked handkerchief resting on his leg, then collected the water pail and hurried through the pecan grove to the creek. Maybelle, the town's healer, always boiled her water and instruments before tending an injury. She said boiling made the water cleaner somehow and minimized the threat of infection.

Helen's stranger couldn't afford any more infection, so even though it meant moving like a snail when her instincts demanded she streak like a thoroughbred across the countryside to find help, Helen took the time to stoke a fire once she returned to the cabin and poured half the water into the kettle to heat. She poured a second portion into a glass retrieved from her supply box, which held one plate, one glass, and one set of flatware. She never expected company. Never wanted it. Now that she had some, she feared she'd lose him before she could extend better hospitality than hurling his unconscious body onto a bed made for someone considerably shorter in stature.

She peeked at the wound and murmured a prayer of thanks when she noted the bleeding had slowed. Looking around the sparse room for something to use for bandages, she frowned. A sheet would be ideal, but the stranger's heavy carcass lay sprawled atop the only ones she had in the cabin. And she wasn't about to move him.

The curtains? She smiled at the thought of binding his wounds with red floral calico, but she cleaned the cabin so sporadically that the curtains not only had dust coating their length, but spider webs in their corners.

That left her petticoats. She was wearing two. Her favorites. The ones that had softened with use and many washings, instead of the stiff, itchy new ones back in her wardrobe. Helen sighed, then reached beneath the front of her skirt to untie the waist string. She'd prefer to tear up the ugly black dress she wore, but if she showed up at the farm house without a skirt, she'd be pelted with questions from every angle and would never get away in time to fetch medical help.

While the water heated, she tore her top petticoat into strips. She rolled several strips into bandages but set aside two to use as bindings. As much as she hated the idea of tying her stranger up, she had more than herself to consider. He might be a noble hero to Rachel, but if he planned to harm Grace, even to save another, that made him the enemy.

Steam rose from the kettle spout and a low hiss started to build, indicating a boil was close. Helen dragged her chair next to the bed, placed the rolled bandages in her supply box, and set the box on the floor beside the chair.

"Time to clean out that hole," she whispered, needing to say the words aloud to galvanize her into action. She'd nursed her mother hundreds of times and knew every trick in the book for dealing with bruises and black eyes and sore ribs, but she knew nothing about gunshot wounds. And though she was ashamed to admit it, the few glimpses she'd had of the hole in the stranger's leg had made her rather queasy.

"Get over it, Helen," she grumbled softly as she marched over to the small stove in the corner. "There's no one but you to do it, so quit bein' a sissy about it." Wrapping a towel around her hand for protection, she clasped the kettle handle and poured most of the hot water into the chipped basin she kept for her personal needs. Steam rose to moisten her face. As if she wasn't damp enough already after gathering pecans and wrestling a full-grown man into bed. If he ever did regain his senses, she'd have to hope the Lord would strike him with temporary blindness. Seeing a five-foot, bedraggled black crow bent over him would surely send his health into a sharp decline.

Helen touched the tip of her finger to the surface of the water, then immediately yanked it back with a hiss. Too hot. She'd scald him and herself. Taking the glass of water she'd set aside earlier, she poured a third of its contents into the basin and stirred with a wooden spoon. She tested the water again. Still hot, uncomfortably so, but not unbearable. She rolled her sleeves to the elbows, then, gritting her teeth, plunged her hands into the water and rubbed them vigorously with a small cake of soap.

Taking the basin in hand, she pivoted to face her patient. "Your turn, mister."

Helen set the basin on the seat of her chair, then lifted her stranger's leg and placed every spare towel she had beneath his thigh. Then, washrag in hand, she got to work. Kneeling beside the bed, she dipped the rag into the hot water and squeezed it out over his wound, letting it flush out as much dirt and debris as possible. The stranger moaned slightly, but thankfully there was no thrashing about. Not until she soaped up the rag and started scrubbing.

He bucked, and his arms swung wildly. Not knowing how else to stop him, Helen jumped to her feet and threw her body across his chest. She grabbed for his shoulders and used her weight to pin him to the bed.

"Easy," she crooned next to his ear. "No need to get all worked up. You're safe. Just got a hole in your leg that needs tending."

His flailing subsided as she spoke, but the tension in his muscles remained taut. "Rachel?" His lashes fluttered and finally parted. His gaze met hers, and his brow furrowed. "Not . . . Rachel."

Helen pulled back a bit, not sure if she was glad he was lucid enough to realize she wasn't his sister. She knew he'd never hurt Rachel. But Helen Potter? That was an entirely different basket of nuts.

"No, I'm not Rachel. My name's Helen. I found you outside. Shot." Something flashed in his eyes. Not surprise. A memory, maybe? Then his focus returned to her, and all at once Helen became aware of her position pressed against his chest. She ducked away from his gaze and lifted off him, keeping her palms braced against his shoulders to make sure he stayed down. "I'm . . . ah . . . trying to clean your wound." Why was *she* the one embarrassed? It was *his* fault they were in this predicament. *He* was the one who got himself shot. And *he* was the one who'd started thrashing around like a kid having a tantrum. She scowled at him. "You think you can manage to stay still long enough for me to finish?"

His mustache twitched. Was he *smiling* at her? It was hard to tell with that giant caterpillar on his lip.

"Yes . . . ma'am."

Would that caterpillar be soft or prickly, should a woman get close enough to feel it? Not that she was considering such a thing, of course. She was simply curious. Curious and apparently dimwitted, for she still hadn't removed her hands from him, even after he promised to lie still.

She scrambled away and reclaimed the washrag that had fallen on the bed. She'd already cleared away the worst of the dirt and dried blood from the outer edges of the wound, but she needed to clean as much as she could from the inside. She soaped up the rag and folded it over her smallest finger.

He must have pieced together what she intended, for his muscles tensed even further. "Can't you just pour some whiskey on it and be done with it?" he grumbled.

"Sorry." Helen shook her head. "I don't have any."

His eyes slid closed again and his jaw clenched. "Figures." He curled his hands into fists. "Do what you gotta do."

She did. And it nearly killed her, watching his face drain of all color and his fists press hard enough into the quilt to lift his torso several inches off the cot. She moved as quickly and as gently as she could, afraid to cause more damage, yet more afraid to leave something to fester inside him.

"There. It's done."

His hands unclenched, and his face relaxed a fraction, but not completely. He was still in pain. Helen rinsed the blood from the rag then folded it over and used the damp cloth to wipe his brow.

Slowly, his lashes lifted. "Thank you," he croaked, "Helen."

She froze. Hearing her name from him set her heart to sputtering and her lips to muttering nonsense like, "Well, I couldn't just let you die."

"You could have," he argued as his lashes lowered again to hide his green eyes, "but I'll be sure to thank God that you didn't."

A smile touched her lips. She might just thank God herself. If he lived.

"I need to fetch someone with medical training," Helen murmured as she set aside her basin and pressed a dressing to his wound. Taking another bandage, she held the end in place atop the dressing, then bent his leg at the knee so she could wrap it around his thigh. "We have a healer in town, and her apprentice is a friend of mine. She'll know how to treat the infection that's building and can finish patching you up."

The stranger's eyes flew open. His razor-sharp gaze slashed at her as his fingers latched onto her wrist. "No one can know," he ground out. "No one can know I'm alive." His hand fell away, his strength suddenly depleted. "A woman's life . . . is at stake." His eyelids began to droop. "Only chance . . . is for him to think . . . I'm dead." His body went lax.

Well, at least they agreed on one point. They needed to keep his presence a secret. Helen just wished she knew which woman he was protecting. Grace or someone else?

"I'm gonna tell Claire whether you like it or not," she whispered as she tied off the bandage and gently straightened his leg. She stood and, on impulse, brushed his disheveled hair to the side. Heat seeped from his forehead into her fingertips. Helen frowned. The fever was getting worse. "Unless you want to be dead for real, we gotta get help."

She glanced at the cotton strips she'd set aside for binding. The poor man was in such sorry shape, she didn't have the heart to tie him up. Thankfully, her mind overrode her heart, just as she'd trained it to do all those years ago in her father's house.

Taking care to make the strip tight enough to be effective but loose enough not to chafe, she lifted each limp arm and tied it to the iron bedstead, close enough to the mattress to allow him to rest comfortably with his arms bent near his head. He'd be none too pleased when he awoke, but maybe she'd get lucky and return with Claire before he regained consciousness.

"Sorry, mister." Her heart panged in sympathy even as she backed toward the cabin door. "I hate to leave you like this, but until I know I can trust you, I won't be taking any chances."

Ignoring the guilt jabbing at her chest, Helen stiffened her spine, lifted her chin, and walked out the door.

18

Helen approached the clinic from the east to avoid riding through the middle of town. It had been tricky retrieving a horse from the farm without rousing suspicion, but she'd managed to avoid Katie by dropping off the half-full basket of pecans by the back door instead of taking them into the kitchen, and Betty's respect for her girls' privacy kept the older woman from pressing for details when Helen proved reticent. Now all she had to do was get to Claire without attracting any undue notice.

After dismounting, she tied her horse to a fence post then pushed through the gate. Before she reached the porch, the front door opened, and a middle-aged woman with a black leather doctor's bag stepped out.

"Helen." Maybelle Curtis drew up short and raised a concerned brow. "Has something happened out at the farm? I was on my way to check on Daisy at the boardinghouse, but if there's an emergency, I can visit her later."

"No, no." Helen waved away her offer, silently thanking God for removing another obstacle for her. "I'm here to see Claire. You go on and tend to Daisy. I remember that awful cough she was struggling with at the town meeting two nights ago."

Maybelle nodded. "It's settled into her chest, a dangerous thing for someone of her age. Claire mixed up a mustard plaster for me, a recipe her mother swears by. I thought I'd try it and see if it helps break up the congestion."

"I'll pray it does."

Maybelle patted Helen's shoulder and gave her a grateful smile. "I'm off, then. Claire's in the examination room. Just go on in."

"Thank you." Helen moved past the midwife-turned-doctor and into the clinic, saying a quick prayer for Daisy's recovery as she went, then adding a petition for her stranger, as well. Heaven knew he needed it.

Helen passed through the front parlor that doubled as a waiting room and knocked on a partially open door on the far side. "Claire?"

The young redhead spun around from where she'd been staring at something in the glass cabinet across the way. A gasp echoed loudly through the room.

Helen winced. "Sorry. It's only me."

The Irish woman scowled. "Merciful stars, Helen. Ye nearly had me droppin' the digitalis. Maybelle would've boxed me ears for sure." She relaxed her fisted hand from against her bosom, where it had flown when Helen startled her, and revealed a small brown vial.

"I'm sorry," Helen repeated. "I ran into Maybelle outside, and she told me to come in. I didn't mean to startle you."

"Och! Pay me no mind. I'm only snappish because me own clumsiness served me a fright." An apologetic smile bloomed across Claire's face a moment before she turned, carefully placed the vial back on its shelf, then closed and locked the cabinet.

Claire was more girl than woman, having only turned eighteen a month ago, but she had the kind of disposition that put the sun to shame. Always vivacious, eager to learn, and more importantly today, always ready to help. As if on cue, Claire tucked the key she wore around her neck back into her bodice and spun to face Helen. "So? What can I do for ye on this lovely day?"

"I found a patient in need of medical attention. Gunshot."

"Lord preserve us! We must fetch Maybelle at once." Claire grabbed Helen's arm and started dragging her toward the entrance. "Whisht, lass. Why did ye not stop her when ye saw her in the yard? She's the one ye'll be needin'. Not the likes o' me."

Helen tugged her arm free. "No, Claire. I need *you*. And you mustn't say anything to Maybelle about it. It has to be kept a secret."

"Why? If someone's in trouble, Maybelle—"

"Will report to Emma and Malachi," Helen interrupted. "And that can't happen. Not yet. Other lives are at risk."

Claire stepped backward and frowned. "I don't hold with keepin' secrets from me employer, Helen. It isna honorable."

"But it's necessary in this instance. It's also what the patient demanded." Helen stepped closer, desperation clawing at her insides, urging her to grovel if need be. "If it's too much to ask, I'll understand. I don't want to pressure you to do anything that violates your conscience." Actually, she *did* want to pressure her if it meant getting the stranger the help he needed, but not at the cost of Claire spilling the secret later when guilt wore her down. "If you aren't comfortable keeping this quiet, say so, and I'll leave. No hard feelings. I might ask for some medical advice, but I promise not to ask you for anything more."

For a nerve-wracking minute, Claire paced back toward the examination room. "Tell me about the wound," she finally said, and Helen's heart thumped with hope.

"It's in the upper thigh. I'm not sure if the bullet is still inside or not. I cleaned it as best I could, but I'm worried about the pus. I think there's an infection."

Claire stared at the medicine cabinet, a thoughtful look on her face. "Does she have the fever?"

"Yes." Helen didn't correct her friend on the patient's gender. She couldn't afford to until Claire committed to confidentiality. "And is unconscious more than awake."

"It sounds bad, it does. I better come with ye." As if that decided matters, she immediately started rummaging through drawers and shelves, collecting various supplies and stuffing them into a small carpet bag she'd dragged out from under the examination cot.

"Does this mean you'll keep quiet about the situation?" Helen hated to pester, but she needed confirmation.

Claire paused long enough in her packing to meet Helen's gaze. "Aye. Me conscience would fret more if I did nothin' and the poor lass died than over keeping a little secret. I'll hold me tongue."

Helen coughed in an effort to find her voice in a throat that had suddenly shrunk in on itself. "Thank you."

Understanding softened Claire's gaze, but only for a moment before she started calling out orders. "Fetch me the day-old loaf from the kitchen and the jug of milk from the pie safe. Me mam says there be nothin' better at drawin' out infection than a good bread and milk poultice. I'll jot a quick note to Maybelle to let her know I left with ye on a house call so she won't fret when she finds me gone. Then I'll meet you out front."

Helen nodded and dashed to the kitchen to collect the items Claire had requested. She had just walked into the parlor, arms full, when the front door opened and a man she'd never seen before stepped across the threshold.

He pulled his hat from his head and curved his lips in a seductive smile that immediately put Helen on her guard. The Colt that rode his hip as if it were an extension of his body didn't set well, either.

Never in a hundred years would she picture this man working in a telegraph office and riding bicycles through the streets.

"Miss Nevin, I presume?" His deep voice purred but left her feeling like a cat that had just had its fur stroked against the grain.

Distaste soured Helen's mouth. It was her usual reaction to men, but the intensity surprised her, perhaps because the sensation hadn't once afflicted her in all her interactions with the man at the cabin.

"No, sorry. Claire's in the office." She tipped her head toward the examination room. "Maybelle handles most of the doctorin' around here, though. If you've got an ailment, you can find her at the boardinghouse down the street." She mentally shooed him with all her might. She'd left her stranger alone too long as it was. She didn't need some crazy velocipede-riding fruitcake holding them up longer.

"Oh, I'm not here seeking treatment. Just answers to a few simple questions." He advanced a step closer, his smile warm and friendly, yet Helen felt about as reassured as a rabbit in the sights of a coyote. "I'm Detective Dunbar," he said, pulling a badge out of his pocket. "Pinkerton Agency."

Detective? Pinkerton? Helen froze where she stood, her pulse throbbing. This wasn't Grace's harmless bicycle beau. This was a threat. One who wore a gun slung low on his hip and projected enough steel in his bearing to assure her that he knew how to use it.

Perhaps he already had.

Helen swallowed the trepidation softening her insides and instead armed herself with the familiar spikes of animosity that usually sprouted in the presence of swaggering men like this, ones who thought they had the right to interrupt a woman's schedule with their personal agendas.

"Does Emma Shaw know you're pestering her citizens?" No way was she going to let this slick newcomer steer her into a corner with *questions.* "If you don't need medical assistance, there's no reason for you to be here, so I'm gonna have to ask you to leave."

The detective's brows rose a fraction, and his smile slipped a bit, but the appendages she cared about most—his feet—remained stubbornly fixed to the floor.

"With all due respect, ma'am," the Pinkerton said as he pulled his hat from his head—a blatant thumb of his nose to her demand that he depart, "if you're not Miss Nevin, and you're not Mrs. Curtis, you aren't in a position to ask me to go anywhere."

He wanted to challenge her? Fine. He'd learn she wasn't one to be intimidated.

"That's where you're wrong, mister." Helen glared up at him. "This is a women's colony, and we look after each other." She took a step forward. His expression lost a touch of its smugness. Satisfaction surged inside Helen, making her bolder. She took a second step. "We protect each other from men who think they can barge in and make demands. Pinkerton or not, you and your questions are not welcome."

"You got something to hide, sweetpea?" *He* advanced a step. A long, man-sized step that brought his too-large, too-cocky self within about a yard of where she stood.

Helen's pulse ratcheted up from a canter to a full-out gallop, but she didn't back away. Her gaze remained locked on the Pinkerton.

"Helen? Is everythin' all right?" Claire emerged from the examination room, her face a mask of concern as her gaze swept from her friend to the man standing in her parlor.

In a blink, the Pinkerton's eyes softened from cold stone to warm chocolate as he turned to smile at Claire.

"Ah, you must be Miss Nevin. There's no reason to be alarmed, I assure you." He pivoted away from Helen and strode toward Claire, all traces of hostility swept under the rug. "I'm with the Pinkerton Agency. Elliott Dunbar, at your service." He dipped his head. "I was just stopping by to ask a few questions, if you have a minute to spare before you leave on your"—he glanced from the small carpetbag Claire carried to the bread and milk in Helen's arms—"outing."

Claire shot a nervous glance Helen's way, one the far-too-perceptive Pinkerton no doubt picked up on. The girl's face displayed her emotions like a shop window showed off the latest bonnet styles.

"I asked him to leave." Helen jumped in before Claire could give anything away. "We have a commitment that we're already running late for." She directed her comment to the detective, praying that Claire understood the need to be vague about their errand. "If you have questions, I suggest you visit with Emma Shaw. She runs this town and knows everything that goes on here."

Emma might know everything that went on in town, but thankfully she was ignorant of happenings out by the pecan grove.

"I've already visited with Mr. and Mrs. Shaw," Dunbar said, shooting a frown at Helen before turning a smile on the more susceptible Claire. "And while they were helpful, I'm sure they don't know *everything*. In my experience," he murmured in that panther purr Helen despised while sidling closer to the redhead, "it's the quiet observers who notice the most pertinent details, especially ones with the intelligence to process what they see and make meaningful conclusions. And you"—he pointed his hat toward Claire—"are exactly that kind of person. I can see it in your eyes. You're clever, kind, and—"

"Late for our appointment." Helen lunged forward and physically inserted herself between the detective and Claire. "Sorry, Pinkerton, but we've got to go. There are people waiting on us." She grabbed Claire's hand and started tugging her toward the front door. "This town is full of smart, kind women," Helen tossed out over her shoulder. "Go pester one of the others with your questions. Start at the boardinghouse for the largest selection."

Helen didn't stop until she had Claire out on the porch, but once there, the younger girl stood fast.

"I can't be leavin' him inside, Helen," she whispered in an urgent undertone. Then she raised her voice to carry to the snail-paced detective still in the parlor. "If ye'll kindly exit the clinic, Mr. Dunbar, sir. I be needin' to lock up afore we set out."

The irritating man moved as fast as a tortoise stuck in molasses. Finally his boots cleared the threshold, and Helen yanked the door closed behind him, enjoying the little jolt of annoyance that flashed through his eyes when the wood smacked him in the rear.

He fit his hat back on his head and nodded to Claire. Helen, he ignored. "I'll call again tomorrow, Miss Nevin, when you're less . . . occupied."

He was still going to be here tomorrow? Helen clenched her teeth. Not only were the men multiplying in Harper's Station, but their quality was deteriorating rapidly. And the one person she'd chosen to share her secret with now had a date with the man who was probably responsible for her stranger's injuries.

"I can't imagine what help I'd be to ye," Claire said, and Helen's hope began a cautious glide upward at her friend's evasion, "but if our paths cross, I suppose I could find time to answer a question or two."

And just like that, hope dropped out of the sky like a duck peppered with birdshot.

Dunbar sketched a bow. "I'll look forward to crossing your lovely path tomorrow then, Miss Nevin." He barely flicked his gaze toward Helen before tipping his hat to Claire. "Good day, ladies."

And finally—*finally*—he strode away.

"Good riddance," Helen muttered under her breath. Then she turned to Claire. "You can't tell him anything about what you see today. Promise me."

"I'll do me best to keep mum, but he's a lawman. I can't be lyin' to the law."

Helen grabbed her friend by the arm and steered her toward the waiting horse. "He's not the law, Claire. Malachi's the law. He's just a detective snooping around where he don't belong."

They passed through the gate, and Claire twisted to pull it closed behind them. "There ain't no law that says you have to answer his questions."

"But don't ye suppose refusin' to answer makes us look a mite suspicious? He might not be the law, but I'm thinkin' he's got a nose that can sniff out secrets. If ye don't want him sniffin' too close, ye gotta throw him off the scent with something sweet enough to satisfy him."

Helen paused in stuffing the milk jug into her saddlebag. "You might have a point." She shot a stern glance over her shoulder. "But you've got to be careful with that one. I saw the way your eyes went all dewy when he turned the force of his charm on you. He's dangerous."

"Aye, he's bonny, all right, but I got more sense than to let a fine-lookin' lad turn me head into a mush pot." Claire reached up to loop the leather handles of her carpetbag around the saddle horn. "Ye can trust me, Helen. If ye say our errand today must be kept secret, I'll not tell a soul." She smiled, and her blue eyes twinkled. "With seven younger sisters at home, I've had me share of secret-keepin' experience."

Helen managed a small smile in return, then she untied the horse's reins and mounted. Removing her foot from the left stirrup so Claire could mount behind her, Helen reached for the young nurse and helped her gain a seat.

As best she could figure, her stranger had been shot sometime early this morning, long enough ago to lose a bunch of blood and develop a fever. Which meant this newcomer could be the culprit. But while she didn't trust this Dunbar fellow more than a wooden nickel, he was still a Pinkerton, and as such, the shooting could have been justified.

A ribbon of doubt wove through Helen's heart at the thought of Rachel's brother being in the wrong, but logic rose to snip the thread. A lawman—an *honest* lawman—wouldn't shoot a man and leave him to die, even if the fellow were a criminal. He'd drag his carcass to jail.

So either this Mr. Dunbar didn't shoot her stranger, or he was pretending to be something he wasn't. Either way, Helen needed to put as much space between her and the Pinkerton as possible.

Touching her heels to the mare's flanks, she urged the sturdy animal to a canter. Once they reached the cabin, Helen drew the mare to a halt and waited impatiently for Claire to slide down so she could dismount. After Claire retrieved her supplies, Helen led the horse a few paces away to a shaded spot with plenty of grass to forage. She had just turned back to escort Claire into the cabin when the creak of the door hinges warned she was too late.

"Umm . . . Helen?" Claire's voice wobbled and pitched upward in obvious distress.

Helen bounded through the doorway then skidded to a halt, arrested by the same sight that must have frozen Claire where she stood.

"Have me eyes suddenly opened to the world of the Fey, or is that a verra angry man tied to yer bed?"

19

Amos spied two women exiting the clinic and immediately realized who would be walking through the door next. Without taking the time to explain, he grabbed Grace's hand and dragged her down the road a few yards. When they reached the oak tree that grew between the café and the first of three houses on the edge of town, he twirled her around and pressed her against the oak's trunk, all while keeping the third house, where the clinic resided, in his peripheral vision.

"Amos," Grace gasped, "what are you—?"

"Shh." He positioned himself half in front of her, his bent arm casually braced against the tree trunk beside her head. "Gaze up at me as if I'm the most interesting man you've ever met."

Her cheeks colored slightly, and Amos smiled, partly because it fit with the character he was trying to project, and partly because he just plain liked being the one to pinken her complexion. Much better than the blushes that snake Dunbar elicited.

Grace blinked at his authoritative tone, but she obeyed. He didn't normally dictate unilateral decisions, but he could assert command when the situation warranted. And this situation more than warranted. Barking orders might not be the most successful wooing technique, but Grace's safety was too important to worry about the possibility of hurt feelings.

When she'd convinced him to help her keep an eye on Dunbar as part of their *investigation*, he'd almost regretted mentioning the strategy earlier in the day. But he had to admit that sharing this adventure held its own thrilling appeal, and it offered a compelling reason to stay close to her side.

Grace lifted her chin and looked at him, her eyes soft and thoughtful. "You just might be," she murmured.

"Might be what?" he asked, only half-listening to her as his ears picked up a horse nickering a short distance away and heavy footfalls approaching.

"The most interesting man I've ever met."

That got his attention. Every one of his five senses honed in on the woman in front of him. He leaned in closer, drawn to her as everything else faded.

The clean scent of her skin teased him, tempting him to bend down and nuzzle her neck so he could breathe her in more completely. But then his eyes drank in her sweet face, the curve of her cheek, the way the wind blew a few loose strands of hair across her chin until they snagged at the corner of her mouth, and he was captivated anew. She reached a hand up to free the hairs from her mouth and tuck them behind her ear, and suddenly he wished it were his fingers touching her face. To brush across the plump softness of her lower lip, to skim along the edge of her jaw, to caress the delicate shell of her ear. Then her lashes fell and her tongue darted out to moisten her lips, and a new hunger rose within him. A hunger to taste, to savor, to—

"You know, Bledsoe," a dark baritone rumbled behind him, jerking Amos back into reality with a start, "if you're gonna court a gal, you should do it somewhere a little more private." A large hand slapped against Amos's shoulder blade, nearly sending him toppling into Grace. "That way, there's less chance of being interrupted by a suitor who's far more handsome and roguishly charming."

Amos scowled at Dunbar, not at all surprised to find the Pinkerton blatantly making eyes at Grace right in front of him. The cad. Grace's cheeks had darkened from pink to scarlet.

"Fortunately, the lady I'm courting is more concerned with substance than surface," Amos said, forcing a confidence he didn't feel into his tone. "But thank you for the advice just the same."

Really, he should be grateful that his quickly formulated ruse had worked, convincing Dunbar that he and Grace were simply out for an afternoon stroll, not following the detective around in order to ascertain his motives. Yet the cocky, far-too-handsome Pinkerton left Amos's nerves raw every time they interacted. Dunbar personified every insecurity Amos possessed. And worse, the detective knew it.

"Are you out for a walk as well, Mr. Dunbar?" Grace said, her voice breathy and . . . did her lashes just bat?

"Yep. Getting the layout of the town mapped in my brain." Dunbar tapped the side of his head and grinned that arrogant, I-can-do-anything-better-than-that-dullard-you're-with smile that set Amos's teeth on edge. "Gotta be ready to protect my mission and the lovely lady tied to it should Haversham's man show his face. I've been asking around, too. If anyone sees anything unusual—another man about, or signs of a trail or campsite—I'll be sure to check it out." He reached out and touched Grace's face with the back of his hand. Her face! "Don't you worry, Miss Mallory. I won't let anything happen to you."

Amos clenched his fist, bit his tongue, stuffed down the raving beast inside him demanding he take retribution against the scoundrel who'd touched his woman. *His* woman.

It helped when Grace stepped away from the Pinkerton, letting his hand fall away from her. But hearing her syrupy sweet tones stroke the man's already inflated ego made it a challenge not to gag.

"You're so good to watch out for me, Mr. Dunbar." She gave a shiver that actually looked genuine, then rubbed her arms. "I pray this whole ordeal is over soon."

That made two of them. Amos was more than ready to send Dunbar packing. Or have him arrested. Whatever method of eradication proved appropriate.

"As soon as we get those books from your friend, this will all be behind you. I'll take charge of the documents, give them to Whitmore, and Haversham won't be able to touch you." Dunbar absently kicked at an acorn near his boot. "Did you . . . ah . . . hear back from your friend yet? Is she sending the books?"

"No . . . she hasn't responded yet." Grace fidgeted with her sleeve and inched a hair closer to Amos. "But I suspect she will soon."

"Then shouldn't one of you be manning the wire?"

Grace shot a look at Amos. He sensed her fear and understood it. Dunbar was no idiot. He knew an operator wouldn't leave his or her post during business hours. Did he suspect they were keeping tabs on him? They'd monitored his comings and goings from the telegraph office, either through the window or via an occasional stroll outside, until he'd headed for the clinic and left their field of view. Grace had insisted they follow him and dashed out of the office without even fetching her shawl. Amos hadn't been about to let her go after Dunbar alone, so he'd hied after her, doing his best to keep her enthusiasm in check and her pretty self out of danger.

Dunbar frowned and shot Amos a hard look. "Maybe the courtship should wait until *after* Haversham is dealt with. Miss Mallory's safety must come first. Don't you agree?"

Was it Amos's imagination, or was there a deeper threat beneath that not-so-friendly warning? Admittedly, it was hard to make a proper inference when jealousy tainted his perception. Either way, as much as it galled him to agree, Amos had to admit that Dunbar made a valid point.

Amos straightened to his full height, which was still a frustrating three or four inches shorter than the Pinkerton. "I assure you, Miss Mallory's well-being is my chief concern."

Dunbar glowered. "Then perhaps you should return to your post to ensure you don't miss any important messages."

Amos tamped down the surprisingly fierce urge to smash his fist into the condescending man's face. It required significant effort to resist, seeing as his blood was running hot and sloshing through his veins with all the delicacy of a rampaging river, but he wasn't so far gone that he'd lost hold of reason. Fisticuffs wouldn't curry Grace's favor. As richly satisfying as it might be to plow his hand into Dunbar's chin, the retribution that would surely follow would only highlight his deficiencies. Dunbar would pummel Amos into the ground. Probably in a matter of seconds. Not that Grace wasn't worth being pummeled for, but it wasn't *her* honor that had been impugned. Dunbar's disdain had strictly been aimed at Amos.

So, forcing his gaze away from the Pinkerton's jawline—the spot he'd been eyeing as the target for a swift uppercut—Amos turned to Grace and held out his hand. "What do you say, Miss Mallory? Are you ready to return to the telegraph office?"

She laid her fingers across his palm. Fingers, he noted, that trembled slightly. "I believe I am, Mr. Bledsoe. Thank you." She dipped her chin slightly toward Dunbar as she stepped away from the tree and moved back into the road. "I'll send word if I hear from my friend. Oh, that reminds me. Where will you be staying, Mr. Dunbar? I might not get word until later this evening and need to know where to find you."

"The marshal's letting me bunk in the jailhouse." He grinned and rubbed a hand over his well-trimmed beard. "Not the most glamorous of accommodations, I'll grant you, but I've stayed in worse. Got me a cot, a stove, and probably a cricket or two to sing me to sleep. All the essentials."

Grace smiled yet continued edging closer to Amos. "I'm glad to hear it. I'll be sure to get a message to you when I learn how soon we can expect the rest of my father's belongings to arrive."

"Excellent." Dunbar touched the brim of his hat. "I'll wish you a good day then."

"Good day."

Amos said nothing, but then, neither of the others seemed to expect him to do so.

Dunbar took his leave without further question or comment, and Amos escorted Grace back to the office, keeping her hand locked in his the entire way.

Once the door was secured behind them, Amos ushered her behind the counter and gave her a stern look. "You can't stay here alone tonight. It's too dangerous. What if Dunbar suspects you're stalling and decides to break in and search for your father's documents himself? You'd be at his mercy."

"Not completely." Now that they were away from the Pinkerton, her pluck had returned, and her voice echoed with a firmness he couldn't help but admire. She moved a few steps away from him then turned her back and rummaged with her skirts.

What in the world was she—

Pivoting to face him again, she held out a small pistol for his inspection. "I'm always armed."

Amos stared at the derringer. "Where . . ."

"I have a garter holster." She didn't even blush as she made that announcement, just stated the fact as if it were nothing out of the ordinary. Maybe it wasn't. Maybe all women walked around with weapons strapped to their garters. How would he know? "Sometimes I carry it in my handbag, but I prefer keeping it closer to hand. A lady never knows when she might have her bag knocked away. At night I keep it on my bedside table, always within reach. Between that and the sturdy locks on my door and window, I'll be safe enough."

Amos didn't know if he should be awed by her preparedness or cowed by her independence. Truthfully, it was hard to concentrate on either one after she mentioned garters. Visions of shapely legs and bits of lace securing silky stockings kept flashing through his mind, distracting him.

"At least now we know where he'll be." Grace slid into the office chair and leaned an elbow on the desk next to the telegraph. "I imagine Malachi offered the jailhouse so he could keep an eye on him."

"Well, if the marshal can see the jail from the station house, that means I can help keep watch as well. I'll speak to him tonight about taking shifts. If Dunbar starts roaming during the night, I want to know about it."

"Mmm."

Amos frowned at the distracted sound. Wasn't she taking this seriously? Had the Pinkerton's blathering about protecting her from Haversham lulled her into a false sense of security? She needed to be on her guard. Dunbar could be a coldhearted killer. Or at the very least, a money-hungry opportunist. All right, he could also be a legitimate detective, but Amos doubted it. Dunbar was too sly by half.

Determined to make sure Grace understood the peril of the situation, Amos planted himself directly in front of her. But before he could start his lecture, she glanced up at him and smiled. Not one of her polite smiles or even the shy curvings of her lips that made his heart flip. This grin was full and toothsome and stretched upward toward eyes that danced with mischief and intelligence. The brilliant show stopped Amos in his tracks and drove all thoughts of lecture from his mind.

"You need to collect Tori's order," Grace said.

Amos usually considered himself a man of astute mind, but in the face of that particular smile and the dramatic turn of topic accompanying it, he found himself at a loss. "What order?"

"The bicycles. From San Antonio." Her tawny eyes glowed with barely banked excitement.

"Right now?"

She nodded. "Yes. With all due haste." She launched from her chair and clasped his hand. "I have an idea," she boasted, her enthusiasm bubbling over. "One that involves bicycles and shipments and me developing a rather speedy friendship with one of your wheelmen compatriots."

20

Y ou won't find her," the stranger growled, his eyes feral as he strained against the restraints.

Helen's heart tripped over itself. She'd tied him like an animal and then left him. Surely she could have come up with some other way to ensure he didn't leave. Why hadn't she—

"Even if you flay the skin from my back, I won't tell you." He glared his defiance at Claire, his mouth drawn in a tight line, his face red from anger and fever. "You might be bigger, but my mind is stronger. You'll never touch her again."

Claire glanced at Helen, the fear that had held her frozen relaxing a little. "The poor man is clearly out of his head," she whispered. "Whisht!" She chuckled softly and looked down at herself, holding her arms wide at her sides. "He thinks me bigger than himself!"

Helen smiled a little at the ludicrous idea of the young nurse being anything but diminutive when compared to the long, lean stranger. Yet she couldn't summon more than a slight upturn of her lips. Not when her heart ached.

He was speaking of his sister again. Protecting her from a man who would restrain him and whip him to try to gain information.

Helen strode forward. She had to get him out of those bonds. No doubt they were fueling his fever-induced memories. No one should be locked in such an ugly, cruel past. His body would never heal if his mind stayed focused on the source of his greatest hurt.

"Wait, Helen." Claire grabbed for her arm, but Helen side-stepped her. "He could strike ye. A man in the grip o' fever is unpredictable. It might be better to leave him tied."

"I can't. It's hurting him." She crossed the few steps to the bed and immediately reached for the closest restraint.

"No, it isna," Claire said from behind her, making no move to follow. "Ye did a fine job with the cotton. 'Tis barely tight enough to hold him."

"It's not his arms I'm worried about," she murmured. It was his mind.

Her stranger continued glaring at Claire, barely paying Helen any heed until she started tugging on the knot at his right wrist.

He turned his head then, and in a flash his defiance melted under a wave of confusion and fear. "Rachel!" His frantic whisper broke Helen's heart. "You've got to run. Hurry. Before he sees you." He bucked his hips and increased his struggles against his bindings, tearing the knot from her fingertips. His movements were so violent, she feared he'd damage his leg with all his flailing. "He's got me tied up again. I won't be able to stop him this time. Please. You've got to run!" His voice broke, and his eyes misted.

Helen nearly crumpled to the floor. What this man had endured. And some of it was at her hand. Well, no more!

"Shh," she pleaded as she reached out to stroke his face. "It's all right. We're safe. No one's going to hurt either of us. It's just a memory. He can't hurt us anymore. We're safe. You kept us safe."

She repeated the litany of safety over and over, stroking his stubbled jaw and smoothing the hair from his forehead until he calmed. Her heart hiccupped at the contact. She'd never imagined touching a man so—with tenderness, caring, comfort. Emotions she wasn't accustomed to feeling flared in her chest, making it hard to breathe, yet she kept up her ministrations, his well-being outweighing her upheaval.

His forehead singed her fingers. Fever raged inside him. Yet as she reached for the knot at his wrist once again, his gaze followed the movement, and some of the fogginess cleared from his eyes.

"Helen?"

He remembered her! She nodded, a tremulous smile twitching her lips. "Yes, I'm here." She glanced over her shoulder. "I brought help. This is Claire. She's a nurse."

"I told you not to tell anyone." He scowled at her, the expression transitioning into one of confusion as if he were trying to hold onto thoughts that kept slipping away from him. "There are . . . lives at risk."

Helen frowned right back at him. "I know. And one of those lives is yours, fool man. You've got a hole in your leg, your veins are nearly empty, and you've got an infection driving you into delirium. You need more help than I know how to give."

He grumbled something under his breath about contrary females, but Helen ignored it as she freed the first knot. She unwrapped his wrist and threw the offending scrap of petticoat to the ground. The chafing marks were light but still stabbed guilt into her heart. For a crazy moment, she considered lifting the man's arm to her mouth so she could kiss away the soreness. Thankfully, her wits sharpened in time to check the ridiculous impulse. But not quickly enough to keep her from holding onto his wrist longer than a sufficiently detached person would have.

Which he noticed.

At least she assumed that was the reason his gaze locked with hers and something . . . personal passed between them. An awareness. A *pleasant* awareness. She couldn't recall the last time she'd actually experienced pleasant sensations during an interaction with a man. A few males had developed neutral sensations—

the marshal and Benjamin Porter came to mind. They'd proven trustworthy, thereby dulling her negative reaction thanks to increased exposure.

But these tiny tingles dancing along her nape and the lightheadedness that made her feel as if she were floating an inch above the floorboards? That was new. And disturbing. Yet . . . enticing.

"Claire can be trusted," she blurted, desperate to break the charged moment. "She's vowed to keep our secret." She stretched across him to untie the second arm.

"Can *you* be trusted?" The soft words drew her eyes back to him. "You tied me up."

Helen's hands fumbled with the knot. Shame made her voice quiver. "I'm sorry."

She ducked her head away from his accusing eyes and yanked on the cotton strip until it finally gave way and pulled free. She straightened, gaining some much needed distance from this man who seemed able to pluck her emotions with the ease of a child plucking the petals from a daisy.

She cleared her throat as she lifted her chin. "You're a stranger," she reminded him, while the intimate pull between them belied her words. "I don't know who you are or why you're here. I couldn't take the chance that you'd slip away while I was gone and hurt someone I care about." She made herself hold his gaze. "I have people to protect, too."

"I'm not here to hurt anyone. I swear." His green eyes bored into her, and the well-honed instincts she'd developed from years of watching her hypocrite of a father smooth-talk everyone he met failed to detect even a hint of insincerity.

"I believe you," she whispered. She tossed the second binding into the corner next to the first. "I won't tie you again."

She stood there, staring at him, until Claire moved up alongside the bed and entered Helen's field of vision.

"While he's coherent," Claire murmured, "you might ask him

if he has any injuries besides the gunshot to the leg. Even a small wound, if overlooked, can hinder the healing process."

Helen nodded, but before she could ask, her stranger responded.

"Leg's the worst. Feels like it's on fire. Head smarts, too. Makes it hard to focus. Think the fellow pistol-whipped me." He reached for the back of his skull as he tried to raise up off the bed a little, then hissed in a breath and grimaced.

Helen rushed to help support his shoulders. "Don't try to move." She gingerly ran her fingers through the hair at the back of his head until she encountered a large bump. "There's a goose egg back here." She slowly drew her fingers away. Evidence of blood long dried dusted her knuckles and fingertips, but she encountered nothing wet. "I think it's already clotted, though. No fresh blood."

"Hot." Her stranger tugged at his shirt as if trying to remove it.

Helen snatched up the half-empty glass of water she'd left beside the bed earlier in the day and held it to his lips with her right hand as she wedged her left beneath his shoulders to lift him. He didn't notice the offering at first, and she grew alarmed at the growing lack of focus in his gaze.

"Here. Drink something. It will help." She tipped the cup enough to send a tiny stream of water onto his mouth. After that, he drank greedily.

"Not too much," Claire warned as she moved closer to inspect the wound on his thigh. "It might upset his stomach."

Helen reluctantly moved the glass away and lowered her stranger's head back to the mattress.

Peripherally, Helen was aware of Claire lifting his leg and examining both the entrance and exit wounds. Helen was more concerned with his fever, however, so she skirted around the nurse and crossed to the washstand, where she wet a small towel. By the time she returned to the bed, her stranger's eyes were closed, and he was grunting softly as Claire prodded him.

His pain made Helen's chest ache. *Lord, please don't let him die.* She gently laid the cool rag on his forehead and crooned to him as she combed his hair away from his face with her fingers.

"Shh, now. You're safe. Claire and I are gonna take real good care of you. You'll be back to Rachel before you know it."

At the mention of his sister, his lashes parted. "Helen?"

Her hands stilled. "Yes?"

He blinked a few times as if trying to clear the fever's fog from his brain. "If I don't . . ." He swallowed. "If I don't make it . . . tell Rachel . . . I'm sorry. She's in . . . Missouri. Carthage. Married name's . . . West. Give her my Bible . . . in my saddlebag."

Hearing him voice the same fears she been working so hard to banish made her stomach turn. No way was she going to tell him he had no saddlebags. She couldn't steal his hope. Heaven knew the scoundrel who had shot him had stolen enough from him already. Her hand trembled, and Helen fisted her fingers to stop the show of weakness. She gritted her teeth. Enough of this soft stuff. There'd be no surrender on her watch.

"Don't you be giving up on me, mister." Helen grabbed his chin like a mother taking a recalcitrant child to task and refused to let him turn away. "Rachel doesn't want your Bible. She wants *you.* And I—" Good grief. She'd nearly blurted that she wanted him too. "I . . . I still have questions for you."

The corners of his mustache lifted a fraction. Was he smiling at her while she railed at him like a cranky fishwife?

"What questions?" His voice wobbled, growing weaker, but she could still make it out.

She should ask him about his purpose. See if he knew anything about Grace or the man hunting her. Or get him to describe the man who attacked him. But none of those sensible questions popped out of her mouth. Her heart beat her head to the punch.

"What's your name?"

His eyes slid the rest of the way closed, but the smile curving his lips stayed in place. "Friends call me . . . Lee."

His face went lax. Helen released his chin but lingered to stroke his hair again, not quite ready to cease touching him. Her stranger wasn't a stranger any longer. He was a friend.

"Lee," she whispered, enjoying the feel of the simple syllable on her tongue. She brushed his hair back a final time then ran her fingertips along the line of his jaw and down to his shoulder. She closed her hand around the well-muscled joint and squeezed, wanting him to hear her even through his unconsciousness.

She bent down until her mouth hovered a bare inch above his ear. "Fight, Lee. Fight with everything you've got. I'm not finished with you yet."

21

Grace spent the remainder of the afternoon burning up the telegraph wires, shuffling the pieces on her imaginary chessboard until they lined up to her satisfaction. Thanks to a cycling enthusiast with a spinster sister on friendly terms with every bookseller in San Antonio, Grace now had a crate of tomes shipping to Harper's Station with her name on it. Tomes that just happened to include copies of *Oliver Twist* and *Guy Mannering*.

"Do you think it will work?" Amos asked after she closed the circuit for the final time and leaned back in her office chair.

Grace blew out a breath, the excitement that had driven her the past three hours fading now that her course was set and she could no longer turn back. "I don't know. But it seemed like a risk worth taking. If Detective Dunbar falls for the ruse, he'll take the books and leave, giving me time to make a run for Philadelphia without him being aware."

Having come to the conclusion that she was never going to trust Elliott Dunbar with her father's documents, there'd been only one recourse: travel to Philadelphia and place the items in Detective Whitmore's hands personally. The trip would be expensive, requiring a loan from Emma on top of clearing out most

175

of Grace's meager savings, but it wasn't the money that had her worried. Haversham knew her whereabouts and could be lying in wait even now. If she left the safety of the town, she painted a target on her back. Yet she saw no other resolution, and it was past time to bring this matter to a close.

Amos rose from the striped chair and tugged at the bottom of his brown worsted vest, drawing Grace out of her troublesome thoughts. He was so fastidious. Barely a wrinkle marred his clothes, even after a vigorous day of spying and plot contriving. His matching suit coat hung on the wall hook. The rest of his apparel remained formal—shirt buttoned to the chin, tie neat and unloosened. When Amos stood, straightened his shoulders, and cleared his throat, Grace felt a bit as if her old schoolmaster was about to address the class. It was adorable, really. Amos fidgeting yet formal all at the same time.

"It would be my honor to escort you on your journey, Miss Mallory." A slight reddening of his neck and ears accompanied the pronouncement. "It is not proper for a young woman to travel such a distance unescorted. Nor is it safe, in your current situation." His light blue gaze glimmered with sincerity and concern. "I realize I'm not a family member"—his ears darkened another shade—"yet I hope you consider me a close enough friend to accept my offer."

Grace's mind spun at a dizzying speed. Good heavens. She'd never considered . . . Did he feel obligated? His company would be a boon for sure, yet there'd be ramifications for him. "Amos," she sputtered, trying to find the words, "the fare to Philadelphia is so expensive. I had to arrange a loan with Emma just to cover my cost. I couldn't ask you to—"

"You're not asking me. I'm offering." He strode over to her with all the purpose and confidence of a band leader on parade. He halted in front of her chair and extended his hand.

Grace slowly fit her palm to his. He pulled, bringing her to her feet. The sweet, nervous Amos was endearing and comfortable to be around, but this more masterful version? He made her toes tingle.

The same sensation had washed over her earlier when he'd grabbed her arm and pressed her against that tree. For a heart-stopping moment, she'd thought he was going to kiss her, and oh, how she'd wanted him to. But that had been for show. Now they were alone, with no need for pretense or subterfuge. Yet here they stood, her hand in his, light blue eyes gazing down at her with such tenderness and determination that her pulse fluttered like a hummingbird's wing.

Rarely did a person sense a life-changing moment before it occurred. Usually only hindsight revealed its significance. Grace had experienced such a premonition once before, in the moment she watched her father step into that Denver street. She felt it again now. A weight of importance. A buzz of excitement. An anticipation that shallowed her breath.

"Grace." Amos rubbed his thumb over the back of her hand. "I came to Harper's Station for you. Not because I overheard your friend's warning, although that did expedite my arrival, but because I had started falling in love with you over the wire. I had already made up my mind to arrange a meeting before we started talking that evening. I wanted—no, I *needed* to meet you in person, to determine if we might be compatible in more than simply wire chatter."

Grace's mouth grew so dry, she feared she'd be unable to speak. Not that her mind was functioning properly enough to form a coherent sentence anyway, but such a soul-baring speech merited some kind of response.

"Amos . . . ," she managed, though she had no idea what would follow his name.

He shook his head. "No, let me finish."

Oh, thank heavens. His finishing meant she could delay beginning. She needed all the time she could get to scrape together the remnants of her scattered wits. Not to mention the fact that she really, *really* liked hearing what he was saying.

"I don't know what will come of this situation with Dunbar and your father's missing documents, but I do know that your safety means more to me than my own life. More than my worldly goods. I may not be a rich man, but I have enough to support a mother, and before Lucy married, a sister as well, while still squirreling away funds for a rainy day. If that rainy day arrives because the woman I . . . I care for needs my assistance, then I will gladly reach for an umbrella to shelter the two of us as we move forward together."

Grace smiled. Well, it started as a smile, then it stretched into a full-out beam of a grin. An umbrella? Oh, Amos. Delightfully gawky when it came to romance but so wonderfully sweet.

He hadn't changed. He was still the friend who made her laugh, the man who wore spectacles and tapped the sounder like a regimented woodpecker, the unconventional sportsman who preferred a bicycle to a horse. However, seeing this new side of him made it clear that he was also a man a woman could depend on when life's burdens grew too heavy to carry alone. A man unafraid to step forward and take the lead. Not with bullying swagger or excessive posturing, but with decency and gentle authority. He was a man worthy of respect. A man who made her feel stronger just by holding his hand.

"I have feelings for you, Grace," he said, shifting slightly and raising his free hand to adjust the perch of his spectacles on his nose even though they were already straight. "Feelings that have only grown stronger during the time we've spent together the past few days. I'd like . . ." He paused, glanced down at his feet and swallowed, then lifted his gaze to hers again. His bright, unapologetic, incredibly courageous gaze.

How brave he was to speak such words. She might have thought along similar lines, but saying such things aloud? So bold and forthright after such a short acquaintance? She'd be a trembling, stammering, tomato-red mess. Admiration swelled in her breast as she held her breath, waiting for whatever came next.

"I'd like to pay court to you, Grace. Officially. With the intention of asking for your hand if the idea proves amenable after a sufficient wooing period."

The smile that had faded to respectable lines when his proposal began fought to break free again, but she restrained it. Some women might consider his intellectual recitation dry and lacking passion, but they would be wrong. Grace could see the depth of emotion glittering in his eyes and recognized his formality as a tribute to the importance he placed on the occasion. She would respond in kind.

Forcing her eyes to maintain their connection with his despite the nearly overpowering urge to glance away, she gave a slight nod. "I accept your suit, Amos Bledsoe. And I accept your generous offer of escort, as well."

His eyes crinkled at the corners, and Grace loosened the reins on her smile, allowing it to welcome his suit, his affection, his . . .

Kiss?

Amos fit his hand to her cheek, cupping her face so tenderly, so intimately that Grace's heart stumbled in its rhythm. The gentle pressure of his hand tilted her face upward, and the sweet curve of his lips as he gazed at her made her feel beautiful and treasured and horrendously nervous all at once.

She'd never kissed a man before. Well, none except her father, and those cheek pecks surely didn't count. What if she did it wrong? She couldn't bear being a disappointment to Amos, not after all those wonderful pledges of devotion he had given her. Yet she couldn't escape either. Pulling away at this juncture would only hurt and confuse the man she'd just accepted as suitor. The man she was quickly coming to admire above all others.

So she held fast, her focus dropping from his heavy-lidded eyes to the lips that hovered a scant inch above hers.

"May I kiss you, Miss Mallory?" His husky whisper sent shivers dancing across her skin.

Land sakes! Did he actually expect her to verbalize an answer? Simply keeping her legs beneath her required every spare faculty at the moment. Somehow she managed a slight dip of her chin, and Amos—possessed of considerably more of his faculties, apparently—astutely recognized the minuscule motion as assent.

When his lips touched hers, the gentle contact soothed her fears even as it lured her in for more. He brushed his mouth over hers once, twice. On the third pass, he lingered, his fingers on her face drawing her closer as they caressed her skin with the lightest touch.

She tried to stay still, to let him direct things, since he seemed to have an inkling of how to accomplish this particular feat. However, when he let go of her hand in order to wrap his arm around her waist and drag her against his chest, she could no more hold back her response than she could hold back avalanching snow.

She lifted up on her tiptoes and kissed him back, praying she didn't do something gauche and embarrass them both. He didn't thrust her away, which she took as a good sign, but neither did he react. It was as if her sudden participation shocked him into paralysis. Until she tentatively reached out and laid her palm over the place she imagined his heart to be. Then, as if a jolt of lightning had passed through her fingertips into his chest, he clenched his arms and tightened his hold on her, his lips pressing deeper, tasting her more fully.

Sensations bombarded her, making her dizzy. Her knees weakened beneath the assault, but Amos held her firm, her anchor in the vortex. She found the idea of a future with this man very amenable indeed.

Yet as much as his kiss exhilarated her, the loss of control it inspired unsettled her. She pushed more firmly against Amos's chest, a tricky feat in itself, since her arms currently held all the strength of wet newsprint. Nevertheless, Amos reacted immediately. He loosened his grip and separated his mouth from hers.

They stood there for a long moment, silent except for the breathless huffs filling the air between them. Grace couldn't quite bring herself to meet his gaze, so she stared at a spot about an inch above the *V* of his vest, oddly comforted by the fact that his chest rose and fell with the same erratic rhythm as her own.

"Forgive me, Grace," he finally said, taking a step back from her and tugging on the hem of his vest in that nervous way of his she was starting to find charming. "I'm afraid my ardency got a bit out of hand."

"You weren't alone in that," she admitted softly, unwilling to let him place all the blame on himself.

"Still . . ." He cleared his throat. "A gentleman never places a lady's reputation at risk. We are in a public office. Anyone could have come in." His body turned slightly. "Or seen through the window."

Grace lifted her head to peer through the paned glass, relief washing over her when she saw nothing but dirt and trees and a handful of buildings. Most people were at home this time of day, preparing for the evening meal.

However, despite her gratitude over not being caught in a private embrace, she sensed an increasing awkwardness about Amos that tugged at her heart. She recalled the humorous, self-deprecating stories he'd entertained her with over the wire about his nemesis, one Harriet Dexter, who believed it her calling in life to point out his shortcomings to the female population of Denison. Now Amos was apologizing to her as if worried he'd *embarrassed* her with his attentions.

Well, Harriet Dexter was an idiot, and as soon as Amos and Grace returned from Philadelphia, she intended to travel to Denison and rub the woman's face in her mistake. Amos Bledsoe was a man any woman would be proud to have by her side. And if he continued to find Grace amenable after their *sufficient wooing period*, she intended to make the arrangement permanent. Permanent and so blissfully happy that all those foolish Denison girls who let him slip through their fingers would kick themselves for their stupidity.

"We're courting, Amos. Officially," Grace said, her voice firm, her attention capturing and holding his gaze hostage. "There is nothing improper about a courting couple sharing a celebratory kiss. And if anyone *did* happen to spy our embrace, I would accept whatever teasing resulted with good grace because I know how fortunate I am to have a man like you as my beau."

A warmth came into his blue eyes that made her pulse flicker. "I am the fortunate one, Miss Mallory. And whatever transpires over the next few days with this scheme of yours, know that I will remain steadfastly by your side. Come what may."

Come what may, indeed. Grace could only hope that what came was a successful double-cross and an uneventful journey to Philadelphia. Everything hinged on Detective Dunbar being less clever than he was pretty. Generally, those who relied on looks to get through life spent little time harnessing their intellect, but the Pinkerton didn't strike her as a fool. He was canny. How canny was yet to be determined. Only time, and a box of musty books, would tell.

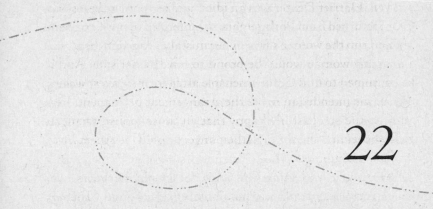

22

Two days later, Helen snuck out of church early and ran for home. Katie had given her an odd look when she muttered an excuse about her stomach aching as she exited their pew while everyone stood for the closing hymn. It hadn't been a lie. Her gut had been tied up in knots ever since Tori Adams made an announcement about a riderless horse her son Lewis had spotted down by the river the day before. Mr. Porter had taken the boy fishing and had tried to catch the still-saddled beast, but being on foot, he'd not been able to keep up with the animal when it spooked and ran.

Mr. Porter was about as good with horses as Miss Bertie Chandler was with blackberry syrup, and Miss Bertie's syrup had won enough blue ribbons to fill an entire kitchen drawer. If Ben Porter couldn't catch the horse, Helen didn't know why she thought she could do any better, but she had to try.

Because she wasn't the only one whose ears had perked up at the announcement. That Pinkerton fella had shown up at services too, making Helen's stomachache even worse, and he'd volunteered to track down the runaway.

Claire had told Helen about the detective's questions when

she'd come out to the cabin to check on her patient yesterday. Dunbar had asked her some generic questions about Grace and then probed her about unusual occurrences around town. Had anyone unfamiliar come to the clinic for medical assistance? Anyone try to buy supplies? He made it sound like he was only asking as a way to prevent someone from getting close to Grace through dishonest means. He had urged Claire not to treat any strangers without first checking with him or the marshal.

He was looking for Lee. Helen was sure of it. Which meant he was the one who'd shot him. The vile thought stirred her simmering anger to such a pitch, she found a new burst of energy as she ran toward the farmhouse. She couldn't let him find Lee's horse. Not if the animal still wore its saddle and bags. She had to rescue Lee's Bible.

Her stranger had been burning with fever the last two days, more unconscious than not. Tossing, turning, flailing, moaning. Calling for Rachel. Every once in a while, even calling for Helen. She had bathed his face and neck with cool water throughout the day and had even sneaked away at night to tend him, careful to leave the farmhouse after everyone was asleep and to return before the roosters crowed in order to avoid suspicion.

She'd followed Claire's directions in cooking up the milk and bread poultice and applied it four times a day. But still, Lee's fever raged. If it didn't break soon, she might have to fulfill his request to find Rachel and give her his Bible after all. Not that she would mind meeting Rachel. Lee's sister had endured the same crucible Helen had as a child. They were bound to feel a kinship of sorts. Yet she didn't want a kinship based on mutual loss. Not when that loss meant Lee's death.

Please, Lord, she prayed as a stitch in her side caused her to slow to a brisk walk. *He's the first man I ever met who didn't make me want to run in the opposite direction.* She glared at the scattered clouds that lollygagged their way across the sky. *Isn't that why you recruited me for nursing duty? Because you knew Lee was the one man on earth who would actually make me feel safe? You can't take him from me now. Not after I've gone all soft for him. That would be a trick my old man would pull. Not the act of a loving Father.*

Like the time her pa had waited just long enough for her to grow attached to Corky's runt pup. All the spaniel's siblings had been sold or given away, but no one wanted little Percy, with his mismatched eyes and uneven gait. No one but Helen. To her, he was the most perfect friend a girl could want. Loyal and full of love, licking her face and following wherever she went. Even making her laugh when no one else was around to hear. Her affection-starved heart hadn't stood a chance.

She'd been careful not to let her delight in the puppy show around her pa, but he must have guessed. Two months after Percy had been weaned, just long enough to make her believe she might get to keep him, her pa brought a gunnysack out to the barn. He snatched Percy by the scruff of his neck, tossed him inside, and marched down to the river.

Helen had screamed and wailed, chasing after her pa, begging him not to drown her pup. But it hadn't stopped him.

"The pup is *mine*, not yours, brat. And if I don't want to spare the food to feed it, I can do what I want to rid myself of the critter. Just like I can with you. So shut yer mouth."

She had. She'd shut everything down that day. Turned off the tears. Turned off her heart. Vowed never to give him a weapon to use against her like that again. Caring only made you weak. Vulnerable.

You're supposed to be better than that, she accused the Father she'd always believed to be worth her devotion, unlike the earthly model she'd been stuck with. *You're supposed to give good gifts to your children. Isn't that what you promised?*

Oh, she knew the Bible promised God's children hardship as well as blessing. Hardship didn't scare her. She'd dealt with it her entire life. God could send all the suffering, persecution, and fiery trials he wanted. What he couldn't do was tease her with hope, break open her sealed-up heart, then yank the gift away. That would make him cruel. And she'd never serve a cruel master. Ever.

The stitch in her side suddenly sharpened to a full-blown cramp. Helen grimaced and stumbled to a halt, pinching her waist between her thumb and fingers. As she did so, the verse the traveling preacher had read from the pulpit that morning tripped through her muddled mind. *The earth is the Lord's, and the fullness thereof; the world, and they that dwell therein.*

Helen shuddered, the passage from Psalm 24 echoing far too closely the words her father had spouted when he'd stolen Percy from her. Ownership. God owned everything. The world. The people. Helen.

No. She would not be owned. She'd not simply lie down and let someone else dictate her life, meekly accepting whatever happened.

If any man will come after me, let him deny himself, and take up his cross, and follow me. For whosoever will save his life shall lose it: and whosoever will lose his life for my sake shall find it.

The words of Jesus slammed into her heart and shattered her arguments. Helen grabbed her middle and doubled over, though not because of the cramp in her side. This pain went deeper, to the pit of her soul. She was the *whosoever* trying to save her own life, which meant she was destined to lose it. Unless she found a way to deny herself. Give up control and fully surrender her will to that of her Savior. If she truly wanted to follow him, she had to be willing to go wherever he led. Even through the valley of the shadow of death.

She'd always thought that meant *her* death. But what if it meant the death of another? One she cared about? Tears welled in her eyes. She hadn't shed tears since the day her pa had drowned her puppy. She hadn't even allowed herself to cry when her mother died. Tears equaled weakness. Yet it wasn't weakness that brought the moisture to her eyes as she stood in the middle of the farmhouse road. It was contrition. By refusing to deny herself, she had denied her Lord. Throwing ultimatums in his face as if she had the right.

Fail to heal Lee, and I won't love you anymore, she'd threatened. *I'll turn my back on you. Call you unjust, a betrayer.* Was her love for him so shallow that she'd turn her back like a petulant child if she didn't get her way?

The first tear rolled down her cheek, followed by a second and a third, until a stream flowed. Helen tightened her grip on her midsection and rocked slightly as she released the last vestiges of her control. "O, God, you are good," she said softly, her voice cracking as her throat grew thick. "Your love is perfect. Your ways are perfect. You are worthy of my trust. No matter what comes. You are able to save Lee from death, but even if you do not, I will still follow you. I will still love you. Because you are not cruel or unjust or petty. You are holy and righteous and full of compassion. You are God, able to see not only into the past but into the future, and I trust you to know what is best."

The tears continued to fall, and Helen made no move to wipe them away. She needed the cleansing, needed to let go, needed to let the Shepherd lead.

A soft whinny echoed in her ears.

Her head jerked up and a smile stretched her mouth wide. *O, Lord. You are good.*

For there, not a hundred yards away from her, stood the very thing she'd sought when she'd bolted from church. A chestnut gelding. Saddle. No rider.

Lee's horse.

She laughed. A tear-clogged, croak of a laugh, but a laugh nonetheless. One that felt so free, she did it again. She'd thought she'd felt true freedom on the day her father died, but she'd only lost her jailor, not her chains. Today she was truly free.

Unwrapping her arms from about her middle, Helen straightened and smiled again. She felt lighter, buoyant almost, and so full of hope that she thought her heart might burst.

She still didn't know Lee's fate, but the Lord had sent her his horse, so she'd be thankful for that blessing and leave the rest in the Almighty's hands.

After pulling a handkerchief out of her pocket and cleaning up the mess she'd made of her face, Helen approached the horse. She moved slowly but confidently, speaking to the animal in low tones.

"Hey, boy." She held her palm open in front of her as her skirts rustled the tall grass near the shallow creek that must have drawn the animal to this particular spot. The big horse blinked at her and swished his tail but showed no signs of fear. "Looking for Lee? I'm helping him. I'd like to help you, too. I could get you out of that saddle if you hold still for a few minutes. What do you say?"

As she neared the horse, she could see the scrapes where the chestnut had tried to free himself from his tack with no success. Helen recalled sleeping in her clothes several days in a row when traveling and the sore places she'd developed from her corset pressing into her skin with no relief. How much worse must a saddle be? So heavy and unwieldly.

She moved within reach. The chestnut snorted and sidestepped. "Easy, boy." She offered him her hand to smell, and when he calmed a bit, she reached up to stroke his cheek. She continued petting him and murmuring praise, moving along his neck and over his shoulder until she reached the cinch strap. Acting as if they were in a confined barn stall instead of out on the wide-open prairie where the horse could spook and run for days, Helen lifted the stirrup and hooked it over the saddle horn to get it out of the way. Then she tugged on the cinch strap. The chestnut blew out a breath, as if eager to assist. The fastening loosened, and the girth fell free. Quickly, Helen tied up the extra strap length and, keeping a hand on the horse's body, made her way behind him to the other side. He was a little too tall for her, but she managed to drag the saddle and pad off without tumbling onto her rear.

The chestnut bolted the moment he was free of his burden. Helen made no move to stop him, just grinned at his exuberance. As he scampered off, she turned her attention to the tack at her feet. Lee's saddlebag hung from the side of the cantle, still affixed. She hunkered down in the grass and unbuckled the leather pouch. Inside were a fresh shirt and a small book—the Bible he'd asked her to take to his sister. A brown ribbon marked a passage near the end.

Helen pulled upward on the ribbon until the Bible opened, and immediately her eyes were drawn to the underlined verse in the middle of the left page. The first verse of Galatians 5.

"'Stand fast therefore in the liberty wherewith Christ hath made us free, and be not entangled again with the yoke of bondage.'" Helen turned her face to the sky. "I will," she vowed.

Never again would she allow her fear of being hurt to shackle her.

23

"Here's my supply list for the week." Tori Adams handed Grace a half-sheet of paper. Grace scanned the items, thankful for the shopkeeper's tidy script. She never had trouble deciphering Tori's handwriting.

Emma, on the other hand, was the worst. The banker's numbers always stood out clear and precise—no one could accuse Emma Shaw of being careless with her figures—but her rushed penmanship often required mental contortions to untangle.

Emma had brought her Monday financial report by that morning for Grace to wire to the broker in New York, and Grace still hadn't finished translating the document into a legible message. Thankfully, she'd been working with Emma long enough to recognize most of her scrawl patterns, but she still preferred to copy the information onto a clean telegraph blank before sending the contents over the wire. It was much easier to decode Emma's scribbles beforehand than trying to translate mid-transmission.

Grace glanced up from Tori's list and raised a brow. "Only five items? That's a short list for you. Has your delivery business dropped off?"

Tori shook her head. "No. In fact, Mr. Porter and I added two new clients last week." The smile that accompanied her words was small, as usual from the stoic shopkeeper, but satisfaction gleamed in her blue eyes. "I gave the rest of my list to Ben when he visited on Saturday. Knowing that shipment of bicycles would be arriving today, I asked him to load up with staples as well. Flour, sugar, coffee, cornmeal, lard. Those kinds of things. No sense making a trip with a half-empty freight wagon."

Grace quirked her lips as she returned to her desk, opened the telegraph circuit, and started tapping out the message that would be delivered to Tori's supplier in Gainesville. "Something tells me an empty wagon wouldn't stop Mr. Porter from making a trip out to see you."

The freighter appeared in town at least three times a week these days. Tori blamed the extra visits on their delivery business, but everyone in town knew she and Benjamin Porter were courting. After each delivery run, Tori cooked dinner for the freighter, and the two were often spotted sitting together on the bench outside the shop in the evenings, sipping coffee and talking until the sun set. How Mr. Porter managed to find his way home in the fading light of dusk was a mystery that kept the gossip mills grinding. Some ladies presumed those giant horses of his could see in the dark. Others believed he set up camp somewhere along the road to pass the night then rose at dawn to finish the journey. Everyone agreed that he'd do anything necessary to spend time with Tori. The man was besotted. And judging by the faint pink coloring Tori's cheeks, he wasn't the only one.

"Yes, well . . ." Tori fiddled with her reticule strings. "Lewis enjoys spending time with him. Ben is helping him train Hercules."

Grace finished sending the message, confirmed the content, then signed off. She moved back to the counter and collected the coins Tori had set out for her. "I'm sure he enjoys helping Lewis with his puppy, but he comes for you, Tori. Everyone knows that."

"Ben is a good man." Tori jutted her chin slightly, ready to rush to her man's defense.

Grace immediately reached across the counter to touch her friend's arm. "I meant no criticism. Mr. Porter is a fine man. One of the best I know. I'm thrilled that the two of you are finally courting. The man adores you, Tori. Lewis, too. And with your similar business interests? Well, I'd say you two make a perfect match."

"And what about *your* visitor?" Tori's eyes sparkled as she neatly turned the conversation around on Grace. "A man with *similar business interests* and an attention to your welfare that goes well beyond that of a casual acquaintance."

Grace blushed, and not the delicate touch of pink that Tori had displayed earlier. Grace's cheeks ignited with instant inferno-level heat. It didn't help that talk of courtship had already brought Amos to mind. Amos and that *kiss* the two of them had shared. In this very room. It was all Grace could do not to turn and stare at the area behind her desk where he had held her in his arms and swept her away with unexpected passion. Who knew a bespectacled, gawky cycling enthusiast could steal her breath so completely?

"Aha!" Tori smirked. "There *is* something between you two."

Grace withdrew her arm and retreated behind the half-wall separating them, a wall that suddenly felt far too short. Not that this stopped her friend from following. Tori just leaned over the counter, making it clear there would be no escape.

It was time to put her shyness aside and stand tall for the man whose name she hoped to share one day. Straightening her shoulders, Grace forced herself to meet Tori's gaze. "Mr. Bledsoe asked to court me, and I accepted."

The shopkeeper's teasing challenge dissolved into an expression of sweet joy. Had Emma been here, she probably would have squealed and dashed around the counter to sweep Grace up in a hug, but calm, unflappable Tori simply smiled. Yet that smile somehow filled the room with such warm acceptance that all Grace's nervousness drained away.

"That's wonderful." Tori's smile dimmed slightly as her gaze roamed to the open doorway and scanned the street. She turned back and lowered her voice slightly. "After seeing you and Mr. Dunbar in the café a few days ago, I worried you might be developing feelings for the handsome Pinkerton agent."

Grace's attention sharpened. "Is there something about Mr. Dunbar you dislike?"

Tori had never been terribly fond of men in general, but she was as close to an objective third party as Grace and Amos were likely to get without giving away their suspicions.

The shopkeeper shrugged. "Nothing I can put my finger on. He's always polite, and I suppose the questions he asks are just part of his detective work, but sometimes . . . I don't know. His eyes go cold." She rubbed her arms. "Yesterday after church, I stopped him from questioning Lewis about the runaway horse he and Ben saw, because I could tell his pressing was making my son uneasy. Lewis kept ducking behind my skirts as if trying to escape. Something angry and almost mean flashed in Mr. Dunbar's eyes. It only lingered for a second before Ben stepped in and offered to answer all of his questions, but it left my heart pounding. I'll be glad for him to leave."

"Me, too," Grace concurred. "He shouldn't be here much longer. He might even leave today."

If he took her bait.

"Oh?" Tori's eyebrows lifted.

"A package should be arriving for me with the shipment of bicycles from San Antonio. Hopefully the contents will satisfy Mr. Dunbar's curiosity and send him on his way."

A jangling harness sounded outside, and Tori's head jerked toward the door. Her eyes lit up. "That will be Ben with my supplies. And those crazy bicycles, no doubt. He was going to meet the train to collect them this morning before heading out."

Grace came around the counter and followed Tori outside. Sure enough, Mr. Porter's large freight wagon was rolling toward the store. But he wasn't alone. Nearly every lady in Harper's Station had come out to welcome him, buzzing with curiosity. Henrietta Chandler pushed through them all, shouting at Mr. Porter to stop already so she could get a gander at her new velocipede.

"Oh, dear." Tori shared a laughing look with Grace. "I better lend a hand before the swarm drags him down."

Grace grinned. Then she spotted a familiar figure joining the crowd, one whose tidy suit and bespectacled features made her pulse flicker. She pointed his direction. "There's Amos. He'll distract the hordes long enough for you to extricate Mr. Porter."

Tori took several steps into the street, her smile bright as she glanced back at Grace. "Your Mr. Bledsoe might be the one who ends up needing to be rescued. Better keep an eye out."

Grace laughed as she waved to her friend. "I will."

Knowing how busy her Monday mornings always were, Grace had shooed Amos away from the telegraph office. He'd volunteered to keep tabs on Detective Dunbar while she worked, so the Pinkerton was probably close by as well. Not that she had expected anything else. He'd be as eager to examine the freighter's load as anyone, waiting for her shipment. Though at the moment, the ladies appeared to be taking over.

Grace smiled as Ben handed down the first women's Yukon to Amos from the back of the wagon. Females engulfed the poor man before the tires even touched the ground. Henry and Emma clambered around in the heart of the fray, taking hold of the handlebars and pushing at the pedals with the toes of their shoes.

It seemed Amos was about to get roped into cycling lessons.

Grace wished she could join the others and watch her man in action, but work came first. Emma's broker needed the financial report before noon.

With a last fond look at the wheelman in the eye of a calico whirlwind, Grace headed back inside.

After deciphering the final line of the report, Grace set her pencil down and lifted the completely filled telegraph blank to review. She wanted to scan it for errors one last time before sending and cross out as many unnecessary words as possible in order to save her friend the extra expense. She'd just crossed out her third *and* when the office door banged open, startling her so badly she jumped.

"Sorry about that," Detective Dunbar said as he stepped into the office carrying a large crate. "My hands are full." He smiled and lifted the box a few inches higher to emphasize the truth of his words—and the breadth of his biceps. As if such a manly display excused his kicking her door in. The peacock.

Amos would have set the crate down and opened the door like a regular human being. Because Amos cared about protecting her property and not scaring her out of her wits.

Grace did not return the Pinkerton's smile, but she did rise from her chair and walk toward the counter. "What can I do for you, Mr. Dunbar?"

"It's what I can do for *you*, Miss Mallory." He thumped the crate down on her counter, the loud *bang* making her wince. Then he patted the top of the box and winked. "I believe this is the package we've been waiting for."

Personally, Grace would have preferred waiting a little longer. And having a different deliveryman. Amos or the marshal, for instance.

"From San Antonio? My, that was fast." She forced a small smile to her lips as she stepped closer and pretended to examine the address on the box. Dunbar loomed over her, close enough that she could feel his breath on the top of her head. Too close. Too . . . unsettling.

Grace stepped back and cleared her throat. "Thank you for delivering this. I should have time to sort through the contents later this afternoon. I'll send word—"

His palm slapped the wood of the crate. Grace flinched. "Why wait?" Dunbar winked at her again as if he were laughing at her puny efforts to shoo him away. He flung the outer door closed with a flick of his wrist, then strode down the counter to the half-door that separated her office from the customer area. He reached over the top, unlatched the small bolt that held it closed, and pushed through, crossing bold as brass into her inner sanctum.

"Mr. Dunbar!" Grace protested. "Customers are not allowed in this part of the office. Western Union officers only."

"Aw, who's gonna know?" He marched over to where the crate sat and hefted it up off the counter as if the box of books weighed little more than a crate of goose down.

Grace scuttled backward.

"Besides, I've seen Bledsoe back here with you. If it ain't off limits for him, it ain't off limits for me." He swept past her and dropped the box onto her desk. On top of the message she'd just copied for Emma.

That put some starch in her spine. Grace marched over to the desk, grabbed the corner of the document she'd been working on, then tried to lift the edge of the box enough to slip the paper out. The box didn't budge. Not until Dunbar, drat his too-muscled hide, lifted it back up for her. His smirk sparked her indignation even higher as she yanked the page out from under the box and tucked it under her logbook to keep the contents confidential.

"I'll have you know that Mr. Bledsoe is a Western Union agent, as well," she pronounced. "From Denison. He has privileges that you do not."

Dunbar leaned an elbow on the crate and ran his gaze over her. "Oh, I think we all know about his *privileges*."

Grace bristled. "How dare you make such ugly insinuations. I insist you leave. At once."

"You want me gone?" He shrugged as if her desires were really of no consequence to him. Which they weren't, obviously. "Then I suggest we open this box and retrieve the items you promised me."

He leaned closer, his eyes losing their teasing light.

Tori had been right. His eyes *were* cold. And hard.

"Once I have what I came for," he said in a menacing tone that sent shivers of alarm shooting down her spine, "I'll be on my way."

24

Helen woke from her doze with a start. Her neck, stiff after falling asleep in the least comfortable chair known to man, sent a sharp jolt of protest through the muscles at the base of her skull as she jerked her head around to check on her patient.

"Sorry," Lee mumbled with a grimace as he reached for his injured thigh. "I didn't mean to wake you."

Helen lurched forward, grabbing the Bible in her lap at the last second before it slid to the floor. Carefully, she set the book next to a glass of water on the small table near the head of the bed, then stood and checked his injury. "Is it paining you?"

What a stupid question. He had a hole in his thigh. Of course it was paining him.

"Not too bad." He glanced at her, a guilty, little-boy-caught-red-handed look on his face. "Until I try to move."

"Well, don't move then," she scolded.

Good grief. She'd finally found a man she wanted to impress, and here she was dousing him with vinegar instead of honey.

He chuckled, though, and the sound muted her self-recriminations. Perhaps this one actually preferred tart to sweet. What a boon that would be. Tart was her specialty.

Lee shifted a bit on the mattress. "I . . . uh . . ."—his gaze dodged hers—"got to make use . . . of the chamber pot."

"Oh!" Helen snapped upright. "Um . . . do you . . . need help?"

She and Claire had cut away his denims to make sure there weren't any hidden wounds, so all he wore were his drawers. The quilt covered his lower extremities, though, exposing only his thigh so she could change the bandage or apply a new poultice.

Still, the man was injured. He needed a nurse, not a shy female nervous about seeing a man in his underclothes. If he required assistance, she'd do what needed to be done.

Just as she stiffened her spine, he cleared his throat and rubbed his mustache. "If you can help me sit up and swing around a little so my legs hang off the bed, I should be able to . . . handle the rest on my own."

Oh, thank heavens.

"Here." She slid a supporting arm behind his back as he started to lift away from the pillow. He winced and hissed in a breath but made no other sound.

She leaned in close for better leverage, and her cheek pressed against his temple.

Cool. His head was blessedly, wonderfully cool.

Helen smiled and sent a heartfelt *thank you* heavenward.

Lee's hair might be sweat-slicked from battling fever, his jaw thick with stubble, and his personal aroma drifting toward sour milk thanks to the poultice mixture she'd dribbled on him over and over, but he was still the best thing she'd ever had the pleasure of holding in her arms.

The worst had passed. Her man was on the mend.

Her man? Listen to her putting the cart before the horse. He barely knew her. His only truly conscious moments had occurred when she'd been in her black crow's dress, or now, when she was so weary from tending him that her eyes surely sported dark circles and bloodshot streaks. Not exactly her most attractive moments.

Still, she couldn't stop the possessiveness from swelling inside her as she held him close and gently scooted his injured leg to the side of the bed. As he shifted with her, his good leg jostled the bedside table. Already unsteady due to age and uneven legs, the table wobbled. Fearing the half-full glass of water would spill on Lee's Bible, Helen made a grab for the glass with her free hand. She caught the glass, but in her haste, her forearm knocked the very item she'd been trying to save to the floor.

"Oh! I'm so sorry." She gently extricated her arm from his injured leg and bent to retrieve the fallen book.

"Don't worry about it," Lee grunted as he braced his arms against the cot's frame. He huffed out a heavy breath. "That Bible's seen worse and survived. A little tumble won't hurt it."

Helen still felt bad about it, though. The book had landed open—spine up, pages down. The pages had been pushed under and bent at the corners. She dusted off the cover with her sleeve then set about unfolding the worst of the bent pages. Most had been squished in a large chunk, so they unbent easily, but the pages at the front sported more definite creases. As she smoothed one of the front pages, she noticed the handwriting at the top of the page. *To Lee, with love. Rachel.* Her hand slowed and a smile began to build. No wonder this Bible was so important to him. It had been a gift from his sister.

She scanned the rest of the page as her hand moved down the genealogy list. As her fingers passed over the top line of record, however, her smile vanished. Her chest throbbed as if an unseen band had suddenly compressed her ribs.

"Lee? What is this?" She held the opened page in front of him then slowly turned her face toward his.

His breath came in heavy pants and his face looked ashy beneath his scruff of a beard, but for the first time in a long while, his health was a secondary concern. She needed an answer. And she needed it now.

"Right here." She pointed to the top line of the family record.

His forehead scrunched, and his green eyes regarded her with confusion as he tilted his head back to look at her. "My name. Why?"

"Because if that is *your* name, my friend is in an awful lot of trouble."

Helen's trembling fingers traced the name scripted in Rachel's handwriting.

Elliott Leander Dunbar.

She clenched her hand into a fist and scowled at the man who had made her mind go soft, who had made her forget where her true loyalties resided. "Tell me what you know about Grace Mallory," she demanded as she flung the Bible away from her and onto the bed. "Now!"

Grace swallowed as Detective Dunbar stared down at her. For a fleeting moment, she considered making a run for the door, to find shelter among the throng of ladies just a few yards away, but the Pinkerton stood too close. She'd never make it. And if she bolted, he'd be certain of her suspicions and would never trust the books in the crate. Better to play along. Act as if she weren't scared out of her wits to be alone with him.

Using her indignation over his siege of her office to mask her fear, Grace scowled up at him. "This is highly irregular, detective. I'll have to report this incident to the Western Union home office."

"Do what you gotta do, lady. What I've gotta do is complete my mission and get those documents back to Whitmore. I've wasted enough time in this petticoat prison already." Dunbar grasped the lip of the wooden crate's lid, and with a single yank, pulled the small nails from their moorings and ripped the cover away.

Grace flinched at the raw display of strength but held her ground. When he turned the crate upside down and dumped the nearly two dozen books onto her work table, she lurched forward and grabbed his arm.

"Be careful! You'll damage my—"

"Your daddy's books will survive." He shook her fingers from his arm with a light flick of his elbow, like a horse shooing an annoying fly with its tail. "Leave me be."

She'd been about to warn him against damaging her equipment, not the books, being more concerned about the telegraph machinery than the random volumes of poetry and prose that held no sentimental value to her whatsoever. Thankfully, his rude interruption kept her from exposing herself.

He tossed books left and right, obviously looking for specific titles. Apparently, he didn't just know there were books missing from Tremont Haversham's library, he knew *which* books.

The knot in her belly tightened a notch.

He checked the spine of a thick, red, cloth-covered book then gave a little grunt of satisfaction before tucking it under his arm. Judging by the size of the book, it must have been *Oliver Twist*. Two tossed-aside books later, he latched onto a dark green hardback with a gilt title line that blazed *Guy Mannering* in bold fashion.

Grace took a single step back, anxious to put some space between her and the large man siphoning all the air out of her tiny office space. He had the books, now she just needed to get him to leave. "I searched my father's collection for the documents after he died," she told him, thankful that her voice sounded relatively steady, "but I never found them. Maybe you'll have better luck."

Please take them and go.

But the detective appeared to be in no hurry. He started examining the covers, the spines. Flipped through the pages.

Not here! Don't look for them here. She needed to get him out of her office. Out of the town.

"Those books have caused me no end of grief," she blurted.

"Just take them back to Agent Whitmore. The two of you can tear them apart for all I care. I never want to see them again."

Please leave. Please leave.

He paused and stared at her, his icy gaze freezing her from the inside. Then he brought up his left leg and planted his boot on the seat of her office chair, making a table out of his knee. He set the books on his thigh, opened the top cover, and ran his fingers over the inside panel. He closed *Oliver Twist*, shuffled it to the bottom, then performed the same procedure on *Guy Mannering*.

What was he doing? Grace's pulse raced as her eyes followed his every movement. He looked like he was feeling for something. The seal? But how would he have known about it? It was the one weak spot in her plan she could do nothing about—the Haversham seal embossed inside each book. If the Pinkerton knew about it, then . . .

Dunbar turned his face to her and smiled, a cat-with-bird-feathers-hanging-from-its-mouth kind of smile.

"I knew you were a clever one," he purred as he dropped his foot back to the ground and stalked toward her. "Had to be to elude me for so long."

Grace retreated a step. Dunbar advanced. She withdrew farther, until the backs of her knees bumped into the blue-striped chair.

"I thought you'd trust a Pinkerton, but somehow you saw through me, didn't you?"

He knew!

Grace didn't wait to see how much. She ran. But the counter's half door slowed her down. As she fumbled to pull it open, Dunbar's arm snaked around her waist and his hand slammed over her mouth.

She kicked and flailed, but he only chuckled. "A fighter. Good. I like a good tussle. Gets the blood flowing."

Grace tried to scream, but his large palm smothered all but a tiny, muffled squeak. If only she could reach her derringer! The thought had her clawing at her skirt, but his hold kept her from bending at the middle, leaving her sole source of protection out of reach.

He toted her like a rag doll to the window and, holding her away from view, peered out, his smile growing wider at whatever he saw. "Everyone's nice and occupied with those crazy contraptions Bledsoe was good enough to order. Getting out your bedroom window unseen will be easier than shooting a deer with a broken leg. No one will even know we've gone."

No! Grace squirmed and shimmied, desperate to get away, but his arms circled her like iron bands.

"Yep, your little ruse almost worked," he said, his voice conversational and not the least bit winded as he toed a fallen book out of his path and dragged her through the doorway into her private rooms. "Too bad Chauncey told me about the stamp his father used on the inside covers of his books. A seal embossed with his initials. Neither of those books had one."

Grace stilled. *Chauncey?* As in Chaucer Haversham?

Dunbar wasn't just working for him. They were friends. Long-standing friends, by the sound of it.

She should have joined Amos and the rest of the town ladies when she'd had the chance.

Dunbar braced a hip on her windowsill then wrapped a long leg around both of hers to free a hand for raising the window. While he shoved the window to its maximum height, she fought the only way she could, scratching at his face. One nail drew blood. He cursed then slammed his forehead hard against her skull. She went lax. Silver diamonds winked in her vision.

"Do that again, Grace, and I'll take my knife to you. See how much *you* like having your face slit open. Not even Bledsoe would have you then."

He bent his big frame around her much smaller one, and while she was too disoriented to slow him down, he ducked through the window and exited into the open field behind the telegraph office. A field completely hidden from the rest of Harper's Station.

25

"How do ya keep the wheels from running away with ya?" Henrietta Chandler demanded as she kicked out her skirt and stepped over the low section of the bicycle frame. Her strident voice brought Amos's head around.

He'd been searching the crowd for Dunbar. He'd last seen the Pinkerton conversing with Ben Porter, no doubt questioning the freighter about who or what he'd seen on his trip into town. The man seemed obsessed with the whereabouts of any newcomers. Only fitting, with what they knew about Haversham, yet something about the man's insistent curiosity raised Amos's hackles.

"Mr. Bledsoe," Henrietta Chandler snapped.

"Sorry, ma'am." Amos smiled at the feisty, gray-haired lady, then immediately lurched forward and grabbed the back of her seat.

Good grief. She'd been about to mount. Even now, her hands clutched the handlebars with purpose and one foot was lifting to fit itself against a pedal.

"Hold on a minute, Miss Chandler. Let me explain a few things first."

The woman had too much gumption for her own good. She'd

proven that when she held him at gunpoint that first day. He still shivered when he thought about her beady eyes staring him down over the barrel of her revolver. Those eyes hadn't changed. They stared at him now with a similar demand for answers and equally little patience.

"Well?"

Amos cleared his throat. "Backpedaling usually aids in the slowing process," he instructed, "and there is a spoon brake you can apply by pressing this lever here." He pointed to the slender rod that extended beneath the right side of the handlebars. "However, engaging the brake tends to cause wear on the pneumatic tires, so I only use that apparatus in emergencies."

Miss Chandler raised a pointed brow. "So how do *you* stop?"

Amos pushed his spectacles up the bridge of his nose and straightened his shoulders. "A well-timed dismount from the seat usually does the trick." He didn't like to brag, but he was practically an expert at the maneuver. "When my feet hit the ground, I keep hold of the handlebars, and the bicycle halts as I do."

Not that he would recommend such a stunt for an amateur. In fact, he hoped to harness Miss Chandler's enthusiasm with that daring description. But he might have miscalculated.

Her mouth tightened at the corners. "Jump off. Got it."

Good grief. At her age, she'd probably break a hip. "No, Miss Chandler. No leaping for you. I'll teach you to backpedal and engage the spoon break. Besides, the ground is fairly level here in Harper's Station." Thank the Lord for small favors. "You shouldn't have need for any high speeds. At a slow pace, you can simply put your foot down to bring the machine to a stop."

Emma Shaw came up beside her aunt, pushing another bicycle through the throng of ladies who had come out to witness the spectacle. The hum of their excitement filled Amos's ears, leaving him oddly on edge.

He darted a glance over to the freighter, but Mr. Porter was busy carting a load of supplies up the steps to the store. The shopkeeper walked by his side, and a young boy held the shop door wide for them.

Where was Dunbar?

His grip on Miss Chandler's seat loosened as he stretched his neck to peer over the crowd. The bicycle wobbled, and a squeak of surprise cut through the crowd's buzz.

Amos immediately returned his attention to the bicycle, taking hold of the seat with both hands and steadying it as Mrs. Shaw reached for her aunt's arm.

"Easy, Aunt Henry."

The older lady must have thought she'd been holding the bicycle steady on her own and attempted to mount when Amos let go. Her left foot slid awkwardly off the pedal, and her ankle twisted a bit before she finally found purchase upon the ground.

"Let's not get ahead of ourselves," Emma Shaw admonished, instantly becoming Amos's second favorite female in town. "When Malachi taught us to shoot, you didn't rush off and start pulling triggers before learning the proper technique. Riding a bicycle is the same. We must first receive instruction—"

"Bah, it's not the same at all. I can't hurt anyone by pedaling improperly."

Amos scowled at her, taking *his* turn at wielding a beady-eyed glare. "Actually you can. Not only can you injure yourself by taking a tumble, but if you ride before understanding how to steer or stop, you could run someone else down."

The shopkeeper's son chose that particular instant to rush around the wagon and skid to a halt right in front of Miss Chandler's front tire. "Are we all gonna get a turn? I bet I could go the fastest." He made a whooshing noise and proceeded to demonstrate his natural speed by sprinting past the giant black horses hitched to the freight wagon and pounding up the store steps, his puppy barking excitedly at his heels the whole way.

Miss Chandler's eyes widened at the boy's unexpected appearance in front of her, and her knuckles whitened as she tensed her grip on the handlebars. Amos could kiss the boy for his timely interruption.

"Maybe we should wait for the crowd to thin a bit," the older lady conceded, though her bristly tone warned that she'd not be put off for long.

Amos glanced over his shoulder toward the telegraph station. He didn't see Dunbar, which would have been reassuring were it not for the fact that he hadn't been able to spot the Pinkerton anywhere else, either.

"Why don't you ladies settle your accounts with Miss Adams?" he suggested.

Henrietta Chandler's brow furrowed mulishly at that suggestion, but he couldn't bow to her whims. Not anymore. He needed to find Dunbar. Or at least confirm that Grace was all right.

"We'll have a lesson this afternoon in the field behind the station house." Amos released his hold on Miss Chandler's bicycle seat and backed away. "Learning to balance on two wheels takes a significant amount of practice at first, and having a soft bed of prairie grass to fall onto instead of the hard-packed street will reduce the likelihood of injury."

His gaze darted back to the telegraph office. Was that movement by the window? He prayed it was Grace, distracted by the commotion of the delivery. Yet his gut still clenched.

Henrietta Chandler harrumphed somewhere behind him as he began weaving through the crowd. "Just like a man to make a woman conform to *his* timetable. It's not like he's got a job here to run off to, is it?"

"Let him go, Aunt Henry." Emma Shaw's voice hinted at a concern that only added to the wave cresting within Amos. "He needs to check on Grace."

Yes, he did.

He pushed past the last of the females fluttering around the delivery wagon and stretched his legs into a jog, then a run. When he reached the office, he slowed just enough to avoid crashing through the door.

"Grace!" he called as he flung the door wide. His gaze immediately swept toward her desk, where she should be gasping and glaring at his boorish entrance. But she wasn't there.

His heart seized. "Grace!" His shout echoed in the empty room as he pushed through the half-door that led to the inner office. He took in the scene—books scattered over the desk, a few fallen to the floor, her chair overturned, and a discarded crate tossed onto its side in the corner by the stove.

The crate.

Amos located the lid where it had been tossed against the far wall and snatched it up. All hope that Grace might have simply gone for a walk shriveled in his chest. A crate from San Antonio. One that Mr. Porter must have brought in on the freight wagon. A crate only one other person would have been interested in opening.

Dunbar.

The slatted lid fell from Amos's fingers.

Dunbar had her.

Amos rushed into Grace's personal chambers, illogically hoping he'd find her asleep or huddled unharmed in a corner somewhere.

The Pinkerton was dirty. Probably on Haversham's payroll. The very man they'd been warned about.

Amos scanned the floors, behind the bed, anywhere Grace could be hidden.

The lying snake. No wonder they'd seen neither hide nor hair of a Haversham henchman. The villain had been right under their noses the entire time, his comely sheep's clothing throwing them off the scent.

And Amos had let an old lady and her bicycle distract him from keeping watch on the fiend.

A gust of wind blew over his heated neck. Amos spun around to face the open window. The *wide* open window.

He rushed toward it, planted his hands on the sill, and stuck his head through the gaping hole.

Nothing. He saw nothing.

He dropped his head in disgust and slammed his palm against the whitewashed sill. Footprints. Right beneath the window. Deep, man-sized boot prints.

A trail.

Amos had one leg through the window opening and was ducking his head under the frame when the marshal's voice stopped him mid-straddle.

"Bledsoe?" Heavy footfalls echoed in the outer office.

"Here!" Amos called, not bothering to pull more than his head back inside. He bit back his impatience at the delay but retained enough sense to recognize that rushing around willy-nilly on his own when there was a capable lawman available to assist would be foolish. The more help he could recruit for Grace, the better.

Malachi Shaw burst into the bedroom, gun drawn. His eyes scanned the chamber. Finding the same thing Amos had—nothing—he holstered his revolver and strode to the window. "Where's Grace?"

"Dunbar has her. I think he carted her out this window." Amos nodded toward the disturbed dirt outside. "I found footprints leading away."

"Did you catch sight of them?" Shaw asked as he shoved his head into the same space Amos occupied.

Amos leaned out of the way, just in case the marshal could spot something he'd missed. His spectacles focused his distant vision a great deal, but it was possible some clue had eluded him.

"No," Amos answered, willing his spirit not to sink at the admission. "He must have had a horse tethered nearby."

Shaw craned his neck to the west. "Station house is the closest cover. Let's check the direction of the footprints then head to the house. Henry was busy with the bicycles, but Bertie might've seen something."

Amos nodded and ducked through the window again, leaving the marshal to use the door. Thank heavens Shaw wasn't one of those ponderers who had to know all the facts before taking any action. He'd accepted Amos's assumption of Dunbar's guilt without batting an eye. Probably because Dunbar was the only outsider to suspect. Other than Amos. But he was here and the Pinkerton was not, so no debate was required.

What he *did* require was a horse. Or a bicycle. Something to carry him at greater speed than his legs. For the marshal was right—the footprints headed west.

Amos pushed up from his crouch just as Shaw rounded the corner. "This way." Amos waved for the marshal to follow him and jogged toward the station house. The greater the distance from the telegraph office, the higher the grass, which meant he couldn't see the footprints, but that didn't matter. The station house was the only logical place for Dunbar to secrete a horse.

Shaw loped up beside him, his longer legs carrying him into the lead.

"Mal! Wait!" An out-of-breath female voice rang out behind them.

The marshal skidded to a halt.

Amos kept going. Shaw could wait if he wanted. Amos was under no such compunction. The town could be under Indian attack, and he'd still find a way to go after Grace.

He reached the house, ran past the front porch, and slowed as he rounded the far corner. Even without his glasses, he would have been able to see the evidence he'd been dreading. Ground chewed up by horse hooves. Boot prints and marks from a smaller shoe. Indistinct, as if the feet that had left them behind had been dragged.

Amos's chest squeezed. *Oh, Grace.* If only he had left the ladies to unload their bicycles on their own. If only he'd kept a better eye on Dunbar. If only—

A hand gripped his shoulder. Amos lifted his head and met the marshal's resolute gaze. "We both let her down, but that doesn't mean we can't make it up to her. We'll find her, Bledsoe."

"Mal knows every inch of the land around these parts."

Amos turned to find Emma Shaw striding toward them, her face taut with worry even as her eyes radiated faith in her husband and in a source greater than all of them. Another woman tagged behind. Dark hair, a bit wild and unruly, and a frown that turned her otherwise pretty face into a pinched mask that warned him to keep his distance.

Fine with him.

"We need horses." Amos turned his attention back to Shaw. "They can't be too far ahead."

"You can take mine," Emma offered, and Amos found himself suddenly grateful for her intrusion.

"Thanks." He gave her a quick nod. "He's after the documents, and judging by the mess I found in her office, he figured out she's not going to hand them over willingly. I'm certain he's working for Haversham, but I'm praying that as a Pinkerton, he'll have enough moral fiber left to keep him from going so far as to torture an innocent woman to get the information he seeks."

"I wouldn't count on that."

Amos scowled at the dark-haired woman. "Why not?"

She stared right back. Angry, defiant. And clutching a book in her right hand that looked like a Bible. "Because he ain't a Pinkerton. And he's already proved himself a killer."

26

The man in glasses paled at her words. Helen inwardly winced. Perhaps she'd been too blunt, but they didn't have time to sugarcoat things. Not since that name-stealing skunk had Grace.

"How do you know?" Bledsoe took a step toward her. The marshal put a restraining hand on the fellow's chest and halted his progress.

Helen took her own step closer. She wasn't afraid of the man bristling in front of her. She knew how fragile hope could be and how hard a person would fight to hold onto the thinnest thread. But he needed to understand what they were up against. The truth might be brutal, but it would serve Grace better than wishful thinking.

"I know because I found the real Elliott Dunbar left for dead out in the pecan grove near the farm." She handed Lee's Bible to Emma. "I found this in his saddlebags yesterday when I ran across his abandoned horse on my way home from church, but I didn't realize what it meant until this morning when I saw the Family Records page. That's when the truth clicked, and I rushed straight here."

Emma flipped a couple pages then read the top name out loud. "Elliott Leander Dunbar, born April 7, 1865." She frowned. "So the man you just told me about, the one you've been nursing, is the *real* Pinkerton agent?"

Helen nodded. "Yep. That other fella stole Lee's papers. Right after he shot him off his horse, bashed him in the skull, and left him to bleed to death in the scrub brush."

Bledsoe shrank back. "Oh, Grace . . ." His voice cracked.

Emma moved past Malachi and touched Bledsoe on the arm. "Grace is a fighter, Amos. And she's clever. She'll be all right."

The marshal placed his palm at the small of Emma's back and nodded, as if a few sappy words would make a difference. They didn't need platitudes. They needed action.

"She carries a derringer," Shaw said, the first practical thing to come out of this conversation. "And she knows how to use it. Pulled it on me once."

"I know about the gun." Bledsoe paced to the station house wall and kicked it with the toe of his shoe. "But if she has it, why didn't she use it already? If nothing else, the sound of the gunshot would have alerted the town and brought us running."

"Maybe in the panic she forgot or . . . didn't get a chance." Emma tried to make it sound harmless, but she wasn't fooling anyone.

A big burly fellow versus the tiny telegraph operator? Helen's mouth tightened. He could overpower her in a snap of his fingers.

"Whatever her reason for not firing it," the marshal said with a firm voice, "she still has the weapon with her, and it's concealed. Dunbar, or whatever his name is, won't even know she has it. That will give her an advantage."

Only if the imposter didn't keep her tied up, which of course he would. Helen kept that thought to herself, though. Stating the obvious never helped. They were all worried about Grace, and Helen had pieces of the puzzle that could help find her friend.

"His name's Lockhart," Helen announced.

All three heads swung around to look at her.

"The man at my cabin has been either unconscious or delirious with fever since I found him on Friday, but his fever broke this morning, and he told me that he recognized the fellow who attacked him. Milton Lockhart, Haversham's second-in-command at the mine." She glanced at Emma, then the marshal, then finally screwed up her courage to face Bledsoe again. "Lee suspects that Lockhart's the shooter who took down Grace's father."

Bledsoe grabbed the marshal's arm. "We've got to go. Now!"

"I know, but we've got to play this smart, too." Malachi tugged free of the other man's hold, then hunkered down to examine the markings Lockhart had left behind in the dirt. Then his gaze lifted to the road. "There's no distinguishing marks, no nicks in a hoof or missing shoe. And his path leads straight to the road. We'll have to ride slow and watch for a trail that leaves the main path if we hope to find him holed up somewhere."

The marshal pushed to his feet and rubbed a hand over his face. "A man like Lockhart doesn't strike me as the hole-up-in-the-middle-of-nowhere type, though. He's used to his comforts, to getting whatever he wants with a wink and a smile, especially where females are concerned. Even staying in the jailhouse, he convinced Ann Marie to bring him breakfast the last two mornings and flirted with Katie enough after church that she brought by extra pillows and blankets for his cot yesterday afternoon along with a dozen of her famous pecan pralines."

Helen frowned at the knowledge that the pecans she'd harvested had gone to feed a monster's sweet tooth.

"He still has Detective Dunbar's credentials," Emma added, her face growing more troubled. "It would be easy for him to convince someone that he's a lawman transporting a prisoner. And since Grace has made a point never to venture outside Harper's Station while she's lived here, very few people would recognize her."

"So we bang on every door between here and Seymour," Mr. Bledsoe insisted, undaunted.

Helen had to admit to being impressed by his persistence. Most men would be hesitant to go up against a gunman with a history of putting bullets into people who got in his way.

"We will," the marshal said, but there was an odd reluctance in his voice. He turned to Emma, his jaw clenching. "But I've got to be back here before nightfall."

Emma's forehead scrunched. "Why? Finding Grace takes precedence over everything—"

"Not everything," Malachi ground out. "I'll do all in my power to find her, Em, but if he gets her to talk . . ."

Bledsoe blew out a harsh breath. "He'll come straight to the bank. And to the one person who can open the vault and retrieve the books."

"I can't leave you unguarded, Em. Don't ask me to." The tortured look on the marshal's face was too much to take. Helen glanced away.

Emma stepped close to her husband, her eyes fierce as she placed her palm against his cheek. "Then I guess you better find her before nightfall." She gazed steadily at him, her emotions raw and exposed but her conviction strong.

Helen swore she could feel the air thickening around her. What must it be like to feel such a connection to another person, as if speaking aloud were superfluous?

The charged moment ended when Emma stepped back. "I'll fetch Ben Porter from Tori's store. He knows the area farms and ranches better than anyone. Maybe he can help you narrow the search."

Malachi nodded. "Good. Then I need you to gather the women and put them on high alert. If Lockhart comes back to town, everyone needs to be ready. And armed."

"I'll tell Betty and the others at the farm," Helen volunteered.

"I'd offer to help keep watch in town, but I've got to get back to Lee. If Lockhart figures out he's alive, he'll be a target, too. And I didn't nurse him back to health just so that skunk could put another bullet in him."

"Are you sure he can be trusted?" the marshal asked.

Helen paused, met the lawman's gaze square on, and nodded. "Yes. He's the most protective man I've ever met. When I told him I had seen Lockhart in town, he tried to crawl out of bed, determined to get to Grace. I had to bar the door from the outside and shutter the window when I left just to make sure he'd stay put. The man's so weak he can barely feed himself, yet he's ready to take on Lockhart to save a woman he's never met. He can be trusted."

Bledsoe's fist unclenched and something nearing acceptance softened his features. Then his forehead scrunched. "Does he wear a mustache?"

Helen started a bit at the unexpected question, then smiled. Emma's brows shot up to her hairline, but Helen didn't care. "Yep. A real thick brown one, trimmed at the edges."

Bledsoe nodded. "Grace contacted the Pinkerton Agency about Detective Dunbar when he first arrived," he said. "Asked about his appearance. Brown hair. Mustache. Just like Lockhart. Beard was questionable, though."

"Lee doesn't wear a beard," Helen added, excited to help prove Lee's identity. "He's grown some stubble over the last few days while he's been recovering, but no regular beard. Oh! And his sister . . ." She snatched the Bible away from Emma and shoved it at Mr. Bledsoe. "Rachel." She pointed at the name written in the inscription. "Her married name is West. She lives in Carthage, Missouri. You can wire her. Get all the details on her brother you could ever want."

"Right now I'm more concerned with finding Grace than sorting out identities." Bledsoe handed the Bible back to Helen. "Although getting on the wire is a good idea. I'll telegraph the area lawmen, let them know about the false Pinkerton credentials and Lockhart's physical description." He turned to Malachi. "Would it be all right if I sent the information in your name? It would give the message more immediate credibility."

"Absolutely." The marshal thumped Bledsoe on the back. "I'll grab some extra weapons from the jailhouse. You need to be armed with something more than a bunch of dots and dashes."

Helen couldn't agree more. Bledsoe might have sufficient brainpower for the hunt, but only a fool would chase down a killer with no firepower. Thankfully, the telegraph operator felt no compulsion to argue.

"Thanks," Bledsoe said. "I can have the telegrams sent in ten minutes. I'll wire Seymour and Wichita Falls directly, then get my colleague in Denison to spread a wider net while we start the search."

Malachi nodded and strode toward town, taking his wife's arm as he went. "I'll have the horses saddled and ready in fifteen."

Bledsoe hurried after them. "Mrs. Shaw?"

Emma glanced around. "Yes?"

"When you gather the women, would you ask them to pray?" His voice thickened. "Grace is out there—alone—with a killer. She's going to need divine protection."

Emma touched his arm. "We will pray without ceasing until Grace is returned to us."

Bledsoe nodded his thanks, then set off at a jog toward the telegraph office. Malachi and Emma continued on to town, their steps long and hurried. Helen hesitated, leaning a hand against the station house wall.

Divine protection. How often had she prayed for that very thing when she lay huddled in a corner, begging the Lord to hide her from her father? To shield her from his fists? And how often had her father found her anyway?

Scripture calls you a hiding place, a mighty tower, a shield to those who put their trust in you. Yet sometimes evil penetrates your defenses. Helen bit her lower lip. *I never understood why.* She lifted her chin and squinted at the sky. *But deep in my soul, I believe you are good. I believe you are strong. And I believe that I don't have to understand everything. I just have to trust. So that's what I'm going to do. Trust you to take care of my friend. Please be her shield. And don't let evil win.*

27

"S he looks so normal." A muffled, unfamiliar feminine voice tickled the periphery of Grace's consciousness.

Grace struggled to open her eyes, but her lashes seemed to weigh a hundred pounds each. Something hazy tugged at her memory. Like a dream, it dodged her grasp as wakefulness pulled her in the opposite direction. She considered surrendering to sleep in order to chase the elusive dream, but in the center of the fog filling her mind, one small pebble of certainty refused to blow away in the mist.

Danger.

She was in danger. She had to wake. Had to fight. Escape.

"She doesn't *look* mad, but she must be if she drowned her own child."

A child? Was it a child who was in danger? Grace needed to shake off this unnatural lethargy. Now. She tried again to lift her eyelids and managed the tiniest slit.

"Will she hang, do you think?" A dark-haired woman in a black dress stood a few feet away, sniffing her disapproval. Only a touch of white lace at her collar and cuffs softened the severity of her appearance—that and the flirtatious smile she aimed at the man beside her between sniffs. The smile vanished, however, as she leaned forward and scowled at Grace. "She *should* hang, if you ask me, mad or not. Any mother who would kill her own child deserves to die."

Grace tried to shout a denial, but all that escaped her raspy throat was a quiet moan. The woman jumped back at the sound.

"There's nothing to fear, ma'am. Not while I'm around."

That voice! That slick, arrogant, womanizing voice. Grace's stomach clenched as memory raced back. Dunbar.

He strutted into Grace's narrow field of vision with a cocksure smile on his face and swagger emanating from every pore. The woman gazed up at him hungrily, as if he were a slice of chocolate cake with buttercream icing.

Which was odd since there was a heavy odor of—Grace sniffed—manure hanging about the place. She pried her lids open another smidgen, careful not to moan again and draw unwanted attention.

"I'll make sure no harm comes to you or your father," Dunbar assured the woman. "But as a precaution, when you bring dinner out later, just leave it on the ground outside the door and knock to let me know it's ready. She'll be awake by then, and I don't want her to frighten you." He stepped closer to the woman and reached out to cup her cheek. "When the madness comes upon her, she can chill the bones with her screams."

The woman shivered and leaned closer to him. The deceitful detective wrapped an arm around her shoulders. "If you happen to hear strange noises, just ignore them, darlin'. I do my best to keep her calm, but I can't keep her sedated all the time. The doctor warned that too much laudanum can be dangerous, and while her destiny lies either at the end of a rope or in a locked room at an asylum somewhere, I wouldn't be able to live with myself if I unintentionally hastened her demise. She's still a child of God, even if Satan has broken her mind."

"You're such a good man, Detective Dunbar. This world needs more men like you."

Grace's stomach roiled, either as an effect of the heavy dose of laudanum Dunbar had poured down her throat or from the naïve woman's syrupy adoration.

The two stood together by a dark wooden beam. Gardening implements and pieces of harness hung on the wall behind them. Straw littered the floor between them and where Grace lay on her side.

A barn. They must be in a barn. But where? On whose property?

Grace stared harder at the woman, trying to make out her features. Thin streaks of gray threaded through the brown bun pulled tightly at her nape. Her face showed a few lines but no discernable wrinkles. Not a young woman, but not terribly old, either. Yet Dunbar mentioned a father, not a husband. So a spinster? A widow?

Whoever she was, she was ripe for Dunbar's picking. And since the father was not the one seeing to the Pinkerton and his *prisoner's* comfort, Grace concluded he was probably infirm or, at the very least, uninterested in the people taking shelter beneath his roof.

Dunbar had mentioned dinner, so it must still be daytime. Grace strained to hear noises from outside the walls. Anything to help her piece together where she was. People. Horses. Wagons. A train whistle.

Nothing.

So they weren't in a town, which made sense. He'd not want to move too far from Harper's Station if he believed she'd hidden the documents there.

The fog continued receding from Grace's brain, and her eyelids felt lighter, but she didn't open them further. Better for Dunbar to believe she remained insensate. What she did do was rock forward very gently. He'd laid her down on her right side, and her derringer was strapped to her right thigh. When she moved, she felt the bruising from lying atop the hard metal. Thank God! Dunbar hadn't found the weapon.

She gently tested her arms. Her left arm refused to budge. She glanced away from her captor to examine her hands. Rope bound her wrists. She wiggled her fingers and silently breathed a sigh of relief when they moved on command.

"You get on back to your father, now, Irene," Dunbar drawled. "And be sure to thank him again for his hospitality. My horse couldn't continue on much longer with the double load. I'll try not to inconvenience you for long."

Irene smiled. "It's no inconvenience, I assure you. Father and I are glad to aid an officer of the law. Besides, you paid well above what lodging and food would require."

Dunbar dipped his chin and doffed his hat. "The Pinkertons thank you for your gracious assistance, ma'am. But I do have one request. You must not tell anyone of our presence here, for your own safety. The woman's brother insists she is innocent despite all evidence to the contrary and has attempted to cut me down on more than one occasion in a misguided effort to rescue his sister."

Irene gasped, her gaze raking the detective from head to toe. "You're not injured, I hope?"

The cocky grin reemerged. "No, ma'am. The fellow's a telegraph operator. Worthless with a gun. Outwitting him was no hardship, but I'd hate for you or your father to be caught in the crossfire should he somehow track us down."

"I'll not say a word," Irene vowed, "and I'll ensure that Father keeps quiet as well."

"You're a fine woman, Irene Gladstone. God surely blessed me when he brought me to your door."

Irene Gladstone. Grace filed the name away even as she cringed at the blasphemy of her abductor claiming God's guidance. The scripture was true indeed about Satan masquerading as an angel of light.

However, as soon as the door closed behind the starry-eyed Miss Gladstone, the demon showed his true colors.

"You can stop pretending to be asleep, Grace." Dunbar stalked across the dusty floor and leaned his face close to hers. "Now that we have a little privacy, we can get down to business."

Rough arms jerked her into a sitting position. The straw beneath her shifted, and her head spun at the sudden movement.

"I don't know where the documents are!" Grace hunched forward, desperate to stop her stomach from revolting. The effects of the laudanum might be clearing from her mind, but they lingered in her belly. Not that she would mind spewing what little was left of her breakfast all over the man in front of her, but she'd rather not cover herself with it in the process.

"Now, Grace." Dunbar dragged a milking stool over to where she sat and planted himself on its seat directly in front of her. Then he winked at her as if this were some kind of game. "I like you, sweetheart. I really do. Not many people are clever enough to fool me, but you managed. At least for a while. I can appreciate that. Respect it even." He smiled as he paid her the ridiculous compliment, leaning forward to rest his forearm on his knee. "But Chauncey is paying me good money to retrieve those papers, and if he loses *his* fortune . . . well, I'll be losing mine as well, won't I? Can't have that."

Grace glared at him.

He chuckled. "Still got your spunk, I see. Well, that won't last long." He flattened his palms against his thighs and pushed to a standing position. Then he strode over to her, grabbed her bound wrists, and yanked her to her feet.

"Let me go!" She struggled against his grip as he pulled her toward the wall, but he paid her as much heed as a buffalo would a fly. So she screamed, loud and long.

Dunbar shot her an impatient glance, then spun her around and shoved her against the wall, pinning her arms above her head with one hand. "No one's going to come, Grace. They think you're deranged, remember?"

She did. She remembered how Dunbar had told Irene to ignore any screams she heard, which meant he expected her to scream. Because he was going to hurt her.

The dull sense of danger that had weighed on her since he'd barged into her office that morning sharpened into a fine point, swiftly honed by the terrifying images springing to mind of blood and bruises and death.

Dear heavens. What was he going to do to her?

Her fear must have pleased him, for he smiled, his cold eyes crinkling at the corners. "Now you're starting to understand, my dear." He ran a finger along the edge of her face in a calculated caress that made her weak stomach lurch. She jerked her head away from the touch, but her defiance failed to deter him. His hand cupped the inside of her exposed upper right arm where it bent near her ear and slid upwards, straightening her arms overhead, the rough wood of the wall catching on her sleeves. By the time his left hand met the right at the rope around her wrists, her arms were fully extended.

"Here we go." And with a flex of his biceps, he lifted her slightly to the right and snagged her bindings on a vacant hook. He stepped back to inspect his handiwork and gave a nod of approval.

Her feet still touched the floor—barely—and the wall offered a bit of support, but the hook kept her arms immobilized.

So much for reaching her derringer.

"Now, Miss Mallory, let's get down to business, shall we?" He stripped out of his coat, hung it neatly on a second hook about two feet to her left, then rolled up his sleeves.

While he fiddled with his clothes, Grace fiddled with her ropes. She raised up on her tiptoes to try to unhook herself, but her arms were already too extended. The inch she gained made no difference. She tugged downward, testing the strength of the hook, but it was anchored to the wall. It didn't so much as wiggle.

"Writhing around like that will only tire you, Grace. If you want down, all you have to do is answer my question. Where are the documents?"

She ceased her struggling, realizing he was right. Even if she somehow managed to get herself free of the hook, she'd not get any farther, not with him less than three feet away. "I already told you that I don't know. Nothing has changed." She eyed him warily. "Torturing me won't work, because I can't tell you what I don't know."

His hand flew up to cover his heart, and he staggered back a mocking step. "You wound me, Grace. Torture? How uncivilized. I'm a businessman, not a monster. We're simply here to negotiate a deal. You have the books—the *real* books—that your father removed from my employer's library. I wish to acquire them."

He extracted a very long, very pointed hunting knife from a sheath at his belt. He stepped close to her, lifted the blade between their faces, and ran his thumb along the sharpened edge. Then his left hand came toward her face. She cringed, tried to pull away, but he didn't touch her skin. Instead he captured a piece of hair that had fallen free of its pins. He stretched the tress out in front of her, lifted the knife, and sliced off a lock with a single twist of his wrist. He held the severed hair between his thumb and forefinger, then rubbed it until it scattered strand by strand onto the floor.

He lifted his icy gaze to hers, that smug smile still curving his lips. "You'll give me what I want, Grace. There's no question about that. All we have left to haggle over is the price to be paid." He lifted the knife again, examined the blade, then pointed the tip at the tender spot beneath her chin.

Grace's pulse thundered in her veins. She lifted her chin away from the sharp point and blinked terrified tears from her eyes. He couldn't kill her, not if he wanted the information she held. Yet as a warm droplet of what could only be blood ran slowly down the front of her throat, she found little comfort in that logic.

"The price is up to you, sweetheart," her captor taunted, his grip on the blade steady. Inescapable. "The longer you hold out, the higher the cost."

28

Amos sat atop his borrowed horse, a borrowed gun belt around his waist, and a borrowed revolver in a holster that made his thigh itch. He'd never carried a gun. In Denison there'd been no need. In fact, the businessmen of the community frowned upon such behavior and bemoaned the presence of uncivilized ranch hands who insisted on riding into town armed. Amos had supported the ordinance banning weapons within the city limits and felt a bit hypocritical wearing one now. But this wasn't Denison, and with Grace in Lockhart's hands, civility was the last thing on Amos's mind.

"Well?" Amos tossed out as soon as Malachi Shaw rode within shouting distance, though the frown on the marshal's face boded ill.

Shaw reined in his dun gelding and leaned forward in the saddle. "No clear path. An equal number of tracks lead north and south. I looked for deeper prints, knowing they'd be riding double, but the ground is so hard, all the markings look the same. If I were to guess, I'd say south toward Seymour. It's smaller than Wichita Falls and closer to Harper's Station, but he could have just as easily taken the road north. I can't be sure."

"Then we need to split up." Amos knew the marshal wouldn't like it, but it was the best option. He wasn't about to trust Grace's safety to guesswork or gut instinct. "I'll head south."

"I'll go with you." Shaw gave him a hard look, promising retribution if Amos argued.

Amos gave a single, hard nod.

"Good." Shaw eyed the large man at the rear of the party seated on a black elephant. Well, in truth it was a horse, but the massive creature looked like it carried a healthy dose of pachyderm blood in its veins. "Ben, you go north," the marshal delegated.

The freighter nudged his monster horse forward and pulled a pair of folded papers from his front pocket. After unfolding each one and giving them a quick glance, he handed the top one to Shaw. "Tori gave me the lists she keeps of all the farmers and ranchers in the area whom we've approached about our delivery service. I've put stars by the names of the folks I think Lockhart would be most likely to target. Bachelor residences and smaller families with unmarried daughters or discontented wives who might prove susceptible to Lockhart's charm."

"Thanks." Shaw scanned the list then refolded it and stuffed it inside his vest. "A narrowed search will save valuable time."

But it could also cause them to miss Grace entirely if their assumptions about Lockhart's patterns were inaccurate. Amos would rather leave no stone unturned, but the more time he wasted looking in the wrong places, the more time Grace spent at Lockhart's mercy. And Lockhart had no mercy.

Amos nudged the dappled mare Shaw's wife had loaned him and trotted to the junction site. He turned the horse south, then urged her into a canter, trusting the marshal to catch up.

He tried to comfort himself with the fact that they were tackling the problem intelligently. Culling their search options, like striking unnecessary words from a long telegram. Smart. Efficient.

But if they cut the wrong name from the list, Grace would pay a hefty price.

"Arms sore?"

Grace glared at Dunbar. He sat in front of her on the milking stool, enjoying a plate of roasted chicken, carrots, greens, and cornbread slathered with butter. He'd offered the second plate to her in exchange for the information he sought. She'd refused, of course, which led to him dumping the contents onto the barn floor in front of her and grinding the delicious-smelling food into the straw with the heel of his boot.

He pointed a fork toward the hook above her head. "I can let you down whenever you're ready. Just say the word."

The temptation was growing harder to combat. Her shoulders screamed for relief from their unnatural position. She'd lost feeling in her hands thirty minutes ago, about the time her lower back started throbbing.

"All you have to do is answer my question, Grace, and the pain will stop."

She couldn't. It would put Emma in danger. She just had to hold on until help arrived.

If it arrived.

No. *When* it arrived.

Amos would have noticed her disappearance. He would have informed the marshal, and the two of them would be searching for her.

But would they get here in time?

Please, Lord. Help them find me.

Because as much as Dunbar enjoyed playing the nonchalant businessman, he was running out of time, and he knew it. His cocky smiles had grown ragged around the edges, his questioning more frequent and pointed. When he'd first snagged her wrists on the hook, he'd seemed content to let gravity and her imagination do the convincing for him. Every time she moaned and shifted her weight to a different leg or rolled her neck in an effort to stretch her aching muscles, he'd offer to let her down, just as he was doing now.

And like all the previous offers, Grace refused this one as well, with a shake of her head and pressing her lips into an uncompromising line.

The way his eyes narrowed in response worried her as he dragged his last piece of cornbread through the chicken grease on his plate and shoved it into his mouth. His patience was thinning.

Yet it was the thinning of her resolve that truly had her concerned. The weakness in her body was wearing on her mind.

All at once, Dunbar lurched up from his seat and hurled his plate against the wall, mere inches from her head. Grace yelped and twisted away from the shattering stoneware, closing her eyes against the shards that peppered her face.

Rough fingers grabbed her cheeks and jerked her head forward. Her eyes flew open. Dunbar glared down at her, his painful grip tightening to the point that her teeth ached. "Where are the documents, Grace?"

She said nothing.

"Tell me!" Still gripping her cheeks, he slammed her head back against the wall. Grace cried out as pain ripped through her skull. Tears welled in her eyes, but she held her silence. Dunbar cursed and released her, tossing her head backward as he did so. It bounced off the wall a second time, and Grace whimpered.

She could last a little longer. She had to. For Emma. For her father.

Give me strength, she begged. At the same moment the prayer lifted from her heart, a promise from scripture settled in her mind.

"'Ye are of God, little children, and have overcome them.'" The words fell from her lips of their own volition. "'Because greater is he that is in you, than he that is in the world.'"

Dunbar scowled. "What?"

Grace lifted her head from where it lolled against her chest and spoke again. Louder. "'Ye are of God, little children, and have overcome them: because greater is he that is in you, than he that is in the world.'"

Dunbar turned away from her and stalked toward the milking stool. "I guess we don't have to pretend anymore, do we?" he scoffed. "You've gone mad for real."

She smiled, feeling more powerful in that moment than she had ever felt in her life. The fact that she was bound, bruised, and fettered to a barn wall didn't signify. She had a weapon. A sword. The Word of God. And the Lord had just unsheathed it for her.

"'The foolishness of God is wiser than men,'" she quoted, "'and the weakness of God is stronger than men.'"

Dunbar gave a dismissive wave. "Keep telling yourself that, honey."

Oh, she planned to. Over and over.

"'In God have I put my trust: I will not be afraid what man can do unto me.'"

"You should be," Dunbar growled. "I can do quite a lot unto you. None of it pleasant."

He reached for the knife sheathed at his waist, but when his hand closed around the hilt, he hesitated. Then he smiled, his arrogance surging back to life as he lifted his hand away from the blade and stalked back toward her like a jungle cat ready to toy with its prey.

"Not only can I do unto you," he purred, "but I can do unto those you care about."

Grace flinched before she could stop herself.

Dunbar chuckled. "Aha. Now we're making progress. Just had

to find the right currency." He stroked a single finger along her hairline, past her temple, over the curve of her ear.

She grimaced at his touch but refused to let him cow her again. God had given her strength, and she would not forfeit that advantage, no matter what he did. She just had to stay focused.

"It's obvious to me that the documents are hidden somewhere in Harper's Station."

Focus, Grace. Don't let him see your reaction.

"And they're not in your rooms." His finger passed beneath her earlobe and drew a line down her neck. "I know because I searched them last Sunday after good old Amos collected you for church."

Grace blinked. He'd been in her room? Touching her things? A shiver ran over her skin. How had she not noticed? Was he really so good that he'd left no trace, or had she been so distracted by her own scheming that she'd failed to see the signs? Now that she thought about it, he had been late for the service, sneaking into the back sometime after the singing had begun.

"And if they aren't in your rooms, that means they're somewhere else. In someone else's rooms." His finger traced her collarbone through the fabric of her blouse. "Perhaps with the shopkeeper. Or stashed at the clinic." His hand crept up to her neck, his fingers gently cupping her throat. "Or maybe they're with that banker lady who's always sticking her nose into everyone's business."

His fingers tightened. Not enough to truly choke her, but enough to let her know he could. Easily.

Grace lifted her quivering chin and forced herself to keep breathing.

Slowly he slid his hand away. "How badly do you want to protect your friends, Grace? Enough to give me what I want?" He moved his hand to the back of her neck and tugged her close as if he wanted to kiss her.

She pulled away, not that it did any good. His strength dwarfed hers.

He lowered his face, his eyes locking on hers, his mouth inches away from her own. "I have friends, too, Grace," he said, so close she could feel the words more than hear them. "Friends who would be more than happy to sweep into Harper's Station and help me look for those missing documents. Friends with guns and low moral character who might get a bit distracted by all the unprotected females running about the place. We would come in the dead of night when only one man stood in our way. A man who sleeps in a second-story room on the west side of the station house and could be taken out with a well-aimed bullet." Dunbar inched closer, until she could feel the rasp of his beard against her chin. "So you see, it's up to you. Tell me where the documents are, and I'll sneak back to town tonight and retrieve them with minimal disruption to the people you care about. Or don't tell me, and I'll call in the cavalry to help me . . . look."

A devil's bargain. One with no good outcome. If she told him about the books in the bank vault, he'd head there straightaway while Malachi and the other men were out searching for her. Emma—beautiful, stubborn Emma—wouldn't cooperate. She and the aunts would probably try to take Dunbar out themselves. No telling how many ladies would end up injured or dead.

Holding her tongue wasn't much better. She'd buy a little time, but the results could be even more catastrophic. Harper's Station would be annihilated.

Lord, what am I to do?

"Oh, and just to give you one more thing to think about," Dunbar continued, finally leaning away from her and allowing her to catch a clean breath, "if I have to go hunting with my friends, I promise to personally take out Bledsoe. What do you think? A bullet to the heart, so it's over nice and quick, seems like the most humane way to go."

Grace's heart stopped. She lunged toward her captor, the hook pulling her up short. "You can't!"

"I've done it before." He smirked. "Oh, that's right. I haven't told you my secret yet, have I?"

He leaned close and whispered in her ear. "I'm not really a Pinkerton. Not even a dishonest one." He straightened and crossed his arms over his chest. "Name's not even Dunbar. It's Milton Lockhart." He winked at her. "You can call me Milt." He watched her like a mean-spirited boy about to tear the wings from a butterfly. "I shot the real Dunbar and left him for dead after helping myself to his badge and papers."

Grace flinched at the complete lack of remorse in his tone.

"Kid followed me from Colorado, so I had to get rid of him. But stealing his identity? Well, now, that was just downright fun. Fooled that imbecile marshal of yours—shoot, the entire town."

He rocked back on his heels, his chest puffing up as if he were actually proud of himself.

"But you know what was even more fun?"

Grace closed her eyes. *Stop listening.*

"What I enjoyed most was sitting atop the bank building in Denver . . ."

Grace squeezed her eyes more tightly shut. *Stop listening.* A tear formed behind her lids and leaked from the corner of her lashes. *Stop listening!*

" . . . aiming my rifle . . ."

She whimpered, then hummed in her throat as if the noise would block out what was coming.

" . . . and shooting your father right in the chest."

No! She struggled anew against her bonds, uncaring that the rope cut deeper into her wrists. She saw her daddy fall. Saw the blood. Remembered the helplessness. The anger. The abject grief. And the beast responsible stood in front of her. Chuckling.

"I lingered, you know. Watched him fall. Watched the crowd

scatter. Watched for you. But you didn't show. Just let your father bleed all over the street. Alone."

She opened her eyes but didn't see her captor. All she saw was her father lying in that street, rubbing his spectacles. Signaling her to run. To spare her life, but more than that, to resist evil and protect the cause of right.

That final act of courage, of selflessness, crept under her skin. Sharpened her wits. Stiffened her determination.

Lockhart thought to weaken her spirit, to force her into a corner with an impossible choice.

Well, she happened to know someone who specialized in the impossible. She'd not leave the future in Lockhart's hands, not when there were better hands for the job.

Grace drew in a steadying breath, then stared *Milt* directly in the face. "'The salvation of the righteous is of the Lord: he is their strength in the time of trouble.'"

His mouth pursed and the veins in the side of his head started to bulge. "Not this garbage again."

She ignored him and continued on, her soul and her voice growing stronger with each word. "'He shall deliver them from the wicked, and save them, because they trust in him.'"

Eyes glowing with rage, Lockhart uncrossed his arms, lunged forward, and slapped Grace across the face. "Shut up!"

Her cheek stung and her jaw ached, but her heart clung fast to hope.

29

"G et back in that bed, *Leander*, before I fetch the rope and tie you up again." Helen stood, hands on hips, and glowered at her hardheaded mule of a patient, who didn't have the sense God gave a blind armadillo.

"Get out of my way, *Helen*, before I pick you up and move you myself." The fool stood in his bare feet, shredded trousers, and mussed hair like some kind of crazed warrior, ready to defy any obstacle that dared block his path.

Well, she dared. And she wasn't backing down.

"You were practically dead yesterday. It's too soon to be out of bed, and you know it. Let the marshal handle it."

He strode toward her without a wince, the crutch he'd fashioned from a tree branch and a wad of old rags supporting him as he moved. Bearing weight on his injured leg must have been excruciating, yet he didn't let on.

Helen had to admit that he'd accomplished more than she'd ever thought possible while she'd been gone. He'd found his discarded trousers, somehow managed to get his one good leg into the right side and fastened the top about his waist with a white braid that seemed to have been woven from strips sliced from one of the extra bandage rolls. Not only that, but he'd bypassed her barring of the door by taking the entire thing off its hinges. Then he'd proceeded to make his way to the pecan grove, find a suitable branch to use as a crutch, and drag it back to the cabin.

Helen eyed his flushed face and perspiring brow, then frowned. The starch went out of her spine as she hurried to his side and lifted the back of her hand to his forehead. Warm.

"You're pushing yourself too hard, Lee. Please. I know you want to help Grace, but killing yourself in the process does no one any good. Think of Rachel. Think of—"

His rigid posture relaxed just a bit, and something softened in his eyes. "Think of who, Helen?"

She turned away, marched over to the stove, and started slamming pans around. Well, pan, really. There was just the one. But she made the most of it, getting a spoon in on the action. She needed to fill the silence with something, *anything*, other than the words burning on the tip of her tongue.

Then a hand touched her shoulder.

Slowly, taking special care not to move too fast and throw him off-balance, Helen turned toward the man who was trying to walk out of her life. She might be an expert at avoiding men, but that didn't make her a coward.

Lee met her gaze, his eyes penetrating. "Think of who, Helen?"

"Think of me. All right?" She twisted sideways and tossed her spoon back into the pan on the stove. The rattle echoed loudly in the room, but not as loudly as the thumping of her heart. "I gave up four days of my life saving your sorry hide," she spouted, "and you just want to throw it all away, as if it doesn't matter. Well, it does matter. *You* matter."

"So does Grace Mallory." His quiet voice, so calm and controlled, stoked her outrage.

"You think I don't know that? That I don't care?" She sidestepped him and paced to the hole where her door used to be then pivoted sharply to face him. "Grace is my friend. I want to do whatever I can to help her. But you killing yourself won't do her any good. You're barely strong enough to stand. How do you think you're going to mount a horse with that leg? If you can even *find* a horse. Yours is roaming the countryside at the moment."

The softness left Lee's gaze. His eyes narrowed in warning. "*Helen.*"

"Do you think I don't understand? That I don't know what it's like to feel powerless when someone stronger steals away something you are responsible for? Something you love?" She stormed back toward him and jabbed a finger in his face. "You're not the only one to grow up in a house filled with violence, under the thumb of a man who thought he controlled you. Who stole everything you ever loved and used it against you.

"I watched my mother die, Lee." Helen's arm fell to her side. "Watched her body break and her spirit wither away. And I was powerless to stop it. I know how helplessness eats at your soul and drives you to take crazy risks. I went so far as to purposely incite my father's wrath so he would take his nightly anger out on me instead of her, but it didn't save her. She died anyway."

He looked like he wanted to say something, but she shook her head. She wasn't finished.

"I know how much you want to help Grace. How you feel like she's your responsibility, your victim to save. But you're not the only one shouldering this load. There are good men looking for her. Smart and capable men who know Grace personally and care about her. Doesn't the Bible say there's a time to kill and a time to heal? Well, this is your time to heal, Lee. So stay put and heal. Please."

"I can help, Helen." He limped toward her, a muscle in his jaw twitching each time he put weight on his left leg. "I might not know Miss Mallory as well as these friends of yours, but I know

Lockhart. I've studied him for months. I know how he thinks, the games he plays. My information can aid their search."

Helen swallowed. He was right. And heaven help her, when he looked at her with those heroic green eyes, glowing with the fire of determination, she melted inside.

Yet not to the point of becoming a mindless puddle. The man still needed a keeper, and she was the only one fit for the job.

"All right," she said. He blinked, no doubt stunned by her capitulation. *Well, brace yourself, cowboy. This bronc ain't done buckin' just yet.* "I want Grace found as much as you do, and if you have information that will help, I'll get you in on the rescue action. But on my terms."

The smile stretching beneath his mustache faltered. "What terms?"

"The men will return to town at nightfall. Hopefully, they'll have found Grace by then. But if not, I'll be sure you're there to meet them. I'll borrow Betty's buckboard and drive you there. You are *not* to get anywhere near a horse."

His mustache twitched suspiciously, but his lips didn't curve. "I suppose I can live with that." He gave her a pointed look. "For now."

Helen ignored the qualifier. "And while we wait for the marshal and the others to return, you'll do nothing more strenuous than lie around and run your mouth with all that essential information you feel so compelled to impart."

"Anything else?" He spoke in a stern tone, but Helen was almost certain she saw a twinkle in his green eyes. It set her pulse to jumping like a pack of startled katydids.

"As a matter of fact, there is." She eyed him from top to bottom. "You're not going anywhere until we find you a decent pair of pants."

Lee laughed. The deep, rich sound echoed through the tiny room and flooded Helen's chest with an unfamiliar yet thoroughly delectable warmth. She wanted to grasp it, nestle it close, and never let it go.

But that would mean holding fast to the man before her. A man she had no right to hold.

Unless, of course, she was holding him in order to help him back to the bed, which might be required. As his laughter faded, so did his color, leaving him pale and bit unsteady on his feet.

Helen moved to his side and slid an arm about his waist. He smiled his thanks, a sheepish grin that seemed to admit his show of strength had been a thin veneer all along. It brought an answering smile to her lips, because it meant he trusted her enough to expose his weakness. Something people who'd grown up in their circumstances rarely did.

As she helped him to the bed, he wrapped his right arm around her shoulders. Surely just to ease his balance, but little frissons of awareness danced over her skin anyway. He limped, she supported, and the crutch mostly got in the way, but they managed to get to the bed in one piece. Not wanting to drop him into place and jar his wounded leg, Helen eased him down by sitting with him. His fingers dug into her upper arm as he let the crutch clatter to the floor and reached for the mattress with his left arm.

Thinking to fetch a cool cloth to wipe his brow, Helen started to rise, but Lee's grip held firm on her shoulder.

She turned to him, her brows arching in question.

"I'm sorry about your mother."

Five simple words shouldn't have such a profound impact on her, but they did. Helen's chin trembled slightly. She gritted her teeth to still the reaction. "Thank you," she whispered as she dipped her head, the empathy radiating in his gaze too much to absorb.

People had said the same words to her countless times at her mother's funeral, and even Betty and Katie had murmured similar sentiments when they learned of her history. Yet no one had ever spoken them with such depth of understanding, as if they recognized her pain because they had lived through it themselves. Somehow it hurt and healed at the same time.

He didn't say anything else for a long minute. Just sat next to her and gently rubbed her arm with the fingertips that draped over her shoulder. Then, after a final squeeze, he withdrew his arm and braced it behind his back to better support his weight.

"Lockhart is a master manipulator." Lee frowned at his injured leg, and Helen imagined the thoughts running through his head. Frustration at his limitations. Regret, perhaps even guilt, for letting himself be shot in the first place. As if he could have stopped such a thing from happening.

"We know," Helen tried to reassure him. She pushed to her feet and crossed to the washstand to pour him a glass of water and fetch a cool rag. "The marshal is taking that into consideration." She wrung out the excess water from the cloth, the droplets tinkling as they splashed into the basin. "Before I left town, I heard Tori say something to Emma about grabbing a list of all the ranchers and farmers in the area from her delivery records. She and Ben were going to mark the households that would be the most likely targets for a confidence man like Lockhart. Secluded places, homes with adult daughters or widows who would be susceptible to his flattery."

Lee straightened, his forehead wrinkling. "Wait. There was a woman. On the train." He shut his eyes tight. "Dark hair, I think. She wore a straw hat trimmed with a thick black ribbon. A schoolteacher."

Helen stilled halfway around the bed. The water sloshed slightly in the glass, but it made no sound. Neither did she. Not even to breathe. She wanted nothing to distract Lee from his recollections. This could be the key to finding Grace.

"She boarded the Fort Worth & Denver City line in Washburn." He moved his hands in the air as if physically arranging the train car and its passengers. "I was in the rear of the car, pretending to sleep with my hat pulled over my face. Lockhart sat four rows ahead, chatting across the aisle with some drummer selling patent medicines. The only females in the car were attached to families. Up front, a young wife, giggling and hanging on her husband's arm as if they were on their wedding trip. And in the rear opposite me, a middle-aged woman traveling with four children who seemed determined to either climb on her, climb on each other, or climb over the seat in front of them to annoy the other passengers. Then the teacher boarded, and Lockhart lost all interest in the drummer."

Lee finally opened his eyes, but his gaze remained unfocused and distant.

"Lockhart jumped to his feet to help her with her bag then offered to share his seat with her. She tried to refuse at first, but the only completely unoccupied seat was the one in front of the mother with the monkey children. When she pursed her lips in disapproval, Lockhart made some comment about how she reminded him of his favorite teacher, who'd been a strict disciplinarian but who'd also gone out of her way to ensure that he didn't fall behind when he had to miss school to work the family farm. He quoted a poem or something fluffy and romantic, and the woman smiled. A gentle steering was all it required after that for him to get her to sit with him.

"I tried to follow their conversation but only caught snatches of it here and there. She said something about her mother passing, which made sense because she was dressed in black. Probably traveling for the funeral." Lee turned his head, and his gaze sharpened as he met Helen's eyes. "Which means she wouldn't have been on your friend's list. If they were picking out homes with single women, they wouldn't choose an elderly couple."

Helen winced. "And if Lockhart had already made inroads with this woman on the train . . ."

"She would make the easiest mark," Lee finished. "He'll go to her."

Helen handed Lee the glass of water and draped the damp cloth over the end of the bed frame. "But where is she? Do you know her name?"

Lee chugged about half the water, then set the glass on the floor, the lines around his mouth tightening at the movement. Once upright again, he glanced at the ceiling. "The beginning of her name had something to do with feelings. Mad . . . Glad . . . Sad . . ."

"Madison? Gladney? Sadler?" Helen rattled off the first names that came to mind, but Lee shook his head and frowned.

"No." He heaved a sigh and stroked his mustache in a slow movement that tugged his cheek downward. "I need to see your friend's list. I'd probably recognize it if I saw it."

Helen gave a sharp nod. "I'll head to the farm and get the buckboard." She glanced through the open doorway. The afternoon sun already dipped lower in the sky than she would like. The sooner she got Lee to town, the sooner they could help find Grace. "Betty should have some overalls or trousers from her late husband that you can wear. I'll grab the first thing I see and be back in less than an hour." She shot him a pointed look. "In the meantime, get as much rest as you can. If we're going to find Grace, we need your mind sharp, not dull from exhaustion. Understood?"

He nodded. Helen turned to leave, but when his hand grabbed hers, she paused.

Twisting to face him, she tried to concentrate on the matter at hand and not on the distracting warmth of his fingers surrounding hers. "Yes?"

"Seymour." His green eyes bored into hers. "The woman disembarked in Wichita Falls like we did, but stayed at the depot. Lockhart waited with her, seeing to her luggage and whatnot.

If she wasn't continuing on to Fort Worth on the original train, she had to have been taking the spur to Seymour. It was the only other option."

Helen squeezed Lee's hand, trying to offer a generous portion of the one thing she usually kept in very scant supply—hope. "We'll find her."

He squeezed her hand in return. "I pray you're right."

30

That's the last one on the list." Malachi Shaw sighed heavily, then glared at the rapidly darkening sky.

They had just finishing questioning Mr. Bedford, father of two grown daughters—one of whom was betrothed to a ranch hand from the Rocking T over in Knox County, and one who was so painfully shy that she never once looked the marshal in the eye. She'd glanced briefly at Amos when he asked her a direct question about Lockhart, but even then, she stammered her answer and blushed furiously. Not exactly a woman who could be counted on to keep secrets. However, they'd searched the premises anyway. The house, the cellar, the barn. And came up empty. Again.

"I know you don't want to hear this, Bledsoe, but we've got to head back. We'll be pushing it as it is to get back before full dark hits."

Amos shook his head. "I can't go back. Not without Grace."

The marshal folded his hands over his pommel. "And I can't leave my wife unprotected."

"I know." Amos met his gaze. "I'm not asking you to."

Shaw's saddle creaked as he shifted his weight. "Look, Amos, I know what it feels like to have the woman you care about taken from you. I lived with that terror for hours piled upon hours when Angus got his hands on Emma last summer. It nearly drove me mad. You're desperate to do something, *anything*, to ensure her safe return, I get it, but you're a greenhorn out here. You don't know the land. Probably passable at best with a pistol, and your opponent is a stone-cold gunman. He might have reason to keep Grace alive for her information, but there's nothing to keep him from shooting you on sight."

"Then I'll have to make sure he doesn't see me." Amos set his shoulders, pretending he wasn't already saddlesore and exactly as green as the marshal portrayed him. His inexperience didn't matter. Grace mattered. And the longer they debated his retreat, the longer she remained in Lockhart's hands.

"Porter might have already found her," Shaw said, though they both knew it was a long shot at best. "Miss Mallory could be waiting for you in Harper's Station even now."

"If so, have her telegraph the depot in Seymour. I'll check a few more houses in the area with what little light is left, then head to town. I'll stop by the railroad's telegraph office, touch base with the sheriff to see if he has any news to report, then find a room for the night and start fresh at dawn."

Shaw raised a brow at him. "Folks aren't going to let you search their property without my badge to gain you access."

Amos shrugged. "Maybe not, but I can still ask questions. Still observe whatever is in the open. If nothing else, I can keep an eye out for Lockhart's horse."

"An animal with no distinguishing markings." The marshal sighed, his frustration palpable, surpassed only by Amos's own. "Lockhart must have chosen it for its very lack of memorable qualities. A chestnut quarter horse with no socks, no blaze, no fancy tooling on the saddle, nothing to make it stand out from any of a hundred others."

Amos jutted his chin forward. He refused to be discouraged.

He couldn't afford the luxury. "The man's clever, but he's not perfect. One of us will find him. And Grace. I have to believe that. And I have to keep pressing on in the meantime." He nudged his mount a few steps closer to the marshal. "Go home to your wife, Shaw. Keep her safe. That's your job. Mine is to find Grace, whatever it takes."

The marshal nodded and handed over the list they'd been working from. "Seymour's only about two miles away." He jerked his head toward the southwest. "If you spot something suspicious, don't go in on your own. Fetch Sheriff Tabor. He and his deputies have the authority and the experience to handle Lockhart."

Amos agreed without hesitation. He might be resolute about finding Grace, but he was no fool. Getting himself killed wouldn't set her free, it would only remove another obstacle from Lockhart's path. His opponent had captured the queen, but if Amos played a stealthy game, he just might get a pawn far enough across the board to get her back.

"God be with you, Bledsoe." Shaw tipped his hat.

"And with you," Amos returned.

As the marshal touched his heels to the flanks of his ugly dun gelding and urged the horse into a canter, Amos studied the list Shaw had handed him. Two homesteads that had not been marked for a visit lay between him and Seymour. About two dozen lay behind him, on the road back to Harper's Station. Grace could be at any one of them. Logic and laws of probability had already failed. Prayer and faith were still in play, but as much as Amos longed for clear direction from the Lord, he had yet to see a finger from heaven point the way.

"So what am I to do?" he mumbled under his breath. "Which way should I go?"

With the marshal heading north, it seemed illogical to cover the same ground, so Amos reined his mare toward Seymour.

About a quarter mile down the road, a narrow path veered

off to the west, not wide enough for a wagon. It was probably a shortcut the area children took on their way to the schoolhouse. Yet when Amos drew nearer, he discovered small arcs cut into the thin line of hard-packed dirt. Hoofprints.

His pulse ratcheted up a level. It could be nothing. After all, he didn't know the difference between a fresh track and a week-old one. But it could be something.

Riding on instinct and the hope that more than his gut was leading him down the narrow path, he nudged his mare to a trot and scanned the rapidly darkening area for anything out of the ordinary.

There, to the right. A small light bobbing as it moved east.

A lantern?

Pressure built in Amos's chest until he feared he might explode. He nudged his mount off the path, toward a stand of juniper bushes. The gray of twilight made it difficult to distinguish shapes in the distance, but it also offered cover in a land where flat terrain and few trees did little to hide a man's approach.

Amos dismounted, his eyes locked on the bobbing light. It disappeared around a dark shadow that must be a building. No light glowed from within, so a barn, perhaps?

Nervous energy flowed through Amos's veins as renewed hope surged to life in his heart. He looped his horse's reins over a low-hanging juniper branch, ran his palm over the handle of the Colt he'd borrowed, then crouched to make his height about the same as the scrub brush and slowly made his way toward the barn. After cresting a small rise, a second building came into view to the west. Light glowed around the edges of doorways and windows. A house. Would Lockhart be there instead?

No. The lantern light had moved east.

Carefully withdrawing the Colt from its holster, Amos held it ready as he dodged from bush to bush. Fifty feet. Twenty. Ten.

A female voice drifted toward Amos, freezing him in position.

He crouched as low to the ground as he could manage, hiding behind a pitifully thin juniper while he strained to decipher the conversation a few scant feet away.

" . . . brought you a pot of coffee too, warm from the stove."

A pause.

"It was no trouble, I assure you. Would you like anything else? A book to help pass the time, perhaps? . . . My father keeps a pair of carriage lanterns in the tack room. I could come in and light them for you, if you like."

Another pause. Amos tried to make out the second voice, but the low tones were too quiet. Muffled from inside the barn.

"Oh, well, if you're sure." The woman sounded disappointed, which speared hope through Amos's chest. Whoever she was speaking to didn't want her inside the barn. And it was *her* barn.

Only someone wielding recognizable authority could commandeer the control of another's property without an argument. Someone like a Pinkerton agent. Or a man posing as a Pinkerton.

"I know." The woman sighed. "I appreciate you taking such measures to protect us. You're a noble man, detective."

Detective. It had to be Lockhart. It *had* to be.

But Amos needed to be sure. The sheriff would require more than suspicions to mount an attack. He'd want proof. And Amos needed to see Grace with his own eyes, to confirm she was alive. His stomach churned at the thought of what state she might be in after being alone with Lockhart for so many hours, but he couldn't allow his mind to settle there. Wounds would heal, and he could love her through any other trauma that lingered. The important thing was that she be alive.

His legs started to cramp from holding their unnatural position for so long, but Amos didn't move as he waited for the woman with the lantern to return to the house.

"I'll bring breakfast out at first light," she said. "I know you want to get an early start." Something her companion said made her titter. "You're too kind . . . Well, then, good night."

The sound of a large wooden door dragging closed rumbled in the night air. At the same time, the lantern bobbed back into view around the corner. The woman carrying it was nearly invisible, dressed all in black, but she was a no-nonsense sort and marched back to the house at a smart clip, leaving Amos a clear path to the barn.

Stretching the kinks out of his legs, Amos stood and cautiously approached. Careful to make as little sound as possible, he crept forward and hid himself in the shadows of the barn wall. Holding his revolver aloft, he inched along the side of the building. When he reached the corner, he hesitated. A drop of perspiration trickled down the side of his face.

He could do this. For Grace.

Amos adjusted his grip on the gun, set his jaw, then slowly stepped away from the side of the barn and craned his neck around the corner.

No one in sight.

The breath he'd been holding whooshed from his lungs as he ducked back to his original position and gently pressed his spine against the wall. He closed his eyes, counted to three in an effort to calm his palpitating heart, inhaled a pair of deep breaths to settle his nerves, then strode around the corner, gun ready.

Only there was nothing to use it on. Which was good, of course, but as he stood back to examine the front of the barn, he realized he had a problem a gun couldn't solve. There were no open windows or doors. Everything had been shut up tight, and anything he tried to open would draw Lockhart's attention.

Amos frowned. There had to be something he could use. A loose board, a crack, some way to see inside. He ran his fingers lightly along the wood seams, finding nothing. Then he rounded the far corner, and a small beam of light grabbed his attention.

He hurried forward, weeds and prairie grass muffling his footfalls, until he stood opposite the glowing knothole aimed at his navel. In a heartbeat, Amos dropped to his knees and pressed his eye to the hole. What he saw sickened him.

Grace—beautiful, sweet, kind-hearted Grace—was tied to the wall like an animal. Arms above her head, hair falling in straggles around her face. Her head lolled forward, and an angry red mark blazed across her cheek.

Amos's heart ached at the evidence of exhaustion and abuse. Yet Lockhart was still here, so he must not have broken her spirit. She must still be fighting.

Good girl, Grace. Don't give up. I'm here. I'll help you.

Somehow.

The sound of something heavy scraping against the floor made Amos shift so he could look to his right.

Lockhart. Bent at the waist, dragging a half barrel across the barn floor. He grunted and strained against the weight of the makeshift trough, water sloshing over the edges as he moved. When he reached a spot a few feet from where Grace dangled, he halted.

"The price has just gone up again." Lockhart straightened, strode over to Grace, grabbed her arms near the elbows, and hoisted her down.

She collapsed against him, her legs unable to support her. Amos bit back a moan, the sight causing him physical pain. Lockhart hauled Grace toward the trough and tossed her to the ground in front of it.

Amos tensed. His grip on his gun tightened.

"Where are the documents, Grace?" Lockhart asked as he fisted his hand in the back of her hair and forced her head down toward the water.

Grace's eyes widened. Her bound hands latched onto the side of the barrel near her chest. "No!" She fought against his hold. "Please. Don't."

Lockhart jammed her head down. *Splash.* Her body jerked and her fists pounded the side of the barrel, but Lockhart held her down. Helpless. All she could do was scream, her underwater gurgles lashing Amos with desperate fury.

He lurched backward, away from the horrifying vision and thrust the end of his pistol into the knothole. Lockhart was *drowning* her. He had to do something. But shooting blind wasn't the answer. He might hit Grace.

As he hesitated, something hit *him.* Hard. Across the back of his head.

Amos crumpled.

31

Terror squeezed Grace's chest as Lockhart forced her head under the water. She pushed against the side of the wooden tub, trying somehow to gain leverage. Water filled her nose, increasing her panic. She squirmed and writhed, her mouth coming open in a desperate bid for air that didn't exist.

I don't want to die!

Her head grew light. Her body went limp. She couldn't fight anymore. Couldn't—

Lockhart yanked her hair and pulled her head out of the trough.

Grace coughed and sputtered. Gasped for air. Lockhart released her, leaving her on her knees, heaving. Wet hair draped over her face. She reached her bound hands up to push it away from her mouth, wanting nothing between her and the air. Her lungs burned and spasmed, rasping as they tried to expel the liquid from their depths.

"Feeling more cooperative yet?"

She ignored his question, too consumed with breathing to care about anything else.

When her lungs finally started to relax into a normal rhythm,

Lockhart's hand clasped her head again and pushed her back toward the barrel.

Grace's heart seized. "No!" Her neck muscles tightened in a vain attempt to halt the downward motion. "*Please . . .*" Hot tears ran down her cheeks.

The pressure eased slightly. "Where are the documents, Grace?"

"I—I don't know. I couldn't find them."

The pressure resumed, forcing her face closer to the water. Her chin broke the surface.

"Then where are the books?" Lockhart insisted. "The *real* books. The ones your father took from Haversham's library?"

Grace wept. She wanted to tell him, God help her. She wanted this torture to end. But telling him wouldn't spare her life. Lockhart would surely kill her as soon as he had what he needed. And then he'd go after Emma.

"*Where are the books?*" His deep voice boomed like thunder next to her ear.

"I . . . can't."

He shoved her down. This time she didn't fight. Not until her lungs pinched and instinct took over. Then she thrashed against his hold, not that it did any good. His weight pressed her down so deep that her forehead scraped the bottom of the barrel.

Then all at once his hold vanished. Her head flew up. Streaming hair whipped against her back as she threw her chin toward the ceiling and sucked in the air she craved. It took her a moment to realize her captor was striding away. Even longer to register the banging on the barn door.

Escape her only thought, Grace used her bound hands to tug herself onto shaking legs. Stumbling forward, she ran in the opposite direction. Away from the water barrel. Away from Lockhart.

Her derringer! Grace grabbed the fabric of her skirt and drew it upward as she ran. She should be able to extract it from the holster, but with her wrists bound, getting a proper grip on it would prove difficult. She only had one shot. If she fumbled it—missed—any advantage would be lost.

As she staggered deeper into the barn, her petticoats at half-mast, her toe collided with something metal hidden in the straw. She glanced down. A small pair of pruning shears. Dropped. Forgotten. An answer to the prayer she hadn't even uttered. Grace dove to her knees and snatched up the handles. The shears were stiff and rusty, but if she could pry them open . . .

" . . . man you warned me about, the telegraph operator. He's here!"

Grace froze. *Amos?*

Irene Gladstone's excited voice bounced through the rafters. "I caught him sneaking around the barn when I stopped to check on the stock in the paddock. He was peeping through a knothole then pulled a gun. I remembered what you said about your prisoner's crazy brother. I couldn't let him shoot you! So I extinguished the lantern, crept up behind him, and bashed him over the head with it."

"Where is he?" Lockhart's clipped tones contrasted sharply with Miss Gladstone's animated recounting.

"Just around the corner. I'll show you."

"I have to secure my prisoner first."

Footsteps echoed. Closer.

Grace fumbled the shears. She had to hide them.

Dragging her bound wrists across her body, she searched for the opening to her skirt pocket, but the slit eluded her. She whimpered. *Please. Oh, please.* She strained against the bindings, her right elbow poking out at a painful angle, but finally the tips of the shears found the opening. *Thank you, God!*

Grace jostled them all the way in a heartbeat before a vise closed around her protruding right arm.

"Come, Miss Mallory. No more hiding." Lockhart jerked her forward and dragged her back to where she'd first awoken, on the lopsided pile of straw outside the first stall.

"Good heavens!" Miss Gladstone declared. "What happened?"

Lockhart exuded a beleaguered sigh as he tossed Grace down on the straw and wrapped a leather strap around her middle, pinning her arms down atop her belly in the process. He pulled her back to her feet, cinched the strap so tight behind her back that it pinched her ribs, then fastened the remaining length to a metal hoop anchored in the wall behind her.

"I thought she might like to wash her face and clean up a bit after the long day, so I dragged the water barrel out here for her to make use of. Unfortunately, when I went to find the carriage lights you mentioned, she tried to drown herself." He wagged his head as he turned to consider Grace's sodden clothes and stringy hair. "The guilt is too much for her, I'm afraid. It's rotted what is left of her mind."

"Thank heavens you got to her in time." Miss Gladstone placed a hand to her throat. "I certainly feel no love for the pitiful creature, but I wouldn't want her to do herself in. Not in Papa's barn." She shivered at the grisly thought.

Grace considered arguing but decided to save her breath. Heaven knew she needed it.

"Well, my good timing was surpassed by your own, Irene. Subduing an intruder with only a lantern for a weapon? Such a courageous, resourceful woman. I'm overcome with admiration." He took the woman's arm and steered her toward the entrance as she beamed up at him. "I best see to him quickly, though. I would hate for him to escape only to return and seek revenge. If one hair on your lovely head were harmed, I'd . . . well, I'd never forgive myself."

The rest of his nauseating claptrap faded from Grace's hearing as he exited the barn. And as soon as it did, she immediately went to work on retrieving the shears. Only, with the strap pinning her arms down, she couldn't reach her pocket. She contorted and tugged and bounced, all to no avail. Then she remembered the hoop that served as her hitch and scooted back against the wall.

Bending her knees, she dragged herself down, scraping the bumps of her spine against the metal ring, but the thin strap refused to catch. Her back was too bony. Not enough give. Grace twisted sideways, exposing the fleshy part of her side, yet the stiffness of her corset offered little improvement.

Grace darted a glance at the barn door, her pulse racing. He'd be back any minute. With Amos. An unconscious, defenseless Amos. She had to be ready. Had to get free.

Grace set her jaw. If she couldn't snag the strap, she'd just catch something else. Lifting up on tiptoes, she jabbed her hip against the wall, digging the metal ring under the lip of her corset until it cut into her waist. The boning at the top of her corset stabbed into her breasts and ribs, drawing a groan from her, but she didn't back away from the discomfort. She pushed farther into it, determined to win.

She wouldn't be weak. She wouldn't relent. God had provided the shears and the privacy. She must supply the heart.

She gritted her teeth and dragged herself downward. The metal ring pushed the corset upward. Whalebone spines jabbed the tender parts under her arm.

An arm she could now lift several inches higher than she could a moment ago.

Grace twisted, folded at the waist, and grabbed for the shears through the fabric of her skirt. Her fingers closed around the metal, and she immediately worked them upward.

When the handles emerged, she fit them between her bound wrists. Drawing her hands closer to her body with bent elbows, she pressed the handles into her ribs as her fingernails clawed at the blades to separate them.

She'd just started to pry them apart when a sound at the door announced Lockhart's return. Heart pounding, Grace dropped to her knees and grabbed at her pooling skirt to cover her hands and the shears.

Lockhart strode through the doorway, his arm crooked around Amos's neck. He dragged the semi-conscious man into the barn and pulled the door closed behind them.

"See what I found, Grace? Your loyal lapdog. So kind of him to pay a visit." Lockhart threw Amos to the floor.

Grace cried out.

Amos braced his arms beneath him and lifted his head, his gaze locking on hers. "Grace? Are you—?"

The click of a hammer being cocked cut off the rest of his question. Lockhart, his expression having lost all trace of humor and gentility, snarled as he grabbed Amos by the collar and jerked him up onto his knees. Then he pressed the barrel of his pistol against Amos's skull.

Lockhart's cold eyes bored into her. "Ready to talk now, Grace?"

Her heart lurched. "Please. He has nothing to do with this. Let him go!"

She knew he wouldn't, but she had to do something to gain herself time. To get the shears open and slice through the bindings.

"I don't think so." Lockhart glared at her. "Tell me what I want to know, Grace. Now. Or Bledsoe dies."

Grace fidgeted, digging her hands deeper into the cover of her skirt, praying Lockhart would mistake her movements for agitation and fear when what she was really doing was hooking the curved pruning blade she'd managed to open around the inside of her ropes.

"How will you explain a dead telegraph operator to Miss Gladstone?" Grace challenged. "She's sure to come running when the gun goes off. Executing an unarmed man isn't exactly the action of an honorable Pinkerton detective. She'll know she's been duped."

Lockhart narrowed his eyes. "Irene will believe whatever I tell her to believe."

"And if she doesn't?" Grace sawed the blade in tiny motions against the hemp. *Please, God. Please help me get free.*

Lockhart shrugged. "Then I'll kill her. The old man, too. And you'll have three deaths on your hands."

"Not on your hands, Grace." Amos's voice, so unexpected and so calm, drew her gaze to his. "He's the one responsible. No matter what happens, nothing is your fault."

She heard the meaning behind his words, the forgiveness freely given. He wasn't begging her to tell her secrets and spare him. He knew as well as she did that as soon as Lockhart had the information he wanted, they were both as good as dead. Amos wasn't thinking of himself at all. He was thinking of her. Letting her know that if he died at Lockhart's hands, he had no regrets and laid no blame at her feet.

Grace stilled, her entire focus on the man who had crept into her heart. The one who could not be any more a hero than he was at that moment. "I love you, Amos."

His lips curved in the sweetest smile she'd ever seen. "I love y—"

"Shut up," Lockhart growled and kicked Amos in the gut with enough force to double the smaller man over.

"Stop it!" Grace screamed.

Lockhart pressed a knee between Amos's shoulder blades and jammed his gun against the back of Amos's head. "Tell me where the books are, Grace, or I'll shoot Bledsoe and cut the answers out of you piece by piece."

"If you kill him, I'll never tell you." She leaned forward against her restraint, the leather digging into her chest. "No matter what you do to me. But if you let him go, I give you my word that I'll tell you where they are."

"Grace, no," Amos groaned, straining against Lockhart's weight, but the larger man restrained him with ease.

Lockhart looked from one prisoner to the other. Grace could

practically see the thoughts running through his mind. He knew what she'd endured already. Knew her mental fortitude. He also knew he was running out of time. If he didn't get the answers he sought tonight, his best window of opportunity to retrieve the books without fully exposing himself would be lost. He might very well follow through on his threat to gather his compatriots and storm Harper's Station, but that would take time. Time that would allow Malachi to bring in reinforcements of his own.

On the other hand, letting Amos go meant running the risk of the telegraph operator fetching Sheriff Tabor. Lockhart would have to abandon the security of the Gladstone farm. Would he take the risk, or would he give up on the books, kill them all, and make his escape?

32

Grace stared at Lockhart, daring him to take her offer.

He rubbed his jaw, scowled, then cursed. "All right. I'll let Bledsoe go. But on my terms." He removed his knee from the center of Amos's back, then grabbed his arm and yanked him to his feet. "There's a clearing half a mile east of here," Lockhart said with a wave of his gun. "Far enough away to muffle any necessary gunshots."

He shoved Amos forward, pointed his gun at his back, and marched him toward Grace.

Bending forward to shield her hands, Grace slipped the shears from her lap to beneath her knees, praying her captor's view was sufficiently obstructed by his prisoner.

Amos caught the action, though, and met her gaze. His eyes burned like blue fire, his jaw set. *I'm not leaving you with him*, his face all but shouted.

She lifted her chin and stared back. *You must.*

A muscle ticked in Amos's cheek and his eyes blazed, but he nodded. Just a tiny dip of his chin, yet it conveyed everything Grace needed. He would escape and protect the ladies of Harper's Station.

"On your feet, Grace," Lockhart barked. "You're gonna fetch my horse."

"Hard to do when I'm strapped to the wall," she sassed as she struggled to get her feet under her while keeping a grip on the fabric of her skirt to camouflage her hands. She hadn't had time to saw through all the rope, but it had definitely frayed. Whether it was frayed enough to allow her to break free was yet to be determined, but she couldn't afford Lockhart suspecting anything amiss.

Unable to use her arms for balance, Grace rose awkwardly, nearly tumbling sideways. Amos took hold of her shoulders, steadying her. Grace smiled her thanks until Lockhart leaned around Amos and knocked his arms away. Grace glared at him.

Lockhart shrugged. "Consider me your chaperone, darlin'. Rest assured there'll be no hanky-panky on my watch."

"I'm so relieved," Grace said, sarcasm dripping from her tongue as thick as molasses from a spoon. She turned to present her back to the men. Someone would have to loosen the leather strap.

"Unbuckle it, Bledsoe. But only the strap, mind you. The lady's clothes must stay where they are."

Grace wanted to slam her fist into Lockhart's mouth. Not that it would help matters. It probably wouldn't even dent a tooth, not with him being so tall and her being so wrung out. But the thought buoyed her flagging spirits. This was a war, after all, and it was time to fight.

Once Amos released her from the strap, Grace circled her shoulders and stretched her elbows wide, reminding her arms how to move. Amos's hands lingered at her waist, squeezing gently, instilling hope. It would have been a lovely moment had Lockhart not snatched her arm and jerked her away.

"Fetch my horse. Last stall."

She glowered at her captor, then met Amos's gaze as she walked past. How she wished they had more time. There was so much she wanted to say to him, so much of life she wanted to share with him. She wanted to meet his sister and his mother, play with his nephew, and perhaps even give young Harry a cousin or two to boss around during family outings.

She even wanted to learn how to ride that ridiculous veloci-pede. She'd seen pictures of bicycles fashioned for two riders. She and Amos could cycle together on the same machine. Laughing, causing havoc in the streets. It would be paradise.

Lockhart's fist crashed into Amos's jaw. Amos's head snapped sideways, his spectacles skewed across the bridge of his nose. Grace gasped.

"Move faster, girlie," Lockhart ordered, "or next time I'll use my knife instead of my fist."

Grace blinked away the shards of paradise lost and dashed deeper into the barn, searching out the last stall. Lockhart's geld-ing lifted his head from the feedbox as she approached. All his tack remained in place—saddle, bridle, pack. All she had to do was tighten the cinch to make him ready. Her captor obviously preferred keeping his getaway options open. He might be cocky, but he wasn't stupid.

Well, she wasn't stupid either. Nor was she helpless. And if everything went according to plan, she just might live long enough to make the future she'd envisioned with Amos a reality.

Grace unnotched the buckle on the cinch, then did her best to tighten the strap despite the awkwardness of bound hands. Once satisfied with the result, Grace took hold of the brown gelding's reins and led him from the stall. The clop of his hooves echoed dully in the barn as they struck the packed dirt floor, but Grace barely registered the sound. She was too concerned about the frayed edges poking up around the center of her wrists. Her work with the cinch had frayed the rope further, and with her arms exposed as she led the horse, there was no way to hide the evidence. Would Lockhart notice?

She stole a glance at her captor. Holding Amos at gunpoint, he was ordering his prisoner to open the barn door. Which meant his back was turned to her. Thank God. With Lockhart's focus on Amos and the increasing shadows as dusk darkened, she just might make it. Grace clasped her palms together around the reins to keep from putting any undue pressure on the weakened rope and strode forward, careful to keep on Lockhart's right so her body would impede his view of her arms.

Amos slid the door open, and Lockhart pushed him through the opening. A dark spot at Lockhart's back caught Grace's notice for the first time. A second pistol was tucked into the waistband of his trousers. It must be Amos's weapon, confiscated after that deluded woman bonked him over the head. That made two pistols, at least one knife, and the rifle in the saddle boot. Against a single-shot derringer with a short range and a woman whose arms were so exhausted from hook-hanging that she couldn't hold them chest-high without trembling.

Yet David needed only one stone to fell Goliath.

Odds didn't matter when God fought at one's side.

Guide my hand as you did David's, Lord. I can't succeed without you.

It took fifteen minutes of tromping over uneven ground to reach the clearing and another five for Lockhart to decide on the perfect centralized position to make his stand.

A three-quarter moon shone in the charcoal sky, and cricket song filled the night air. The wind cut through Grace's wet hair and clothing until she shivered so severely that she lost her grip on the gelding's reins. Not that it mattered. Lockhart had stopped. Unable to wrap her arms around herself for warmth, Grace settled for hunching her shoulders and turning her back to the wind.

"Come here, Grace." Lockhart jerked his head forward, signaling her to approach on Amos's side.

She obeyed, eying the gun pointed at Amos's head and Lock-hart's punishing grip on his arm. Her heart throbbed.

This was it. In a few minutes Amos would either be free or dead. Her too, though that outcome was secondary.

"Do you see that scraggly mesquite about eighty yards to the north?" Lockhart tipped his head that direction.

Grace eyed the shadowy outline of a short, gnarled tree not too far away. "Yes."

"I figure with the low visibility, that's about the extent of my range for hitting a moving target." Lockhart tapped the pistol barrel against the side of Amos's head, making him wince and duck away. "In a minute, I'm going to let Bledsoe go, and he's going to walk in a straight line to that tree. You have until he gets there to tell me where the books are. If you don't, I shoot him." He met her gaze, his voice menacing. "And we all know how good a shot I am."

Grace swallowed, desperately fighting off images of her father bleeding in the street.

"What happens to Grace after she tells you what you want to know?" Amos demanded, his voice strong and sure despite the threat of death hanging over his head.

Lockhart shrugged. "I'll have no more need of her. She'll be free to find her way back to the main road or to a homestead nearby. Probably won't find much of a welcome at the Gladstone place, but there are others around who might be more sympathetic to her plight."

Grace didn't believe a word coming out of Lockhart's mouth, and judging by his clenched jaw, Amos didn't either. Nevertheless, it was essential Amos went along with the plan.

She stepped close to his side, drinking in his warmth as he wrapped an arm around her shoulders. "Don't worry about me," she urged. "I'll be fine."

He stared hard at her.

She stared back. "I need you to go, Amos. Please."

His fingers tapped against her arm. At first she simply absorbed the comfort, but then she realized it was code. *I'll come back for you.*

She wanted to return the message, to tell him again that she loved him, but her hands were pinned between them, and Lockhart was too impatient to give her the chance. He yanked Amos away from her and shoved him forward.

"You heard the lady, Bledsoe. She needs you to go."

Amos stumbled a few steps, then turned to look at Grace. She nodded and mouthed the word, *Go.*

Lockhart was less subtle. "Get a move on," he ordered as he planted a boot on Amos's rear and pushed. "I don't got all night."

Amos found his balance, favored Grace with one final, incredibly fierce gaze, then pivoted forward and started walking toward the tree.

Grace watched him go. Each step he took farther away filled her heart with hope. This would work. It *had* to work.

When Amos reached the halfway point, Lockhart chanced a quick glance at her before refocusing his attention on his quarry. "Where are the books, Grace?"

Not yet. Amos was still within range. She needed to make sure he put as much distance between himself and Lockhart as possible.

Amos halved the remaining distance.

"Grace?" Lockhart's voice hardened, demanding she give him what he sought.

She held her tongue.

Ten steps from the tree.

Eight.

"I'm going to count to three, and if you haven't held up your end of the bargain, I'll shoot him." His gaze remained fixed on Amos.

Grace backed up a few paces. Started testing the strength of the rope at her wrists.

Five steps from the tree.

"One . . ." Lockhart counted.

Grace paced back another stride, twisting her hands. The right one was nearly free.

"Two . . ."

"The bank," she blurted as Amos's silhouette blended with that of the tree. He was out of pistol range. "The books are locked in the vault at the bank."

"Thank you, my dear." In a seamless motion, Lockhart holstered his pistol, spun toward his horse, and slid the rifle free of the boot. He'd just doubled his range by changing weapons.

"Run, Amos!" Grace screamed as she wrenched her hand free of the binding.

As Lockhart took aim, Grace hitched up her skirts and pulled her derringer.

She didn't look for Amos. Didn't worry about her shivering, trembling arms. This close to her target, it wouldn't matter.

Holding the tiny pocket pistol with two hands, Grace disengaged the safety and raised the barrel.

The two shots concussed almost simultaneously.

Grace didn't wait to see where hers had hit. Nor did she search for Amos, even though her heart yearned to know his fate. With Lockhart's howl of pain echoing in her ears, she did the only thing she could. She used the last of her depleted energy to mount Lockhart's horse, leaned low over the saddle, and raced for the road as a volley of gunshots exploded behind her.

33

R un, Amos!"

At Grace's shout, Amos dodged sharply right. But instead of running as instinct and the woman he loved demanded, he lunged for the mesquite that stood a mere two steps away. Its twisted trunk and curving limbs might be thinner than his own frame, but they offered more cover than the knee-high scrub brush dotting the rest of the prairie landscape.

Even as he leapt behind the gnarled tree, a gunshot boomed. Then echoed. A second shot?

The question pierced Amos's brain at the same moment a bullet pierced his sleeve.

Amos hissed and spun to his left, planting his good shoulder against the tree trunk and making himself as thin a target as possible. An animal-like roar, deep and angry, blasted across the clearing.

Lockhart.

Grace must have gotten free and retrieved her derringer. Thank God!

Another shot rang out. Then two more. Amos sucked in a breath and tensed for impact, his eyes squeezed shut, but no bullets peppered the tree. No lead ripped through his skin. Amos's eyes popped open. The shooting wasn't aimed at him.

Grace!

No longer concerned with his own protection, Amos ducked beneath the mesquite's low-hanging branches and stared back across the clearing. Lockhart lay sprawled on the ground, firing his repeating rifle one-handed. He'd tucked the butt of the rifle into the crease between his legs and waist to hold it steady as he shot.

At a woman on horseback.

Grace leaned low over the horse's neck. The too-long stirrups flapped against the animal's sides, keeping the beast racing at top speed. Amos's breath caught. As dark as it was, her mount could lose its footing and crumple. Grace could break her neck.

But if she slowed, one of Lockhart's bullets would take her down.

Ride, Grace, he silently urged. *Ride.*

A movement caught Amos's eye, drawing his attention away from Grace. Lockhart was pivoting toward him, working the lever of his repeater.

Time to go.

Amos dodged around to the back side of the tree again and sprinted cross-country, keeping the tree between himself and Lockhart to make the gunman's shot as difficult as possible. Unfortunately, that meant running in the opposite direction from Grace, but he'd veer east to search for the road as soon as he put adequate distance between himself and Lockhart's rifle.

Grace must have gotten in a good shot to leave the gunman favoring his left side so significantly. With any luck, Lockhart would be too wounded to chase down either of them. Yet Amos couldn't count on that. Vengeance would fuel the imposter now, and that could be a powerful motivator. Amos had to find Grace and keep her safe until Lockhart was either behind bars or dead.

So he kept running. In the dark over uneven terrain. He stumbled more than he didn't, but he never went down. As if the Lord's mighty hand had a steadying grip on his collar, keeping him on his feet.

The landscape changed, steepening into sloping hills and slowing his progress. Yet he ran on. Through the cramps in his side. Through aching lungs that screamed at him to rest. He ignored it all, keeping his eyes focused on a tall cylinder that began to separate itself from the rest of the darkness. Too tall to be a juniper. Too thin to be a mesquite.

If it was what he thought it was, it just might be their salvation.

So fixed was Amos on the pole that he failed to notice the road until he practically tripped over it. Even then, he paid it little heed as he crossed to the wooden pillar on the far side. A dark wire extended along its top on either side.

Telegraph wire. The very wire that led from the depot in Seymour to Grace's office in Harper's Station.

Amos stumbled to a halt and braced a bent arm against the pole. He rested his forehead on his wrist as he struggled to catch his breath. His chest heaved, but his mind churned, testing and discarding theory after theory for climbing the pole. If he had his clawed climbing boots, he could reach the top in a heartbeat. But he didn't. Neither did he have a ladder. The gun belt he'd borrowed from Shaw would not expand enough to encompass both himself and the pole, which rendered it useless as a climbing belt. So he was left with good old-fashioned arm and leg coordination. Not exactly his forte.

Give me strength, he prayed as he straightened. He dug his pocketknife out of his front trouser pocket, extended the blade, then placed the handle between his teeth. Amos glanced upward, eying the distance. Twenty-five feet. Maybe thirty.

Not a problem, he told himself. He could do this.

He stepped close to the pole and hugged it at chest height. A stinging in his right arm reminded him of his injury. A tear in the fabric a few inches below his shoulder caught his eye, but he didn't see much blood. Probably just a graze. Still hurt like the dickens, though, not that it mattered. His arm could be on fire, and he'd still find a way to get up this pole.

Amos grunted as he tightened his abdominal muscles and drew his legs up to cling to the pole, bending one foot behind the pole while pressing the instep of the other against the side. Holding firm with his left arm, he lifted with his right and pushed up with his legs. One hand up, then the other, thigh muscles straining to maintain his hold on the pole, his feet already aching from the awkwardness of their position. As he reached a third time, the soles of his shoes slipped. Down he slid, splinters stabbing his palms before he landed hard on his rear.

The shoes had to come off.

Amos yanked them from his feet, followed by his stockings. He spared a few moments to pull the worst of the splinters from his hands, then replaced the knife between his teeth, set his shoulders, and tried again.

He contorted his legs around the pole and slowly inched his way upward. He glued his gaze to the round, glass insulator at the top of the pole. That was where he needed to be.

The back of his right foot curled around the pole, keeping him from sliding down as his left foot craned sideways to find purchase. Hand over hand he crawled. Muscles fatiguing. Sweat beading on his upper lip and rolling down the back of his neck.

Just . . . a little . . . farther.

The insulator was nearly within reach. A groan ripped from his throat as Amos forced his exhausted body to pull one more time.

Finally, the top. The insulator sat at eye level, and telegraph wire bumped against the side of his head. Amos stretched his left hand up to cup the pointed top of the pole and support his weight while he crossed his legs for a more stable grip.

With his right hand, he took hold of the telegraph wire and pulled in some of the slack. Wires needed extra length so they wouldn't snap when the wind gusted. Thankfully north Texas had plenty of wind, so he had a decent amount of play to work with. Feeding the extra line to his left hand, he held it steady a couple inches from where the main line was fastened to the insulator with a twist of support wire.

Then he eased his jaw open and grasped the handle of his knife. Working carefully, he cut a section of wire between the thumb and forefinger of his left hand. Once he had it cut, he dropped the knife to the ground, no longer needing it. Keeping one end of the wire pinned between his left thumb and the top of the pole, he took the other end in his right hand and started tapping out a message.

When he'd put the local operators on alert before leaving, he'd asked them to stay late in case anything urgent came through. Hopefully the operator in Seymour remained at his post.

Lockhart spotted in clearing half mile east of Gladstone farm. Injured, armed, angry. Grace making escape on horseback. Send sheriff at once.

Without a line tapping clamp with a portable sounder and key, there was no way to tell if his message had been received. He'd have to leave that part of the equation in God's hands.

Amos twisted the wire ends back together, crimping them as best he could with his fingers. He'd put in a request for a maintainer to come out and splice it properly later.

As he released the wire to drape back into place, his feet slipped. Gasping, he grabbed for the pole with his right arm. His cheek smashed against the wood. His heart throbbed in his chest, and his muscles clenched. But his limbs were too fatigued. He couldn't support his weight any longer. He started to slide.

Hoofbeats pounded on the road. Riders? Amos dug deep, hope of rescue lending him an extra dose of strength. Keeping his knees tight, he dragged his bare feet underneath him and pressed both insteps into opposite sides of the pole. The pads of his feet found a crevice and stopped his descent. Taking a careful breath, Amos tucked his hips and leaned his torso away from the pole, assuming the position he would have used if he'd had proper lineman boots and a climbing belt. The change in leverage relieved the pressure in his arms. As long as his feet held, he just might—

"Bledsoe? That you up there?"

He'd been so focused on not falling, he'd failed to notice the arrival of the horsemen. One of them held a lantern aloft, making it hard to see his face, but Amos had no trouble recognizing his voice.

"Mr. Shaw. Thank heavens. Is that Mr. Porter behind you?"

"Yep, I'm here. What are you doing on that pole?" The second rider urged his massive elephant of a horse past the marshal to get a better view.

"Sending a telegram, of course," Amos replied, as if it were an everyday occurrence to find a shoeless Western Union man clinging to a telegraph pole in the middle of a country lane. "Though I could use some assistance returning to the ground. Might I make use of your horse?"

"On my way." Porter clicked his tongue, and his giant black horse walked forward, his thick, steady hooves thumping against the ground with satisfying firmness. Once directly beneath Amos, Porter reined in the beast and patted its neck. "Stand steady, Hermes," the freighter's deep voice rumbled in calm, comforting tones. "Stand steady."

Amos couldn't see much, since Porter was directly below him, but he heard saddle leather creaking, something thudding against the ground, and a grunt as the big man shifted.

"Careful, Ben," the marshal warned. "You're not exactly the acrobatic type."

Amos chanced a glance under his elbow. Good heavens. Porter was in the process of *standing* on his horse's back. Amos caught a glimpse of the freighter's white feet in the lantern light and nearly laughed aloud. He had discarded his boots. It seemed to be the theme of the night—daring *feets*. He did chuckle then.

Amos lifted his head and bit back a groan. The strain of gripping the pole must have pickled his brain. He was laughing at his own puns now.

"I'm in position," the freighter said. "Let go with your legs and stand on my shoulders."

Amos glanced down again. The big man's palms and splayed fingers grasped the wood, nearly matching the circumference of the pole. His head bent toward the pillar, exposing his wide shoulders and muscled back.

"I've got Hermes's head," the marshal assured them. "He won't shy."

"Hermes would never shy," Porter countered. "Would you, boy?"

The horse snorted as if in answer and held his position.

Tightening his arms, Amos slowly released his left leg. He needed to descend a few more feet before he'd be able to reach Porter. He willed his muscles to hold out a little longer and gritted his teeth through the painful descent. Once within range, he hooked his right foot around the pole to keep from dropping all of his weight onto his rescuer at once, then stretched out his left toward Porter's shoulder. After that foot found purchase, he unhooked the other and brought it down as well. His arms sagged in relief as the weight transferred to his legs. Using his hands to maintain his balance, he bent his knees and walked his palms down the pole until he crouched on Porter's shoulders. From there, he crawled down the man's back until his feet made contact with the saddle.

"Here." Shaw held out a hand.

Amos clasped it and jumped down to the ground. His cramping legs crumpled beneath him as he hit, but the marshal's grip kept him upright. Amos nodded his thanks and immediately commenced collecting his knife, stockings, and shoes. "God brought you two at just the right time. I don't think I could have held on for much longer."

"I'm impressed you got up there in the first place," Shaw said, respect ringing in his tone. "Not sure I could have."

Amos sat, yanked one particularly large splinter from his right instep, then shoved his feet into his socks before starting in on the shoes. "You would if your wife's life depended on it."

"Nah," Ben said, dismounting and taking up his own boots. "He'd have just blown the thing out of the ground."

Malachi chuckled, but Amos didn't join in. Now that he had himself put back together, they needed to make tracks.

"We have to go after Lockhart." Amos finished lacing his second shoe and scrambled to his feet. "I can lead you to him, or at least to where he was twenty minutes ago."

"Near the Gladstone place?" The marshal shared a look with Porter as the two of them remounted their horses.

"How did you . . . ?"

Porter leaned down and extended his arm to Amos. "Dunbar—the real one," the freighter clarified as he swung Amos up onto the horse behind him, "was waiting for me in town when I returned. Told me about the Gladstone woman."

"Ben headed out immediately and caught me on the road. Convinced me the Pinkerton was in good enough shape to help guard the women, so I turned around."

Amos pointed at a spot across the road. "There's a clearing through there. Grace managed to wound Lockhart and steal his horse, but we can't take anything for granted. He knows the books are in the bank vault, and beyond that, he's got a personal vendetta to settle against Grace." He met the marshal's quickly hardening gaze with an unyielding stare of his own. "Neither of our women will be safe until that man is behind bars."

The marshal handed the lantern to Porter and slid his revolver from its holster. "Lead the way."

34

The closer they came to the clearing, the harder Amos's heart pounded in his chest. Not from fear this time but from righteous anger. Flashes of Lockhart forcing Grace's head into that water barrel rose in his memory to heat his blood, fueling his need for justice.

A gunshot pierced the quiet. The lantern Porter held aloft to light their path shattered. Hermes spooked and reared. Amos grabbed for Porter's waist, but without stirrups to brace himself, he was helpless against gravity. He tumbled to the ground. Recalling the size of the draft horse's hooves, Amos immediately rolled away from the skittish animal.

Porter settled the beast in admirable time, while Shaw circled his own mount to keep him under control.

"Bledsoe!" Porter hissed into the darkness. "You all right?"

"Yeah." Amos got to his feet and brushed the dirt from his trousers. "Which direction did the shot come from?"

"West." Shaw's answer was definitive, as was his gaze as he searched the shadows for any sign of their attacker. "Toward the Gladstone place. Probably going for a horse. Gotta cut him off before he gets there. We need to split up, try to surround him.

Bledsoe, take the rifle from my saddle boot. It's got fifteen shots. There's a box of cartridges in the side pouch, too."

Amos did as instructed, the rifle heavy yet comforting in his hands.

Another shot rang out, and Amos ducked. Shaw's horse side-stepped out of reach before Amos could retrieve the extra ammunition.

"Porter?"

"I'm good," the freighter called from a few feet away. "But we can't stay here and let him pick us off."

"I'll circle left. You go right. Bledsoe, take cover in that juniper over there." Shaw pointed to a cluster of brush about twenty feet away. "Keep low to the ground. Flat on your stomach is best. Rifle aimed and ready. With as dark as it is, the closer you are to the ground, the harder it will be for him to distinguish you from the landscape."

A third shot blasted.

Shaw spurred his mount. "Go!" He laid down cover, firing three shots in Lockhart's general direction as they all took up their positions.

Amos ran toward the juniper, rifle in front of him. A yard out, he dropped to his belly and crawled on bent arms to the far side of the brush, not wanting Lockhart to see precisely where he was going to ground.

Then chaos ensued. Gunshots to the right, the left. They seemed to come from everywhere. Amos stared into the night, trying desperately to make out shapes. To identify his friends. He kept his rifle aimed low. Porter and Shaw were mounted. Lockhart was on foot. Yet Amos didn't pull his trigger and add to the storm of bullets. He couldn't risk shooting the wrong man.

The sounds grew closer. Louder. As if Shaw and Porter were herding Lockhart toward him, like dogs flushing quail for the hunter. Only Amos was the least qualified hunter of the pack.

Amos's hands shook as he shifted the rifle to cradle it more securely in the hollow of his shoulder. He braced himself on his elbows and tried to relax his legs, recalling what his father had taught him about shooting when he'd been a boy. The prone position was the easiest and most accurate, his father had explained, because the ground would steady his shot. Amos lowered his head to sight along the barrel. The easiest and most accurate. He could do this. He *would* do this.

He might not be a lawman or have muscles the size of boulders, but he had heart. A heart that belonged to a beautiful woman who'd been willing to die rather than put the people she cared about in danger. A heart that demanded he protect this woman, no matter the personal cost.

His panic ebbed and his pulse steadied. Amos clenched his fist, then slowly unfolded his fingers one at a time before fitting his forefinger once again to the trigger.

Out of the darkness, a figure emerged. Hunched. Lumbering. Lockhart.

He couldn't be more than ten yards away. He looked nothing like the cocky, coldhearted ladies' man he'd been the last time Amos had seen him. His hat was gone, and his hair stood on end as if he'd crawled through a bramble. His shirt had been torn off and fashioned into some kind of bandage around his left shoulder and across his torso. Dark streaks stained his chest and side—blood. Yet it was his eyes in the moonlight that made Amos catch his breath. Wild. Animalistic.

Lockhart pivoted back toward his pursuers and fired off another two shots from his rifle. He pumped the lever for a third shot, but nothing fired. With a growl, he threw the weapon to the ground and yanked a revolver from his waistband behind his back. The very revolver he'd confiscated from Amos. A revolver with six shots, any one of which could end Shaw or Porter's life. Amos's life. *Grace's* life.

Amos took aim.

"I've got a bead on you, Lockhart," Amos called. "Throw down your weapon."

Lockhart paused. He raised his right hand, pointing his pistol harmlessly toward the sky. He started to turn.

"I said, throw down your weapon!" Amos couldn't let him turn with the gun still in his hand. He was too good a marksman.

Hoofbeats echoed, coming closer. Shaw and Porter would be here any second. He only had to hold Lockhart a little—

Lockhart spun, dropping to a crouch. His eyes found Amos through the juniper and his jaw tightened. The revolver came around.

Amos pulled the trigger.

But his wasn't the only shot to ring out. Three others blasted through the night. Lockhart's body jerked as each one hit from a different angle. Finally, he fell forward onto his face, the revolver tumbling from his hand unused.

"Nice of you to join the posse, Tabor." Shaw tipped his hat to someone on Amos's left, then dismounted and made his way to the body.

Amos got to his feet, his legs shaky and his mind numb. He'd never shot a man before.

"Well, I had me a personalized invite."

Amos slowly turned his head toward the unfamiliar voice. A man on horseback with a star on his lapel was returning a gun to his holster.

The sheriff's gray mustache twitched slightly as he crossed his wrists over his saddle horn, leaned forward, and scowled down at Lockhart. "Terrible business, this. Kidnapping womenfolk. Impersonatin' lawmen. Pulling sheriffs away from perfectly good suppers to give chase. My stew's gonna be stone cold by the time I get back to Seymour." Sheriff Tabor shook his head as if that were the biggest crime of the night. "He dead, Shaw?"

The marshal stood from his crouch and nodded. "Yep. Though it's impossible to tell whose bullet did him in."

"Since you folks got no undertaker over in Harper's Station, let's say it were mine. That way, the county'll pay for the pine box." The sheriff eyed Shaw and Porter, his wily gaze lingering on the freighter's mount. "I'll let you younger fellas drag in the carcass, though. That Shire of Porter's could probably carry all three of ya plus Lockhart's dead weight without breaking a lather."

"We'll see to it," the marshal agreed.

Sheriff Tabor tapped the brim of his hat in thanks and reined his mount back toward the road.

"Wait!" Amos darted forward, dropping his borrowed rifle near Malachi's feet before intercepting the sheriff. "Could you take me back by the Gladstone place on your way? I stashed my mare near the barn, and I'll need her to track down Miss Mallory." He glanced back at his friends, hoping they'd understand his desertion. "Grace left here fleeing for her life. She's terrified and most certainly injured. I have to find her and let her know she's safe."

"Whoa now, partner." Sheriff Tabor leaned forward in his saddle. "Yer throwin' words faster than my ears can catch 'em. This female yer talkin' 'bout, she got brown hair, all wet and in a tangle, with a dark blue skirt?"

Amos nearly leaped from his shoes. "Yes! Have you seen her?"

The sheriff nodded, unhurried. "Crazy woman nearly ran me off the road. She had no business ridin' a horse two sizes too big fer her. Stirrups floppin' all over the place. Had to fix those for her before lettin' her go on to town. All the while, she flapped her gums about some poor fella named Bledsoe being hunted down." Tabor tilted his chin toward Amos. "I'm guessin' that's you. Anyhow, she demanded I leave her be and hurry over to Gladstone's place to apprehend the same reprobate you wired about. Which I did. Thankfully in time to add my lead to the bullet sandwich you boys were offerin' up."

"So she's in Seymour?" Amos fought to hide his impatience. The sheriff chewed his words like a cow did cud. Slow and circular, when Amos needed quick and direct.

"Yep. Told her to take the horse she *borrowed* to Bart Porter's livery. Figured his wife would tend to her."

"Their house is behind the livery," Ben Porter said, blessedly concise and to the point. "On Main Street. A block north of Fischer's Emporium. Not the stable near the depot where you rented that mule."

Amos nodded, took the hand Sheriff Tabor offered, and swung up behind him.

"Addie's a good woman." The freighter's endorsement of his sister-in-law's character relieved Amos a bit, but the urgency to see Grace for himself refused to abate. "She'll take good care of Miss Mallory."

"Sorry to leave you to deal with Lockhart." Well, not really. Amos's stomach roiled every time he glanced at the fallen body, knowing he'd had a part in bringing him down. No matter how justified the killing, it still left him rather ill.

Shaw waved him on. "Don't worry about it. Go see to Grace. She needs you."

She needs you. The words did something strange to Amos's chest, flooding it with warmth and protectiveness. And love so rich and soul-stirringly deep it left him rather shaken.

Grace needed him. Loved him. And heaven knew he needed her. Needed to be with her, to care for her, keep her safe, and never let her go.

Sheriff Tabor tossed a glance over his shoulder. "Ready, Bledsoe?"

Ready didn't even begin to describe it. "Yes, sir."

"Then hold on." With a nudge of his heels, they were off, and for once Amos found himself glad to be on a horse instead of a bicycle. Transport involving four unwearied legs and superior night vision had its advantages. And he'd take any advantage he could wangle to get him to Grace's side as fast as possible.

35

Grace couldn't remember the last time someone else had brushed her hair. It should have been soothing, sitting in a chair by a warm fire, sipping tea while another woman gently removed the tangles from her matted tresses. Her scalp tingled pleasantly enough, yet her nerves refused to be assuaged.

"Relax." Addie Porter's southern lilt stroked as gently as her brush, yet both proved equally ineffective at releasing Grace's tension. "You'll do your man no favors if you fret yourself ill waiting on his return."

Grace spun around on the footstool she was sitting on, her gaze imploring her new friend to understand the severity of the situation. "But he's out there alone with the man who killed my father. A man who wants both of us dead."

"And what, exactly, can you do that isn't already being done for him?" Addie's quiet question stole some of Grace's steam.

The livery owner's very pregnant wife took hold of Grace's shoulders and repositioned her on the stool so she could resume working on her hair. "You've shot the scoundrel, stranded him without a horse, and alerted the sheriff—who apparently already knew about the situation because your man had somehow sent a telegram from the middle of the countryside. I still have no idea how he pulled that off."

"He must have climbed a telegraph pole and cut the wires." Though until this very moment, Grace hadn't taken the time to fully digest what that meant. No ladder. No climbing gear. How had Amos accomplished it?

Addie chuckled softly. "Sounds to me like you have yourself a very resourceful fellow there. Have faith in him, Grace. There's nothing worse for a man than for his woman to doubt his abilities."

"I don't!" Grace started to turn again as she voiced her protest, but Addie's pointed look kept her in place. "Amos is the most intelligent, capable person I know. But he's unarmed, running from a gunman who kills without conscience."

The brush stilled. "And will your worry bring him back any faster?"

Grace sighed, knowing the answer but not knowing how to stop. "No."

Wood clicked against wood as Addie set the brush on the end table beside her seat on the sofa. A moment later, her fingers separated Grace's hair into sections and she began to plait. "Then let's fill your mind with more worthy thoughts. Tell me about Amos. What is it about him that captured your heart?"

Grace sat silent for a long minute, sorting through all the wonderful memories she'd collected of the man she loved. The stories he'd entertained her with over the wire before they'd ever met in person—tales of his mother's meddling, his sister's teasing, and his young nephew's exploits in the sports of glasses-grabbing and mud pie-eating. His genuineness. No unnecessary frills to dress up his tales and make them more titillating. No drive to impress. He was simply himself. Warm. Kind. He made her laugh and reminded her what it meant to be part of a family. The connection. The joy. The dedication to one another.

"He makes me feel like I've come home," she finally said, her voice barely above a whisper. "He took on my enemies as if they were his own and vowed to remain by my side no matter the danger. And he has. He's so brave, Addie. So honorable."

And if she lost him, she wasn't sure she'd recover.

Addie must have sensed her melancholy, for she tied off the braid she'd fashioned with a bit of white ribbon then spun Grace around to face her. Her eyes twinkled, and her lips turned up impishly at one end. "And has he kissed you yet, this brave, honorable fellow?"

Heat rushed to Grace's cheeks. She ducked her head.

"Aha! He has." Addie's laughter was infectious.

A smile crept onto Grace's face.

"Was it a gentlemanly peck on the cheek, or something more . . . daring?" Addie leaned close, eager eyes wide and ready to absorb the secret.

And despite the fact they'd known each other for less than an hour, Grace wanted to tell her. Share confidences as if they were best friends with their heads bent together behind the schoolhouse after class. Addie had welcomed Grace into her home, after all, and given her dry clothes to wear—everything from undergarments to stockings to a lovely pink calico dress that had been one of Addie's favorites before her pregnancy. A pregnancy that proved she knew a thing or two about kissing a man.

Grace's gaze dropped to her lap, but her smile widened. "More than a peck."

Addie hooted loudly enough that Grace feared Bart Porter might hear at the livery.

"Shhh!"

Addie clamped a hand over her mouth, yet her eyes continued to dance. Grace grinned. How could she not, when her hostess was such a delight?

And truly, remembering the kiss she and Amos had shared

in the telegraph office—his strong arms around her, the way he'd looked at her as if she were the most beautiful creature he'd ever seen, his ardency as he'd taken control and led her down a road to passion she'd never travelled before but couldn't wait to travel again, with *him*—her spirits couldn't help but lift. She'd use her dreams of the future to hold the worries of the present at bay. She'd trust in the Lord to watch over the man she loved and continue praying for his safe return.

"Thank you." Grace met Addie's eyes as her friend's hand fell away from her mouth. Understanding and comradery flowed between them. Addie nodded. Fear was an enemy best battled with an ally.

A dog barked outside, and Addie's forehead crinkled. "We must have a guest. Scout wouldn't carry on so if it were Bart. Though it's awfully late for a caller." She grabbed the arm of the sofa and started to lever herself up, the baby she carried making the movement awkward.

Grace hurriedly set down her nearly empty teacup and motioned for her friend to stay seated. "I'll see to the door."

"You don't have—"

Grace narrowed her eyes in a mock scold. "I insist. It's the least I can do after all you've done for me tonight."

Scout's barking grew more insistent, and footsteps pounded on the porch as Grace made her way to the door. A burst of three knocks in quick succession echoed loudly in the room.

Grace set her hand to the latch but hesitated. What if Lockhart had tracked her somehow?

The knocks came again. Three rapid beats.

"Mrs. Porter?" a male voice called through the door. "Your husband sent me. My name is Amos Bledsoe. I'm looking for—"

Grace threw the door wide and launched herself into Amos's arms.

"Grace!" His arms closed around her. "Oh, thank God." His

embrace tightened, and a sob born of pent-up worry and immense gratitude erupted from her throat.

He released her immediately, setting her away from him and running his gaze over her from head to toe. "Are you hurt?"

She shook her head even as her body trembled from the sudden emotional release. "I-I'm just s-so happy to s-see you!" She threw herself back into his arms, yearning for the comfort of his embrace.

Amos, smart man that he was, caught on and held her close, one hand pressed against her spine, another reaching up to cup the back of her head.

She sighed and snuggled against his chest, her tremors abating as the reality of his presence soothed and comforted her. After a long, heavenly moment, Grace pulled back slightly so she could look into his eyes. Her arms moved up to twine about his neck. "Oh, Amos, I'm so very, *very* glad that you're all right."

The blue of his eyes darkened. "I love you, Grace Mallory."

She toyed with the hair at the nape of his neck, all her recent talk of kissing putting rather scandalous thoughts in her head. If he didn't take care of the matter soon, she just might have to pursue the business herself. "And I love you. With all my heart."

Tugging gently, as if she were made of the most delicate lace, he drew her face close, his fingers tunneling into her loose braid as he tilted her mouth up to meet his. When his lips finally met hers, she sighed. This was where she belonged. With this man. Loving him and basking in the gift of his love.

His kiss started as a tender caress, sweet but far too careful to Grace's way of thinking. They had escaped death tonight. She wanted to feast on life and love.

She tugged on his neck to bring him closer and lifted up on her tiptoes to deepen the kiss.

Amos reacted instantly. With a little growl that vibrated in his throat, he clutched her to his chest and gave her the kiss she'd been longing for. Passionate, possessive, and just the tiniest bit out of control. His fingers massaged her scalp as his lips crossed over hers at a new angle. Shivers danced down her neck and along her arms.

A throat clearing softly nearby penetrated their celebratory haze. Amos broke off the kiss to lift his head and peer behind her shoulder.

"As much as I hate to interrupt such an . . . enthusiastic reunion, I think we ought to at least move it off the front stoop and away from prying eyes."

Grace could hear the smile in Addie Porter's voice and knew she meant no censure, but her cheeks flamed anyway. She'd completely forgotten where they were and that they had an audience.

Amos's neck flushed red, too, but he stood straight and tall and kept a hand at Grace's back as they moved inside and closed the door. He might be embarrassed to have had their private moment witnessed by another, but there was nothing about him that indicated shame. In fact, the look he gave her as he led her to the sofa radiated a pride so rich, she felt like the most highly sought girl at the fair instead of the practically invisible telegraph operator she knew herself to be.

Amos Bledsoe wanted her. Loved her. Had chosen *her* from all the ladies of his acquaintance. And when this mess with Lockhart was concluded, she planned to show him that she had chosen him as well.

Addie lowered herself into a rocker. "Did you happen to run across Sheriff Tabor, Mr. Bledsoe? Grace was worried the two of you might not find each other out there in the dark."

Grace swiveled in her seat, her gaze intent on Amos's face as he gave a solemn nod. The joy humming through him a moment ago seemed to sputter and fade. Something had happened out there. And whatever it was, she wanted to be the one to shore him up. Taking his hand, she twined her fingers through his and squeezed.

His eyes met hers, yet it felt as if something deeper than their gazes connected.

"Yes, ma'am," Amos answered, turning his attention back to Addie. "I met up with Sheriff Tabor along with Malachi Shaw and your brother-in-law."

"Benjamin was out there?" Addie sat a little straighter in her chair, her brow puckering slightly.

"Yes, and he's fine, by the way." Amos rubbed the edge of Grace's thumb as he glanced sideways at her. "They all are."

Grace exhaled in relief.

"Shaw and Porter split up when we began the search then headed back to town when dark began to fall."

Grace heard what he didn't say. The others had returned to Harper's Station, but not Amos. He'd continued hunting for her alone. Even knowing how badly Lockhart outgunned him. He truly was her hero.

"Apparently the Pinkerton who Lockhart had been impersonating had recovered enough for Miss Potter to bring him to town."

"Helen?" Grace couldn't stop herself from interjecting, too shocked by this piece of information to remain quiet. "*Helen* brought the Pinkerton to town? But she hates men."

"Not this one." Amos's grin was downright mischievous. "Apparently she's been nursing him for several days and has become rather well acquainted with the gentleman."

Grace flopped back against the cushions of the sofa. Helen and the Pinkerton. Who would have even fathomed such an occurrence?

"Anyway," Amos continued, "the real Dunbar recalled seeing Lockhart with the Gladstone woman on the train and figured he'd try to take advantage of that relationship. So Shaw and Porter left Harper's Station in the hands of the Pinkerton and hightailed it out to the Gladstone place. The sheriff showed up as well, right when . . ." Amos glanced down at his lap and swallowed. "Well, let's just say we had Lockhart surrounded, and he didn't make it past us."

Grace's heart fluttered. "You mean . . . ?"

Amos lifted his face toward hers and nodded. "Lockhart's dead, Grace. You're safe."

Her vision blurred.

Safe. After all this time. Mercy, she'd nearly forgotten what such a state felt like. Then, as if a dam had broken, the tears fell, purging her heart of all the grief, fear, and dread that had hounded her heels for the last year.

Amos curled her into the crook of his arm and gently pressed her head onto his shoulder. "Shh." His lips brushed the top of her head. "I've got you, love. I've got you."

Yes, he did.

36

Grace waved farewell to her new friend early the following morning. After the men had caught a few hours of sleep in the livery, they'd been up at dawn, readying the horses for the trip back to Harper's Station. Not that Grace could blame them. She was more than eager to be home. Lockhart might no longer be a threat, but Chaucer Haversham could send another henchman. She had to end this matter for good.

The men surrounded her as they rode, the marshal on her left and Amos on her right. Porter rode behind. Their protectiveness eased her mind and made her smile, as did their efforts to keep the conversation light.

"Tabor said Miss Gladstone nearly shot his toes off when he dared to imply that Lockhart had been less than honest in representing himself to her." Malachi grinned and shook his head. "Gotta appreciate the woman's dedication. She's got spunk."

Amos rubbed the back of his head. "A little *too* much spunk, if you ask me. She brained me with a lantern."

Grace winced, recalling how limp he'd been when Lockhart dragged his semi-conscious body into the barn. "Make sure you get Maybelle to take a look at that when we get back."

He shrugged. "It's just a knot and a few scrapes, nothing requiring stitches."

"Still . . ." Grace stared at him.

The marshal chuckled. "Better do what the little woman wants, Bledsoe. Trust me, it'll go a lot easier on you that way."

"I have a mother and a sister," Amos quipped as he tossed a teasing glance at Grace, throwing in a wink for good measure. "I know all about the words that buy a man's peace."

All three men looked at each other then said in near perfect unison, "'Yes, ma'am.'"

Grace rolled her eyes but smiled, unable to resist their amusement. It felt good to laugh. To smile. To . . . relax.

But when they reached Harper's Station, relaxation gave way to intentionality. It wouldn't take long for Haversham to learn of Lockhart's demise, and the best way to protect herself and those she cared about was to find the documents her father had hidden.

So while Amos visited the clinic and Malachi sought out Lee Dunbar, the true Pinkerton, Grace retrieved her father's books from Emma's vault and invited everyone involved in the affair to join her at the telegraph office. The time for secrets had passed. The more minds they had working on the problem, the more likely they were to find a solution.

Within twenty minutes, her small office nearly overflowed with occupants. Helen hovered over a man with a thick mustache, who sat in the blue-striped chair along the wall, his leg propped up on the crate her false shipment of books had arrived in. Malachi Shaw and Ben Porter moved her desk and telegraph equipment against the back wall to create more open space by the window, while Emma and Tori helped Grace tidy the books Lockhart had scattered over her floor and work area. Amos arrived last with a scowling Claire traipsing behind him.

"Daft man saw ye all gatherin' and decided he'd had enough doctorin', but I aim to finish the job I started." The redhead marched Amos straight to the office chair and directed him to sit with a point of her finger.

Amos chanced a quick glance at the marshal as he walked past then turned back to Claire. "Yes, ma'am."

Malachi and Ben snickered, earning glares from their women.

Grace ignored them all and came up beside Claire. "How is he?"

The young healer waited for Amos to seat himself then pointed to a wet spot on the back of his head. Grace winced at the size of the knot showing through his flattened hair.

"That lump will pain him fer a wee while," Claire said, "but I've cleaned the cuts and brought along an unguent of St. John's Wort that'll speed the healin'. As long as he keeps the area clean, the sun will shine on him."

Grace placed a hand on Amos's shoulder, needing to touch him, to comfort, thank, and somehow convey how much he meant to her. His own hand came up to cover hers.

Amos craned his neck around and smiled at her. "See? I told you there was nothing to worry about." The teasing left his eyes as his attention drifted to the edge of the table, where her father's books lay. "At least regarding my health. Haversham, on the other hand, is a different matter." He glanced at Grace, his thumb rubbing the back of her hand as he tilted his head toward the books. "May I?"

She nodded. "Of course."

He released her hand and pulled away from her hold on his shoulder in order to lean over the edge of the table where the books sat.

Malachi strode away from the window, his eyes locked on Amos. "Did you figure out where those papers are hiding?"

Amos met the marshal's stare, then looked at each man in turn—Porter first, then Dunbar. However, when Amos gave his answer, his attention focused solely on Grace. "A suspicion has been gnawing at me since the day we last examined them.

However, I wasn't able to test my theory while Lockhart was snooping around."

"We need those documents to build a case against Chaucer Haversham." Dunbar's jaw ticked as he sat forward and rubbed a spot on his leg. Helen placed a gentle hand on his arm, and the tightness in his neck seemed to ease.

The sight of Helen voluntarily touching a man, and in such an affectionate manner, distracted Grace from the seriousness of the discussion, but as the Pinkerton continued, her focus sharpened.

"Lockhart was smart," Dunbar said. "He kept no evidence on his person linking him to Haversham. Shaw searched his body last night, and we both went through his saddlebags this morning. Nothing turned up to connect him to Haversham beyond a leather pouch filled with silver nuggets that, while circumstantial with Haversham owning a silver mine, offers no definitive connection of payment for services rendered."

Dunbar sighed as he released his leg and leaned back against the cushioned chair. "I can testify that Lockhart worked for Haversham and that the two were often found in each other's company, but I cannot swear under oath that the two were colluding. All Haversham has to say is that he was unaware of Lockhart's activities, and he'd be exonerated."

"I could testify against him," Grace said, her voice trembling as much as her legs at the thought of facing down the man who'd ordered her father's murder. But she'd do it if it meant bringing a killer to justice. "When Lockhart had me in that barn, he admitted to murdering my father and shooting Mr. Dunbar in order to steal his credentials."

Dunbar shook his head. "Sorry. As awful as that is, it doesn't tie Lockhart to Haversham."

"But Haversham is the one who gained from my father's death, not Lockhart." The fire of injustice heated her belly. She paced toward the Pinkerton, spitting words at him like bullets. "Lockhart said that Chaucer knew about the books, told him which ones to look for, and how to find his father's library stamp inside the front cover. That has to prove collusion."

Malachi came alongside her and placed a hand on her shoulder. "It's not enough, Grace. Haversham's lawyer would simply say the two had been talking about the library and a pair of missing books—which your father was technically guilty of stealing."

Dunbar stroked his thumb and forefinger over his mustache, his eyes sympathetic. "Don't go givin' up just yet, though." He tipped his head toward Amos. "If Bledsoe finds those papers, we can cripple Haversham. Take away his inheritance, and you steal his power, not to mention his reason to come after you. We might not be able to convict him of murder, but we can ruin him financially."

"And who's to say something won't turn up later in the investigation?" Helen added, her chin jutting forward. "Lee said that the new will would establish motive, and if they can find a suspicious payment in one of Haversham's account books, it could be enough for a conviction."

Dunbar smiled at Helen, his mustache stretching as he beamed. "There ain't no guarantees, but I'll sure give it my best effort."

"As will I." Amos drew Grace's attention as he opened the front cover of the top volume, *Oliver Twist*, then reached into his trouser pocket and extracted a small knife.

No one spoke as Amos slowly unfolded the blade. Grace held her breath, her heart pumping in a wild rhythm as Amos slid the tip of the knife along the inner edge of the cover. It seemed to take days for him to slit the cover from bottom to top. After he reached the top corner, he paused to push his spectacles higher on the bridge of his nose then went back to work, his face a mask of concentration.

As he started along the top edge, the truth clicked into place in

Grace's mind. He wasn't cutting away the cover. He was separating it from the endpaper—the glued-down sheet that gave the book its finished look. A sheet that could hide fraying cloth edges or uneven cover folds . . . or secret papers.

"Are they there?" she breathed, pressing close, her shadow blocking his light.

He didn't answer. Instead, he set down the knife, despite the fact that he was only halfway across the top, and began tugging on the corner of the brown endpaper. The soft tearing sound made Grace cringe even as it sent her pulse into a gallop.

There, beneath the brown paper. Something else, ivory in color. Was it just the back of the cover, or . . . ?

Amos released the endpaper and grasped the ivory sheet secreted beneath. He tugged gently, then more firmly when it didn't pull free. "It might have been glued in accidentally when your father hid it."

"Just yank off the endpaper." She couldn't stand the slowness. She needed to know. Had they found the will?

Amos ignored her demand and took up his knife again, carefully separating the endpaper from its moorings. Finally, the brown paper was freed from the three outer edges. Amos peeled it back and plucked the folded ivory paper from its hiding place with a sharp tug. He didn't open it, simply handed the sheet to her.

She looked at him then accepted the paper, her insides rioting with nerves. Her father had dealt with books all the time, appraising rare volumes for collectors, recommending acquisitions to buyers. It made sense that he would know how they were put together. How to repair or restore a damaged copy. How to secrete an important document in a place few would think to look.

With trembling fingers, she unfolded the paper then had to place one hand on the edge of the table to support her suddenly limp knees as she read *Last Will and Testament* inscribed in fancy script along the top of the page.

"You did it," Grace whispered as she set the first page of the will onto the table top. Glancing down into the face of the man she loved, she beamed. "You did it!" With a happy squeal, she threw her arms around Amos's neck and pressed her lips to his cheek, uncaring that she had an audience.

"How marvelous," Emma enthused. "To think the documents were there all this time and we never realized. How did you ever puzzle it out?"

Grace released her hold on the hero of the hour and stepped aside, eager to hear his answer. Amos's blue eyes glowed with joy and love as he grinned at Grace before turning to Emma and the others.

"Mr. Mallory died protecting these books. He wouldn't have done that if he'd removed the documents and stored them elsewhere, so I knew the will and the Pinkerton report had to be in the books themselves somehow. We all examined the pages, the bindings, and found nothing. The only option left was to look inside the cover. If the documents hadn't been beneath the end-papers, I would have pulled the cloth from the pressboard next, then unsewn the binding." His gaze found Grace's. "Whatever it took."

"Good work, Bledsoe." Detective Dunbar eased his injured leg down from the crate and made to stand. "Think there's another page or two under the back cover?"

"Don't you be gettin' out of that chair, Leander Dunbar," Helen scolded. "I'll fetch the paper for you."

She made it two steps before Lee grumbled, "I'm fully capable of fetching the paper myself, woman."

"Wrong answer," Ben Porter remarked in a stage whisper. "You're supposed to say, 'Yes, ma'am.'"

Tori swatted his arm, but the big man gave no indication that he felt it, just shared an amused glance with Malachi. Grace ignored their antics, much more concerned with what Amos was doing.

Working meticulously, Amos separated the endpapers from both books and extracted all three pages of Haversham's will along with a single-sheet report from Detective Whitmore regarding the identity of Tremont's daughter.

"Margaret Flanders of Worcester, Massachusetts." The name felt surreal slipping from Grace's tongue. How many times had she read the letters between Tremont Haversham and his seamstress bride, Deborah, and tried to picture their daughter? "Raised by Horace Pierce, a machinist, and his wife, Ann. Their only child. Margaret married Owen Flanders, an employee of Crompton Loom Works, in 1891." She glanced up from the report. "Can you imagine how this woman's life is about to change? The money. Ownership of a mine in Colorado. All the people, the responsibility. It's bound to overwhelm her."

"Worcester women are strong," Emma said.

Grace's brow scrunched. "How can you possibly know that?"

Emma grinned. "Worcester hosted the first two National Women's Rights Conventions in 1850 and 1851. Strong, forward-thinking women make up the backbone of that place. She'll be fine."

"Don't forget she's got a husband to help her deal with all the changes, as well," the marshal added, giving his wife a telling look.

Helen snorted. "Unless he turns out to be a weasel and steals everything out from under her, leaving her high and dry."

Detective Dunbar, safely seated back in his chair, reached for Helen's hand. "Not all men are scoundrels."

She ducked her head. "I know. But more are than ain't."

Dunbar smiled and brought the back of her hand to his lips. The gallant gesture seemed to flummox Helen and turned her cheeks bright pink, but she didn't tug away or flay him with the sharp side of her tongue.

"I'll investigate her husband's work history and reputation

before I deliver the news," Dunbar promised, "to avoid any surprises." Without releasing Helen's hand, he shuffled the papers lying in his lap, grasped the second page of the will, and scanned the contents. "Though it might not matter. Haversham's will stipulates that the money belongs to Margaret Pierce Flanders in her own right. The only way her husband will be able to access the funds is with her permission."

A dark thought tripped through Grace's mind. "You don't think Chaucer Haversham will try to harm his half-sister in order to reclaim his inheritance, do you?"

The Pinkerton shook his head. "No. The will stipulates that the monies will pass to Margaret's children in the event of her death. If she has no children, the funds will be disbursed among several Philadelphia charities supported by Tremont's first wife. Margaret should be in no danger."

Grace nodded, relief trickling through her. She wouldn't want any woman to go through what she had this last year. "I guess all that's left for me to do is turn over Tremont Haversham's letters to you, then, so you can be on your way."

Grace expected the Pinkerton to readily agree—after all, he'd been pursuing these answers as long as she had. Surely he was eager to bring his case to a close. Yet his face went oddly blank at her words, and his grip on Helen's hand tightened.

Regretting her careless words, Grace moved toward Helen, trying to think of something reassuring to say, but the tapping of an incoming message from the telegraph made her reverse course.

Amos scrambled to get out of her seat so she could respond to the call. Grace smiled her thanks, reached for a telegraph blank and pencil, then sat and tapped out the code signifying that she was ready to receive.

"The message is for you, Marshal." Grace glanced quickly at Malachi, her pencil continuing its stilted scribbling as she deciphered the incoming code. "From Bart Porter."

"Bart?" The freighter's questioning tone hushed the room. "We just left his place this morning. What could he possibly—?"

Amos's sharp pivot toward Grace cut off Ben's words. The sounder continued tapping out code, but Grace had stopped transcribing. She looked up, met Amos's eyes, and saw her own shock reflected there.

"Bart Porter just spotted a man in a fancy suit with a silver-headed walking stick leaving the undertaker's building," she reported, breaking Western Union's confidentiality policy for the first time in her career. "It appears he's rented a horse from Stranton's Livery and is planning a visit to Harper's Station."

Lee Dunbar shot to his feet, a grimace the only evidence of his pain. "Wire Sheriff Tabor to gather some men and meet us here," he ordered through clenched teeth. He shoved the will at Grace and pointed to Emma. "Lock the documents back in the safe and spread the word to the ladies to keep off the street." His penetrating stare moved from one man to the next in the room. "Looks like Chaucer Haversham is paying us a visit."

37

Chaucer Haversham rode into Harper's Station like some kind of visiting dignitary, tipping his hat politely to each of the armed men he passed on his way. Malachi Shaw at the station house. Ben Porter in front of the store. Lee Dunbar at the bank where Helen, Claire, and Maybelle had decided to wait things out—Helen to stay close to the Pinkerton, and the healers to be on hand in case their services were required.

Amos stiffened as the man who'd instigated all of Grace's hardship guided his horse toward the telegraph office. Sheriff Tabor shadowed him and deputies rode behind, but that offered small comfort. Amos adjusted his grip on the rifle he'd borrowed from the marshal. Whatever Haversham thought to accomplish by coming here, Amos intended to see he left unfulfilled.

"Good day to you, sir," Haversham said as he drew his horse to a halt in front of Amos. "I'm here to see Miss Mallory. Would you be so kind as to fetch her for me?"

"I'm afraid Miss Mallory is unavailable." Amos widened his stance as he eyed the man in the black tailored suit. Sunlight glinted off a silver ring on Haversham's little finger as he lifted his hand to tip his hat to Amos just as he had done to all the others, who were now closing in on their visitor, surrounding him on all sides. Feeling the strength of their numbers, Amos grinned. "I'd be glad to convey a message to her on your behalf, if you would like."

"I'm afraid that would be quite unsatisfactory." Haversham met Amos's gaze with eyes as smug as they were falsely solicitous. "You see, I've come to offer my most heartfelt apologies. I understand that a man formerly in my employ harassed Miss Mallory in recent days and caused her some manner of distress."

"Some manner of distress?" A muscle ticked in Amos's jaw. "Lockhart tried to *kill* her. And me."

"Well, you can imagine my relief at learning that he was unsuccessful," Haversham continued, his gentility so sickeningly sweet it was all Amos could do not to retch. "I would like to express my deepest regrets to the lady and assure her that I had nothing to do with the incident."

"Then why are you here?" Amos glared up him, not believing a word that passed his lips. "If you're so removed from this incident, as you claim, how is that you came to be in Seymour on the very day that your employee abducted and attacked Miss Mallory? Doesn't seem very removed to me. Seems more like you had a vested interest in the matter."

Haversham sighed. "I can see that you've already painted me guilty by association. Understandable, given the situation. But in truth, I followed Milton Lockhart to Seymour in order to stop him from doing anything . . . untoward. Milton could get rather fixated on things, you see, and when he realized how upset I was about the theft of a pair of books from my library, he took it upon himself to get them back. I insisted that we wait to get a court order, but he wouldn't hear of it. As soon as he learned of Miss Mallory's location, he set out to retrieve my property."

The way he emphasized the words *my property* set off alarm bells in Amos's head.

"And now, I really must insist on seeing Miss Mallory." Haversham dismounted and strode forward until he stood directly in front of Amos. "She may meet me of her own accord, or I can have the sheriff drag her out and throw her in jail, if that is her preference."

The marshal pushed his way through the deputies to flank Haversham from the rear. "Tabor? What's he talking about?"

Sheriff Tabor dismounted as well, then reached inside his jacket and pulled out a paper folded in half. "He's got a writ. Signed by a judge. It compels Grace Mallory to produce two novels marked with Tremont Haversham's seal." Tabor unfolded the paper and held it up to his face. "*Oliver Twist* and *Guy Mannering*," he read. "She's to return them to their rightful owner, Mr. Chaucer Haversham, or face arrest on charges of theft." He handed the paper to Malachi. "I got no choice, Shaw. The law's the law. Best if she just hands over them books. Then we can send this jackanapes on his way."

"That jackanapes shouldn't be sent on his way. He should be arrested for murder." A feminine voice laced with steel echoed behind Amos.

Grace! Amos wanted to shout at her to get back inside, to stay as far from Haversham as possible. He'd nearly lost her yesterday. He couldn't bear to think of anything happening to her today.

But Haversham couldn't harm her. At least not physically. He was only one man, unarmed by all appearances, and surrounded by no less than seven men who'd not hesitate to put him down should the occasion call for it.

"Ah, the lovely Miss Mallory." Chaucer Haversham removed his hat with a flourish and sketched a gallant bow. "What a delight to finally meet you in person. Let me say—"

"No. I won't let you say."

Amos nearly choked at the startled look on Haversham's face as Grace marched past Amos and planted herself directly in front of her nemesis. Shy, quiet Grace Mallory had not only interrupted a conversation, but she'd placed herself directly in the center of attention. Every eye was locked on her, and she held herself like an avenging angel ready to pronounce judgment.

Clutching the books Haversham sought against her chest with folded arms, Grace raised her chin and stabbed him with an icy stare. "You killed my father."

Haversham darted a glance toward Sheriff Tabor as he straightened and replaced his hat on his head. "I assure you, I did no such thing."

"You might not have pulled the trigger yourself, but you ordered it done."

He shook his head, a condescending smile sneaking onto his face. Amos wanted to smash it with his rifle butt. "My dear girl, I fear you're laboring under some misguided notions."

"I'm not your dear anything," Grace ground out, "and everyone here knows you are guilty."

Haversham made a *tsk* sound. "Miss Mallory, perhaps you are unaware, but in this country a man is presumed innocent until proven guilty." He opened his arms and gestured to the men encircling him. "And since none of these fine, upstanding lawmen are rushing forward to take me into custody, I must assume that proof of my guilt does not exist. However, proof of *your* guilt does." He nodded toward the books she held. "I believe those belong to me."

Not for long. Satisfaction filled Amos at the thought of the arrogant rogue finally getting his comeuppance.

Grace thrust the books at Haversham, but as he closed his hands around them, she kept a grip on her end. "God knows the truth," she said in a low voice that only those standing closest could hear. "And if justice does not find you in this life, Chaucer Haversham, it will find you in the next."

With those words hanging like sharpened swords in the air,

Grace released her hold on the books, turned around, and walked back toward her office.

Such courage and conviction. Amos grinned at her as she came alongside him. She was extraordinary.

"Oh, Miss Mallory?" Haversham called to her retreating back. Grace slowly pivoted to face him.

"It seems the books have been damaged." He ran his finger along the inside cover then held the volume up for her inspection.

Amos had helped her glue the endpapers back into place earlier, but the paste had not had time to dry completely, nor was there any way to hide the slit that Amos had cut along both spines.

Nonplussed, Grace met the man's stare. "Yes. I believe my father intended to restore them, but he died before he could finish the job. I'm afraid you'll have to be satisfied with my efforts."

Haversham's eyes narrowed, his gentlemanly veneer slipping. "Did you remove anything from the books, Miss Mallory?" His voice tightened to fit though his clenched jaw. "The court order specifies the books *and any foreign contents contained therein* are to be turned over to me."

Sheriff Tabor nodded. "That's true." He looked at Grace. "You remove any *foreign* contents from them there books, Miss Grace?"

A slow smile spread over Grace's face. "No, sir. I never removed anything from those books of a *foreign* nature. Everything I saw inside the book was written in English."

"Good enough for me. Take yer books and skedaddle, mister."

Haversham lunged forward and grabbed Grace's arm. "You conniving—"

The sound of seven guns being cocked simultaneously cut off the rest of his words. In a flash, Malachi had Haversham's arms pinned behind his back. The instant Grace was free of the man's grip, Amos pulled her into his side, leaving the sheriff to collect the books that had fallen to the ground in the scuffle.

"You see that, Tabor?" Shaw asked as he fastened a leather strap around Haversham's wrists.

"Unhand me, you cretin!"

"Yep," the sheriff replied, completely ignoring Haversham's protests. "Assault on a female. I'll charge him and keep him locked up until the judge comes to town."

Haversham struggled against his bindings until Ben Porter laid his big hands on the man's shoulders and forced him to be still.

"This is outrageous!" Haversham cried. "I barely touched her. No judge will find me guilty."

"Maybe not." Lee Dunbar limped into the circle, revolver in one hand, crutch in the other. "But the judge won't even hear your case for . . . what, Tabor, a week?"

The sheriff rubbed his chin. "More like ten days, I'd say. Circuit judge only comes once a month."

"Plenty of time for me to return to Philadelphia and make my report to Whitmore, then," Dunbar said. "Excellent."

Haversham paled as the truth finally sank into his brain.

He had lost.

38

The next morning, Helen stood in front of the station house, watching helplessly as Lee checked the ties on his saddle-bags. Maybe it wasn't too late to tie him up again in her cottage and keep him from leaving. She'd hoped the difficulty of finding and capturing Lee's horse would postpone his departure, but Ben Porter, drat his hide, was apparently the pied piper of mustangs. In less than two hours, he and the marshal had the horse caught, saddled, and ready to carry Lee away.

"I packed you a cold supper for the train," she said as she held out a small sack that she'd stuffed with enough food to feed him and probably half of the other passengers as well. "I tucked extra bandages and salve into your satchel, too. Claire says infection can set in even after healing has begun, so you'll need to change the dressing regularly."

He accepted the bag of food from her and hooked the knotted end over the pommel. "Helen—"

"I'm still not sure you're healed enough to ride," she interrupted. She didn't want to hear him say good-bye, to politely thank her for nursing him, then ride out of her life. "And on the train, you should keep your leg elevated. Claim a bench for yourself and don't let anyone crowd you out of the extra space. It's a long trip to Philadelphia."

"Helen." His voice echoed a little louder, a little more insistent.

Yet she rambled on, determined to delay the inevitable. "With Haversham locked up in Seymour, he won't be able to interfere with you getting the documents to Whitmore, but that doesn't mean there aren't others in his employ who could cause trouble. Keep your eyes peeled. Since Mrs. Flanders's identity is still a secret, she should be safe from—*oomph.*"

Soft, warm, *determined* lips pressed against hers. Helen jerked in surprise, her eyes popping wide. Lee's hands came up to cup her cheeks and his crutch clattered to the ground. Helen wrapped her arms around his waist, worried he might take a tumble, but his muscles felt like iron. So strong, so sure. In a heartbeat her grip changed from trying to hold him up to reveling in the vitality of the man she cared about.

All right, maybe more than cared. There was no point in lying to herself about it. And if he wanted to kiss her good-bye, she wasn't about to argue. Her hands slid up his back, her lashes dropping closed as she immersed herself in sensation. His mustache tickled in the most delightful way. His thumbs caressed her cheekbones as he held her close, gentle yet firm at the same time. It was the most perfect moment of her life. Because for this one moment, Lee belonged to her. She savored the wonder of his kiss and seared the memory into her heart for the lonely days to come.

All too soon, he pulled away.

Lee peered down at her, his gaze heated, his breath a little labored. Yet a disgruntled frown wrinkled his brow. "Are you gonna let me talk now?"

Helen swallowed and gave a shaky nod. She couldn't speak now if she wanted to, anyway. Too many emotions whirled in her stomach.

Lee's hands gently skimmed down her cheeks, along her neck,

and came to rest atop her shoulders. "I have feelings for you, Helen. Stronger feelings than I've ever experienced." He squeezed her collarbone and raised an eyebrow at her as if warning her not to interrupt. "And it's not just gratitude for saving my life either, so don't think you can just explain it away."

As if she would. Not when he was saying exactly what she'd dreamed of hearing from him. Her pulse fluttered wildly, joy swarming like hungry grasshoppers inside her chest.

He grabbed the nape of his neck. "I *am* grateful. Don't think I'm not, but there's more to it than that. There's a . . . a connection between us. I feel it. And I think you do, too."

He paused, his gaze searching her face.

Helen bit her lip, dug deep inside herself—past the fear of being hurt, past the mistrust, past the bad experiences of her youth—and leaped. "I do," she whispered. "I feel it, too. But you're leaving, Lee. You're leaving."

"Not forever." His voice softened, his gorgeous green eyes glimmering with promises she wanted so much to believe. "Only long enough to finish this job." He took her hands in his. Inhaled. Exhaled. "Can I write to you, Helen?"

Her pulse stuttered. This wasn't simply an offer of friendly correspondence. Not with the way he was looking at her. This was more. This was courtship.

"Yes." Her voice scratched, so she cleared her throat and answered again. "Yes, Lee. Please write to me."

He smiled and lifted one of her hands to his mouth. He pressed a tender kiss to the back of her knuckles then cradled her hand against his chest, where she felt the thumping of his heart.

"Ready for a leg up?" The deep tones of Ben Porter rang out behind them, and Helen felt her cheeks flush.

Lee hesitated, holding her hand a few heartbeats longer before nodding to the freighter and releasing his hold on her.

Blinking to keep the annoying moisture collecting behind her eyes from forming tears, Helen stooped to retrieve his fallen crutch.

"Be careful with that left leg," she warned as Mr. Porter hefted Lee into the saddle.

Thankfully the two managed the mount without much more than a pair of grunts and a clenched jaw from Lee.

He looked down at her, his eyes soft and full of promises. "Be watching for my letters, Helen."

She gave a jerky nod and sniffed, far too close to losing her composure. "I will," she rasped, reaching up to pat the horse's flank near Lee's leg.

Her heart throbbed with both doubt and hope, each battling for dominion. Meeting Lee's earnest gaze, Helen chose hope.

I'm trusting you, Lee. Please don't let me down.

"Are you sure you don't want to take your bicycle?" Grace walked side by side with Amos as he led his mount out of the station house paddock. "I could ask Mr. Porter to take it in the wagon for you."

Amos smiled, his blue eyes shining behind his spectacles in a way that made Grace's stomach flip. "No. I'll leave it here so I have something to ride when I visit. I still owe Revolver Granny some cycling lessons, after all. Got to come back for that."

Grace stifled a giggle at the nickname he'd given Henrietta Chandler. She slipped her arm through his and leaned close. "Is that the *only* reason you'll be visiting?"

Amos gazed up at the sky and feigned great thought. "Well, I should probably check on that telegraph line I cut. Make sure it's repaired properly." Then he dipped his chin to face her, his features serious. "Oh, and then there's the matter of Western Union relations."

Grace scrunched her forehead. "Western Union relations?"

He nodded sagely. "Yes. It seems there is a great need to enhance relations between personnel from various Western Union offices in the area. I thought for sure you'd heard about this new measure. It's a mandate intended to boost morale."

Catching on, Grace fought back a smile. "I see," she replied, trying to match his thoughtful tone. "I suppose I should plan a trip to Seymour to visit with Elmer Donaldson then. He's the closest operator to my station, and he's always been pleasant on the line. I suppose meeting him could boost my morale."

Amos frowned. "Elmer Donaldson? No. As I recall, Harper's Station has been assigned to Denison for morale-boosting meetings."

"You're sure?" Grace tried to tame her smile, but she couldn't quite manage it.

"Positive." Amos nodded sharply, his own eyes twinkling with humor.

Grace hugged his arm and looked up into his face. "Good. I tend to prefer Denison operators to the ones from Seymour, anyhow."

Amos pulled his mount to a halt a few feet from where the others waited. He turned to Grace and stroked her cheek. His gaze captured hers with such sweet intensity that her pulse skipped a beat. "I'll be on the wire tonight after hours if you want to get an early start on nurturing those relations."

"I'll be listening for you." Grace turned to face him more fully, slid her hands up to his coat lapels, and smoothed them flat against his chest. Not because he needed the grooming, but simply because she wanted to touch him. To feel his heart beating beneath her fingertips. "Be safe," she whispered.

"You, too." He bent and kissed the top of her head.

Her eyes slid closed at the contact. Heavens, she was going to miss him.

She opened her eyes and spotted Helen—someone who would have to wait much longer to be reunited with her man.

As Amos mounted the horse Bart Porter had loaned them after Lockhart's attack, Grace walked over to Helen and wrapped an arm around the other woman's waist. They stood together quietly as their men met up and waved their final good-byes.

"They're good men, Helen," Grace said, squeezing her friend close as much to offer comfort as to gain it for herself. She lifted her hand in farewell then watched as Amos and Lee turned their horses and set off down the path to Seymour. "They'll be back."

Helen leaned her head onto Grace's shoulder. "I pray you're right."

EPILOGUE

A February chill stung Grace's nose and cheeks. Wind buffeted her face as she raced down the slope. Dual wheels bumped over the hard-packed earth, and her arms absorbed the shock as she steered the velocipede onto the straightaway. Laughing with delight, she pumped the pedals faster and faster, determined to catch the fine figure of a man who rode a few feet in front of her. No longer a novice rider, she kept up with Amos quite well these days on their little jaunts around Harper's Station.

She'd spent the last few months attempting to train Flora Johnson to take her place at the telegraph office. Flora could use the funds such a position would provide, and Grace could use a capable substitute to cover the wire whenever Amos came to visit. Unfortunately, Flora struggled to distinguish the dots and dashes, but her son Ned had a real ear for code. He wasn't yet old enough to apply for a position himself, but with additional training, he would have a marketable skill to provide for himself and his mother one day. Recognizing that fact, he'd gladly volunteered to mind the wire for her while she and Amos took their ride.

Amos slowed his bicycle and raised an arm to point to something colorful on the ground a few yards from the east bank of the Wichita River. "Let's stop over there," he called over the noise of the wind and wheels.

Taking advantage of his slowing pace, Grace grinned and pedaled past him. "Last one there forfeits a favor!"

"You're on!"

Amos rose to the challenge, as she knew he would. He loved a good race. Of course, that was probably because he always won. The man had a competitive streak and insisted that he respected her too much to *let* her win simply because she was female. As if she would want to win in such an underhanded way.

However, getting a head start when the competition was distracted was another matter entirely. That was simply using one's wits. A perfectly acceptable advantage. All was fair in love and cycling.

Grace raced for the blue cloth pinned to the ground by eight large stones. The fabric flapped between the rock anchors, urging her on.

She was going to win this time. She felt it.

Leaning forward over the handlebars, she drove her legs faster, her heart pounding with excitement. The finish line loomed, but she dared not slow down. Better to simply steer away from the rocks.

"Be careful!" Amos called out from behind her.

From *behind* her! Grace laughed and continued pedaling. At the last moment, she steered to the left to avoid the rocks, but the jerk of the front wheel threw off her balance. She wobbled.

"Brake!" Amos yelled.

Grace reached for the braking lever, but when she loosened her grip on the handlebars, what little control she'd managed to maintain was lost. The bicycle tipped. She jumped from the seat, but the wheels kept rolling. The frame clipped her legs.

Grace tumbled, bracing herself as she fell. One hand hit the blue blanket, and the other grabbed for a corner rock to ensure she didn't strike her head.

"Grace! Are you all right?"

Grace rolled onto her side in time to see Amos execute a perfect, full-speed dismount, clearing the metal frame with an agile leap while the bicycle rolled past and toppled harmlessly to the ground a few feet away.

It really was quite impressive—and patently unfair—that he should be so graceful in his dismount while she lay sprawled on the ground in an inelegant heap. Yet she couldn't help but admire his athleticism.

Grace smiled as Amos reached her, his worried gaze scanning her for injury. "Are you hurt?"

She giggled and shook her head. She might have a bruise or two on her hip, and her wrist might be a tad sore after the awkward grab of the rock, but she was fine. Glorious, really.

"I won!" She grinned up at him and poked him in the chest. "*You* owe *me* a favor."

He frowned, obviously not quite as delighted as she by her victory. "If you wanted a favor so badly, all you had to do was ask. Goodness, Grace. You frightened me half to death."

He helped her gain her feet, then took her by the arm and led her to the middle of the blanket, where a picnic basket sat waiting for them.

Her heart melted at all the trouble he had gone to: finding a beautiful spot by the river, setting out a blanket, arranging a basket of refreshments. He must have been working on this all morning. But then, Amos was like that, going out of his way to make her feel special.

Like the code he created to tell her he loved her over the telegraph lines without anyone else understanding: •–––   •••••   •••–– Anyone who happened to be on the wires after hours would simply think it was a call sign, when in fact the numbers 143 stood for the number of letters in each of the three words that made her heart sing. *I love you.*

Not only had they resumed their evening chats, but over the last three months, Amos had made a point to visit Harper's Station nearly every two weeks. He even surprised her once with an extra return fare so she could travel to Denison and meet his family. She'd stayed with his sister and instantly felt at home with the vivacious Lucy. Amos's mother was a dear too, welcoming Grace without the slightest hesitation. And two-year-old Harry was about as adorable as little boys came, even with his penchant for grabbing bonnet strings while one's bonnet was still attached to one's head. Apparently, if spectacles weren't available, the little scamp had no trouble improvising. She loved Amos's family and couldn't wait for the day she'd claim them as her own.

"Are you sure you're all right?" Amos asked as he helped her take a seat on the blanket.

Grace nodded. "I'm perfect." She glanced around at the river, the blue sky, the birds soaring on the currents overhead. "How could I not be? It's a beautiful day"—she looked at the man at her side—"I'm in wonderful company, and I just bested Amos Bledsoe in a bicycle race!"

He smiled at her, the tender playfulness in his expression heating her insides enough that she could probably remove her heavy wool coat without fear of setting her teeth to chattering.

"What will you claim as your favor?" His voice deepened, grew richer, darker. The sound of it set her heart to fluttering. Every time he'd won, he'd claimed a kiss.

She thought of asking him for the same but held back. As much as she loved his kisses, she wanted to savor her victory a little longer. "I'm going to hold onto it for a bit," she said, a healthy dose of sass in her tone. "One never knows when a favor will come in handy."

He chuckled, raising his gaze from where it had been resting on her lips, and turned to open the picnic basket.

Hmm . . . maybe she shouldn't have given up her claim to that kiss so quickly.

Amos pulled out a glass jar full of apple cider and two lovely engraved goblets in a pattern she thought she recalled seeing in his mother's china cabinet.

Grace sat up a little straighter, her stomach dancing.

Amos said nothing as he poured the cider into the two glasses. He handed her one and kept the other for himself. Then he reached inside the basket a second time and pulled out a small box wrapped in a red ribbon.

Grace toyed with her goblet, not sure if she should sip her cider or wait for her companion to speak. He was obviously setting the stage for something. Her gaze darted from the box to Amos to the box again. She swallowed.

Amos set the box on the blanket in the few inches of space that separated him from her. Then he held his goblet toward her and met her gaze with his beautiful blue eyes.

"For years, I searched for a woman to call my own. For the *right* woman. One who valued character over charisma and intellect over broad shoulders. For a while, I despaired of finding her. Then came a delicate tap across my sounder. A tap that complimented me on my 'fine hand at the key.'"

Grace dropped her attention to her lap, her lips curving into a soft smile. She remembered that day. Emma had had some urgent banking business to convey to New York, but the operator in Seymour had been out sick and Grace had needed to find another telegrapher to relay her message. Mr. A had always impressed her with his precision on the key, so she'd approached him about her predicament, and he'd responded with speed and efficiency. It had seemed only right to thank him afterward and show proper appreciation. Little did she know, that single interaction would spark a friendship that would deepen into a life-transforming love.

Amos reached between them and gently lifted her chin until her eyes met his. "I thank God that he made me wait, Grace. Because no other woman could make me even half as happy as you do."

The smile that stretched across her face was so wide it nearly hurt. How she adored this man!

"Grace Mallory. I love you with all my heart. I want to share my life with you, my home with you, my future with you. I know you treasure this place," he said as he looked away from her for the first time in order to gesture toward Harper's Station with a tip of his head, "but if you'd be willing to take me as your husband and follow me to Denison, I vow to do everything within my power to ensure you never regret it."

Her heart full to bursting, it was all Grace could do not to toss away the fancy goblet and fling her arms about her beloved's neck. Instead, she sat up on her knees and lifted a hand to touch his smoothly shaven jaw. "I would follow you anywhere, Amos Bledsoe." And she would. As much as she loved Harper's Station and the friends she'd made here, it was time to move on. This had been her sanctuary, her place to hide from danger, but now it was time to stop hiding and start living. Shoot, she might even retire her derringer.

Amos leaned into her touch, his eyes never leaving hers. "Does that mean . . . ?"

"Yes, I've decided on the favor I want to claim."

He blinked a couple times as if dazed by her random change of subject. It wasn't nice to tease a man at a time like this, but she couldn't help it. It was just so fun to keep him off-balance.

"Oh?" he asked, pulling slightly away from her. "What favor is that?"

She found his free hand on the blanket and covered it with hers. "Make me your wife, Amos. My heart will never recover if you don't."

His eyes glimmered behind his spectacles, and his mouth curved into a smile so sweet, it made her insides ache. "Well, I certainly can't let your heart suffer such a fatal blow, can I?"

"Not if you wish to be considered a gentleman." Grace tried to make her face prim and prudish but failed miserably.

Amos bent his head close to hers. "Would I be considered a gentleman if I were to kiss my newly betrothed?"

Grace tipped her face up to meet his, her breath growing shallow. "I suppose it would be acceptable if the lady was willing."

His attention dropped to her lips then languidly lifted back to her eyes. "And is my lady willing?"

"Oh, yes," Grace murmured, her voice breathy in anticipation. "Very."

His lips brushed hers, the contact light and tender. She lifted up to meet him, to deepen the connection. Some of the cider from her goblet sloshed onto her hand as she moved, but she didn't care. Amos had finally proposed! If ever an occasion called for a little celebratory mess, this was it.

He tugged his hand from under hers and reached up to cup the back of her head. He drew her close, exactly where she longed to be. She wanted to be by his side forever, loving him, supporting him, partnering with him as they maneuvered through the challenges of life.

When Amos pulled away, Grace's eyes slowly opened. She peered into his face for a long moment, then, as passion receded, she settled back on her heels. "I have one more favor to ask of you, Amos."

He quirked a brow. "Oh?"

"Let's have a short engagement."

Rich, masculine laughter rang out across the countryside. "I think that can be arranged." He raised his glass to her and winked. "So, a toast. To us!"

Grace held her half-empty goblet up as well. "To our future. May it be filled with love, laughter, and family."

"Hear, hear." Amos gently clinked his glass against hers, then sipped.

Grace did the same. The cool liquid refreshed her, its sweetness a promise of good things to come.

When they finished their toasting, Amos set his goblet aside and pushed the beribboned box toward her. "Open it."

She handed her goblet to Amos, then gently picked up the box and tugged the bow free. The red ribbon fell into her lap as her fingers found the edge of the hinged box and pried it open. In the center lay a beautiful, heart-shaped gold locket. Delicate raised flowers decorated the pendant. "Oh, Amos. It's lovely." She ran a fingertip over the raised design, her touch light, reverent.

"I thought you might like to carry a photograph of your parents inside."

She looked up from the gift to the giver, her eyes growing misty. "I love you, Amos Bledsoe."

He smiled. "And I, you."

Determined not to turn into a watering pot, Grace thrust the jewelry box toward him. "Put it on me. Please?"

He hesitated. "But there's no photo inside yet."

"I don't care," she said. "There's love inside, and that's what really matters." She turned her back to give him access to her neck and to keep the earnest look in his eyes from melting her into a puddle of sentimentality.

He reached around her head and positioned the gold heart at the base of her throat, then fastened the clasp at her nape, his touch stirring the tiny hairs there.

She covered the locket with her hand and pressed it against her chest, her heart brimming with love for the kindhearted man who would soon be her husband. "Perfect."

They lingered on the blanket for an hour, talking of everything and nothing and thoroughly enjoying being together. But when gathering clouds moved in to block the sun and the wind began to blow from the north, they recalled that this was, in fact, February, and outdoor excursions could become uncomfortably cold in quick order.

"Has Helen heard any news from Dunbar?" Amos asked as he packed away his mother's glassware.

Grace pushed the rocks off the blanket then shook the worst of the dry grass from it. "She received a letter last week. The judge denied Chaucer's appeal. Tremont Haversham's amended will stands valid. Margaret Flanders's inheritance is secure."

"Excellent. And the investigation into Chaucer's involvement with Lockhart?" Amos collected the two blanket corners closest to him and stood.

Grace grinned. Most men would wad the fabric up or leave the woman to deal with it. But not Amos. He was chivalrous to the core.

"Last I heard, they had uncovered enough circumstantial evidence to press charges, but nothing to guarantee a conviction." They folded the blanket in half, then halved it again. "Chaucer has retreated to Boston, and he and his mother are circling an army of lawyers around them." She stepped forward to meet Amos. She collected his corners then waited for him to bring up the folded edge. "Lee doubts the man will spend any time in prison, but with his fortune out of reach, he should no longer be a threat to anyone."

"Doesn't sound like a sufficient penalty compared to the crime." Amos frowned as he handed off the last fold.

Grace crouched down to fit the blanket inside the basket. "To be honest, I'm more concerned about Helen. Lee's been writing her every few days, but his work with the Flanders family concluded several weeks ago, and he still hasn't returned. Helen's afraid he won't come back, that his letters will slow to a trickle and eventually stop. I've tried to reassure her that he wouldn't have written with such regularity if he didn't care about her, but the longer he stays away, the more despondent she gets. She hides it well behind that tough exterior, but she's cracking inside, and it breaks my heart."

She and Helen had bonded over the last few months, sharing confidences about their long-distance beaus over daily tea at the telegraph office. Helen came to town every day to check for a letter at the store, and afterward she'd drop by the telegraph office to visit. At first, the visits had been out of courtesy. She'd come to share the latest news on the Haversham case as it unfolded. But gradually, the visits had become longer and the conversation more personal as the two ladies shared their hopes about the future. Marriage, leaving Harper's Station, how to be a proper wife.

Helen had opened up a bit about her past, her story tugging on Grace's heartstrings even as it helped her understand the insecurities Helen carried regarding men. Yet even as close as they had become, Helen had withdrawn lately. The more Amos visited, the less Helen sought out Grace's company, as if seeing her friend find happiness was too painful to endure when her own lingered in the haze of uncertainty. Grace prayed for her friend every night. For Mr. Dunbar too. Nevertheless, the waiting continued to eat away at Helen.

Amos retrieved Grace's bicycle and rolled it over to where she stood. He took the basket out of her hands and held the bike steady as she straddled the frame and clasped the handlebars.

He hooked the basket handle over his own handlebars then swung a leg over the frame in preparation for mounting. Both feet still on the ground, he looked over at Grace. "I wouldn't worry about Dunbar's return."

"How can you be so sure? He was here for such a short time."

Amos grinned. "I saw the way he kissed Helen good-bye. That wasn't a passing fancy kind of kiss. That was a *my-life-has-been-permanently-altered* kind of kiss. I happen to be well-versed in that particular variety." He winked at her and set his foot to the pedal. "He'll be back."

Amos pushed his velocipede into motion. Grace hesitated, offering up a brief prayer on Helen's behalf, hoping Amos was correct. She wanted so badly for Helen to find the same happiness with Detective Dunbar that she had found with Amos. Her fingers found her locket, and she gave the treasured charm a stroke. Gaining the love of the right man made the pain and uncertainty of the wait worthwhile in the end.

Grace mounted her bicycle and pedaled hard to catch up to Amos. The ride back to Harper's Station was colder than the ride out, but her heart held too much warmth to mind. She was to be married to a man she adored. To her best friend—the man on the other end of the wire who had brought light into her lonely life before she'd ever seen his face. God truly was adept at bringing good out of even the most horrible situations. For if she hadn't been on the run from Haversham, she never would have met the wonderful ladies of Harper's Station, and without Harper's Station, she never would have met Amos. Only a master weaver could intertwine dark and light threads in such a way that all one saw was beauty when looking back at the finished tapestry.

So caught up in watching Amos's back and counting her blessings was Grace that she failed to notice they had veered off course, past Betty's chicken farm onto a small rutted path, until Amos halted on the outer edge of a grove of pecan trees.

"Look," he said, pointing through the trees toward a tiny, ramshackle cabin on the far side of the grove.

A man on horseback—Amos must have spotted him as they rode and decided to follow—dismounted and called Helen's name.

The cabin door opened. Helen stood in the doorway, frozen. Then all at once her face beamed. Even from a distance, Grace could feel the force of her smile.

"Lee!" Helen ran to him and threw herself into his arms.

He caught her easily, his leg fully healed and strong, then twirled her around in a circle as their combined joy erupted in laughter.

"Told you he'd be back." Amos wiggled his brows in a gesture of overblown masculine smugness.

Grace slapped at his arm with the back of her hand. She couldn't let such arrogance run *completely* unchecked. Yet at the same time, she couldn't hold back the smile that burst directly from her heart to her face at the sight of her friend reuniting with the man she loved.

As Lee and Helen's reunion transitioned into something decidedly more romantic, Grace and Amos turned their bicycles around and quietly pedaled away.

A hope deferred maketh the heart sick: but when the desire cometh, it is a tree of life.

The verse from Proverbs eased its way into Grace's mind as she rode, its message striking a sweet chord in her soul. A tree of life, indeed. Full of promise and vitality, and ready to offer shelter from whatever storms might come. A gift of love that would never die.

Nothing could compare.

Christy Award finalist and winner of the ACFW Carol Award, HOLT Medallion, and Inspirational Reader's Choice Award, bestselling author **Karen Witemeyer** writes historical romances because she believes the world needs more happily-ever-afters. She is an avid cross-stitcher and shower singer, and she bakes a mean apple cobbler. Karen makes her home in Abilene, Texas, with her husband and three children.

To learn more about Karen and her books and to sign up for her free newsletter featuring special giveaways and behind-the-scenes information, please visit www.karenwitemeyer.com.

Sign Up for Karen's Newsletter!

Keep up to date with news on Karen's upcoming book releases and events by signing up for her email list at karenwitemeyer.com.

More from Karen Witemeyer

When the women's colony of Harper's Station is threatened, founder Emma Chandler is forced to admit she needs help. The only man she trusts enough to ask is Malachi Shaw, whose life she once saved. As Mal returns the favor, danger mounts—and so does the attraction between them.

No Other Will Do

◊ BETHANYHOUSE

You May Also Like . . .

When unfortunate circumstances leave Rosalyn penniless in 1880s London, she takes a job backstage at a theater and dreams of a career in the spotlight. Injured soldier Nate Moran is also working behind the scenes, but he can't wait to return to his regiment—until he meets Rosalyn.

The Captain's Daughter by Jennifer Delamere
LONDON BEGINNINGS #1, jenniferdelamere.com

Growing up on the streets of London, Rosemary and her friends have had to steal to survive. But as a rule, they only take from the wealthy. They've all learned how to blend into high society for jobs. When, on the eve of WWI, a client contracts Rosemary to determine whether a friend of the king is loyal to Britain or Germany, she's in for the challenge of a lifetime.

A Name Unknown by Roseanna M. White
SHADOWS OVER ENGLAND, roseannawhite.com

Evelyn Wisely has a heart for orphans. She works daily to help get children out of her town's red-light district, but she longs to help the women there as well. Intrigued by Evelyn, David Kingsman lends his support to her cause. Though they begin work with the best of intentions, complications arise.

A Love So True by Melissa Jagears
TEAVILLE MORAL SOCIETY, melissajagears.com